Barbara in the Bush

The Army Cadets

C.R. Cummings

Also By
CHRISTOPHER CUMMINGS

Barbara in the Bush

The Army Cadets

C.R. Cummings

DoctorZed
Publishing
www.doctorzed.com

Published 2020 by DoctorZed Publishing

DoctorZed Publishing books may be ordered through booksellers or by contacting:

DoctorZed Publishing
10 Vista Ave
Skye, South Australia 5072
www.doctorzed.com

ISBN: 978-0-6487107-3-8 (hc)
ISBN: 978-0-6487107-2-1 (sc)
ISBN: 978-0-6487107-1-4 (ebk)

National Library of Australia Cataloguing-in-Publication entry

    Author: Cummings, C. R., author.

    Title: Barbara in the bush/ Christopher Cummings.
    ISBN: 9780648710738 (hardcover)

    Series: Cummings, C. R. The army cadets.

    Target Audience: For young adults.

    Subjects: Adventure stories, Australian.

    Military cadets--Queensland--Fiction.

Cover image © Sakdam | Dreamstime.com
Cover design © Scott Zarcinas

Printed in Australia, UK & USA

DoctorZed Publishing rev. date: 14/01/2020

Special Thanks
to
the Officers of Cadets
of
the Australian Army Cadets

This book, while a work of fiction, is dedicated to all the Officers of Cadets and Instructors of Cadets of the Australian Army Cadets who attended the North Queensland Combined Army Cadet Promotion Courses at Macrossan 1986-1993 and whose hard work made those courses a success and shared in the trials, tribulations and dramas of such activities. You have done a magnificent job in preparing young people for life as good citizens. By being good role models and by showing compassion and sympathy to young people under stress and in need you have done good work for Australia and helped many.
Thank you.

Special thanks also to the cadets of Heatley State High School Cadet Unit (130 Regional Cadet Unit and now 130 Army Cadet Unit (Heatley) who attended those courses. You provided the motivation and inspiration for me to battle through the two worst crises of my life. May your lives be long and fulfilling and may you serve your country well.

Chapter 1

AN UNPLEASANT REUNION

Seventeen-year-old Army Cadet Warrant Officer Barbara Brassington walked out of the side door of the Townsville Coach Terminal. She was wearing casual civilian clothes: blouse, shorts and gym boots. In each hand she carried a cup of fruit juice. Carefully she threaded her way through the jumble of luggage and cadets on the footpath. As she reached the rear of the army coach parked there, she recognised the bull-necked shape of a cadet she knew. Her nose wrinkled in distaste.

It was that arrogant creep Weismann from Broadsound.

He was standing side on to her and looking down at her friend Wendy, who was hauling kitbags from a pile.

"Hello Wendy," he said. "My, my! Haven't you grown in a year!"

Wendy looked up at him and realised he was leering down the front of her blouse. Blushing she straightened up, holding her a kitbag in one hand and a suitcase in the other. She went to walk around him.

Weismann sidestepped to block her path. "Now that isn't very friendly. I was just paying you a compliment. You were only a little girl last year, but you aren't a little girl now are you? Not with a shirt full of tits like that!" he said.

Wendy stepped back as though she had been struck. Her mouth fell open and her face flamed crimson.

Barbara could hardly believe her ears. Poor Wendy! She was only 15, a year and a bit younger than her, but Weismann was right. In the last year Wendy's boobs had grown as though they'd been pumped up. They had become so prominent that Wendy's nickname at school had become 'Wobbles'. Barbara knew that her mother had said it was just puppy fat and that, as the rest of her grew, she would get back in proportion. But that was no immediate comfort. She knew that Wendy was very self-conscious about it.

Barbara stepped across some bags to stand beside Wendy and glared at Weismann. "That's not a compliment Weismann. That's sexual harassment," she snapped.

Weismann turned his grey eyes to meet hers. "Well, well! Hello 'Ginger Top'. Fancy meeting you here! Aren't you pretty when you're angry! The red face matches the hair."

"Leave Wendy alone!"

"There's no need to bite my head off. I'm just saying hello to the girl," Weismann replied.

"There's no need to leer at her or make insulting suggestions!"

"I wasn't insulting her. It was a compliment. Anyway, you've got a nice pair of tits yourself if it comes to that," he said. He lowered his gaze to deliberately eye her front.

Barbara felt a surge of white-hot anger. "You disgusting creature!" she cried. She hurled the fruit juice into his face.

Weismann stepped back and swore. "You fucken moll!"

"Stop your gutter language and leave us alone, you foul-mouthed pig!" Barbara hissed.

"Don't you talk to me like that, you red-headed bitch or I'll belt you in the mouth!"

"Just try it," Barbara replied between clenched teeth.

Weismann took a pace forward, his face mottled with anger. He raised his fists.

A person stepped between them. Barbara found herself staring at a broad back as the male newcomer confronted Weismann. The newcomer snapped, "No you won't buster! Leave the girls alone." The strange youth said this in a deep voice which seemed to resonate in Barbara's ears.

Annoyed, she stepped forward and shouldered the newcomer aside. "You keep out of this. I'll fight my own battles," she snapped.

The youth turned and looked at her. "He's right. You are pretty when you are angry. Look at that green fire sparkling in those eyes!" He was smiling and Barbara had a vivid impression of clear blue eyes, firm chin and a tanned, handsome face.

She had a momentary urge to close her eyes and she bristled, even as the deep timbre of his voice sent an involuntary thrill through her. She snapped, "Don't you start! You keep out of this!"

The youth smiled and gestured towards Wendy. "But you weren't fighting your own battles. You were helping this damsel in distress." The blue eyes twinkled and his cheeks dimpled into a grin. He turned and smiled at Wendy.

To Barbara it seemed she had received an electric shock and the realization of it nettled her even more. "So who are you, Sir Galahad? We don't need a knight in shining armour. We can look after ourselves," she retorted, then instantly regretted the words because they had been exactly the concept which had crossed her mind.

The young man gave a soft chuckle. "No, I'm not as pure as that."

He would have said more but Weismann now stepped belligerently forward and yelled, "You keep out of this and mind your own business Farr." He glared at the youth and raised his clenched fists.

The young man turned to face him. Barbara saw that they were well matched for size but Weismann had a more solid build. The young man, Farr, said coolly, "Grow up Weismann. If you want a fight you can have it, but this is hardly the place or the time."

Weismann sneered. "No guts eh?" he snarled.

A chubby man in a camouflage uniform with captain's rank slides pushed his way towards them. He was Capt Conkey and Barbara knew him well because he was the OC of her cadet unit.

"What's going on here?" he asked.

"Nothing sir," replied Weismann, lowering his fists and starting to turn away.

"Just a minute!" Capt Conkey ordered. "You're Weismann aren't you? You were on the Sergeants Course last year, weren't you? Are you going to this promotion course?"

Weismann gave a surly nod. "Yes sir."

Capt Conkey turned to the youth beside Barbara. "And who are you? Do you have anything to do with the Army Cadets?"

"Yes sir. My name is Gordon Farr. I'm a sergeant in the Broadsound Cadet Unit. I'm a candidate for the Cadet Under-Officers Course."

Barbara looked up at him in surprise. "Oh, are you? So am I," she said. Then she mentally kicked herself for saying it.

Gordon turned to her and gave her a mischievous grin, half-teasing, half-questioning. "Oh good!" he replied.

Barbara felt her heart turn over. Then she blushed and felt angry with herself for being so weak, so scatter-brained and schoolgirlish.

But, gosh! He's handsome, she thought.

Capt Conkey turned to her. "Well Barbara, what was that all about?"

"Nothing sir. Just a bit of a disagreement," she replied. Part of her mind told her she should report the incident as Weismann's behaviour was a clear breach of Cadet Regulations, but she hesitated, not wanting to cause that much unpleasantness and upset at that moment.

Capt Conkey looked from one to the other, apparently unconvinced. "Yes, well. Get your gear and get on the bus and we'll have no more trouble." He looked meaningly at Weismann then turned on his heel and walked away.

Gordon Farr turned his back on Weismann, who also walked off muttering. Gordon looked at Barbara and said, "Hello. I'm Gordon. We haven't been introduced."

"No we haven't. Excuse me!" Barbara replied as frostily as she could. She turned and stepped past him. Gordon shrugged and smiled but a blush mounted his neck and cheeks. He turned on his heel and left.

Wendy hurried to catch up. "Oh Barbara! You shouldn't have been so rude. He was only trying to help," she said.

"Who? Oh him? He can mind his own business and leave me alone."

"Oh Barb. Don't be so hard on him," Wendy said. Then she sighed. "Isn't he handsome!"

Barbara shrugged. "He's a male and they're all the same. They only want one thing! I hate them all!"

Wendy shook her head and smiled. "That's not true and you know it. He seemed very nice to me. Very well mannered."

"Just a 'Mr Smoothy'," Barbara said, giving Wendy a wry grin. She held out her left hand. "Here's your fruit juice. I'm sorry I spilt most of it."

Wendy smiled. "That's OK. It was worth it just to see Weismann's face."

They both burst out laughing.

Another youth called to them. "Come on you two. Grab your gear and load it on the bus." It was Sergeant Roger Dunning from their unit.

"Yes Roger," Barbara replied. The two girls looked at each other and burst out laughing again.

Roger looked from one to the other in puzzlement. "What's so funny?"

"Nothing Roger," Barbara answered. Then she chuckled and picked up her bags. Wendy finished the drink and walked over to toss the paper cup into a rubbish bin.

Roger turned and called to her, "Come on Wobbles, hurry up!"

Barbara hissed. "Don't call her that, Roger! Don't you start."

Roger looked at her with a hurt look on his usually cheerful face, obviously not sure what he had done wrong. Wendy picked up her bags and followed. Because of their weight her body moved with an exaggerated swing as she walked and she really did wobble. She put her nose up and said, "Yes Sergeant Dunning, Corporal Werribee to you." With that she pushed past him.

Roger looked at Barbara, one eyebrow raised questioningly. Barbara liked Roger. He was a bit overweight and fairly plain in looks but was normally very considerate of other's feelings.

"Don't ask, Roger. Here, grab this," she said, tossing him one of her bags.

He placed this in the luggage compartment of the coach, then helped Wendy put hers in. The three then walked to the door where the tubby captain, Captain Conkey, stood checking them on. They were the last cadets to board.

Wendy climbed aboard first, followed by Roger, then Barbara.

Barbara saw Gordon Farr as soon as she stepped up into the aisle. Her eyes seemed to seek him out of their own volition. She saw that he was sitting near the front of the coach, just behind Miss McEwen. Their eyes met and he smiled.

Barbara looked hastily away, and met Weismann's angry glare. Again she looked away, annoyed that she felt she had to. She followed Wendy along the aisle past him.

Weismann was sitting next to a blonde girl she vaguely recognised. As Barbara passed him, he hissed quietly, "Bitch! You'll get yours!"

Barbara felt her stomach turn with distaste. Despite an urge to speak her mind she ignored him and walked on. Luckily there were two empty seats well to the rear. Wendy chose one of these and slid in to sit next to the window on the left. Barbara settled next to her.

Fiona Davies, another CUO candidate from Cairns and a long-time friend leaned across the aisle. "What was that all about while we were loading the bus Barb?" she asked.

"Oh, nothing. Just an unpleasant reunion," Barbara replied.

Chapter 2

BACK TO BUNYIP RIVER

The coach headed out of Townsville along the Flinders Highway towards Charters Towers. On board were 47 army cadets, all high school students, and 6 Officers of Cadets. It was December and the cadets were all candidates for 12 days of training to prepare them for promotion.

Barbara, Wendy and the others from Cairns had already travelled for five hours. They had left Cairns at 0400 hrs that morning. All the others had come from the south, from Mackay, Sarina, Broadsound and Rockhampton by commercial coach. Now all were on an army coach headed for the Bunyip River Stores Depot, 110 kilometres inland.

For over an hour the coach raced at 100 kph through seemingly endless and mostly uninhabited bush, the open savannah woodland of inland North Queensland. The trees were mostly black-trunked ironbarks with their straggly leaves. The grass was short but green, indicating recent rain, but there were many bare patches. The reddish, sandy soil showed through almost everywhere. In places there was more deadfall of twigs and dry leaves than grass.

Barbara spent most of the time reading a training manual. Beside her, Wendy was absorbed in a romance novel. Loud laughter from in front made them look up. It was Weismann telling jokes. Barbara saw Captain Conkey turn and frown.

She nudged Wendy, then asked, "Who's that girl beside Weismann, the blonde? Wasn't she on the Corporals Course last year?"

Wendy nodded. "Yes, she was. She wasn't in my section, thank God! Her name's Monica Malone and she's a real little tart," she replied. Wendy was only a corporal herself, being a year and a bit younger and a grade behind Barbara at school.

Barbara nodded. "I remember. She was the one all the rumours were about, the one who was always sneaking off to meet the boys, and to smoke."

Wendy nodded and made a sour face. "That's her. I suppose I'll have to put up with her again. I hope she's not in my section this year. It makes you wonder how she could be selected to do a Sergeants Course after that sort of behaviour."

"Wasn't she the one who went skinny dipping with some of the boys that day we were down at the river doing fieldcraft?"

Wendy nodded. "That's her. And some girls from Townsville. It's a wonder she was never found out."

"Isn't she from the same unit as Weismann, from Broadsound?" Barbara asked.

Wendy nodded. "Yes, I think so," she replied. "Where is Broadsound anyway? It's somewhere near Mackay isn't it?"

"No. Further south. Somewhere between Sarina and Rockhampton," Barbara replied. She became very thoughtful. Wendy gave her a quizzical look out of the corner of her eye, then settled back to her novel.

As she did the coach topped a gentle crest. On the left the bush gave way to an open paddock studded with clumps of grey rocks. A railway angled in on the far side of the field. Wendy looked out.

"I know where we are!" she said. "This is where we did our resection problem in our Navigation exam last year."

Barbara looked out. A line of rugged hills a few kilometres away held her gaze. She had seen them on every camp she had done in the area and was annoyed she couldn't immediately remember their name. Then it came to her just as the hills were lost to sight behind trees.

The Tucker Box Range. "Won't be long now," she said.

"Thank God for that! I'm getting a numb bum," Wendy replied.

The bus roared down a long gentle slope. Barbara felt a sensation of prickling unease. She leaned out into the aisle to look forward through the front window. They were approaching a short concrete bridge.

FIVE MILE CREEK the sign read.

Barbara raised herself in her seat to look out the window on the right as the tyres hummed on the concrete. She had a glimpse of a creek like thousands of others in inland Queensland: a dry sandy bed lined with Eucalypts. Her eyes took in the gravel area on the right beside the bitumen highway. Beyond it were the inevitable three-strand, barbed wire fence then clumps of rubber vines. She went tense as memories flooded her mind.

That was the fence Miss McEwen ran into when she was trying to escape from those crooks last September, she thought.

Barbara felt herself cringe at the thought of the jagged, rusty barbs ripping her flesh. She leaned into the aisle again and looked forward to where Miss McEwen sat. All she could see was the top of her head, but it told her the teacher, who was also an Officer of Cadets with the rank of lieutenant, was looking out as well.

She is probably remembering that terrifying time, Barbara thought.

Barbara sat back and looked to her left as the coach went up a long, bush-covered rise. "The country looks fairly green, much greener than it was during Annual Camp last September," she commented.

Wendy looked out. "Yes it is. Gosh I'm sick of being in a bus. Are we nearly there?"

"Shouldn't be more than a kilometre or so. Just over this next rise I think," replied Barbara.

The coach had gone down into a dip. As it topped the next gentle ridge, she saw she was wrong. There was one more rise. She moved in her seat for a better view and was surprised how fast her heart was beating. Was it the memories, or just anticipation? She wasn't sure.

They went up and over another long, low rise. The ribbon of black tar stretched down and away for over a kilometre before ascending another low ridge. A tiny spot of colour caught her eye. "There's the sign. We'll be there in a minute," she said.

Wendy nodded and put her book down. "This must be where you crossed the highway that day?"

Barbara bit her lip, her mind flooding with memories from the Annual Camp three months earlier. "A bit further down. There's a culvert. Yes, just up ahead, this side of Scrubby Creek. The crooks had one of those enormous yellow dump trucks parked at the Scrubby Creek bridge."

Memories flooded her mind: crawling through the grass and prickles, then through a concrete pipe full of dust and dead toads to reach the safety of the army camp. To get a better view she leaned across in front of Wendy, but the scene flashed past her almost too fast for her to focus her eyes. She lifted her gaze and saw the grassy embankment of the railway.

Barbara tried to pick out the exact route she had followed on that awful day but found she wasn't sure which side of which clump of thorn bush or rubber vine she had gone.

"Remembering?" Wendy asked, closing her book and bending forward to slip it into her bag.

Barbara nodded. Wendy looked at her. "It must have been awful. Did the police ever catch those revolting pig hunters you rescued Cadet Lillis from?"

"Yes they did. The one I shot, Boyer, he had to be taken to hospital. The police got them both." In her mind, Barbara relived those terrifying minutes: running through the bush being shot at and chased by Berzinski. She shuddered involuntarily. His lust for her had been terrifying. Even now the thought of him filled her with dread. Thank God he was in jail!

Her eye registered the white, bullet-riddled road sign as it flashed by: SCRUBBY CREEK.

She had run along beside Scrubby Creek to escape Berzinski but had to slow to a walk to catch her breath. Rounding a bend she had come on the most incredible scene. In the dry sand of the creek bed was a fire. Tied up to a tree were two cadets, both boys. Roped to another tree, stripped naked, was a girl, one of her cadets, Leanne Lillis.

The two Pig Hunters had been there. The big, pot-bellied one, Lenny Boyer, had a red-hot knife and was just about to torture Lillis with it. The other, the skinny one, Wally, had been standing nearby, leering in a disgusting way.

Barbara had seen a rifle leaning against a tree and in a couple of steps had scooped it up and aimed it. She had told the man Lenny to stop or else. He hadn't believed her, the fool. He had gone to throw the knife, so she shot him. The bullet had broken his leg.

Barbara had then untied Lillis and the others, and as soon as the girl was dressed, they had run into the thick vine scrub beside the creek. She remembered the looks on the faces of the two Pig Hunters as she'd left. Skinny Wally had nearly been dribbling with fear and could hardly speak. Lenny, the fat one, had been groaning in pain and mouthing obscenities as he tried to stop the bleeding.

"Men are disgusting," Barbara said as the coach began to slow down.

"Yes, aren't they," replied Wendy with a smile.

"You take that smirk off your face Miss Werribee. You only think they're nice because of Lofty. But he's only a gentleman ... when it suits him. They all are. Mum was right. They're all the same. They only want one thing from a girl," Barbara lectured.

Wendy smiled again. "You remembering your mate Lenny the Pig Shooter?"

Barbara snorted and looked out the window. The coach turned left off the highway onto a bitumen side road. It went past a large sign painted in blue and red horizontal bands on which the name BUNYIP RIVER STORES DEPOT stood out in white letters above the RAAOC badge.

"How long did they get in jail?" Wendy asked.

"They haven't gone to jail yet. Their trial isn't due till January," Barbara replied. It was an ordeal she was not looking forward to. The trial of those other crooks last month had been bad enough. She remembered Berzinski's eyes just as he'd been led away. He had looked directly at her. "I'll get you!" he had hissed. His eyes had glittered in a way that didn't seem sane. Barbara shivered at the memory.

Wendy again interrupted her thoughts. The coach slowed to a stop at the railway crossing before accelerating up a long driveway lined by white painted railings.

"Do you mean those Pig Hunters are still out free?" she asked.

Barbara felt ill at the thought. "Yes. I think so. They both got let out on bail."

Wendy looked horrified. "Oh! I hope they aren't still around here."

Barbara gave a weak laugh, to reassure herself as much as her friend. "Well, they live in Charters Towers so I suppose they must be in the district, but I wouldn't think they'd be anywhere near here. Anyhow, this is an army camp and they wouldn't even know we were here." She tried to sound confident, but it took an effort to push the spectre of their possible vengeance back under a mental carpet.

The road went between two high-set houses which were married quarters for the Regular Army personnel based at the camp. The coach passed through the camp gate and followed the road left to a low wooden building of bungalow style. This was the camp guardhouse. The army driver stopped the coach and called through her window to a civilian in stockman's clothes who had come onto the veranda. Barbara recognised him as one of the three civilian caretakers. She had met him when on piquet during her Warrant Officers Course the previous December. He waved them on.

The coach started moving again and followed the single bitumen road as it wound along a wide, flat ridge. The camp was spread over a large area, the buildings scattered in no apparent pattern. Between the widely spaced store sheds was open savannah woodland. The trees were mostly ironbarks. The undergrowth and larger deadfall had been removed and the grass was kept mown, giving a rough, park-like appearance.

The camp was in two distinct sections. The main part was the store depot. This consisted of the two houses, guard hut, petrol store, eight large store sheds and a number of smaller out-buildings. The last shed was a colossal 'igloo'; with a curved roof and semi-circular ends. The whole massive structure was made of corrugated iron on a timber frame. It was painted silver and stood out as a local landmark in the otherwise featureless bush.

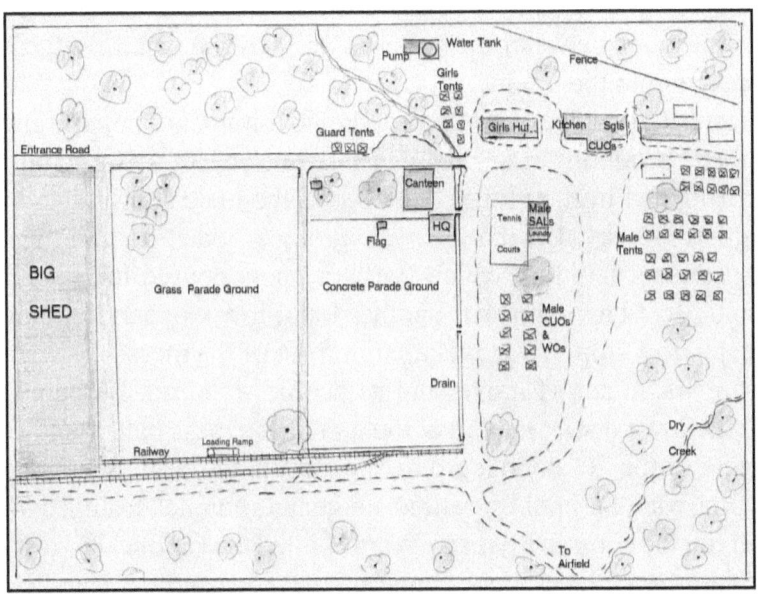

Macrossan Camp

This part of the camp dated from World War II. Here and there concrete slabs marked the site of buildings long demolished. A spur of the railway came in on their right. One of its double tracks passed through huge doors at the far end of the big shed.

The road then ran straight for 300 metres. On the right was a grass parade ground bounded by bitumen roads. Beyond it was a concrete loading ramp beside the railway spur line. Large trees at irregular intervals provided some shade. A huge flat expanse of concrete marked where a second large shed had once stood. Starting at the northern end of the large concrete slab was a cluster of 8 newer buildings on both sides of the road. This was where the cadets would be holding their promotion courses for the next 12 days.

The coach passed three buildings on the right. First was a small toilet and then, beyond 50 metres of green lawn with a large tree in the middle of it, the canteen. At that point the road crossed a deep drain. Twenty metres to the right of the canteen and actually built astride the drain, was a single room building with a shady porch at the east end. Barbara knew this was the HQ. On the left of the road, 75 metres away and near the drain, was a shed that housed the water treatment plant. Beside it stood a huge steel tower topped by a massive water tank. A row of 8 tents stood under some trees between the water tower and the small bridge. These tents backed onto the drain.

Beyond the bridge were a rectangular bitumen car park and then a ring road. Inside the ring road and in front of HQ was a tennis court and a corrugated iron building that housed the male showers and toilets and a small laundry. On the left was a long wooden building and then a T-shaped steel building which Barbara knew housed the kitchen and mess halls. Just beyond it was another long, low wooden building. The coach came to a stop in a gravel area in front of the mess.

There was a stir of movement as people stood up. Barbara looked out. On the low concrete porch at the end of the mess hall which formed the upright of the 'T' stood a group of cadets in uniform. She recognised some. One was the chubby retired lieutenant colonel from Townsville who had run the courses for many years (Called the Colonel by everyone).

Beside the Colonel stood some of the Townsville cadets. Barbara recognised some from previous camps. Wendy pointed at them. "That Townsville mob! Don't they think they are just too good!"

Barbara agreed. "Especially that crowd from Heatley."

Wendy turned to her. "Yeah! Well, this year I'm going to beat them. I'm going to top the Sergeants Course!"

Barbara laughed. "Good for you!" she said.

She couldn't bring herself to say it, but she had the same ambition for her course. The previous year Heatley had taken out top of the Cadet Under-Officers Course and top of the Sergeants Course—and both had been girls. Barbara had been top of her Warrant Officers Course, narrowly beating that big Anthony Glenn from Heatley. She made the resolve she would be top of the CUOs Course this year.

A teenage youth in uniform and with a scarlet sash across his chest and a CSM's cane under his left arm strode past the window, his voice audible above the noise of the motor.

Barker, from Heatley, she remembered. There was a hiss as the doors opened and his voice bellowed in.

"Off the bus! Collect your gear and move into the shade at the end of that hut," he said, while pointing with his cane to the next building.

Wendy grinned and muttered, "Here we go!" Her brown eyes sparkled with excitement. The girls stood up and began gathering hand luggage. On the coach there were 11 cadets from their unit in Cairns, plus their OC, Captain Conkey and Miss McEwen. Even though she was a lieutenant Barbara always thought of her as 'Miss' because she was one of her teachers. Capt Conkey was also a teacher but she never dreamed of calling him 'Mister'!

Four of the Cairns cadets were candidates for the Cadet Under-Officers Course: Fiona Davies, Roger Dunning, Lofty Ward and Barbara. Pat Sheehan was doing the Warrant Officers Course. The remainder, including Wendy, were doing the Sergeants Course.

They filed off the coach. As they stepped out of the air-conditioning into the open the heat and humidity seemed to smite them like a solid blow. Perspiration began to trickle at once.

"Strewth, it's tropical!" grumbled Roger to all and sundry as they began to wrestle ports and kitbags from the luggage compartment.

"Well it is summer," a freckle-faced girl replied.

Barbara looked at her. "Oh hi! You were on the Sergeants Course last year."

The girl nodded. "Yes. I'm Jennifer Bladen from Sarina."

"I'm Barbara."

Roger butted in. "And I'm bloody hot. Grab this kitbag."

"Don't be rude Roger!"

Before Roger could answer the cadet sergeant in the red sash bellowed, "Stop chatting and get that gear unloaded!"

The coach was quickly unloaded and drove off, leaving the cadets standing on the lawn near the male showers amid a litter of kitbags and webbing.

Now it starts! Barbara thought, half-dreading, half-loving the experience.

Chapter 3

THE CUOs COURSE

The new arrivals, all still in casual civilian clothes, gathered in the shade cast by the overhanging roof of the next hut. This was a long wooden building and was the last building at that end of the camp. Beyond it were rows of tents and then bush. Barbara made sure she was standing well away from Weismann. While she waited, she looked around and realised she was standing next to Gordon Farr. She looked quickly away and pretended she hadn't noticed. But for the next few minutes she was a bit annoyed with herself for experiencing a flutter of emotion.

The Heatley sergeant with the red sash directed them into three groups: Sergeants Course, Warrant Officers Course and Cadet-Under Officers Course. Having done the same job the previous year Barbara knew exactly who he was. He was the Orderly Sergeant for the day and had to be on the Warrant Officers Course.

Barbara went to join the group in the shade of the mess porch. As well as the candidates for the CUOs course the adult Officers of Cadets were there, exchanging greetings and gossip. A few earlier arrivals stood nearby, already in uniform. Barbara recognised several faces and nodded a friendly greeting.

The blonde girl who had been sitting next to Weismann on the coach joined them and stood in front of Barbara. For a minute the implication did not register.

Surely not? Barbara thought. *She must have made a mistake and joined the wrong group?*

"You're Malone aren't you?" Barbara asked.

The girl looked over her shoulder. "Yes I am. So what?"

"This is the CUOs Course."

"Yes I know. That's the course I'm doing."

Barbara was amazed. "But you only did the Corporals Course last year. Shouldn't you be doing the Sergeants Course?" she asked.

Malone turned and put her hands on her hips. "No. My OC selected me for the CUOs Course, so mind your own business!"

"There's no need to be like that. I only wondered," Barbara replied. She felt herself blush. To recover her composure she looked away. Fiona gave her a sympathetic nudge.

There was worse to come. Barbara had been hoping Weismann would be on the WOs Course but with that sort of sickening inevitability reserved for such things she heard his name called and saw him march towards them.

Once all the new arrivals were in their groups, they were called a group at a time, starting with the potential sergeants, to where the Colonel stood in the shade. He checked their name on an organization diagram and then directed them to a table where two CUO Assistant Instructors (AIs) had sets of coloured name tags. From previous courses Barbara understood the colours: Blue for Corporals Course, red for Sergeants Course, green for Warrant Officers and yellow for CUOs. This system told the instructors at a glance what course a cadet was on. She told them her name and was handed a name tag. She took this and returned to the front porch.

Once all the new arrivals had been processed and their medical and Next-of-Kin documents checked ('Marched-in'), the Orderly Sergeant then marched over and saluted the Colonel, who was also the Chief Instructor. After a short conversation the Orderly Sergeant saluted again and turned to face the CUOs Course.

"Right, listen. Each group has a Duty Student rostered for the day. They will take charge of you and show you where to go. Lunch is in fifteen minutes. You have until 1330 to get yourselves organised. At that time you are to be in uniform ready for the Opening Address. Duty Students carry on!"

"OK CUOs Course, pay attention," a girl's voice called. They turned to look. A slim, female sergeant stood beside them. She smiled and said, "I'm Karen Harvey, from Heatley. I'm Duty Student." She went on to point out the tents where the boys would camp and their showers and toilets. Then she turned and pointed to the long, wooden hut the other side of the kitchen, between it and the canteen hut. "That is the girls hut. All the female officers are in the rooms at this end. We are in the big room at the other end. We have two showers and toilets at this end of the hut. The female corporals have some temporary showers at the back of those tents behind our hut. So grab your gear and settle in."

Fiona put up her hand. "Can we pick our own bed or do we have to sleep in a particular place?" she asked.

Karen shook her head. "There is a bed plan. CUOs and WOs this side, Sgts the other side. Your names are on your stretchers."

The cadets broke into a cheerful babble as they went to collect their gear. The Sergeants Course joined them. Barbara hefted a bag and called, "Here's your kitbag Wendy."

"Thanks." Wendy bent to pick up the bag.

Weismann's voice cut in. "Nice bum, too!"

Barbara looked around from hauling her suitcase from the pile. Weismann was standing just behind Wendy looking at her.

A spurt of instant anger coursed through Barbara. "Keep your crude comments to yourself Weismann!" she snapped.

"What's wrong Brassington? Are you jealous?" he replied with a sneer.

Barbara threw her suitcase down so that Weismann had to jump quickly back. She put her hands on her hips and glared at him. "Leave us alone and keep your dirty thoughts to yourself, you pig!"

"Don't call me a pig, you stuck-up troll."

"Don't act like one then!" Barbara retorted. Her mouth twisted in distaste. "Your unit must be hard up if you're all they've got to send on a CUOs Course."

"Watch your mouth, you dog, or I'll smack it!" Weismann snarled. He bristled with anger.

Gordon Farr's voice cut in from beside Barbara. "I thought officers were supposed to be gentlemen."

Weismann turned to face him. "You keep out of this shit-face."

Gordon gave him a cool stare. "Shut your gutter-mouth in front of the ladies or I'll shut it for you," he replied.

Weismann put up his fists. "Come on big mouth!"

Gordon sneered. "Don't be a fool. If you want a fight you can have it, but not here and not now. I came here to pass a CUOs Course and a punch-up in front of the officers on Day One doesn't strike me as very sensible."

Weismann checked and looked around. All the cadets near them had stopped and were watching. Several of the officers, including the Colonel, were looking their way.

Gordon spoke again. "Let's move. We can settle this later." He turned to Barbara and bent to take the handle of her suitcase. "Can I help you with that?"

Barbara snatched the case up. "No you cannot! I can carry my own gear."

"Fine, OK!" Gordon replied. He raised his hands placatingly and smiled.

This made Barbara even angrier, partly because it made her heart leap. She stepped forward, brushing the two boys aside. "Come on Wendy."

Wendy followed. "Thanks Barb," she puffed, as she struggled under the weight of her luggage. "Aren't men disgusting animals?"

"I remember you telling me how nice they were on the bus this morning," Barbara replied.

"Yes, well some of them are. Isn't he nice," Wendy said, unconscious of the contradiction.

"Who?"

"Gordon Farr, the sergeant from Broadsound who just saved us then."

"He didn't save us!" Barbara bristled. She stamped up the short flight of steps onto the back veranda of the girl's hut.

"No. But isn't he handsome," puffed Wendy as she followed.

"He's just another ignorant male," Barbara retorted. She led the way past the showers and through a door. This led into a corridor with two rooms on either side. These had the names of female officers on the doors.

Wendy continued talking. "He likes you. Did you see the way he smiled at you?" she asked, a twinge of envy in her voice.

Barbara grunted. She had noticed and it annoyed her that she was affected. However she pretended she was not interested and led the way into the large room at the end. "Which stretcher is mine?" she asked, changing the subject.

There were 30 canvas stretchers (Cots Folding in army jargon) lined up, 15 on each side of the room. There were no lockers or tables and just enough room to walk between the stretchers. The cadet's suitcases and kitbags obviously had to go against the wall.

Barbara found her stretcher on the left side. It was nearest the main door at the far end. Wendy was almost opposite her on the sergeant's side. The girls put their gear down and looked around. There were only 8 girls on the CUOs Course (and 16 boys). Barbara greeted the others she knew from the previous year's course.

The stretcher next to hers had no-one at it. Barbara bent to read the nametag but even as she did she felt her heart sink as she guessed what it would say.

"That's mine," called Monica Malone, bustling in and dumping her gear on the stretcher.

Barbara tried to hide her dislike and forced a smile. She didn't want trouble and would have to live beside her for nearly two weeks.

A girl on the sergeants course asked, "Where do we change?"

Karen gestured around the room. "Here if it doesn't bother you. But if you are shy use either of the showers or toilets."

A tall, attractive brunette whom Barbara knew was from Townsville grinned, "Here will do me, unless any of you guys mind."

A solid, busty girl with fair hair and a mischievous grin nodded. "Me too. I don't mind."

The brunette laughed. "You lot from Black River wouldn't!"

The cheeky fair-haired girl grinned even more. "We have a lot of fun at Black River."

"I'll bet you do!" retorted the brunette who looked at Barbara and then walked over. "Hi! I'm Sharon, and this naughty girl is Camille." she added, while gesturing to the fair –haired girl. "Call her 'Camel'."

"I'm Monica," Malone replied. "Why Camel?"

"'Cause she looks like one," Karen called from the door.

"No. It's because she smells like one," Sharon replied and laughed. Camille retaliated by throwing a pillow.

"Come on you lot," Karen called from the door. "It's lunchtime. Grab your eating irons and line up outside the Mess."

The girls hurried out and lined up on the side of the road. Karen raised her voice and yelled. "Come on you boys, Mess Parade!"

The boys came straggling over from where they had been erecting tents. Barbara found herself looking until she saw Gordon Farr appear. Then she looked away and stood in the ranks pretending she wasn't interested. He joined the rear rank further along. Barbara became very self-conscious, wondering if he was looking at her. She thought he was but she resisted the urge to look and check.

The Orderly Sergeant took control. The Sergeants Course then filed in to be served first.

While the CUOs Course stood waiting Roger spoke up. "We're a bunch of nongs standing here in this blazing bloody sun," he said.

"Stop grumbling Roger," Lofty Ward murmured.

"Well, we could form up in the shade of that tree near the laundry. This is hot enough to melt a man's brains." Roger replied.

"What brains Roger?" Fiona quipped.

Weismann grunted. "Huh! He isn't a man either," he added.

Roger looked around to see who had made that dig. Barbara tensed. She saw a look of hurt and then another of dislike cross Roger's face but to her relief he did nothing.

Karen looked anxious and then called, "OK CUOs, in you go."

They filed in one rank at a time. There were two dining rooms attached to the kitchen. For lack of space these doubled as lecture rooms. The larger one was in the same room as the kitchen and serving counter and was for the Sgts and WOs courses. The smaller one, at right angles to the centre of the building, was for the CUOs and Officers. It had been outside this that they had gathered after being placed in their course groups.

The buildings were made of pre-fabricated steel and, although the walls were mostly louvres the air inside was stifling from the mid-summer sun. It was December in tropical North Queensland and Barbara guessed that the temperature must be in the high thirties. She followed Fiona, aware that Gordon Farr was a few behind her in the queue. When she turned to answer a question from Camille, she saw him but she avoided his eyes. Weismann was further back. She also ignored him.

Barbara filed past the servery and collected her food, then made her way back into the CUO's room. At the doorway she paused in the doorway to decide which table to sit at. There were two empty spaces at the table where Fiona was just sitting down so she walked over to it. She put her mess gear down and sat on the bench seat beside Roger.

Feeling happier she reached for some bread and butter and was just answering Roger's enquiry about whether she had brought a Drill Manual when she became aware of Gordon Farr. His voice seemed to penetrate to the very centre of her being. Her heart skipped a beat, which annoyed her. She glanced up. He was standing at the vacant space opposite her.

"May I sit here?" he asked Fiona.

Fiona smiled and moved along the bench a bit. "Of course."

Gordon settled himself. "I'm Gordon Farr. I'm a sergeant from Broadsound," he said to her.

"Fiona Davis. From Cairns. I'm a sergeant too. You weren't here last year, were you?"

"No I wasn't. I'm from West Australia. My dad moved to Queensland earlier this year."

Barbara was annoyed and tried to shut the conversation out but in spite of herself she found she was listening. But she wouldn't look at him. Instead she carried on a monosyllabic conversation with Roger and concentrated on eating. Just once she glanced up when he talked about the school he'd gone to in Fremantle. Their eyes met and she hastily looked away, but not before he had winked at her.

Winked!

Or was it just a twitch? Barbara didn't dare look up again. She became more aware she was breathing very rapidly and that perspiration was trickling down her back. With feelings of mild panic, coupled with annoyance she almost wolfed down the rest of her lunch. The seat seemed to get harder by the minute and her skin felt flushed.

This is silly, she thought. *It's just the summer sun.*

Because she had been assaulted and nearly raped twice when she was in Year 9, and because of other unpleasant experiences, she had a strong dislike of men. This had been made worse by her experiences a few months before so she was appalled that this youth could have such an effect on her. It made her feel vulnerable. She almost jumped when he spoke to her. Feeling slightly flustered she realised he was repeating a question.

Gordon said, "Excuse me but we've met somewhere before."

"No! No we haven't," Barbara replied, avoiding his eyes.

He chuckled. The sound seemed to draw her gaze up to meet his. He said, "Yes we have. Two hours ago. I don't know your name."

Barbara pushed a spoonful of pudding into her mouth and tried to stare back at him while she chewed. She knew she wanted to tell him but also did not.

To her annoyance Fiona answered for her. "She's Barbara," she said, noting the byplay of eyes.

Barbara turned an accusing look on her, then switched back to meet his steady gaze. It was a friendly, confident gaze, from the bluest of blue eyes. "I've got to go and get changed into uniform," she muttered. She didn't wait to finish her dessert but stood up quickly, gathered her eating utensils and walked out to the washing-up area, very aware that his eyes were following her.

Back in the hut she briefly considered taking her clothes to the shower to change but then shook her head. *I don't really mind if the other girls see me in my underwear,* she thought, although that notion caused her some guilty pleasure. Turning her back on the other girls in the room she quickly changed.

When Fiona came into their hut ten minutes later Barbara was sitting lacing her boots. Fiona put down her mess tins and sipped from a cup. "Want some cordial Barb? It's cold."

"Yes thanks," Barbara replied, putting down her brush and reaching up.

"He likes you," Fiona said, passing the cup.

"Who?"

"Oh Barbara, don't be like that! That big, gorgeous hunk of a sergeant from Broadsound, Gordon Farr."

"Oh him! What makes you think that?" Barbara asked before taking another sip.

"The way he looked at you," Fiona replied with a grin.

"I hate men looking at me. It makes me feel sick. You can see their dirty, little minds at work mentally undressing you when their pupils dilate," Barbara said, wrinkling her nose.

Wendy looked up. She was self-consciously buttoning up her uniform shirt. "I wish his pupils would dilate at me," she said.

Monica Malone turned from looking at her hair in a hand mirror. "His eyes won't dilate over you," she said. "If he sees those whoppers you are trying to hide in that top they'll bloody well pop out!"

Barbara swung her head sharply to look. Wendy was plainly embarrassed. Barbara snapped, "Don't you start any of that crude filth! We've had enough of that sort of thing today. You don't want to be the second person I throw cordial on in one day."

Monica's mouth formed a grin but her blue eyes went cold. "Yeah, Franz told me about that. He said he would get you back for it. Anyway what's wrong with you? Don't you like tits? We've all got them, although some are better than others!"

So saying she unbuttoned her short cotton top and shrugged it off, exposing a pair of almost perfectly proportioned breasts, for she wore no bra. She turned her back on Barbara and bent to pick up her army shirt. The girls looked at each other in a mixture of surprise, embarrassment and outrage.

Barbara had to restrain herself from dashing the contents of the cup over the honey-gold back in front of her. She was about to say exactly what she thought when Camille beat her to it.

"There's no need to flaunt yourself in here. We aren't a bunch of 'Lemons'. How come you're on the CUOs Course anyhow? How can you jump from corporal to CUO without being a sergeant?"

Monica looked at her as she slipped the shirt on. She gave a wide and suggestive smile while swinging her hips. "My OC thinks I'm good. That's how."

She turned her back, picked up her slouch hat and set it on her curls at a jaunty angle. Then, with a laugh, she walked out along the corridor, still buttoning her uniform shirt.

Camille stood speechless, disgust on her face. Barbara and Fiona exchanged glances.

"Bloody tart," Fiona murmured.

Barbara nodded. She realised the hand holding the cup was shaking. Quickly she drained the last of the cordial and handed the cup back. "Thanks," she said sadly. "I've been looking forward to today for months and it just seems to have been one awful thing after another."

With a sigh she settled to finish lacing her boots.

Chapter 4

TRAINING BEGINS

Fifteen minutes later, Barbara hurried out of the hut with the others, in answer to Sgt Karen Harvey's call. Now they were all in DPCU (Disruptive Pattern Camouflage Uniform).On their heads they all wore their Hat, Khaki, Fur Felt (KFF in army jargon, or slouch hat in plain English) with the left side unclipped so it was flat. Normally they wore cloth bush hats but, on this course, they were better dressed. The left side was only clipped up and the 'Rising Sun' badge added for ceremonial parades.

As she marched across to where the platoon was forming up Barbara saw Gordon appear from the direction of the CUO's tents which were on the lawn beyond the male showers. To her own annoyance she found just couldn't seem to resist looking. He was adjusting the angle of his KFF as he walked along.

He looks like the original Aussie 'Digger', she thought.

Then she hastily averted her gaze when he looked in her direction. She joined the front rank next to Lofty and instantly regretted it as Gordon joined the rank behind her. Feeling sure that his eyes were on her she tensed and seemed to burst into perspiration all over.

It's only the sun, she said to herself while looking out at the heat shimmer in the trees beyond the huts.

Weismann came marching up with exaggerated arm swing. He stamped to a halt beside Barbara. She felt something pluck at her sleeve and glanced down. It was Weismann. He was tugging at the crown sewn onto her shirt sleeve. "Warrant Officer eh! What did they call you? With a haircut like that I'll bet it was Butch."

"You're disgusting. Mind your manners or I'll break your face!" Barbara hissed between clenched teeth. She hated her ginger hair with a passion but now she regretted having had it cropped so short that it almost looked like a boy's hairstyle.

"The tough Sergeant Major eh!" Weismann sneered. "I'm glad I wasn't in your company. I bet you were a real Miss Bossy-boots."

Gordon's voice came from behind them. "Shut up Weismann, or we'll both end our course this minute," he warned.

At that moment the Orderly Sergeant's voice pealed out. "Sergeant Harvey! Get the CUOs Course here now!"

The course were called to attention and moved to the right in threes, then given the order 'Quick March'. Barbara found she was boiling with anger, mostly because it seemed so pointless. Her happy anticipation had been well and truly shattered.

What a horrible way to start the course! she thought. *It is going to be a long twelve days!*

The CUOs Course marched past the canteen to the big shady tree on the patch of lawn at the end of the large concrete area. The Sergeants Course and WOs Course were already seated in the shade. The CUOs were directed to join them. Barbara sat on the grass and put down her plastic folder for notes. She looked around and found Gordon sitting right beside her.

Their eyes met and he smiled. To her own dismay Barbara found that she couldn't help herself. She smiled back, then blushed and looked away. The tree was cloaked in yellow flowers and they looked ever so brilliant.

The Orderly Sergeant made them sit at attention and then handed them over to the Colonel. He stood in front of them, a solid man with short grey hair and a determined mouth. But his blue eyes twinkled, and Barbara knew from experience that his bark was worse than his bite.

"Welcome back to Bunyip River," the Colonel began. "If you haven't been here before you have missed one of life's great experiences. Now, I suppose you are wondering why you are sitting here under this tree. The reason is simple..." He paused and looked up.

They all did.

There was a splatter of white on top of the Colonel's KFF.

He roared and shook his fist upwards at the offending bird. "By Gad! Shat on in Period One of Day One! That's a bad omen."

The cadets didn't know whether to laugh or not, but the Colonel did. He broke into a hearty bellow in which they all joined. After a few seconds he held up his hand for silence.

"CSM! Charge that bird with assaulting a Superior Officer. Now, where was I? Ah yes! That reminds me. Just as well I was wearing a hat."

They laughed again. He silenced them. "Seriously. You must all wear your hats. You are under this tree because the heat in the lecture rooms is now about 42 degrees Celsius. Out here it's only a measly 34. That's the air temperature. Luckily, because the climate here is so dry, the Wet Bulb temperature is only about 28 so we can still train safely if we are careful. I could wish for a breeze, but it could be worse. Heat! Remember it. In North Queensland in the bush it is the most dangerous enemy you have."

The Colonel went on to caution them all to avoid Heat Exhaustion by keeping in the shade as much as possible. He reminded them to drink large quantities of water and to have food with it. "If you drink too much without the food you wash out all your body salts and you get sick," he cautioned. He went on to warn them to be on the alert for heat symptoms among their squads as well as themselves.

Nearly all the students were North Queenslanders and were acclimatised to the tropical climate. Barbara found she was a bit bored and had to stifle a yawn. It had already been a long day since getting up at 0300; and there were still seven 40-minute lessons to go.

The Colonel then went on to outline their course programs and to stress what was expected of them in performance and behaviour. This made Barbara glance across at Weismann. To her surprise she saw he wasn't even looking but was gently stroking Malone's fingers!

Barbara squirmed in annoyance and changed her position. As she did her own hand came in contact with someone else's. She drew it away even as she glanced to see whose it was. It was Gordon's!

Oh no! she thought, *I hope he didn't think that was deliberate.* Even so her fingers seemed to tingle. *This is ridiculous! I only saw him for the first time a few hours ago and now I go to jelly at the thought of him. I don't like men!*

The Colonel stopped talking at last and they stood up and formed up in platoons. After a 10-minute break with time for a drink, training began. The first lesson was on Heat; on how to recognize the symptoms of heat illness and how to treat it. This was followed by a lesson on 'Equity' which covered the Army's rule about harassment and bullying. The Colonel gave this and was very grim about it and warned them not to misbehave, or else! During the lesson Barbara could not resist a glance at Weismann. His response was to scowl and mutter under his breath.

After this the courses split up. The WOs and Sergeants were marched off by WO1 Pryor, a tough old regular soldier, to learn about Flags and Regimental Colours. The CUOs were marched to a large gum tree on the edge of the grass parade ground near the railway loading ramp. Crusty old Captain Royston, who also had many years of regular army experience before becoming an Officer of Cadets, was their instructor. The lesson was Sword Drill. He lined them up in an L shape in the shade, spaced well apart.

After an introduction explaining about swords being the traditional weapon and symbol of the Officer and Gentleman and about safety with swords he went on, "We have only been able to get seven swords, for reasons cloaked in Military Security, such as some lazy bugger in a Q Store couldn't be bothered to organise more just for cadets. So...!"

He paused and ran his eyes along the two lines. "You four." He pointed at Barbara and those next to her. "Put on those Sam Browne belts and attach the swords to them." He pointed to the swords lying on a groundsheet. "The rest of you, collect one of these sticks. You will have to practice with them. It won't be the first time the Australian Army has had to train with wooden weapons. Move!"

Barbara picked up a Sam Browne and Fiona and Karen helped her to sort out the leather straps. They buckled it around her. Karen picked up the sword, still in its scabbard. "Gosh! Isn't it light! I thought it would be much heavier seeing how long it is."

She passed the sword to Barbara who was also agreeably surprised. She slid the scabbard down through the leather 'frog' and adjusted it. It gave her a peculiar thrill to touch the hilt.

At that moment Weismann strolled past swishing a stick in the air. "I don't know why they let girls have a sword," he muttered. "I would only let them have a bread knife."

Barbara ignored him but Karen bit back. "I wouldn't even trust you with a butter knife!"

Weismann just sneered at her and walked on. Then he whacked Wilmot on the backside and began a mock sword fight.

Captain Royston went red with anger. "Stop that you pair of drongos and get in line!" he roared.

Barbara couldn't resist a smirk and she saw Gordon grin as well. He looked at her across the L as he lined up.

And he winked again!

Barbara looked away and felt herself blush but she couldn't control a smile.

Captain Royston resumed his lesson. "As the Colonel pointed out in his opening address, at the end of this course we have a Graduation Parade. The Parade Commander will be the top student on the CUOs Course. He or she will get a sword"

As he said this Barbara again resolved that she would do her utmost to be that top student. She resisted an urge to fidget. Sweat made her left hand slippery as it held the leather scabbard. A fly annoyed her. She glanced at Gordon again and their eyes met. He smiled.

Is he thinking the same thoughts? she wondered.

Captain Royston went on, "Because we have only seven swords then six more of the top eight will be the ones to carry them on the parade. The one who misses out, who will be the second ranking student, will have the honour of carrying the Australian Flag. Third, fourth, fifth and sixth will be the company commanders. The next two, seventh and eighth, will be the battalion 2ic and adjutant. They will all get a sword on parade."

He paused to allow them time to absorb this, then said, "Back in your own units, as CUOs, you may get the opportunity to carry swords on a ceremonial parade so you all need to know this." He then went on with the detail of the lesson. First he demonstrated how to draw and return swords. Following the normal sequence of the 'Blueprint' for drill they then learned it by stages, each time practising each movement five times. Once he was satisfied they understood the movements Captain Royston went on to teach them how to salute at the halt with swords.

Barbara found this fascinating and satisfying in a way she could not define. She found it a delight to sweep the blade up in a glittering arc so that the hilt was in front of her mouth. It felt good. It looked good. It made her feel like an officer.

Regretfully she unbuckled the Sam Browne and passed it to Karen. The course kept practising for another hour. While she was standing there going through the motions with a stick Barbara realised she was watching Gordon. He now had a sword. And he held it so well it looked just right. The sunlight sparkled on the chrome blade as he moved it. His well-muscled arm seemed to make it flow with a combination of grace and precision.

They look like nice arms; strong and muscular, Barbara thought. They had a very masculine appeal even with his rolled down sleeves. *He does look good,* she decided. *He's the original bronzed Anzac with his KFF tilted over, the chin strap outlining a firm jaw. Oh! What am I thinking?*

She looked away and concentrated on her drill, working so hard she was soon perspiring freely. At the end of two lessons the CUOs Course marched over to where the Sergeants had been learning to raise, lower and fold flags at the edge of the concrete parade ground. They were fallen out for a break.

Barbara noted that the CUOs Course had already begun to drift into friendship groups. She found she was glad when Gordon joined the group she was with. With an effort she even managed to carry on a normal conversation.

The last period in the afternoon was on Guard Mounting. This involved drill and earned them all some sharp comments from WO1 Pryor. "Come on Cadets! You can do better than that. You are Third and Fourth Years, not First Years! Now lift those feet up! Squaaad Atten.... Shun!"

The problem was simple. Most of the time the cadets were just normal High School students. Cadets was only one afternoon or night a week and a few weekends a year. Not only were they out of practice they hadn't mentally adjusted to the sudden change to a military environment. They were also very tired. When Roger grumbled about being on the bus since 0400 Sgt Millet from Rockhampton acidly pointed out that his group had spent the entire night travelling!

In the last part of the lesson the actual quarter guard or piquet for that night: Duty Officer, Orderly Sergeant, two CUO candidates as Duty NCOs and a section of 8 sergeants—paraded and the flag was lowered.

Barbara found it a real relief to be fallen out beside their hut at 1730. Feeling quite worn out she sat on her stretcher and sighed. She began to unlace her boots but thought better of it and lay back to stretch her tired muscles. With 20 girls and only two showers she had no chance of getting one before tea as several sergeants were already lined up at the door.

At evening mess parade Barbara discovered she was a bit disappointed when Gordon didn't stand near her in line. When she got her meal the disappointment turned to something like dismay. Gordon had been ahead of her in the queue. When she came back to the mess with her food, she saw that he was sitting opposite Monica.

Pretending all was well Barbara went and joined Roger and Fiona again, but she couldn't help darting glances across the room. Monica was all smiles and giggles and Gordon seemed to be chatting away as though they were old friends. 'Bosom buddies' were the first words to come into Barbara's head, but she hastily pushed them out.

Of course they both come from Broadsound and are in the same unit, she told herself. With a jolt she realised that what she was experiencing was jealousy. All of a sudden, she felt all mixed up.

Fiona nudged her. "What's up Barb? You look a bit down in the mouth?" she asked, giving Barbara the impression that she knew perfectly well what the matter was.

"Nothing. I'm just tired," Barbara replied.

She didn't enjoy the meal. Later she couldn't even remember what the food was. She nibbled at it and felt quite miserable. While she ate she couldn't hear Gordon's words but the sounds of his voice reached her. A shrill giggle from Monica made her look across, just in time to see Monica place her hand on Gordon's arm. Seeing that hurt in a way Barbara wouldn't have believed possible.

She went to get up.

"Where are you going Barb?" Fiona asked.

"I can't eat any more. I don't feel well."

Roger, who was sitting opposite, picked up his spoon. "There's dessert to come," he put in.

"Don't eat so much Roger. You'll get fat again," Barbara said. As soon as she said the words, she instantly regretted it as hurt momentarily crossed Roger's face. He had been very chubby when he was in Year 8 and 9 but now he was just a bit big around the waist. She knew he was very self-conscious about his build.

Roger looked at her. "You sit down and eat. This course is a once-in-a-lifetime thing. It's only twelve days and it's more important to keep your energy up than to worry about your weight."

Fiona nodded. "He's right Barbara. You sit down and eat. I'll get us some fruit salad and ice-cream. Want some Roger?"

"Yes please."

Barbara sat and reluctantly put a forkful of mashed potato, peas and gravy into her mouth. Roger was right of course.

Then she made a discovery which cheered her up again. She realised that Weismann was sitting at another table and was glaring furiously at Gordon and Monica.

As Barbara and her friends came out from their meal the sun was just setting beyond the big shed. They paused on the porch and Roger breathed deeply. "That's better. At least it's cooler now," he said before biting into an apple.

Lofty snorted. "Yes, a whole one degree," he added.

Millet, who was walking on Lofty's left added: "It's still 32 degrees."

Roger raised his eyebrows. "How do you know?" he asked.

"I'm very good at estimating such things," Millet replied in a mock-pompous rejoinder.

"Be the only things you are any good at," sniped Cosgrove, another Rockhampton boy. "Besides, didn't I just see you looking at that thermometer in the kitchen?"

They all laughed. Barbara sipped cordial from her canteen cup and quietly enjoyed the sunset. Half the sky was crimson in the way western sunsets are. She sensed someone beside her.

"It's beautiful," said Gordon's voice.

Barbara nodded. "Yes, it is. We don't get sunsets like that in Cairns. It's all clouds and rain there at the moment," she replied. The weather was a nice safe topic.

"You are beautiful too," Gordon added.

Barbara didn't know what to do or say. It was so unexpected. She felt a surge of warmth mixed with panic. After a flustered pause she said, "We were discussing the weather." She knew her voice sounded a bit odd and that embarrassed her even more.

Gordon wasn't put off. "Your hair matches the sky. It is lovely."

Fiona had just come out of the mess, cup in hand. She overheard this and stopped. "Oh! Pardon me. I didn't mean to intrude," she cried delightedly.

Barbara seized the opportunity. "You aren't," she said firmly. "We were just discussing the possibility of rain."

Fiona looked from one to the other, unable to keep the grin from her face. "We could do with some."

"Yes. It would cool things down," Barbara replied with emphasis.

Gordon laughed, a deep chuckle which seemed to make her go weak. She had to join in.

Half an hour later they were seated in the mess, now converted to a lecture room, getting a revision lesson on the organization of Sections, Platoons and Companies. Gordon sat beside Barbara. In fact he had made sure of it by blocking Roger when he had gone to sit there. Barbara was very conscious of his nearness and could hardly concentrate on the lesson.

Fiona kept looking across and smiling which made it worse. Barbara was annoyed with herself for not being able to control her emotions better. Once they bumped elbows and it was as though a spark of static electricity jumped across.

This is silly, she told herself. *I'm acting like someone in a Romance Novel. How could he affect me so much, and so quickly?*

There was then a lesson on 'Compliments' (Who to salute and when). This was to the whole group out on the tennis courts. Here there was a faint breeze which felt positively cool. The lesson was run by Major Wickham, OC of 130ACU, and included demonstrations of various situations and Barbara found it quite entertaining.

The next lecture, the last for the day, was on the duties of the various ranks. Luckily the lieutenant who gave it had a hand-out to give them as they were nearly all so tired they could hardly keep their eyes open. Only the Townsville people were relatively fresh, and they had the duties that night.

At the end of the lesson the officer reminded them of the lessons they had to give later in the course. Barbara knew this and had made a special effort the previous week to come prepared. It was 2130 hrs when they were dismissed.

As they made their way out into the night Fiona tugged at Barbara's sleeve. "Coming to the canteen for a soft drink Barb?" she asked.

"Alright. Just one. I'm whacked."

They walked along past the girl's hut in a group, Fiona on the right, Barbara in the middle, Gordon on the left. Roger and Lofty followed behind with Camille and Sharon. The canteen was just a small wooden hut with a bar and cold storage. One of the lieutenants from Townsville ran it with some of his cadets. It was a cheerful spot but too small. Once they had their Cherry Ripes, Mars Bars, and soft drinks most cadets spilled back out into the night.

Barbara managed to talk normally despite the fact that she knew Gordon was looking at her all the time. She finished her drink but was curiously reluctant to go.

"Bedtime you lot," Camille called. "Lights Out in twenty minutes and I still haven't had a bath."

Sharon giggled. "That's why you smell like a camel," she needled. They laughed and began to stroll across towards the girl's hut. As they came level with it Roger and Lofty called cheerful 'Goodnights' and kept walking.

Gordon hung back and spoke quietly to Barbara in the semi-darkness. "See you tomorrow."

"Yes."

His voice thrilled her. She realised she didn't want to leave him but reluctantly she followed Fiona up into the hut.

Inside Fiona smiled and said, "Oh look at you! You are in dreamworld."

"Is it that obvious?" Barbara asked, blushing as she did.

"Is it that obvious! You two have been flashing signals at each other all day. I thought he was going to manhandle Roger aside so he could sit next to you tonight. If ever there was love at first sight!"

Love! Barbara's mind tried to reject the word in a near panic.

Then it was all half-spoilt. There was loud female laughter and Monica bounded into the hut, her shirt half-unbuttoned and without her hat. She went to her bunk and bent over Barbara who had sat to unlace her boots. Placing her face close to Barbara's she hissed, "You keep your claws off Gordon Farr, you tramp! He's mine."

Barbara looked up in hurt surprise. The whole room, now full of girls preparing for bed, went silent.

"I'll do what I like," Barbara replied. "Besides, it's up to him what he does."

"Keep away from him or I'll scratch your eyes out."

Barbara couldn't believe her ears. She pulled off a boot before looking up. It took her a moment to master her emotions. "Just try it," she said as coolly as she could manage.

"I mean it!" Monica snapped, but she turned away.

The room seemed to heave a collective sigh of relief and the bustle resumed. Barbara peeled off her socks, grabbed her toilet bag and towel and pyjamas and made her way to the shower. She had to wait her turn and it was after 'Lights Out' when she came out. By then the bedroom was in darkness and she had to grope around to organise her bedding. From over at the boy's tents she heard several shouts of 'Get to bed!' and 'Lights Out' in an 'or else' tone of voice.

Barbara had just lain down on her sleeping bag when Sgt Harvey came in and checked with a torch to see they were all in bed. For a few minutes Barbara lay quietly, trying to sort out the mixed memories of the day.

Then sleep claimed her.

Chapter 5

A SAFE TRAINING AREA

B arbara was roused from a delicious dream in which Gordon had just been about to kiss her. It was still quite dark.

"Wakey wakey! Rise and shine," called Sgt Harvey as she clicked on the lights. "Everyone out for check parade. Make sure you have something on your feet."

Barbara sat up and groaned. Bleary eyed she groped for her boots and pulled them on without socks. After checking her pyjamas were decent, she stood up and rubbed her eyes. It was pleasantly cool.

Karen stamped across the room. "Come on, hurry up!" she called. On her way past she kicked Monica's stretcher. "Come on Malone, out of bed!"

Monica's tousled curls appeared out of her sleeping bag. "What time is it?"

"Five past six," Karen replied. "Now get a move on. Come on you lot. Move!"

Barbara hurried out of the hut with the others, wrapping a dressing gown over her pyjamas. Most of the girls were similarly dressed but some were in tracksuits or in shorts and T shirts. They joined the male CUOs under the streetlight in front of the Mess. The first streaks of daylight showed through the trees to the east.

As the girls arrived Roger waved. "Morning all! Lovely day," he called.

Lofty grunted, then replied, "Shut up Roger! It's a horrible day. I couldn't sleep at all last night, between the squeaking of that damned stretcher and your snoring!"

"Quiet in the ranks!" Sgt Harvey called. "Platoon. Atten... shun! Right Dress, Eyes Front! Platoon. Stand at... ease! Answer your names." She opened the roll book and began to call the names.

"Jones?"

"Ma'am!"

"Malone?"

Silence. Then Karen called again, "Malone!"

"Not here," someone murmured.

Karen turned to face the girl's hut and raised her voice. "Malone! Get out here. Hurry up!"

Monica appeared on the veranda. "I'm coming. I'm coming. Keep your shirt on!"

They all turned to look, and an audible gasp escaped the group. Monica was wearing some sort of short negligee of almost transparent material and even in the poor light it was obvious she was wearing nothing else.

A couple of boys gave low wolf-whistles and the girls broke into a scandalised murmur. Monica's only response was to walk with an exaggerated wiggle. She joined the end of the platoon. Barbara looked along the line and could plainly see Monica's nipples through the thin nylon.

And she doesn't look as though she is wearing any pants! she thought.

Barbara couldn't restrain herself. "Oh you shameless tease!"

Monica flared. "Don't you call me a tease." She turned to face Barbara and put her hands on her hips. Roger looked as though his eyes would pop out. The boys goggled. Most of the girls fumed.

Stephens, one of the Townsville cadets, hissed. "Cat fight, cat fight!"

"Shut up you!" Camille snapped at him. Then she too started on Malone. "You go and get some clothes on," she said, also placing her hands on her hips.

Monica scowled back defiantly. "Something on my feet was the order," she replied with a sneer. At the same time she held up one leg to show a rubber thong.

Sgt Harvey yelled above all of them. "Shut up all of you! I'm Duty Student. Corporal Malone, fall out and make yourself decent!"

With a sulky pout Monica stepped out of the ranks. She then deliberately marched across in front of them all, her breasts quivering at every step. As Monica passed in front of her Barbara had a strong urge to kick her wiggling bottom.

Most of the boys were obviously delighted, if not impressed. As Monica walked away Roger rubbed his eyes.

Lofty chuckled and said, "You awake now Roger?"

The joke helped ease the tension. Karen was doubly embarrassed as the disturbance now called forth a reprimand from the Orderly Sergeant. He came marching over to see what the fuss was about. The roll call was completed and they were given 'Fall Out'.

Embarrassed and annoyed by Monica's lewd display Barbara smiled briefly at Gordon but at once turned away and went into a scandalized huddle with the other girls.

"That was disgusting! What will we do?" she asked.

"We should tell one of the lady officers," Sharon said emphatically.

Jennifer Bladen from Sarina shook her head. "That's a bit hard. But she needs to be spoken to," she said.

"Who's going to speak to her?" Camille asked.

"I will," Barbara volunteered.

Fiona spoke next. "No, not you Barb. She won't listen to you. Not after last night," she said, shaking her head.

"I will," Camille said.

They left it at that and made their way back to the hut. When they got there Monica was in the bathroom. Camille went in and the others made their way through to the bedroom. Even before they had all filed in they heard raised voices from the bathroom.

Monica's voice sounded in an angry and strident tone. "Who do you think you are? Don't you start telling me what to do!"

Camille's answer was not audible to them. Then Monica screamed a reply. "I don't care what you think! Get out of here and leave me alone!"

"There's no need to yell," Camille replied. "I was only saying..."

The rest was lost as Monica yelled over her. "So what? I don't care what those boys think, so wop it up ya!"

There was a loud banging sound and Lt McEwen's voice cut in. She was clearly angry as well. "Well I do young Miss! I saw you come back and I'll tell you this; if you parade around like a shameless hussy again you'll be off this course and on the next bus home!"

Barbara looked at Fiona and Wendy. They all grinned and Wendy gave a thumbs-up. They had all seen Miss McEwen when she was steamed up and they knew that, while she looked soft and meek, she was the original 'iron fist in a velvet glove.'

The voices died down. Camille came through and stopped in the doorway. She hugged herself in silent laughter which made most of them snicker and giggle.

When Monica came in a few minutes later, she was wearing only a towel. She ignored them all and walked to her bunk. With a flourish she unwrapped the towel and flung it on the bed. She was totally nude. The room went very quiet as people pretended to be busy polishing and tidying up. Monica slowly dressed herself.

Barbara sat with her back to her thinking unkind thoughts. She was shocked, but as much by her own reactions as by Monica's brazen display. To her own annoyance Barbara found she was gripped by a desire to look at Monica. She sometimes admitted that she was actually very drawn to liking females and that she found nudity both exciting and embarrassing, but she had not fully articulated this into defining her own sexuality.

To add to her annoyance, she knew she was jealous. When she was having a bout of low self-confidence, she sometimes acknowledged that her own body was very beautiful by conventional standards, but so was Monica's. It took a few minutes for murmuring and then proper conversation to spring up again. During that time Barbara took herself to the bathroom and changed into her uniform in private.

What a pity, Barbara thought, *to have the course made unpleasant and split like that.*

She also felt bad about her own unkind thoughts and resolved to try to heal the breach somehow. It was a relief for them to be called out for breakfast.

At the mess Roger again cheered her up. "Day Two. Ten to go," he said as he joined the ranks.

"Don't be such a bloody optimist Roger," Lofty said. "You mean ten and three-quarters."

"Excuse me Lofty." It was Gordon. He gently pushed in between Lofty and Barbara.

Lofty looked at him in surprise. "What the...? Go to the end! Oh...I see. Oh! Sorry Gordon." Lofty moved along and a grin split his face.

Barbara felt a rush of embarrassment mingled with pure pleasure. Gordon had been willing to take on Lofty, who stood a good half-a-head taller, so that he could stand next to her.

Incredibly for her, when they filed in to get their meal, she found herself tongue-tied. She could only nod and smile. Gordon didn't seem to notice. He chatted cheerfully away. Then he then sat next to her while they ate. She found herself looking at him more and more.

The only 'off' note was noticing a sour-faced Monica muttering to Weismann in the corner.

Fiona tapped Barbara on her shoulder. "Come on Babs. No time for that now. We have to be ready for inspection in less than half an hour."

Reluctantly Barbara got up and went out to wash up.

There followed twenty minutes of sweeping, dusting and polishing. Punctually at 0730 Karen called them to attention. Lt McEwen then minutely inspected their bed layout and their uniforms. The minor faults were numerous.

At 0800 they raced out into the already scorching sunshine to form up for Morning Parade. The CUOs Course marched as a platoon onto the concrete parade ground with an air temperature already in the thirties, for a talk-through by WO1 Pryor on the conduct of a Company Admin Parade. The CUOs Course was lined up on the side with their backs to the sun. Four of them: Banaboos (A Torres Strait Islander), Cosgrove, Camille and Millett were then detailed to act in the role of the platoon commanders.

The parade was formed as two small companies. A Coy comprised two platoons of sergeants and B Coy of the other two. Two members of the Warrant Officers Course acted as Coy Sgt Majors and the others stood at the front, near the tree with the yellow flowers, where a temporary flagpole had been erected. All of the Sergeants Course and the WOs carried innocuous rifles. The companies were formed up 'In line' with the platoons side by side and B Coy to the left of A Coy. The formation stretched most of the way across the concrete slab and to Barbara it looked impressive.

Half an hour of sweaty drill improved the cadets considerably. Markers were called by CSMs. The platoons were moved on parade, right-dressed, numbered and the roll called. The Orderly Sergeant, acting as RSM, gave the orders as WO1 Pryor instructed him to.

Only when WO1 Pryor was satisfied with their performance did he relax them for a minute to have a big drink from the water bottles they had been ordered to bring with them. Then he handed over to the Colonel. The parade was called to attention and the Colonel marched on. After saluting the Colonel the Orderly Sergeant and WO1 Pryor marched to the rear. When they were in position the Colonel stood the parade at ease to symbolically demonstrate that he now had command and then called them back to attention. The Platoon Commanders were 'posted' in front of their platoons. The Colonel then ordered, in a very loud and clear voice, "Present Arms!" and "Break the flag!" On that command one of the Duty NCOs broke the flag.

During this Barbara stood rigidly, chest-out. Watching the red, white and blue of the flag as it unfurled gave her a surge of pride and satisfaction.

I am glad to be here and I'm proud to be an army cadet, she thought.

Seeing the flag with its colours so bright in the morning sun against the green backdrop of trees made her feel proud to be Australian. She also enjoyed hard drill that was well done.

The Colonel ordered them back to attention and then stood them at ease. After ordering them all to drink from their water bottles he said, "Your drill leaves a lot to be desired. Remember, tomorrow 128 would-be corporals arrive, and you people will be out in front. You must set them an example. As for you ones keeling over and looking sick!" He paused and shook his head in disgust. "It's only the heat. You were told yesterday to drink and drink. And make sure you have a good breakfast, and some salt. During the break before the next lesson have another drink—at least half a water bottle—all of you. You'll soon toughen up. You're all just unfit."

The Colonel fell out the acting Platoon Commanders, handed back to the RSM and marched off. The Parade was then marched to the side of the parade ground and fallen out. Half a dozen pasty-faced miserables who had fainted or fallen-out earlier sat there in the shade. With a twinge of malice Barbara noted Monica was one of these.

Training then began in earnest. All three courses were formed up on the grass under the big tree where they learned how to carry out an inspection of a platoon. All the CUOs Course took turns with members of the Sgts Course acting as their Pl Sgts. They used the remnants of the four platoons of the Sgts Course to practice on.

After that it was a relief to get out of 38-degree sunlight and 33 degrees in the shade into the 31 degree heat of the lecture room for a lecture on 'The Role of Warrant Officers and Senior NCOs in a Company'. Captain Royston was the Instructor. He handed out a precis detailing the duties of various ranks and postings.

As they sat there, Roger fanned himself with the handout. "Strewth, it's hot!" he muttered.

Barbara could only agree. There was no wind and inside the metal building it was stifling. Sweat dripped from them. It also trickled down their backs, which felt very unpleasant.

"Ah, yuk!" Fiona said in disgust. She peeled away a page which had stuck to the perspiration on her arm.

"Yes, I quite agree," Captain Royston replied, mopping his brow. "It is about forty degrees. Right, let's get on with the lesson."

It was mostly just revision. The subject was something they had all covered before but because some units were not run in a very military way there was some uncertainty.

"But we don't do it that way in our unit sir!" was the comment from several.

"I realise there are problems," Captain Royston replied, trying to dodge around the issue of making implied rebukes of other OCs. "But this is the standard Army procedure."

The lesson went on, mostly in the form of Question and Answer, to make the class read the 'handout'. Capt Royston asked, "Who in the company is specifically responsible for the dress, discipline and behaviour of the sergeants?" He paused and ran his eyes over the squad. "Malone?"

Monica pouted, paused with obvious uncertainty, then answered. "The captain Sir."

"The captain? So, do you mean the OC or the 2IC? In an army unit or full-sized company the OC is a major. Anyway that's wrong. Someone else try now, ah… Brassington."

Barbara silently swore, wishing she had not been asked. *I don't want to upset Monica anymore,* she thought. But she answered, "The Company Sergeant Major, Sir."

Capt Royston nodded. "Correct. I'm glad you got that right, seeing you are a Warrant Officer. Were you a CSM?"

"Yes Sir."

Weismann made a low aside. "I'm glad I wasn't in your company!"

Barbara turned to look at him but before she could comment Gordon cut in. "I wish I had been," he said.

This raised a laugh. Captain Royston raised an eyebrow, sensing but not fully understanding the by-play. "That will do," he said in a mild voice frosted with iron-filings. He went on with the lesson. Luckily, he did not select the same people to answer further questions.

Morning tea—cake and cold cordial at the rear of the kitchen—was a welcome break. Then it was back into the lecture room for a lecture on the types of patrols by Capt Conkey.

During the break at the end of the lesson, Weismann muttered to the group. "What a load of crap! Why do we need to learn all this stuff about patrols?"

"It comes in useful sometimes," Roger replied. "After all it is basic military knowledge and we are supposed to be *Army* Cadets."

Weismann sneered. "Oh sure! But when will we ever use it?"

Roger paused before answering. "Our unit uses it all the time. In fact during our annual camp last September we needed to patrol for real."

"For real! Get real! Don't talk crap. You were just playing silly games," he sneered.

Lofty touched Roger's sleeve. "Don't get steamed up Roger. He doesn't know what happened."

"So what happened?" Weismann asked with insulting disbelief.

"Our unit had some problems with a gang of crooks," Lofty replied.

Roger butted in. "That's right. We had to carry out some real patrols, both types: recon patrols and fighting patrols."

Weismann still did not believe. "Fighting patrols! You lot play with yourselves!" he jeered.

"They were real! Real enough for live ammo and people getting shot," Roger replied hotly.

Weismann paused. It was obvious from his face that he now remembered hearing something about it and that he realised he was making himself look silly. "I suppose you shot someone?" he asked in a disbelieving tone.

Roger hesitated. Barbara could tell that he didn't want to sound like a braggart. Lofty cut in: "No, but he led a bloody good patrol and they certainly got shot at and fired back."

"I shot a truck," Roger admitted with a grin.

Lofty nodded. The whole group were listening intently, most knowing the outline of the story. Lofty went on, "CUO Kirk shot one of the crooks and so did Barbara."

Barbara had been keeping out of it and hoping no-one would mention her but now everyone's eyes turned on her. She felt her stomach churn as horrible memories flooded her mind.

Jennifer Bennett blurted out the question on most minds. "Barbara, did you kill him?"

Barbara blushed. "No. I just broke his leg," she answered.

Karen cut in. "Here comes the Colonel. Everyone take their seats."

That was a relief for Barbara as she didn't want to talk about that horrible incident. Just thinking about it upset her. She took her seat and was very conscious of Gordon's questioning eyes on her.

The lesson was on 'Safety in Training'; on the responsibilities of officers to select safe areas and to supervise to ensure activities were accident free. After pointing out the Safety Regulations and Restrictions in various Manuals and Standing Orders the Colonel went on to how to select suitable training areas. He talked about the importance of having clear boundaries so that lost cadets could be easily found. Then he went on to discuss accidents. By question and answer he extracted the dangers: heat exhaustion, snakebite, broken legs, thorn trees, wild pigs and so on.

The Colonel said, "My rule of thumb, when picking an area, is that the cadets must never be more than 10 minutes' walk from a Safety Vehicle so we can have a serious case in hospital in about an hour. That means training areas must be within 30 to 45 minutes' drive of a hospital. It also means good vehicle access to the area."

The class scribbled some notes. The Colonel then went on: "However, having good road access can introduce another safety hazard. What might that be?"

Fiona answered. "People Sir. Stranger Danger."

"Correct. People. Creepy weirdos, gun-nuts and other undesirables, especially on weekends when all the 'yobbos' go bush in their 4WDs. I gather your Cairns Unit had more than its fair share of problems with unwanted visitors last annual camp?"

"Yes sir, we did," Fiona replied. She made a wry face. "We were just talking about it when you came in."

"Indeed! Captain Conkey told me about it. A fascinating story. You all did very well." He checked his watch. "That concludes my lesson. Any questions? Duty Student, take over."

Karen called them to sit to attention and saluted. The Colonel left the room and they relaxed, except Barbara. The memories swirling in her head made her feel nauseous and she shuddered.

I hope I never have to do anything like that again! she thought.

Chapter 6

STORIES

"Lunch time," Roger reminded them.

Gordon nodded. "Yes Roger. Now come on you lot from Cairns, don't keep us in suspense. Tell us the whole story. What happened?" he asked. He looked at Barbara, but she shook her head. So Gordon turned to Lofty. "Come on one of you, please tell," he pleaded.

Lofty shrugged. "Not me. Roger, you tell it. You were in the thick of it."

Reluctantly Roger agreed. The others crowded round and settled on chairs and tables.

"Well... er... um... we, that is 4 Platoon, we hid this girl," Roger began.

Fiona shook her head and interjected. "No Roger. Start at the beginning. Otherwise you'll just confuse everyone."

Roger paused again to gather his thoughts, then said, "Our unit came here for annual camp last September. The 'First Years' were here in the camp and my platoon, 4 Platoon, which was the senior rifle platoon, was bivouacked across the Flinders Highway on Sandy Ridge. I was the platoon sergeant and CUO Kirk was the platoon commander. On the third day a girl came running through the bush carrying a briefcase. She was being chased by crooks who had just killed her uncle. CUO Kirk hid her and even got us to pretend to help the crooks search for her. Instead we made sure she wasn't found. Then we dressed her as a cadet and hid her in the platoon while we worked out what to do. This went on for two nights and a day."

Gordon looked puzzled. "But why didn't you just get the police?"

"The police were there. That's what had us baffled. They were helping the crooks search and had roadblocks and things," Roger explained.

"Why? Were they crooks too?"

Roger shook his head. "No. They'd been fed a story by the mine manager who was a 'Big Wheel' in the local business community. But we didn't know that at the time."

"What were these crooks doing all this time?"

"They had the area surrounded and were searching everywhere," Roger exaggerated, waving his arms.

Gordon frowned. "Surrounded? How big was this area? How many crooks?" he asked.

"At least a dozen and all armed. Plus they had all the miners and a ring of mine vehicles with radios. They even hired two Pig Hunters to search the creeks. That's when Barbara met the man of her dreams."

When Roger said this, Barbara glanced towards Gordon, and before she could correct the mistake she saw that others had noticed.

Gordon turned to her. "Man of your dreams?" he queried, causing Barbara to blush and several others to smile of smirk.

Roger answered for her. "Two Pig Hunters."

Barbara wrinkled her nose to hide her blushing confusion. "Revolting animals!" she cried.

"So, did the crooks find out you were hiding the girl?" Gordon asked.

Roger hung his head. "Yes they did. It was my fault partly. You see there were always NORMAC security men at Company HQ, which was why we could never get Capt Conkey alone to explain things. Anyhow we, that is 4 Platoon, came down from a hill called Black Knoll where we'd spent the night and I had to collect our ration packs. I included Elizabeth, that's the girl, in the number and the CQMS said that was one too many."

Barbara now spoke up. "I made it worse. I joined in and supported the CQ and got the Roll Book to check. I was CSM you see. And I was sure that 4 Platoon had only 23 on the roll, not 24. Well this crook saw the Roll Book cover and realised we were from Cairns. They knew Elizabeth came from there, so I suppose... sorry Roger it's your story."

"No. You tell this bit Barb."

"OK. So I suppose the crooks put two and two together. It was just after this that I walked down to where 4 Platoon were waiting in the riverbed. It was then I saw Elizabeth. CUO Kirk gave me a letter from Miss McEwen for Captain Conkey and I walked back to Company HQ. When I got there, I explained what I knew to the OC. At that moment the leader of the crooks, a Fijian Indian named Bargheese, arrived. He had more thugs with him and they all had guns. Was he wild! I thought he was going to shoot Capt Conkey there and then," she said.

Barbara paused to collect her thoughts and to calm her emotions. Then she went on: "While Bargheese was arguing with Captain Conkey I walked to the Signals Tent and warned 4 Platoon on the radio. Then the crooks sat us under guard, the whole company I mean, or at least the three First Year platoons and HQ. This Bargheese bloke then went and tried to catch CUO Kirk. He took Capt Conkey and Lt MacLaren as hostages and guides."

Roger grinned. "He didn't get us though. We gave the bastard the slip!" he said.

"How did you do that?" Sharon asked.

Roger then described the events of the next day and night.[1] "CUO Kirk really got stuck into the crooks. He sent me with a patrol to set up a roadblock to stop them escaping from their camp. That's when I shot my truck."

"What with?" Gordon asked.

"12-gauge shotgun. Anyway we harassed the buggers all night. In the morning they came after us to try to get a brown notebook. The notebook was full of incriminating details you see. They shot one of our kids. A mongrel named Berzinski did that. So the boss shot him, CUO Kirk that was, not Capt Conkey. Didn't kill him though," Roger explained.

At the mention of Berzinski's name Barbara tensed. A vivid image of the man's lust-filled eyes ravishing her body and of his violent temper caused her to shiver. "I wish he had!" she said.

"Oh Barbara!" Sharon cried. "That's a bit bloodthirsty!"

"He's a vicious animal. He tried to kill me," Barbara snapped.

"How? Tell us," Gordon asked.

Roger cut in. "We should be getting ready for Mess Parade. The sergeants are lining up."

"Oh Roger! Stop worrying about your stomach for a minute. We want to hear this," Gordon said. "Go on Barbara."

Barbara was reluctant to. Her mind seemed to fill with a picture of Berzinski's eyes leering their disgusting message; and of the wicked black sub-machinegun he carried.

"Please Barbara," Karen asked.

Barbara shrugged. "It's not much really. Bargheese started beating Cadet Nelms to find out where Graham, I mean CUO Kirk, was going.

---

[1] Read *The Cadet Under-Officer* by C.R. Cummings.

Captain Conkey grabbed him and punched him a couple of beauties but they clubbed him with their gun butts."

Barbara felt her stomach churn at the memory. She took a couple of deep breaths and went on, "I helped Mrs Standish put the OC on a stretcher. Then the crooks started to torture Cpl Kenny. That brute Berzinski kicked him in the groin and kept on kicking. Mrs Standish tried to stop him. Bargheese started to hurt her so..." She stopped, sickened by the memories.

"So?" Gordon asked.

Fiona cut in. "She's being modest. She kicked that bastard Berzinski fair in the nuts. Then she flattened Bargheese. We all got up to join in. When Bargheese got up he was like an animal gone mad. He shot CUO Bronsky and threatened us. While all this was going on, Barbara got away."

Barbara blushed. "I didn't like running. I was worried you would think I was a coward, but I wanted to get the police. Berzinski chased me. He tried to shoot me, with a sub machine gun, but I made it into the thick scrub along the bank of the Canning. I was terrified!"

"That's when you met your idea of the perfect man," Fiona said with a laugh.

"No, that was a bit later," Barbara said. She gave a wry grin. "I got away from Berzinski, but while I was heading along Scrubby Creek on my way here I found these two revolting Pig Hunters. They'd captured three members of 4 Platoon." Again she paused. She didn't really want to describe what followed.

"Is that when you shot one?" Gordon asked in a gentle voice.

Barbara nodded. "Yes, they had Lillis, a young girl cadet, tied to a tree naked and they were going to torture her. A disgusting pig of a man named Lenny had a hot knife and was threatening to touch her on the..."

She was too embarrassed to say, but gestured to her breasts. Gordon looked and nodded and she noted the way his gaze flickered to her front and then away. To her own surprise she did not mind that.

She said, "I saw a rifle and picked it up. He moved the knife and held it ready to throw. I warned him but he did not believe I would be game and went to throw it, so I shot him."

"Did you kill him?" Stephens asked.

"No. Broke his leg."

"Well, what happened next?" Sharon asked.

"Nothing much. I set the cadets free and we made our way here. We had to creep past some miners in their dump trucks at the highway. When I got here, I told our QM and he phoned the police. By the time they arrived most of the crooks had snuck away."

"What about their boss, this Bargheese character?" Gordon asked.

"He flew back to their mine in his helicopter. Roger can tell you what happened then."

They all looked at Roger. He shrugged. "Aw! I've told you. CUO Kirk wrecked his chopper. Then we kept at him all night till what was left of his gang fell apart. Then we caught him. Actually it was CUO Kirk who did and it was a lot more exciting than that."

During all this Weismann had been listening. Now he curled his lip. "You lot all think you are just so good!" he said.

"We are," Roger replied calmly. "Now let's have lunch."

To Barbara's relief the moment passed without further unpleasantness and the course lined up at the servery.

Lunch passed in a buzz of conversation. The stories had excited their imaginations and they had dozens of questions to ask. Gordon sat opposite Barbara, his face showing frank admiration. Weismann and Monica sat in a corner sneering and murmuring to each other.

The first period after lunch was 'Fronts and Flanks', to ensure they understood the correct orders to give when marching their platoons. They had all done it on their corporals and sergeants courses, but some were still hazy.

The lesson seemed to lead with inevitability to another series of minor clashes. WO1 Pryor had the squad. He revised the explanation on a 'Blanket' Board using cardboard symbols with sandpaper glued on the back. Then he formed them up outside in three ranks and 'Right Dressed' them to establish the 'Right Marker'. Members of the platoon were then selected to give the orders. Barbara hoped she wouldn't get a go. She was bored by it but still did her best. It was something she was sure she knew well. The cadets were told not to indicate which way the platoon was to turn on the executive order to test that the 'precautionary' was correct.

"Sergeant Farr fall out! Take over," WO1 Pryor ordered.

Barbara's heart leapt into her mouth. *Oh please don't make a mistake!* she thought. She didn't want him to look silly.

"Sir!" Gordon stepped smartly out of the ranks and marched over beside the Warrant Officer.

WO1 Pryor pointed which way he wanted the platoon to go. Gordon nodded, breathed in deeply and called, "Platoon! Move to the Right in threes. (Pause). Turn! By the Left, Quick March!"

For the next few minutes he marched them around, giving a dozen orders. Gordon did well. His orders were clear and delivered in a deep voice, which carried clearly.

He has natural authority, thought Barbara as she marched along. It increased her respect.

After a couple of minutes they were halted. WO1 Pryor then said, "Right Sgt Farr, fall in! Sgt Weismann, fall out and take over."

Weismann was nervous. Barbara could hear it in his voice. He was also unsure of what the correct orders were and quickly made several minor mistakes. After a while he got them marching in line in the 'Retired' position. "Platoon! Turn to the right in threes. Turn!" Weismann ordered.

Chaos resulted. Half the Platoon did a right turn. The others turned left. This wouldn't have been so bad if the squad had split in two but it didn't. As a result there were several collisions. Barbara turned left and ran full tilt into Monica. The two of them lost their balance and fell over.

Monica landed heavily on her backside. She swore loudly. "Ow! Fuck! Watch where you are going, you stupid cow!"

Barbara, along with several others, had started to laugh but the sound died in her throat. She stood up and dusted herself. "Don't swear at me, you coarse baggage!" she snapped.

WO1 Pryor at once intervened. "All right! That is enough of that. Back in line," he commanded.

Monica stood up and pointed angrily at Barbara. "She turned the wrong way the…" she began.

"That will do both of you!" roared WO1 Pryor. He turned to Barbara. "Now Warrant Officer Brassington, what should the order have been?"

It just seemed so inevitable Barbara felt like swearing herself. With an effort she restrained the urge and replied, "We were retired sir, so the precautionary order should have been 'Move', not 'Turn', to YOUR left in threes. The order 'Move to the right in threes' could be given but, as was demonstrated, can lead to possible confusion."

"Quite right!" WO1 Pryor agreed. "So your order was confusing Sgt

Weismann, and," he turned to face Monica. "You turned the wrong way Corporal Malone."

Barbara met Monica's eye. Her lip curled and a glint of dislike showed. That caused Barbara a twinge of regret as she really did not want ill-will on the course.

WO1 Pryor said, "Fall in Sgt Weismann. Fall out Sgt Ying and take over."

Weismann replaced Ying in the ranks. This put him beside Barbara. Out of the side of his mouth he hissed, "Bloody know-all smart arse!"

With an effort of willpower, Barbara did not respond but inside she seethed. The lesson went on for another ten sweaty minutes before they were fallen out in the shade for a drink.

The second lesson after lunch was Map Reading by Capt Conkey on 'Inter-visibility', whether one place could be seen from another or whether some intervening terrain feature prevented this. "It's most important for Line-of-Sight to get good radio communications with the VHF radios you are going to use," he explained. They were all given the local map on a 1:50 000 scale and began to work on an example.

Capt Conkey said, "Locate the highest point in these hills to the Southeast of us, the Tucker Box Range. The question is; can we see that point from the camp?"

Weismann spoke. "Yes we can sir. It is over 500 metres high."

"Can we though? How high are we?" Capt Conkey queried.

The cadets pored over their maps, checking contour intervals and spot heights. Capt Conkey went on, "You will see we are about 260 metres above sea level. The highest point in Tucker Box is 12 kilometres away and is 509 metres." He paused to allow them to check. "But in between, only two kilometres this side of Hill 509 is a ridge 450m high."

He then talked them through how to draw a simple cross section. This proved that, in fact, Hill 509 was not visible. Next he then got them to go outside, saying, "Let's see if we can see the 450 metre ridge."

They orientated their maps and looked in the direction of the hill. Barbara saw that the surrounding bush hid almost everything.

"There it is sir," Stephens said, pointing up the track between the corporals' hut and the corporals' tents.

"No, sorry. That's Hill 376. If we walk over near the showers, we will just glimpse the Tucker Box Range," Capt Conkey said.

They did this, glimpse being the right word for an outline through a tiny gap in the trees. Then they went back in to the lecture room to do another inter-visibility problem. Capt Conkey said, "OK class, try this one. This is for Roger. Can you see this camp from Whaleback Hill? It is 15 kilometres to the West."

"Is that the Whaleback Hill where you had the battle with the crooks sir?" asked Millet.

"Yes, it is. If..." Captain Conkey was side tracked. For the next few minutes he ran over the story again, tracing it out for them on the map.

"And was it line-of-sight Roger?" Sharon asked.

Roger nodded. "Near enough. Didn't make much difference though. The bloody radio was bung!"

"It wasn't all the time. We got you loud and clear once," Lofty laughed.

"Aw yeah! For about a minute at three o'clock in the bloody morning," Roger replied.

Barbara joined in. "It worked when we needed it," she said quietly.

"My word yes. You saved our bacon Barbara," Roger said with feeling, remembering how she had warned them the crooks knew they were hiding the girl.

"You've got plenty of bacon to save Dunning," Weismann said.

Captain Conkey cut in sharply. "That's enough talk like that! Remember the Code of Conduct. No harassment and teasing! Now, let's get back to our problem."

They bent to the maps and worked. The answer was NO. A low rise, unnamed on the map but nicknamed 'Bare Ridge' by the cadets, just blocked it by 20 metres. Barbara found it an interesting exercise. It certainly seemed like a useful skill.

Period 8 was on 'Efficient Time Management'. It was in the stifling heat of the lecture room and Barbara found it very hard to stay awake. Period 9 came almost as a relief. It was Drill and even though it was out in the blazing afternoon sun there was at least a bit of breeze and not the same need to concentrate.

The Drill was revision of Marching in Slow Time. WO1 Pryor kept them hard at it. They went up and down the parade ground in line and in column, the Warrant Officer's voice lashing them to improve. "Cadet Malone! Stop waving around. You're not doing a dance. Cadet Millet, that's very good. Cadet Weismann! Stop that jerky walk. The foot should glide smoothly from one step to the next!"

Barbara heard a murmur and glanced sideways. Roger had a grin from ear to ear. "Show pony high-stepping," he whispered.

Weismann overheard this and turned to glare. WO1 Pryor bellowed. "No talking! Pay attention in the centre rank."

Period 10 was on 'Patrol Planning & Preparation' by the Colonel. Once again Weismann sneered and muttered. After it was over and the Colonel had left the room, Weismann gave vent to his thoughts. "Why do we do all this crap? Our unit never does anything like this."

"What does it do then?" Roger asked.

"We do drill. We're the best in Broadsound. We beat the Air Cadets and Navy Cadets every year."

"What's the point of that?" Lofty asked.

"Discipline," Weismann snapped.

"Hasn't given you much!" Lofty replied.

The others laughed. Weismann glared but didn't reply.

Roger asked, "What else do you do? Do you ever go in the bush?"

"We do a bivouac," Weismann replied.

"<u>A</u> bivouac! Only one a year? We do one a month. What do you do on annual camp?" Roger persisted.

"We go to our school camp beside the sea," Weismann replied.

"Yes, but what sort of activities do you do?" Roger asked.

"We do a range shoot."

"That's one day. What about the other six?"

"We practise for the band competition and the drill competition."

Roger snorted. "How boring! You sound like a mob of show ponies."

Weismann stood up looking angry. "We're better than you lot. You watch what you say or I'll give you a fat lip."

Roger stood up as well and the two stood measuring each other.

Gordon stepped forward. "Stop threatening everyone Weismann. Besides, if you want a fight pick on someone your own size."

"Big talk!" sneered Weismann. "Any time."

Karen cut in. "CUOs Course, outside! Three ranks. The next lesson is drill."

Barbara sighed. *This bickering and rivalry is so unpleasant and so unnecessary!* she thought sadly.

Chapter 7

MORE COMPLICATIONS

Training finished at 1710. The course was marched back to near the lecture room by Karen. As they fell out and began to disperse Weismann bellowed, "Make sure you are all ready in the lecture room by 1855. I am the Duty Student for the next 24 hours."

As the girls tramped up into their room Barbara wiped her brow. "Whew! That was a solid day. Ten to go."

"Shower for me," Fiona said. She hauled off her boots, grabbed towel and soap and ran to join the queue.

Barbara looked and saw five girls already in line, so she decided to shower after tea. Instead she sat on the end of her stretcher to relax. As she did Wendy came in the door, so she said, "How's it going Wendy?"

"Alright," Wendy replied. She also sat down and the two friends talked about the minor dramas of the day. After ten minutes angry voices broke into their conversation. They were coming from the showers. Barbara heard Camille call, "Come on Malone! Get out of there. You've had your turn!"

Barbara looked up. Sharon came along in the corridor drying her hair. Six girls still stood in line. Monica's answer was not audible. Sharon shook her head and said, "Four of us have been through the other shower and Malone's the only one to go into that shower."

There was the sound of fists hammering a wooden door. Camille again called out. "Hurry up Malone! Don't be selfish. There are nineteen of us and only two showers. You've been in there nearly twenty minutes."

Monica said something which didn't please Camille who banged on the door again. "Don't you talk to me like that!" she shouted.

Lt McEwen's voice then cut in. "Stop that banging Sgt Clark! Cpl Malone, hurry up and get out of that shower!"

There was a mutter amidst the splashing of water. Lt McEwen called again, plainly angry, "Don't you back answer me young Miss! You get out of there, right now!"

A minute later a door slammed. Monica flounced into the room, a towel around her waist and a bundle of clothes held over her front. She dumped the clothes on her bed and pulled the towel off with a flourish. Once again Barbara was confronted by the sight of Monica's nude form. To her own annoyance Barbara had to grudgingly admit it was a very nice female form. Monica proceeded to towel herself. Barbara turned her back in annoyance. As she did she met Wendy's eyes and gave a wry smile, then looked at her watch. *Twenty minutes to Mess Parade. I might just have time for a shower,* she thought.

She did. During Mess Parade Gordon stood next to her. They talked the whole time. Barbara was glad she had rushed through the shower as she didn't want to put him off with the odour of perspiration. They sat opposite each other to eat and she found she couldn't keep her eyes off him.

To her amazement she felt an urge to touch his hand and was surprised at the strength of her own feelings. She felt simultaneous regret and relief at the rule about 'No Fraternisation'.

They sat next to each other during the three evening lectures. These were on 'Personal Hygiene', 'Camp and Field Hygiene' and 'How to inspect a bivouac'. Barbara hardly heard them. All she was conscious of was Gordon's nearness. Several times their elbows touched and towards the end she felt his knee press against hers. It seemed to send fire through her thighs and lower body. She was torn between wanting him to stop it and desire for him to keep doing it.

What will I do if we kiss and he starts to caress me? she asked herself. *If I'm like this over a simple touch!*

After the last lecture Barbara and her friends remained in the lecture room. The list of lessons they were to teach had been pinned on the notice board. Barbara was relieved to see that her lessons weren't changed from the ones she had been allocated in the 'Joining Instruction' as she had done a lot of preparation. But she wasn't satisfied and set to work to improve her lessons. She sat with Fiona and Roger to work on her lesson plan. Others drifted out into the night.

Gordon came through from the kitchen with two cups of lime cordial. "I don't know if you like lime," he said, setting one down in front of her. Barbara said thanks and drank it gratefully. She didn't even mind Roger nudging Fiona and winking.

Gordon pointed to her book. "That's a snazzy Training Manual you've got there," he commented. He picked up the book which Barbara had carefully 'flagged' important pages with small coloured tabs. She had also colour coded various sections of it for ease of reference. Gordon flicked through it. "Mind if I use this for a few minutes?"

"Of course you can use it. I'm finished for the moment," Barbara replied.

The two worked contentedly in silence for another ten minutes. From time to time one or the other paused and looked at the other. Their eyes met. They smiled and resumed work.

Roger interrupted them to say, "The canteen will shut soon. Does anyone want something to eat?"

"Get us two 'Cherry Ripes' Roger," Gordon said, reaching in his pocket for money. "Do you like 'Cherry Ripes' Barbara?"

She looked up and smiled. "Yes thanks." Fiona grinned and Barbara felt a blush mount her neck.

When Roger returned they stopped work and stood outside in the cool to eat. Barbara and Gordon stood side by side a little apart from the others.

He's so good looking! she thought, studying Gordon's profile. The porch light made a strong contrast of shadow on his clear-cut features. To her amazement she realised she was feeling an urge to stroke his cheek. *I wish I could hold him,* she thought. She blushed at her own thoughts and tried to suppress even more passionate stirrings. They were emotions and desires she didn't want to admit to.

"What are you thinking?" Gordon asked.

"Oh! Nothing. Isn't it lovely and peaceful here at night, so still," she replied.

Gordon nodded. "Yes, it is. But it won't be tomorrow though when a hundred or so little cadets arrive to start the Corporals Course."

As they stood there a vehicle's headlights came towards them, shone full on them for a moment, then swung away as it turned. Barbara saw that it was a battered and dirty white utility with some old 44-gallon drums in the back. It pulled up at the back of the kitchen. Two men dressed in grimy civilian clothes got out. They began emptying garbage cans of food scraps into the drums.

Gordon turned from watching them. "Do you know what I was thinking?" he asked.

"No?" Barbara replied. The word seemed to catch in her throat.

"Regret."

"Regret?"

"Yes, that we aren't allowed to fraternise. I want to kiss you," Gordon said.

Barbara's heart leapt twice. She was glad that he wanted to kiss her. She was even more glad he had the moral character to do the right thing. In her heart she knew that her respect for him would have gone down if he had suggested sneaking off to meet. It would have been so easy. The camp was a small island in a sea of dark bushland.

She looked into his eyes and smiled. "I'm glad. I'd like that," she confessed.

The Orderly Sergeant's voice broke into their thoughts as he called from over near the boys' tents. "Lights out in five minutes!"

"Come on you two," Fiona interrupted. "Bedtime."

"We know," Gordon murmured.

Barbara saw the twinkle in his eye and couldn't resist a smile.

Fiona snorted. "That's not what I meant!" she said. "Now say Goodnight."

"Goodnight," Gordon said with a grin.

"Goodnight," Barbara responded. She was annoyed at how her throat seemed to constrict as she said it.

The two girls walked across to their hut and went inside.

*****

Barbara lay in her bed in a state close to bliss. She was tired but sleep would not come. Her memory kept reliving every moment with Gordon. She knew that she was strongly attracted to him. Half of her did not want any emotional involvement with boys. The other half whirled in warm dreams and yearnings.

Eventually she drifted into a restless sleep.

The other girls seemed to be restless too. Barbara was dimly conscious of the creaking of their folding stretchers as they turned over. Her own stretcher was annoyingly loud as she changed to a more comfortable position. Then Monica's stretcher squeaked even louder. Barbara was sleepily aware of Monica standing up, pulling on her sneakers, wrapping her gown around herself and padding quietly along the corridor towards the toilet.

That night Barbara had the most passionate dream she could remember. She and Gordon were clutched in a hot embrace in a way her conscious mind would have shied away from.

A hand gripped her shoulder and shook her awake. The lights flicked on. Barbara opened her eyes to find Fiona bending over her. "Wake up Babs. Check Parade. Time to get up."

Barbara groaned and sat up. Her eyes felt sore and scratchy. She rubbed them and greeted Wendy who stifled a yawn to wave back. A glance revealed that Monica still wasn't awake.

Camille shook her. "Get up Malone. Check Parade."

Monica swore and groaned. She threw back her sheet and stretched, displaying for all to see the fact that she slept nude. Barbara blushed and quickly looked away, then slipped her sandshoes on and hurried out as Monica stood up, still naked, and stretched again.

Monica was last on parade again but this time she was well covered with a dressing gown. Barbara glanced at her with dislike, suspecting she had nothing on under it. Weismann was the Duty Student, but while he had yelled at a couple of others who were slow, he said nothing to Monica.

Barbara barely noticed. She was all aglow at the smile Gordon gave her. They stood side by side and their arms brushed a couple of times.

After check parade Barbara went back to the barracks to change. Because the showers and toilets were full she had no choice but to change in the room. Turning her back she peeled off her top and bent down to pick up her bra.

From behind her Fiona said, "Gee Barbara, you have a lovely body."

At that Monica, who was also changing, curled her lip. "Gawd! What are ya, a lemon?"

Barbara covered her breasts and straightened up. She glanced over her shoulder and noted Fiona blushing and looking upset and opened her mouth to speak. But Camille beat her to it. "No. She just appreciates true beauty when she sees it," she said. Turning to Barbara she added, "You are very attractive Barbara."

"Thank you," Barbara replied, blushing with pleased embarrassment. Monica scowled but made no comment. To end the situation Barbara quickly dressed and groomed herself. Then she devoted fifteen minutes to carefully organising her bedspace for inspection. She had everything neat by the time breakfast was called.

At breakfast her stomach felt all a-flutter. She had to force herself to eat and she seemed unable to tear her eyes from Gordon. He sat opposite and talked, his face lit by a cheerful grin.

Fiona interrupted. "Come on you two. It'll be inspection soon, and you still have to make your bed Barb."

Barbara looked up in surprise. "But I've made it! I'm ready for inspection," she replied. A sinking feeling settled in her stomach.

"Well it was a mess when I came to breakfast," Fiona replied.

Barbara swung around, alive with suspicion. Her eyes sought out Malone. Monica was sitting in the corner beside Weismann. She saw Barbara and smirked, then turned and said something to Weismann and snickered. Unable to credit her suspicions Barbara hastily stood and went outside to wash-up.

When she strode into the bedroom a few minutes later Barbara was slightly breathless. Even though she had been prepared for what she might see the shock made her feel physically ill. Her carefully made stretcher was a tangle of sheets. The pillow lay on the floor. The neatly arranged clothes were all awry. For nearly a minute she stood there, speechless with disbelief and mounting rage.

Fiona looked from the untidy tangle to her. "What's wrong Barb?"

"I made it before I went to breakfast," she said between clenched teeth.

Wendy joined them. "She did too. I saw her. I'll bet it was that bitch Malone. She was late on parade."

Barbara shook her head in disbelief that anyone could be so petty. "We've no proof," she said sadly.

"Come on. Inspection in two minutes," Sharon called as she came in.

Barbara set rapidly to work, helped by the other two. They had only just straightened out the worst of it when there was the tramp of boots. Monica came in just as the girl who was Duty Platoon Sergeant for the Sergeants called them to attention. Barbara glared at Monica who smirked again. Tense with anger Barbara had to restrain an urge to scratch at her.

"Atten... shun!"

Barbara moved to the end of her bunk and stood rigid. One of the female OOCs, Lt Curwen, came in to inspect them. She was thorough and exacting. Not one of the cadets escaped some sharp comments. When she reached Barbara her eyes flicked from object to object.

"This is the worst bedspace in the hut," Lt Curwen commented acidly. "Very poor job! Sloppy! Look at the wrinkles in those sheets. There's dirt on your pillow. Get all those shirts lined up. You'll need to improve a lot if you want to do well on this course."

Gritting her teeth Barbara kept her face neutral. "Yes Ma'am," she replied. She burned with shame and righteous anger. But she looked straight ahead. Wendy met her eyes, her own full of sympathy. Then they flicked towards Monica and her lips flattened into a hard line.

As soon as the officer had gone the cadets filed out ready for the Morning Parade. As they formed up Fiona whispered, "What are you going to do?"

Barbara shrugged. "Nothing. We've no proof and I'm not starting a petty feud. I'll just be more careful."

Gordon joined them. "What's wrong Barbara? You look a bit upset."

"Nothing."

Gordon looked from her to Fiona.

"That bitch Malone," Fiona hissed.

Barbara shook her head. "Leave it Fiona," she said.

But Gordon was not to be put off. "Malone? What happened?" he asked.

Weismann stamped to attention out in front. "Stop talking in the ranks. Platoon, Atten...Shun! That was sloppy! As you were," he snarled. The platoon stood at ease.

"Platoon. Atten...shun!" Weismann bawled again. He made a face and yelled, "Still not good enough. As you were! Pick your feet up properly next time Brassington."

Barbara bristled with resentment. She had come to attention as smartly as a good Sergeant Major should. But she refused to be drawn and made no reply. Instead she continued to look straight to her front.

Weismann called them to attention again. He strolled over to where Barbara, Fiona and Sharon stood side by side in the front rank. There was a long minute while he stood in front of them, his gaze moving up and down their bodies. Sweat began to trickle down Barbara's back. He curled his lip and said, "Make sure you are correctly dressed for parade. I don't want to get into trouble because some of you have low standards."

Lofty's voice growled from the centre rank. "Stop buggerizing around Weismann and move us to the parade ground. Don't keep us standing here in this heat."

Weismann looked at him. "Silence in the ranks. I'm the Duty Student."

"Only for today," reminded Roger.

Weismann ignored him. He stepped forward and deliberately and slowly looked Barbara up and down, his eyes lingering on her shirt front.

Barbara fumed. "Stop leering at me or I'll break your face," she hissed. She had to restrain herself from slapping him.

"If you've got it, flaunt it," Weismann replied.

Barbara went to slap him but felt her arm firmly seized from behind. There was a movement either side of her. Gordon's voice grated in her ear. "One more insult from you Weismann and I'll flatten you here and now and to hell with the promotion course."

"Oh yeah!" Weismann sneered and put his hands on his hips.

Lofty Ward spoke quietly from Barbara's other side. "Stop causing trouble Weismann, you obnoxious brute. I'm sick of standing in the sun and I'm sick of your insults to the girls so you'll have to fight me too. Now move us or I'll make your face even uglier than it already is."

Weismann looked from one to the other. He tried to keep his face determined, but his eyes flickered and he put his hands to his sides. "Get back in line so we can move," he blustered.

The two boys stepped back. There was a pause while a collective shudder ran through the platoon. Then Weismann turned them and ordered 'Quick March.'

When they reached the parade ground for the morning parade Barbara felt quite dizzy and thought she was going to be sick. On top of the upset of the two incidents the heat was already intense. She bit her lip, wriggled her toes and jiggled her kneecaps and somehow got through it. Several others fell out or knelt down.

It was a relief to get out of the sweltering sun into the lecture room. The first lesson was by the Colonel on how to conduct an 'Orders Group'; the formal procedure for passing on Verbal Orders for a military operation or training exercise.

Once again Weismann muttered little asides. "Boring!" "What a load of crap!" "We never do any of this so why learn it?"

The Colonel noted his muttering and raised an irritated eyebrow. "Do you have a problem Sgt Weismann?"

"No sir!"

"You will have if you keep murmuring."

"Yes sir."

Roger grinned and winked at Barbara who could not repress a smile.

For Weismann the next lesson was even worse.

It was on 'How to plan a patrol.' They were given copies of the 'Headings for Orders' and then a situation briefing on a theoretical scenario. After that they were given a four-page written order from which they had to plan a patrol and prepare the Verbal Orders.

The Colonel explained, "You have four days to do this task. On Thursday morning you are to give your answer as Verbal Orders. This is a practice. You will then be given another set of Orders and they will be for assessment. The second set will be given to you verbally, as they would be in reality, and you will only have an hour to prepare."

Barbara found the problem quite interesting and settled happily to begin the task. Morning tea came next. They gathered at the back of the kitchen for cake and chocolate milk. Gordon passed Barbara a piece of cake. Their fingers touched. Barbara wanted to keep touching him. The others in the group now treated them as though they were a couple.

'How to indent for Stores from the Q System' came next. Barbara found it boring. She began to yawn and felt her eyelids getting heavy in the stifling heat of the room. The high-pitched whine of cicadas added to the feeling of drowsiness.

During the break she went and splashed water on her face in the bathroom. As she stepped from the shade to walk back the heat of the sun seemed to sear her skin, even through the cloth of her shirt. She found it a relief to reach the next building.

Captain Royston arrived to take them through the theory of accurate rifle shooting. The lesson had been going for ten minutes when there was the roar of engines. Four large coaches pulled up on the ring road outside. Captain Royston looked out and said, "Right-O, this is the Corporals Course arriving. Those people who are Duty Platoon Commanders for them, move out."

Barbara was one of the eight. She found the Orderly Sergeant, four Duty CSMs and her own Duty Pl Sgt, Malcolm Summers from Rockhampton, outside. For the next hour they were very busy sorting out 128 potential Corporals from nine units into eight platoons. Barbara was Duty Platoon Commander for No 4 Platoon. The platoons were a mixture of boys and girls from different units. The roll was checked and they were shown where showers, toilets, laundry, and so on were located.

"Like a mob of bloody sheep," Cpl Summers commented. The Junior Leaders Course candidates were mostly only Year 8s or 9s, 14- or 15-year olds. They looked around themselves with a mixture of curiosity and apprehension.

Barbara smiled. "You were like that last year," she reminded him.

The new arrivals were seated in the shade and were put through the 'march-in' administration by the Orderly Sergeant and the Colonel, who checked every cadet personally to make sure they were allocated to a section and had a bed. The potential corporals were then seated in lines behind Duty Pl Sgts. Once all had been checked in and given name tags and the duty personnel had been given copies of the bed plans, they moved off with their gear. The boys went to four rows of tents on the east of the camp beyond the ring road. The girls were to sleep in the eight tents at the back of the girls' hut near the Water Treatment Plant.

While the roll was being called Barbara had noticed a busty young blonde who she thought looked familiar. *Is that Chloe?* she wondered. Now that she had the group standing together, she turned to the girl. "Do I know you?"

An impish grin dimpled the girl's face. "I'm Chloe," she said, "From Heatley."

For a moment Barbara was too amazed to speak. She shook her head in dismay and disbelief. "So you are still in the cadets?" she managed to say at last. In her own opinion Chloe should have been chucked out for misbehaviour.

The smile vanished from Chloe's face and she looked unhappy. "Yes, and now I'm on the Corporals Course."

"How did you manage that?" Barbara asked.

"By being good for a whole year," Chloe replied.

"You'd better not get up to any of your tricks here," Barbara warned. Then an unkind thought crossed her mind.

We've got enough tarts already, she told herself, thinking of Monica.

Chloe bit her lip and looked sullen. She shook her head and Barbara felt a twinge of guilt at seeing what she thought was a tear forming in the corner of Chloe's eye. To ease the situation she asked, "Is your friend here too?"

Chloe nodded again and pointed to where the girls from 3 Platoon were being led away. "Janie's over there. Don't worry. I want to pass. This is the end of my second year in cadets. It took a big effort to get selected to be here."

Barbara looked at her then said, "I heard that you helped save some lives on a bivouac a few months ago."

Chloe nodded. "I did, but I heard you did better last annual camp," she replied.

Barbara felt a glow of embarrassment. She actually wanted to hear the details but her own emotions were so mixed between admiration and resentful jealousy that she could only nod. "Just watch the boys here," she advised.

Chloe gave a wry grin and shook her head. "They won't bother me," she said. "I can freeze them out."

At that Barbara warmed to her and relented. She knew that most cadets went on a Corporals Course at the end of their first year. Smiling she nodded. "Good, now let's get you girls organised." Leaving Cpl Summers to look after the boys she led the girls over to the tents and showed them how to set up their stretchers and arrange their gear.

This kept her busy into lunch time. Mess Parade took much longer as the corporals had to be fed first, then the Sgts and WOs and only then the CUOs. The officers came last.

Chapter 8

CHLOE

During the meal Chloe was one of the main topics of conversation. Stephens brought her name up by commenting to Camille, "I see that blonde trollop of yours is here on the Corporals Course."

Camille frowned and pursed her lips. "Chloe? Yes she is."

"You lot must be hard up if she is all you've got to send," Stephens retorted.

"Bite your bum!" Camille snapped. "She's alright. Anyway, she's behaved herself this year."

"Not what I heard," Stephens replied.

Millet leaned over. "Is it true she swam the pool naked at your school swimming carnival?" he asked.

"She did," Camille grudgingly admitted.

"Did she get into trouble?" Millet queried.

"Of course, but that was years ago, when she was in Year 8. She hasn't done anything like that since," Camille said.

Stephens gave a leering grin. "I hear she takes her clothes off for money," he commented.

"So I've heard," Camille replied. "I think she poses for artists."

Stephen's gave a derisive snort. "I heard she will strip for anyone who pays her, and do even more than that," he said.

Camille admitted that was a story she had heard. "I don't think that is true," she added, but her voice lacked conviction.

Karen's voice cut across the babble of prurient speculation. "That's enough talk like that thank you! Now stop harming the girl's reputation with rumours and gossip."

"She harms it herself by her own actions," Stephens retorted.

"How do you know what she does?" Karen queried.

"The stories reach our school," Stephens replied angrily.

Karen glared at him. "Leave her alone! And don't go bothering her," she snapped.

That caused the conversation to lapse for a while, but later Barbara overheard more rumours about Chloe. These included letting the boys have sex with her for money and that her mother was a prostitute. Barbara found it all distasteful, if only because of the evident lecherous interest by the boys. She was particularly put off by the way Weismann and Stephens sniggered at some of the comments.

I hope I never get a reputation like that, she thought.

It saddened and confused her. What was really bothering her were her own attitudes. When she was home alone, she often went without clothes and found it very pleasant. But deliberately taking her clothes off in front of other people was a much more worrying notion.

Weismann then really annoyed her by saying to Camille, "So how did she come to be selected for the course? Does she offer it to the officers?"

At that both Camille and Sharon really bridled. "Don't you dare make unfounded accusations against Major Wickham!" Sharon snapped.

"That's right! How dare you!" Camille added.

Sharon went on, "Chloe won her place here by saving 4 Platoon from the Bikies at Mingela."

"Oh yeah! How'd she do that?" Weismann sneered.

"She took command of the platoon when the CUO and sergeant both failed to do so," Sharon replied. "She kept them together; made sure they carried two wounded cadets; did the navigating; and then led the platoon for kilometres through the bush in the dark to meet up with the police. She did a mighty job so Major Wickham forgave her for sometimes being a bit naughty."[2]

"A bit naughty!" cried Sharon. At which they all laughed and the tension eased. The course then moved out to start work.

The afternoon went by in a blur of work: Safety on the Rifle Range, Safety with Water, How to Site a Platoon Bivouac, and Period 10 on How to Plan Search Patrols. This last was by Major Wickham, Chloe's OC, a typical grey-haired veteran. Barbara was irritated to overhear more behind-the-hand comments about Chloe from Stephens. But most of the time they were too busy for idle chatter. Even Weismann knuckled down without grumbling or being obnoxious. Barbara started to really enjoy herself.

After they were dismissed, she saw Gordon waiting at the door. She really wanted to talk to him but knew she had a lot to do. "Sorry. I have

---

[2] Read *Mischief at Mingela* by C.R. Cummings.

to go," she said. "I have to help my platoon get settled in," she added by way of explanation.

"That's fine. I should be studying although I'd rather be with you," he replied.

"Thank you," Barbara said. On an impulse she put her hand on his forearm. The instant she did she knew she was making a mistake and quickly withdrew it and smiled at him "Oh! Sorry! No fraternising," she said. Then she hurried out.

But before she could go to her platoon she was confronted by a problem. Outside the mess she saw Weismann stop Chloe and say something to her. Barbara saw Chloe's lip curl and her face go hard. Then she tossed her head and walked on.

Catching up to Chloe Barbara asked, "What did Wesimann just ask you then Chloe?"

"For sex, what else?" Chloe replied in a matter-of-fact tone.

Barbara was shocked. "He's not allowed to do that! Do you want to complain?" she asked.

Chloe shrugged and smiled. "No. It doesn't bother me. Men ask me all the time, and all the boys think it."

"But... but... but what do you do?" Barbara asked.

"If I like them, I let them," Chloe replied. "If I don't, I tell them to get lost."

"Oh Chloe! But... but you could... You could get hurt."

Chloe nodded. "Yeah, I know. Mum has warned me about getting pregnant and about horrible diseases and AIDs and whatever. I'm a lot more choosy now than when I was young."

At that Barbara had to smile. "Yes Grandma!" she retorted sarcastically. "So, do you want to complain to the officers or not?"

Chloe shook her head. "Nah! He won't try again. Anyway, it's my word against his. His sort always makes sure there are no witnesses."

Chloe said this with such profound cynicism that it saddened Barbara. But she had to agree. *That would be his style,* she thought.

"You take care," she warned.

"I'll be alright. I do Martial Arts," Chloe replied.

By then they were back at the girls' tents and Barbara was at once asked questions by several girls. From then on she had hardly a moment to herself until mess parade and then hurried through her meal to get back to answering the dozens of questions the new cadets had. In what seemed no time at all her platoon was called on parade for the evening lessons. The Duty Pl Sgt marched them away while Barbara stood and watched.

Chloe still looks shapely, even in that baggy camouflage uniform, she observed. *I hope she isn't going to cause problems!* Shaking her head, she made her way to her own lessons.

At the lecture room she was annoyed to discover that real patrols and incidents had again become the topic of conversation. Stephens was jeering at the reputation of 130ACU again. "You lot just think you are so good!"

Sharon at once spoke up. "We are!"

"Not as good as Cairns. You don't battle off gangs of crooks," Stephens said, giving Barbara a sneering look as he did.

"Oh yes we do!" Sharon cried. "I told you, we had a similar problem on a bivouac in May at Mingela."

Jennifer nodded and said, "Oh yes! I heard about that. You were chased by a gang of bikies, weren't you?"

Sharon nodded. "Sort of. It was really only our 4 Platoon. They went off on an exercise and saw these Bikies shoot a bloke. They were going to kill another guy but only wounded him and he ran up the creek and ended up in among our people. There was a real to do and the Bikies shot two of our cadets."

"Were you there?" Millet asked.

Sharon shook her head. "No. I was the 2 Platoon sergeant and we were back at the bivouac."

Camille now joined in. "I was on that bivouac too. I was 1 Platoon sergeant and these Bikies turned up with guns and held us hostage. I really thought they were going to shoot Major Wickham. They bashed him something horrible."

"By Bikies you mean leather jacket motor bike types I take it?" Ying asked.

"Yeah, a real Outlaw Motorcycle Gang, called 'Atilla's Axemen'," Camille said.

"What did they want? Why did they do that?" Fiona asked.

Sharon replied. "Apparently the first bloke they killed was going to testify at a trial against them and they wanted him dead, but the other guy was the gang leader. The bloke who shot him was a rival who wanted to be the boss."

"Did they get him?" Jennifer asked.

Sharon shook her head. "Nope. Four Platoon managed to hide from them and escape across some really rough country during the night. They carried the wounded bikie boss and one of our girls who had been shot all the way to safety."

As the story was told Barbara glanced at Roger. She knew that he had been in some sort of trouble with an Outlaw Motorcycle Gang during the July holidays, but he had never spoken about it. Now she saw that he was listening intently and was making a deliberate effort to keep his face neutral.

I wonder what did happen? she thought.

Sharon then surprised her by saying, "Actually it was Chloe Cummings who led 4 Platoon, even though she was only a cadet. The CUO and sergeant weren't up to it so Chloe took command. That's why she is here on the Corporals Course."

"This Chloe, is she the famous nudist you were talking about earlier?" Millet asked.

Sharon nodded. "Yes."

"I heard she killed a bloke," Millet said.

"That's the story," Sharon replied. "But I don't know if it's true."

There was a babble of talk, all speculation and rumours about Chloe. Included in this were various versions of how she and her friend Jane had been kidnapped the previous year on a weekend exercise near Innisfail and of how they had escaped. "I heard she was raped," Jason Hillditch said.

Stephens nodded. "That's why she killed the guy and fed him to the crocodiles," he said.

Sharon pursed her lips. "A giant croc. It was in a crocodile farm in a huge swamp," she corrected. "Chloe and her friend Jane were kidnapped by these men and taken there. They escaped but had to swim across a swamp and several croc infested creeks in the dark to get away."

During this Barbara's mind flooded with memories. "I was there. I was one of the cadet commandos who were helping search for them," she said.

"Is it true this Chloe ran along the beach naked in front of the whole company and then wouldn't get dressed?" Hilditch asked, his eyes alight with prurient interest.

Reluctantly Barbara nodded. "She did," she agreed.

"Not a stitch on?" Hilditch persisted, "in front of everyone?"

"Yes," Barbara agreed. But then her own mind flooded with memories and her eyes met Fiona's. When they had been on a cadet exercise as First Year cadets, she and Fiona and two other girls had been abducted at gun point by two prison escapees. They had taken the girls to a creek nearby and were preparing to rape them when Barbara had managed to get a gun and stop them. It had all been very traumatic and was one of the reasons she did not particularly like men.

Then her eyes met Roger's and he smiled. She blushed and fervently hoped neither he nor Fiona would mention the incident because when Roger and other cadets and staff had arrived, she had been stark naked and had stayed that way for some minutes. To her relief Roger just gave a friendly smile and nodded but said nothing.

Hilditch frowned. "So what happened to this Chloe?"

"She went off in a motor launch with some navy cadets to try to save her friend Jane," Barbara said. As she did she pursed her lips with disapproval but then could not make up her mind whether she admired Chloe or despised her. Mental images of Chloe mingled with images from her own nude drama and she could only shake her head, knowing she was being a hypocrite. She also found the images of nude Chloe quite disturbing as she did not want to admit to herself that she actually found such scenes very arousing.

Millett spoke next. "What were you all doing there?"

Barbara answered that as more vivid memories of the weekend exercise near Innisfail a year and a half earlier swirled in her head. "It was a commando type exercise between Army Cadets and Navy Cadets from Cairns and Townsville," she explained. "I was one of a group of Army Cadets acting as commandos. On the first night we did a dawn raid in kayaks on several 'targets' defended by the Townsville Army and Navy Cadets. Chloe was a cadet who was one of the defenders and she and a friend went missing during the night. We didn't know it at the time but they had been kidnapped off the beach at Ella Bay by smugglers."

There was a ripple of interest among the listeners. Barbara went on: "For the next two days we searched for the two missing girls. On the Monday morning they turned up on Banfield Beach at dawn, having escaped."

Jason sniggered. "Was that when she ran along the beach in the nude?"

Barbara again experienced vividly memories of Chloe running along the beach to join the group. She had been stark naked and quite uninhibited. The jealous thought that Chloe had a fabulous figure for a girl of her age now returned to annoy her, as did the memories of how all the boys (and men) had ogled her in stunned delight and how she had seemed to revel in their lecherous gaze.

"Yes," she said, "and she completely ignored the officer's orders and ran off to get in the Navy Cadet boat. She should have been chucked out," she said.

At that Lofty shook his head. "Oh, be fair Barb. You got rescued with no clothes on once."

"Yes, but I didn't choose to take mine off," Barbara snapped, embarrassed and annoyed that Lofty had now mentioned the incident.

Gordon raised his eyebrows. "So what happened?" he asked.

Barbara shook her head and didn't want to talk about it but Roger spoke up, describing the incident.

When he finished Hilditch said, "How do you know all this Dunning, were you there?"

Roger nodded. "I was. Cpl Kirk and I were first on the scene," he replied. Again his eyes met Barbara's and he gave her an apologetic look.

"And she had no clothes on?" Hilditch queried, leering at Barbara.

Roger nodded and added: "She was starkers and was holding a gun on these two naked blokes."

"Roger!" Barbara cried, blushing furiously.

Gordon looked at her admiringly. "I wish I'd been there," he commented.

This caused an outburst of laughter. Barbara blushed again but could not help thinking about Gordon seeing her with no clothes on. To change the subject she said, "I don't want to talk about it."

Monica gave her a sour look then said, "No. It was this Chloe girl we were discussing."

Weissmann grinned and looked at Barbara. "So are all these fantastic rumours about her true?" he asked.

"You will have to ask her," Barbara replied shortly.

Stephens gave a leering grin. "There are lots of other stories and rumours about Chloe and boys," he added.

Jason looked very interested. "This is the Chloe who is supposed to have gone on morning check parade naked?"

Camille answered that. "She did. She claims it was because the platoon sergeant told her she only had to wear her boots and hat so she did, but I think she did it because she is a real tease."

Lofty chuckled. "Boots and hat! I like that. You do that tomorrow morning Roger," he cried.

Roger snorted. Jason looked puzzled. "So did she get into trouble?"

Camille shrugged. "A bit. She got a real lecture from Lieutenant Peters and the OC. But it was still pretty dark so you couldn't see much."

"Were you there?" Gordon asked. He also looked very interested and that needled Barbara's feelings.

Again Camille nodded. "I was her section commander."

Lofty was puzzled. He said, "So if this Chloe has done all these wrong things, how come she is here now? Why hasn't she been chucked out?"

Sharon shrugged and said, "Because she is actually very good most of the time."

At that moment Karen came back in and called to them, "OK, sit to attention. Here comes our instructor."

Captain Conkey had the CUOs for a lesson on Platoon Leadership. That was followed by one on 'How to teach a Theory Lesson' by Lt Curwen. After that they mostly remained for study, writing patrol orders, making training aids or rehearsing lessons.

Gordon looked over at Barbara's work. "Heavens! Haven't you got neat writing!" he said. He picked up Barbara's Lesson Plan and looked at it. "You've got the same theory lesson to teach as me: Snake Bite," he commented.

"I've got a book here to help identify snakes," Barbara said. "It's in my suitcase. I'll go and get it if you like."

"I'd like that, but it's supper time. I'll get you a drink while you get it," Gordon offered.

Barbara walked across to her hut. As she did the dirty white utility with the garbage bins swung past and stopped at the back of the kitchen.

When she came back a couple of minutes later two men were talking to the cook and his offsider. They turned to look at her but she ignored them and rejoined the others.

Gordon came in with two mugs of cocoa. "Well, it's not quiet tonight," he observed.

The Corporals Course had just finished their last lesson and they flocked to supper or the canteen. The noise of their excited voices became the dominant sound.

"Here's the book," Barbara said, handing the slim volume to Gordon. "It's got colour photos and diagrams of the arrangement of scales and so on so you can properly identify different snakes."

Gordon flicked quickly through it. "Yes it's good. Mind if I use it for a while?"

"Be my guest," Barbara answered with a smile. She sipped the cocoa and turned back to her work.

Fifteen minutes later Barbara looked at her watch. "Oh dear! Lights-out in ten minutes. I want to have a shower." She began packing her notes.

Roger chuckled and said, "I wondered what the smell was, but I was too polite to say."

Barbara poked her tongue at him and they all laughed.

Gordon handed her the book and said, "Here's your book on snakes. Thanks Barb." He passed it over. For a long moment they looked into each other's eyes. Then Gordon whispered, "Goodnight. Pleasant dreams!"

"If they are like last night's they will be," Barbara replied.

Gordon looked interested. "Oh yes? What did you dream about last night? I slept like a log."

Barbara blushed. Roger saved her from having to answer by saying, "You aren't a log. You were the sawmill cutting up the log. Snore! What a noise!"

Gordon turned towards Roger and the two boys began a mock fight. Barbara took the opportunity to leave and walked quickly to her hut singing happily.

I'm in love! she told herself, marvelling that such a thing could happen to her.

Chapter 9

A MORAL DILEMMA

Barbara wriggled into her sleeping bag feeling deliciously happy. She called a cheery 'goodnight' to the others and lay back to dream. The lights were turned off and she hugged herself and wished it were Gordon's arms around her instead of her own. She was just drifting into slumber land when Lt Curwen came through on a bed check. The OOC shone her torch on each of the beds in turn.

Must be about eleven p.m., Barbara thought. She rolled on her side and was soon asleep.

Sometime later, Barbara opened her eyes. She hadn't been dreaming that she could recall, and all sounded normal. There was only the gentle breathing of the other girls and the faint rustle of leaves from the breeze. Barbara rolled over in annoyance and tried to make herself more comfortable. But sleep had fled. So she lay in the darkness thinking about men and about Gordon. The only sounds she was aware of were one of the girls on the Sergeants Course murmuring in her sleep and Lt Cavendish, one of the female officers, snoring. Otherwise all was quiet.

Barbara's eyes had adjusted to the semi-dark, there being plenty of light from the streetlight and the light at the bathroom. "I wonder what time it is?" she muttered to herself. She turned on her watch light. Just after 0100. She went to lie down but decided a visit to the toilet was needed.

As she swung her feet onto the floor Barbara realised that the stretcher next to hers was empty. She bent over and stared. No doubt about it. Monica was not in her bed.

I wonder where she is? Perhaps she's at the toilet? Barbara thought. Still half asleep she got up and padded quietly along the corridor.

Monica was not there. A puzzled and slightly worried Barbara made her way back to her own bed a few minutes later.

What should I do? she wondered. *Should I wake one of the lady officers? Or should I go and tell the Duty Officer in the Guard Hut?*

Barbara bit her lip. She wasn't sure. This was partly because she did not want to cause trouble unnecessarily. Nor did she want to be a 'dobber' as she had formed a suspicion of where Monica might be, or at least what she might be doing.

It will cause a lot of ill-will, and Malone will blame me, she thought.

Barbara lay down and thought about it. After a while she dozed off again until a noise woke her.

It was Monica getting into bed.

Barbara lay pretending to sleep and then checked the time inside her sleeping bag so Monica wouldn't see the glow of her watch. It was nearly 0200.

Where has Monica been for over an hour in the middle of the night? she wondered, her mind filling with unpleasant suspicions. Feeling slightly upset Barbara rolled on her other side. *Should I ask her in the morning?* she pondered. After considering the idea she shook her head. *No. I will probably just be told a lie or be told to mind my own business.*

Luckily tiredness spared Barbara more unpleasant thoughts. But it did not save her from a nightmare. In the dream she was running or trying to run. It was dark and someone was after her. Her boots got heavier and heavier and she mysteriously she had no boots at all and she could only hobble on stones and prickles. 'It' was just behind her. Where was Gordon? She cried out.

Hands shook her roughly. She cried out again.

"Wake up Barbara. You are having a bad dream," Fiona called in her ear.

Barbara groaned and rolled on her back.

"Sorry," she muttered. Her mouth felt dry. "What time is it?"

"About five I think. Boy, it must be wonderful to be in love!" Fiona said.

"In love!" echoed Barbara.

"You called out his name at the top of your voice," Fiona said with a chuckle.

Monica rolled over. "Shut up you two. I'm trying to sleep," she said.

Barbara was about to say, 'Guilty conscience keeping you awake?' but bit her tongue in time. Instead, she said, "Thanks Fiona. Sorry I woke you." She lay back and tried to get back to sleep. After a while she did, but it was fitful and she woke feeling tired and drained.

As a Duty Platoon Commander Barbara had a lot to do. As soon as she was dressed, she rushed off to worry about her platoon and was so busy she quite forgot about Monica. At breakfast she sat with Gordon.

He gave her an anxious look. "You're very quiet this morning," he said. "You look tired."

"Yes. I didn't sleep very well," she replied. She remembered Monica and looked to see where she was.

"Dreams?" Gordon asked.

"Mmm. Bad dream," she replied. She spooned in some cereal.

Fiona called across, "She cried out for her hero to save her."

"Oh yes?" Gordon asked. "Who is he?" He sounded so anxious Barbara realised with a jolt he was jealous, worried that she might have a boyfriend back in Cairns.

Fiona laughed. "Oh, someone she thinks is wonderful."

Gordon looked into Barbara's eyes with a worried frown but didn't ask. She seemed to be drawn into the twinkling pools of blue.

"You," she whispered, then blushed and busied herself in eating.

Gordon seemed suddenly hungry as well, but he smiled.

He really does like me! Barbara thought.

Her tiredness seemed to evaporate, and she began to talk happily. It was with real regret she had to hurry herself away. She had too much to do. Her own bedspace had to be put in order for inspection, then she had to inspect her own platoon.

As she finished tidying her gear she hesitated, remembering the previous day.

Fiona came in and saved her. "Don't worry Barbara. I'll watch your gear. You go," she said, nodding at where Monica was being told by Camille to do her share of the sweeping.

"Thanks." Barbara picked up her hat and marched out to wait until Cpl Summers came to get her. She chatted to Sgt Oakwood from Mackay, the Duty CSM of B Company for the day, while she waited.

Punctually at 0730 Cpl Summers came and reported the platoon ready for inspection. Having been the CSM for a year the carrying out an inspection held no novelty for Barbara. She started with the girl's tent. Instead of just half an hour the whole first period was also allocated to this first inspection of the Corporals Course so she had time to be very thorough. The girls had dozens of little faults to correct but the boys were even worse.

They were given ten minutes to rectify the problems then Barbara inspected them again. Once she was satisfied, she marched over to the HQ where the officers were sitting under a corrugated iron roof beside their hut.

She halted and saluted. "Capt Buchan sir, Four Platoon ready for inspection."

The OOC, an officer from Heatley, went with her to inspect the platoon. He was generally satisfied. "Good. Good. You can move them to the parade ground ready for parade," he said. They exchanged salutes and the captain wandered off. Barbara turned to the Duty Pl Sgt, who was just returning his notebook to his pocket.

"OK Cpl Summers, move the platoon to the parade ground."

"Yes Ma'am."

The Morning Parade was another 'talk-through' to explain the procedure step by step to the Corporals Course. But this time it was much bigger with 12 platoons on parade, grouped into 4 companies. The platoons of each company were in line, side by side with their Duty Pl Sgts 3 paces in front of them. A and B Companies made up the front line with C and D Companies 15 paces behind them. The CUOs and WOs Courses were in line to the rear of the Cpls. The 12 Duty Pl Comds formed up along the front edge of the parade ground facing their platoons.

When the Duty CSM of B Coy called for markers Barbara saw that 4 Platoon's marker was Chloe. She had obviously volunteered for the job and Barbara was struck by how well she did it. Most of the other cadets marched stiffly and showed their nervousness but Chloe did it with grace and style.

And looks very good too, even in a shapeless camouflage uniform! Barbara grudgingly admitted.

What also intrigued, peeved and fascinated her was how the whole focus of the parade, of all12 platoons, seemed to be Chloe. Equally she was certain that every male eye was following her movements. It was both irritating and amusing at the same time.

Bloody Chloe! she thought.

When the Duty CSMs of each company had dressed the ranks, checked the numbers on parade and satisfied themselves that the parade was ready they did an about turn and stood at ease. RSM Pryor then handed over the parade to Captain Royston. He called four officers by name to move on to the parade ground to take command of each company. While he did this, he had the cadets in the ranks sit on the concrete. This was both a safety measure and to allow the cadets to see what went on. He then explained what the CSMs, platoon commanders and platoon sergeants had to do. Next, he ordered the acting OC each company to take over their company from the CSM and then to post their officers.

The acting OC of B Coy was Capt Hamilton from Heatley. He called the company to attention and did an about turn to face the front of the parade ground. Knowing what was coming Barbara stiffened in anticipation.

"B Company platoon commanders. Take Post!"

"Sir!" The three potential CUOs for B Coy, including Barbara, came to attention, saluted and marched forward to where their sergeants waited out from the right markers. They saluted, reported numbers on parade, saluted again then stepped around the Pl Comds and marched to a position 3 paces in rear of the platoon. Barbara stepped around the sergeant and marched forward to the centre front of the platoon.

As she did Chloe, who was standing in the front rank, met her eye. It took some willpower on Barbara's part not to smile back; and not to shake her head at how Chloe's bosom strained at her shirt front.

Heavens she is busty! she thought. *No wonder all the boys make suggestions to her.* She was mildly puzzled at why she did not intensely dislike her as she did not approve of the kind of activity Chloe was rumoured to be involved in.

While waiting for Cpl Summers to halt Barbara ran her eyes over the platoon. Knowing that they were all looking at her made her anxious and she had to suppress a nervous desire to fidget. She and the PL Sgt then turned to face the front.

It was only her platoon for 24 hours, but it still felt good. It reinforced her determination to pass the course and to get a platoon of her own back in her unit. Barbara stood at ease on Capt Hamilton's command. The acting OCs of C and D Companies then fell their platoon commanders in. When all companies had completed this Capt. Royston stood the cadets up and called the battalion to attention. He then handed over the parade to the Colonel.

Standing with her back to the platoon made Barbara very self-conscious. She was sure that all their eyes were on her, critically appraising her figure. Knowing that she had a very attractive figure did not help much.

I hope my bum doesn't look too big, she worried.

She found it a relief to move. The battalion were given 'Stand at ease' and then called to Attention again. The Colonel's orders carried clear and crisp in the morning air.

"Battalion... Present... arms! Break the flag!"

Barbara saluted in time with the rifle movements of the cadets. The Orderly Sergeant tugged the halyards and the flag burst out as a vivid splash to colour in the morning sunlight. As always it made her feel good to be alive; good to be free; good to be Australian.

The battalion was brought back to attention and stood at ease. The Colonel stood them 'easy', then spoke to them. While he did there was a clatter behind Barbara. She quickly looked. A cadet had fainted in the heat. Barbara became aware that a dozen or more had already trickled to the edge of the parade ground. Her lip curled with contempt. Cpl Summers moved to help the sick cadet.

The Colonel was not amused. "You were warned yesterday. You have just changed environment and lifestyles. You are mostly unfit. You are used to sitting indoors in air-conditioned classrooms. Now you are outdoors in the sun, and working instead of sitting on your blots. You were told to discipline yourselves to eat a full breakfast to get your energy up. You must, or you won't last ten days. You were told to drink lots of fluid. You must, or the heat will knock you."

He paused and gestured to where those who had fallen out were clustering in the shade of the canteen. "Keep wriggling your toes. Keep the circulation moving. Parade, atten... shun! Stand at... Ease! Now, we will practise the parade again. Capt Royston!"

"Sir!"

Captain Royston marched out and took over. The Colonel stalked off to berate the 'sick' who hastily gulped water from their water bottles and came marching back to re-join their platoons.

"Platoon commanders. Fall... out!"

Barbara snapped to attention and saluted. She and the other platoon commanders marched to the edge of the parade ground. Captain Royston handed back to WO1 Pryor. He had the Duty CSMs marched their companies off for a drink, WO1 Pryor all the time prowling and growling.

Fifteen sweaty minutes later, after another quick practice, the platoons marched off to lessons. Cpl Summers marched 4 Platoon to a lecture on Training Aids. When she was sure the platoon was going to the right place, Barbara went to her own lesson.

This was on the use of radios with Capt Hamilton as the instructor. Morning Tea followed. Barbara ensured her platoon was marched around to get their biscuits and cordial. Another signals lecture followed. The heat rose to 36 degrees centigrade. This would have been bearable except the humidity was very high as well, so their perspiration didn't evaporate. Instead, it trickled and dripped in a most uncomfortable way.

"Strewth, isn't it humid!" Roger grumbled as they formed up on the road to march to their next lesson.

Lofty peered out through the steel louvres. "Might get some rain, looking at those clouds out there," he said hopefully.

The CUOs Course marched to the big tree near the railway ramp. All the Corporals and Sergeants were there already, seated in the shade. The CUOs and WOs joined them. The lesson was a demonstration by WO1 Pryor on 'How to teach a Drill Lesson.'

Barbara thought of herself as a good drill instructor so she only half-paid attention. The rest of the time she allowed herself to study Gordon's profile. Sitting on the ground was a bit uncomfortable as the grass was fairly sparse. Small stones and twigs dug into her. She found the heat and cicadas were making her drowsy. Someone yawned. Barbara yawned as well. She dusted her hand, changed her weight to the other hand, watched some red ants.

"You there! Wake up!" Captain Royston bellowed at the group.

Barbara gave a guilty start and looked up. But it wasn't her. Beside her lay Monica, stretched out sound asleep, with her hat over her face. Monica woke and sat up, looking a pasty-white colour. She had dark rings under her eyes.

"Come out to the back of the group and stand with me Corporal Malone," Captain Royston ordered. Monica stood up unsteadily, still half-asleep. As she did she muttered something.

"What did you say?" Captain Royston snapped.

"Just asking where my hat is sir," Monica answered in a surly tone.

"Get it and move. You can have half an hour on the Defaulters Parade at 1730," Captain Royston growled.

Monica went and stood beside the officers, a very sulky look on her face. Barbara smiled to herself. As she did Monica looked at her. A resentful scowl formed on her face and she poked her tongue. Barbara felt a stab of dislike but was also pleased that Monica was getting what she felt were her just deserts. She turned her back to watch as WO1 Pryor resumed his lesson.

Serves the silly little tart right, Barbara thought. Then she felt guilty for making such a harsh judgement and for being so unkind. For the next ten minutes Barbara contemplated whether to report Monica's midnight absence but decided not to. *She will get herself into enough trouble without any help from me.*

There was one more lesson before lunch. Captain Royston took the CUOs on 'How to assess a drill lesson'. He seemed to direct many of his questions to Monica, a process the girl visibly resented.

Lunch came as a real relief. The strain of the course was starting to tell. During the mess parade Barbara went and talked to her platoon as they filed in. Then she checked them while they were eating. As a result she was last in to eat.

"Don't worry about them so much," Gordon advised as she came in with her food.

Weismann was at the next table. "You fuss over them like a bloody mother hen," he sneered.

Barbara ignored him. She was too late to sit next to Gordon so she went and sat at another table and ate as fast as she could.

After lunch the CUOs joined all the others for a lesson in which WO1 Pryor and Capt Royston demonstrated how to teach a skills lesson, in this case how to assemble an army radio. Then they were marched to the bush on the edge of the camp for a lesson by Lieutenant Hamish Hamilton of the Army Reserve, brother of Capt Hamilton, on 'How to Teach a Fieldcraft Lesson'.

The afternoon sun was still blistering and the straggly leaves of the ironbarks cast very little shade. In the distance the towering masses of several 'Thunder Heads' passed to the north, but they seemed to avoid the Bunyip River area. Barbara sat next to Wendy on a large mound of red earth.

"Isn't he handsome?" Wendy whispered, indicating the young officer. "I love his moustache."

"He'll be just like all the others," Barbara replied.

"Just like Gordon?" Wendy asked, her face the picture of innocence.

Barbara sniffed but had no answer. She had to smile though.

At the end of that lesson, when they had marched back to the huts, Barbara stood down from being Platoon Commander. Karen Harvey took over 4 Platoon from her. Monica took over 3 Platoon and Weismann took over 5 Pl (Sgts) from Fiona. By the chance of the rostering system Wendy became Weismann's Duty Pl Sgt.

Oh no! Barbara thought.

Chapter 10

AN AWFUL SHOCK

"You could ask to have the roster changed," Barbara suggested to her.

Wendy bit her lip. "But what reason could I give?"

"The truth."

"Oh, I'll be alright. It's only for 24 hours," Wendy replied, putting a brave face on things.

Within an hour Barbara could see Wendy regretted her decision already. When Wendy marched her platoon in for dinner, she looked pale and strained. Barbara forgot about her while eating her own tea and talking to Gordon, but before she had finished her main course she noticed Wendy go past towards the girls hut. Her face indicated distress.

Barbara stood up. "Excuse me. I'll be back in a minute," she said. She hurried after Wendy and found her lying on her stretcher sobbing. Barbara knelt down and put her hand on her shoulder. "What's the matter 'Wobbles'?"

"Don't (sniff)... call me (sniff) that (sniff) please!" Wendy sobbed.

"I'm sorry. Never again. What's wrong?"

Wendy convulsed with sobs into her pillow. "That animal Weismann. He. He...He asked me for sex. To sneak out and meet him after (sniff), bed check. sob. Oh! He's (sniff) disgusting!"

"What exactly did he ask?"

"I'd rather (sniff) not say. He just leered (sniff) at me and (sniff) asked me straight out. I was too stunned to answer for a (sniff) while."

Wendy rolled over to face Barbara. Tears trickled down her cheeks.

Barbara shook her head and said, "Here, have my hankie. What did you say?"

"Thanks," Wendy said. She took the handkerchief and wiped her eyes. "I mean I told him he was a disgusting pig and if he said one more thing, I'd report him."

There were footsteps in the hall. Fiona, Karen, Sharon and Camille appeared in the doorway.

Fiona came over and bent down. "Is it OK Barb? What's the matter?" she asked.

Barbara told them. The girls looked at each other. Camille pursed her lips. "That turd is getting beyond a joke. It's time something was done," she said.

"But what?"

"Tell Miss McEwen to start with," Fiona suggested.

"But who is going to tell her?" Sharon asked.

"I will," Barbara replied grimly.

Wendy held up her hand. "Oh Barb don't. It's not that serious. I'll be alright," she said.

Barbara looked at her friend's anxious face. "But it's not just for you," she replied.

Wendy looked unhappy. "I don't want you to," she replied in a hoarse whisper.

"Has he threatened you?" Barbara asked.

"No. Not directly, just, well..."

"That does it! I'll tell Miss McEwen. You might not be the only one," Barbara said, the name 'Chloe' forming in her thoughts.

"No," agreed Camille. "That Malone she..."

"She what?" came Monica's voice. The girls whirled around to see her standing close behind them.

There was an awkward silence. Barbara stood up. "Let's go back and eat. Come on Wendy. You need to eat more."

The girls brushed past Monica and made their way back to the Mess Hall. As she entered the room Barbara noted Weismann sitting with Stephens and Wilmot. The two boys snickered as the girls sat down.

Gordon raised an eyebrow. "What was that all about?" he asked.

"Never mind. Secret women's business," Barbara replied flatly. She picked up her knife and fork and attacked the cold steak and kidney pie.

They had night lectures as usual. Capt Royston talked to them about how to 'Advise an Instructor'. Then Captain Conkey came and taught them how to construct a 'Going Map' using a compass and protractor.

Last of all the Colonel took them for a lecture on where Cadets fitted into the Army's Legal System. The second half of his lecture dealt with what were 'Lawful Commands' and what were 'Unlawful Commands'. "It is your duty as leaders to ensure all your cadets understand these so they will not be coerced into doing the wrong thing. Likewise it is your clear moral duty not to obey a superior who gives you what appears to be an unlawful command. We will have none of that Hitler's SS business of 'Ve ver only followink orders'."

"What sort of things sir?" Roger asked.

"Well, in war time the shooting of prisoners or civilians. That's just murder," the Colonel explained.

"Is it an unlawful command for a male officer to tell a girl cadet to take her clothes off?" Jennifer asked.

The Colonel looked appalled. "Most definitely!" he replied. "Remember, Civil Law is superior to Military Law. If it's against normal civilian law, it's a crime. You have touched on a very important issue. In the cadets you leaders, and also we officers, have a particular responsibility to protect the cadets from any sort of sexual harassment. They are only minors, which means they aren't adults in law."

Barbara and the other girls all turned and looked at Weismann. He looked uncomfortable but pretended not to notice. The Colonel noted this and a worried frown crossed his face. He went on with another example related to a sergeant ordering a cadet to steal military stores from another unit or sub-unit.

For the rest of the lecture Barbara sat in a state of turmoil. *Should I tell or not?* she agonized.

Finally she decided she must. The cadets had been allowed an extra half-hour before lights out because they had to teach their practice lessons the following day. When they were dismissed Barbara left the others and sought out Lt McEwen who was sitting in the HQ.

The two walked up and down the concrete parade ground in the dark for twenty minutes while Barbara related Weismann's words and actions. In this she included mention of Chloe, at whose name Lt McEwen gave an unimpressed sniff. Barbara also considered saying something about Monica but held back.

I don't have any real proof, she told herself.

Lt McEwen looked very thoughtful. "Alright Barbara, you go back and prepare your lesson. If Wendy won't make the complaint herself there isn't a lot I can do. I'll keep this to myself for the time being, but I will be on the lookout and if there's another incident let me know. I don't think we have enough proof yet for official action," she said.

"Yes Miss. Thank you. Goodnight."

Barbara marched back to the lecture room barely noticing the swarm of young corporals outside the canteen. When she got back to the lecture room, she said little to the others and settled to her study. Gordon sat opposite but wisely did not ask. For twenty minutes Barbara read her notes and textbooks. She again loaned them to Gordon. He got her some cordial and a biscuit.

After she had taken a sip, she shook her head. "It's no good. I'm too tired," she said, rubbing her eyes. "A good sleep is what I need." Even though she really wanted to stay with Gordon she stood up, put her lesson plan in her folder, picked up her books and said goodnight.

The hut was quiet, only a few girls talking, reading and polishing. Monica was not there. Barbara put her books and folder into her duffle bag and had a quick shower. Back in the room Camille's jokes soon cheered her up a bit. But she was in bed before 'lights out' and then lay awake to see if Monica came back.

Monica did, and only a couple of minutes late, scrambling into her bed just before the bed-check. Barbara turned away and lay quietly. *I must watch and see if Malone sneaks out,* she thought. For a while she lay thinking, pretending to sleep, and fell sound asleep.

The next thing she knew it was Check Parade. The morning routine swallowed her up. There seemed to be more things to do than usual, so she had little time to talk to Gordon. She just gave him an extra-special smile and rushed off to get ready for inspection.

During the morning parade Barbara stood at the rear of the parade ground with the CUOs not rostered as platoon commanders. It was hot and still, and she found it quite boring. Many 'corporals' fell-out from the heat but fewer than the day before.

It was the day for the CUOs Course to give their practice lesson. Barbara was scheduled to teach during Period 3 so she had Period 2 free to prepare and rehearse. As soon as they marched off parade, she went to her hut to collect her Lesson Plan and the book of snakes. It was her intention to use the coloured pictures to illustrate the different species. Before starting work, she had a drink then walked to her bed. She picked up her plastic clipboard and opened it to read the Lesson Plan.

It wasn't there.

Puzzled, she flicked through the pages of notes.

"It must be here somewhere. I put it back last night, I'm sure," she muttered.

But she could not find it. Thinking she must have missed it she went carefully through the folder again, page by page. There was no sign of it. Anxiety formed furrows in her brow. Quickly she searched through her suitcase. It was not there either.

"Where can it be? Oh botheration!" she cried after looking at her watch. "Twenty minutes and I have to present. I'll have to rewrite it. The Assessor will want to see it."

Now feeling a little stressed and flustered she went back to the suitcase to look for her training manual. There was no sign of it either. In mounting concern she rummaged through her belongings, disordering the neatly folded clothes. There was no sign of the missing book or plan. Now feeling somewhat upset she then looked in her webbing and other unlikely places.

As she did it dawned on her she hadn't seen the book of *Australian Snakes* either. Another search of the suitcase failed to produce either book. Barbara stood up. By this time she was perspiring and her pulses raced. An awful sensation akin to nausea seemed to form in the pit of her stomach. An even more unpleasant feeling pulsed outward from her brain as the foul taste of suspicion spread.

"I'm sure I put them back last night. Someone must have taken them. I'll bet it was that bitch...!" She left the name Malone unspoken, unwilling to wrongly accuse. Then she shook her head. "No. That's not fair. Just because I don't like her, or she doesn't like me is not sufficient reason to blame her. I've no proof," she muttered. Now close to tears she wiped the perspiration from her forehead and checked her watch again.

Only 15 minutes left!

Feeling wretched she sat down, took out a blank lesson plan form and began to write furiously. When she went into the lecture room, she felt more like curling up and crying. With an effort she made herself act as though all was well. She saluted Lt Curwen, who was assessing, and took her position in front of the class. This only comprised three other potential CUOs, but one of them was Gordon and this made it worse. She had so much wanted to look good for him.

She opened her folder and took out the single sheet of paper on which she had written key words from memory. This she placed down beside her hastily scrawled plan. After a nervous check of her watch she began to teach the lesson.

To add to her worries she was sure that her voice sounded strange. Her throat felt dry and she had to swallow repeatedly. Her hands became sweaty. She forced herself to keep eye contact with the squad. Somehow, she made the words come out.

Thirty-five minutes later she reached the conclusion. "Does anyone have any further questions? No? Good. In this lesson you have learned how to identify various snakes." As she said this she gestured to her sketches on the whiteboard, "And you have learnt the treatment for snake bite. Your next lesson on this subject is..." She went on to detail the next lessons.

Feeling as though she wanted to throw up she stopped and for a moment just stood there. Lt Curwen spoke up. "Alright Warrant Officer Brassington. Bring me your lesson plan. You others can help with constructive criticism."

Barbara reluctantly took the single sheet and placed it on the table in front of the officer. She looked at it and frowned, then said, "Sit down Warrant Officer Brassington. That was quite a good lesson. Was this all you had written?"

Barbara swallowed and nodded. She had trouble grasping what the officer had said. To her it had seemed an awful lesson. "Yes Ma'am. I actually had a much more complete plan and detailed notes," Barbara explained. Then she hesitated before going on. "I...I seem to have lost them. I mean, I couldn't find my lesson plan this morning when I went to revise, so I had to rewrite it quickly."

Lt Curwen looked at her quizzically. Barbara felt her explanation sounded a bit lame, so she added, "I was also going to show them pictures of the various snakes but I seem to have misplaced the illustrated book I brought to camp."

Stephens, who had been listening, then spoke up and pointed to Gordon. "I saw Sgt Farr with that book this morning."

They all turned surprised eyes on Gordon who first looked astonished as well before flushing indignantly. "I did not have it!" he denied. He turned to Barbara, who felt the sickness in the stomach again.

"You did so!" Stephens repeated accusingly. "I saw you. You were sitting on your bed reading it after breakfast."

"That's not true!" Gordon replied hotly.

Barbara thought she would vomit. She cast frantically around in her memory. *Did I loan Gordon the book?* she thought. He had certainly looked at it the previous night, but she was sure she had received it back and carried it to her room. *Did I leave it here on the table, unnoticed amongst other people's books?* she wondered. To her dismay she couldn't remember.

Gordon looked at her. "I didn't Barbara. I gave it back to you before you left last night."

Barbara opened her mouth to agree but Stephens shouted over her. "Are you calling me a liar? I saw you with it this morning!"

"That will do!" Lt Curwen snapped. She rose to her feet looking worried.

The Colonel came in, attracted by the angry voices. "What's the problem?"

Lt Curwen explained. The Colonel tugged at his chin for a moment before facing Stephens. "This is a serious accusation Sgt Stephens," he said. "Describe exactly what you saw."

Stephens repeated that he had seen Gordon sitting on his stretcher reading the book. "Then he put it in his kitbag sir," he added.

The Colonel nodded thoughtfully and turned to Gordon, who repeated his denial. The Colonel then looked at Barbara. "And did Sgt Farr give you back the book last night?"

"Yes sir."

"You don't sound very sure?"

"I remember picking all my books up sir,"

Stephens cut in again. "Farr's got it sir. It's in his kitbag," he cried. To Barbara he seemed very nervous.

The Colonel frowned at him. "Well, we can easily check that. Do you mind if we search your gear Sgt Farr?"

"No sir. I don't mind. I've got nothing to hide," Gordon replied.

They walked across as a group to the CUO's tents. The Colonel stopped them at the entrance to Gordon's tent. "Which is your bag Sgt Farr?"

Gordon pointed. There were only six stretchers in the tent. The Colonel walked over and picked up the kitbag at the head of the bed. He unzipped it and began to rummage inside. A peculiar expression crossed his face and he paused. Barbara suddenly felt a sickening premonition. The Colonel withdrew his hand and held up a small, hard-cover book with a glossy picture of a brown snake on the cover.

Barbara gasped and thought she was going to be sick. She looked at Gordon and saw that he was staring at it in horrified fascination.

The Colonel turned to Barbara. "Is this your book Warrant Officer Brassington?" he asked. He walked over and handed it to her. Her hands shook slightly as she took it. It was hers alright. Her name was on the inside of the cover. In dumb misery she showed the Colonel.

Gordon found his voice. "I didn't take it Barbara. I didn't! Sir, I didn't!"

The Colonel frowned. "So how did it get into your gear?"

Gordon shrugged. "I don't know sir. I didn't put it there."

"By that are you implying someone else put it there?" the Colonel asked, his voice and eyes hard.

"Yes sir."

"Who?"

There was a strained silence and Barbara saw Gordon bite his lip and a look of near despair cross his face. He opened his mouth but just said, "I did not take the book sir."

"He's lying sir!" Stephens cried.

The Colonel's face went dark with anger. "Silence Sgt Stephens! Well Sgt Farr, who?"

"I don't know sir."

Barbara felt giddy. Her mind whirled in suspicious turmoil. If it had been Weismann or Malone who had made the accusation the deceit would have been clear but she couldn't fathom how Stephens could be involved.

The Colonel turned back to Gordon's kitbag and emptied it onto the stretcher. He held up a half empty packet of cigarettes. Gordon shook his head in disbelief. "I don't smoke sir. They aren't mine."

It got worse. Barbara's Lesson Plan was there, and her 'flagged' Training Manual. Gordon turned to Barbara. "I didn't take them Barbara! Someone's planted them there. This is a set-up!"

"Don't call me a liar Farr!" Stephens yelled. He hopped from foot to foot looking very agitated.

Barbara wanted to believe Gordon but an insidious worm of doubt had intruded into her brain. She shook her head. "I'm sure I took all that to my room last night sir," she said.

The Colonel looked hard at her. Barbara flushed at the realization that he was trying to decide if she was lying to cover Gordon or not.

Our friendship has been very open, she thought.

The Colonel stood up. "This is serious. I shall have to investigate this more thoroughly but if I find you haven't been telling the truth Sgt Farr you will be off the course. Do you understand?"

"Yes sir," Gordon replied, the bitterness clear in his voice.

Chapter 11

SUSPICIONS

The Colonel ordered them to separate locations while he called a hasty meeting of several officers. Feeling utterly wretched, Barbara sat on the porch of the girls hut.

If only she didn't have doubts!

She believed Gordon but the evidence of the expose had been damning. *What will I do if he is taken off the course?* she fretted.

The Colonel convened an inquiry. Barbara saw Gordon called over to the HQ where the Colonel sat behind a table flanked by Major Burnside and Captain Conkey. After ten minutes of questioning Gordon was led away by Capt Royston.

Next Major Ross hurried in and after a few minutes Sgt Stephens was called over. He was then led away by Capt Buchan. Capt Conkey beckoned to Barbara.

Anxiety became so powerful that Barbara had to consciously think to control it. It made her grateful for the military system as all she had to do was march and halt then salute while keeping her face neutral. She had to stop her limbs from trembling as she stood in front of the table. The Colonel asked her a series of questions: When had she last seen the books? Did she lend them to Gordon?; and so on.

Barbara had to swallow to moisten her throat before answering. "I'm sure I had them last night sir. I put them in my duffle bag before I went to bed."

"Did anyone else see you?"

"I...I don't remember sir. Fiona Davies was still studying," Barbara replied. She struggled to remember. Wendy hadn't been there she was sure. What about Malone? She couldn't remember. "Yes. Camille Clark was there."

"Capt Conkey, would you please get Sgt Clark, and Major Wickham if he is not teaching," the Colonel asked.

He turned back to Barbara. "Did you put the books on your bed, or in your echelon bag?"

"In my echelon bag sir."

"Did you go straight to bed?"

Barbara hesitated. "No sir. I had a quick shower. Then I talked to Camille and Karen."

"You're sure you didn't leave the books on your bed?"

"Yes sir. I'm sure."

"You sleep next to Cpl Malone. Was she there?"

Barbara hesitated again. "No sir. She came back just after 'Lights Out'."

"How long after?"

"Only a couple of minutes sir."

"Alright. Go with Lt Curwen and she'll take a statement from you."

Barbara saluted and followed Lt Curwen back to the lecture room. There she spent a miserable half-hour writing out her version of the story. Lt Curwen then left her alone and took the statement to the Colonel.

Ten minutes later Barbara saw WO1 Pryor march Gordon over to the HQ. Biting her lip with anxiety she stood at the door watching. She felt so ill she had to steady herself on the door post.

The interview only lasted a couple of minutes. She watched Gordon salute, about turn and march off towards his tent. He vanished from sight. What was to be his fate? Barbara realised she was holding her breath. She felt dizzy and had to sit down. Even though she felt desperate to know she knew she couldn't go to the boy's tents to ask.

A few long minutes later Gordon appeared. He marched over to her, his face set in grim lines.

Barbara wasn't sure how to ask him.

"Well?" she said at last.

"I am still on the course but I'm under a cloud. I think the Colonel smelled the rats but there was no other proof."

"I'm sorry," Barbara said.

"It wasn't your fault. Someone put those things in my gear."

"Stephens?"

"Or Weismann, and maybe Monica, but I don't get how Stephens comes into things. Why would he lie like that?" Gordon said.

"Did you tell the Colonel?"

"No. I had no proof so I couldn't name names," Gordon replied. His lips compressed into a sour line. "Did you?"

"No. I thought Malone must have taken them but didn't say so," Barbara replied.

"You do believe me, don't you?" Gordon asked.

"Yes."

"You sound a bit doubtful. You either trust me or you don't," Gordon answered sharply.

"Well, it did look suspicious when the Colonel pulled the book out of your gear."

Gordon was clearly nettled. They eyed each other uneasily. Barbara didn't want to talk about it anymore. She sensed that something wonderful was gone.

They were saved by the arrival of a dozen others at the end of Period 4. Lofty joined them and said, "Come on. We've got more lessons to listen to."

They separated and went to the groups on the roster. Barbara sat through a lesson by Sgt Ying on 'How to find Water' but her mind was in such turmoil she was only half aware of it.

At lunch time the CUOs were a very subdued group and plainly split into partisan groups. The story had rapidly done the rounds and they now divided into those who believed Gordon and those who didn't.

It wasn't a spoken thing. It was only revealed by looks and by who sat with whom.

Barbara didn't want to have lunch, but Fiona and Camille made her. She wasn't able to stand next to Gordon in the line, but she made a point of sitting next to him.

It was an uncomfortable meal with a lot of murmured conversations and covert glances. Once Barbara looked up and met Weismann's eyes. To her they appeared to be filled with malicious glee. It made her look to see where Stephens was sitting. He was at a table with the people from his own unit and looked quite miserable.

During the afternoon the CUOs were all together in the lecture room for five periods. Barbara sat next to Gordon, but she felt a bit strained and they said little to each other. The weather seemed hotter than ever and sweaty arms stuck to notepaper. Tempers became irritable. The whole class was plainly on edge.

They were instructed by Capt Conkey on how to plan a Navigation Exercise. He then grouped them into fours to spend a period working out a Navex. "This is for the Corporals Course to do on Sunday afternoon. Half of you will be running this while the other half help assess the Sergeants Course on their Resection Test," Capt Conkey explained.

Roger's hand shot up. "Excuse me sir. Which half of us will be with the Corporals?"

Capt Conkey looked a bit irritated. "We haven't decided yet, why?"

"I just wondered Sir. I thought the bottom half of us would be best with the Corporals as they're a mob of bums."

"Yes Roger. Thank you for that suggestion," Capt Conkey replied. Then he laughed. The others joined in. The feeble joke helped ease the tension considerably and normal conversation sprang up as they went back to their work.

The area allocated to Barbara's group was to the east of the camp. It was only a three-kilometre course they had to plot. Barbara found the mathematics of it easy. Their only disputes were over problems such as where the check-points should be, how the Directing Staff would get to the check points, and issues of safety such as providing water in jerrycans and how casualties might be evacuated.

They had only reached the stage of realising they still had all these problems to solve when Capt Conkey stopped them.

"Right, time's up. You have another lesson Saturday morning to finish this problem, plus two lessons to plan a night 'Navex' after that, so you have plenty of time to get organised before the event. Have a five-minute break. Your next lesson is here with the Colonel on Problem Solving."

That next lesson Barbara found fascinating as they had explained to them by an expert the army's simple system of logical steps to solve problems: the 'Appreciation'. This was followed by one on how to plan a reconnaissance and how to plan the use of time. She found it so intellectually stimulating that for a while the misery of the morning was forgotten.

At the conclusion of the afternoon training Barbara went to the small laundry to do some washing. This was mostly hand-washing as there were only two washing machines, both in constant use. After that she had a shower and changed into a clean uniform. She felt so tired that things seemed a bit unreal.

Feeling stressed and guilty at not studying she lay back on her stretcher and closed her eyes. *Just a few minutes rest,* she told herself. She tried to block out the hubbub of a dozen other girls polishing brass, cleaning rifles and chattering.

Someone hit her boots. Wendy's voice penetrated her consciousness. "You OK Barb?"

"Mmm. Yes. Just a bit tired."

"You were starting to snore. Mess Parade has been called."

"Thanks," Barbara replied. With an effort she sat up and rubbed her face. She felt abnormally hot and drained. The air was very still and humid, but she thought the heat was internal.

"I must have dozed off," she said, getting up and stretching stiff joints.

The CUOs Course formed up on the road outside. Barbara walked over to join them feeling slightly groggy.

As she joined them Roger cried, "What extraordinary light!" Barbara looked around and saw that everything was bathed in a reddish-golden glow. The whole western sky was a rippled sheet like a vast static flame.

Fiona gasped. "What a gorgeous sunset," she said.

"What a gorgeous sunset!" mimicked Weismann.

"Shut up Weismann," Lofty murmured. Weismann scowled but said nothing more.

Gordon looked around. "That looks like a ripper of a thunderstorm building up," he commented.

"We might get some rain," Roger responded.

"We could do with it," Camille added.

Karen nodded, adding, "Come on you lot, dinner time. Let's go."

During the meal Barbara sat opposite Gordon but she said little.

"You Ok?" he asked.

She was touched by the concern in his voice. "Yes thanks. Just a bit tired," she replied. She didn't want to explain that she thought it was mostly nervous exhaustion from the morning.

The evening lectures were by Capt Royston on Military Map Symbols and how to mark a Military Map; followed by the Organization of a Command Post by the Colonel. Barbara found it very interesting and she concentrated hard, excluding everything else by an effort of will power.

What she couldn't exclude so easily were her memories. When the

Colonel detailed how the signaller in a CP should log all messages, she remembered that it was just this routine which had given the leader of the crooks the clue about where CUO Kirk had gone. She had a vivid flashback to sitting in the signals tent calling 4 Platoon on the radio and Cpl Henning, the Sig Cpl, noting her call. At the time she had been terrified the leader of the crooks would overhear her. He had been in the next tent and she could hear him threatening Captain Conkey and the other OOCs.

Then, soon after, she had made her run to get away, to get help. Berzinski had fired his sub-machine gun at her. At the sound of those bullets cracking past she had almost frozen with terror, then the adrenaline had kicked in like a charge of electricity and she had bolted. With a rolling dive she would never have attempted in cold blood she had taken cover, rolling through thistles and prickles. The leader of the crooks had apparently fired a shotgun. She hadn't known it was him at the time but had heard the blast and the pellets rattling through the leaves overhead.

Barbara closed her eyes and could remember every detail of that frantic run, of Berzinski in hot pursuit mouthing foul obscenities, his eyes glittering with...? Lust? Hate? She shuddered. It was after she had outrun him she had met the pig hunters. By then she had been nearly exhausted and drenched with sweat.

She realised she was sweating now.

Fiona nudged her. "You Ok Barbara?" she asked.

Barbara opened her eyes with a start. Everyone was looking at her.

"Yes. Sorry. I was just remembering our signals tent last September," she explained. She met the Colonel's concerned gaze. "Sorry Sir."

When the class was dismissed Barbara went to get a cup of cold cordial. She felt quite shaken. The air was sultry and still. Thunder grumbled away to the west. Perhaps the storm was coming? She went back to the lecture room and sat to finish writing out her Patrol Orders for the following day. Gordon had left but Roger and Lofty were there, so she sat with them.

Fiona came in with Karen and Sharon a few minutes later.

"Coming to the canteen Barbara?" she asked.

"I want to finish these orders."

"We've still got half an hour for that but the canteen shuts in ten minutes," Fiona said.

"Oh alright." Barbara stood up.

"Canteen. Good idea!" Roger agreed.

Lofty declined. "You go. I'll keep working and mind your gear. Bring me a 'Crunchie Bar'," he said.

The group made its way out onto the road and walked into the semidarkness past the girls hut. Lightning flashed and flickered across half the sky ahead of them.

"That storm is a lot closer," Sharon noted.

"I can smell the rain," Karen claimed.

They walked past a group of cadets at the small veranda at the end of the girls hut. In the centre of a group of boys was a giggling Chloe. She had no hat on and her blonde hair was sparkling in the light.

She's enjoying herself, Barbara thought. She had forgotten about Chloe.

Roger then said, "Who's that blonde; the 'Boy Magnet' over there?"

"Roger!" Lofty cried. "Where have you been for the last few days?"

"Here, why?" answered the puzzled Roger.

"That is the famous Chloe," Lofty answered.

"Oh! Oh that Chloe!" Roger muttered.

"Yes, that Chloe!" Fiona mimicked. Then she nodded back to the group and said, "Like bloody flies around the honey pot."

Karen snorted. "Huh! More like blowflies around the cess pit," she muttered.

"She had better behave!" Sharon warned.

"Is she from your unit?" Roger asked.

"Yes she is," Sharon answered. "If she passes the course, she will probably be one of my section commanders." The group walked on and began to discuss rumours about Chloe.

As they neared the canteen Barbara glanced sideways at two figures standing close together out in the darkness of the car park. As she did there was another big flash of lightning. What she saw so stunned her that she nearly stopped walking. She was sure her heart stopped.

Gordon was standing talking to Monica!

Chapter 12

THE THUNDER STORM

Monica was standing very close to Gordon with her face upturned. Barbara couldn't see in the ensuing darkness whether they were touching or not, but she had the distinct impression Monica had her hand on Gordon's arm.

Barbara went into the canteen in a state of confusion. It was apparent that none of the others had noticed. She was glad of the press of sweaty little corporals as it gave her a chance to master her turmoil unnoticed. She and her friends made their purchases amid a cheerful chatter then headed for the door. Barbara led the way. Just as she reached the door Gordon stepped up out of the night. Monica was close behind him.

They halted facing each other in the narrow doorway. Gordon smiled and said, "Hello. I was wondering where you were."

"I was wondering where you were too," Barbara replied, her mind racing. *Is that an innocent smile, or the grin of guilty guile?* she wondered. She said, "But I saw you were busy." Her eyes travelled past him to lock with Monica's.

Gordon half-turned to follow her stare. The implication of her statement then dawned on him.

"No. It's not like that."

"No? Excuse me." Barbara brushed past him and down the steps. Monica had to step hastily aside. Barbara had an urge to push the little minx over. *Trollop!* she thought.

Gordon turned and followed her. The others also followed but she was oblivious to them.

"Barbara please! It's not what you think," Gordon said. He caught up with her and took hold of her sleeve.

"Let me go!" she snapped. She snatched her arm free and whirled to face him. "Well it looked that way, meeting out there in the dark."

"Now be fair," Gordon replied with more than a hint of anger in his voice.

Barbara felt stung and cried, "You shouldn't talk to her. She's a..."

"Don't be ridiculous! She's in my unit," Gordon replied. "She just wanted some advice on a problem. I can talk to people from my own unit if I like. You don't own me. Besides, you lot stick together like..."

"Like shit to a blanket!" Monica's voice called from beside them. A flash of lightning showed her with hands on hips and lips pursed.

"You keep out of this Malone!" Barbara hissed.

"Stop it you two!" Gordon called. His voice was almost drowned out by a crackling roll of thunder.

"Don't tell me what to do!" Barbara cried.

A heavy raindrop fell on her cheek. Other drops began to spatter on the leaves and roofs. A cold gust of wind made her shiver.

Gordon snorted. "Well same goes for me. I'll talk to who I like. You either trust me or you don't!" he replied angrily.

Another spatter of raindrops hit them. A great flash of lightning lit up his face. Barbara noted stark angles and eyes staring in... in what? Pain, anger, misery? A crash of thunder made them all jump. It sounded as though a giant sledgehammer had flattened the huge shed.

"Come on. We'll be soaked. Run for it!" cried Fiona. She tugged at Barbara's sleeve. Barbara hesitated. She could hear the approaching roar of the rain on the trees but it meant little. The others began running. Gordon turned his back and walked off towards his tent.

Fiona cried again and Barbara broke into a reluctant run... too late. The rain seemed to engulf them in a stinging wall. As she ran Barbara saw Gordon in the distance as lightning lit up the camp. The cold raindrops mingled with warm tears.

The girls reached the shelter of their hut just as there was another mighty thunderclap.

"Bloody hell!" Camille cried. "That sounded like a bomb going off."

The rain roared on the roof so loudly they had to shout to make themselves heard. Run-off began to gurgle in the downpipes and pour from overflowing guttering.

"Strewth! What a downpour!" Sharon called, jumping up and down in excitement.

"I'm glad we aren't in tents," Karen observed.

"Oh yes. All the boys will get wet," Wendy replied.

"Perhaps they could move in here," suggested a sergeant from Rockhampton.

Barbara stood with the group looking out the front door, feeling as though she was stunned. She knew she had made a mistake, that she had flared up out of jealousy and made things worse, not better.

Camille hopped up and down with excitement. "Let's look out the other end," she suggested. Most of the girls followed her out of the room and along the corridor. Barbara just stood staring into the blackness, the downpour matching her mood.

"Here," Wendy said, passing her a towel.

Barbara took it and looked around. Fiona was there too.

"Dry the eyes kid," Fiona said gently.

"Oh I'm a fool," Barbara blubbered in reply. Hot tears came. Wendy put an arm around her and hugged her. Fiona took the towel and gently wiped her face. Thunder crashed. Cold spray blew in. Barbara shivered.

Monica came running through the rain from the canteen. She was giggling and shrieking. She dashed up onto the porch and stopped facing the friends. "I was right, you lot from Cairns are all 'Lemons'," she said.

It took all Barbara's self-control not to smack her down the steps into the mud.

Fiona glared angrily. "Don't be disgusting!" she snapped.

Monica just sneered and walked past to her bed and began to peel off her wet clothes.

"Come on," Barbara said. She couldn't bear to have Monica see her upset. Turning on her heel she walked quickly across the room and along the corridor. Her friends followed. By the time they reached the front porch she had wiped her eyes and gained control of herself.

The girls stood there talking and laughing as the rain continued to thunder down. In the distance they could see torches around the boys' tents. In the flashes of lightning they got glimpses of figures hastily improving the storm drains.

A girl on the sergeants course came and tugged at Karen's sleeve. "Come and look!" she cried. "That Chloe is out in the rain and it looks like she is in the nuddy!"

Oh no! Barbara thought. But she followed the other girls through to the back veranda, her heart full of anxiety. *Silly girl! She could be chucked off the course.*

The tent Chloe was in was about 25 metres away and almost in line and even in the dim light of the lights at the front and near the kitchen

Barbara could just make out a pale figure kneeling in the mud at the side of the tent. There were a few other people outside other tents either digging or holding torches and when the beam of one of these flickered around Barbara got a glimpse of naked female. There was no doubt; even in the drenching downpour she could see it was Chloe and it looked like she had no clothes on.

Then a lightning flash lit up the scene and Barbara saw that Chloe actually had on a skimpy bikini. *Wheh!* she thought.

"What's she doing?" the female sergeant asked.

Barbara spoke first. "Keeping her uniforms dry."

"Digging a storm drain," Camille answered.

"She looks like she is pushing mud into the tent," Rebecca commented.

Camille nodded. "She is. That's what you are supposed to do. You need a dam to keep the water from flowing into the tent once the drain is full."

"She could have worn a raincoat," Karen commented.

Camille laughed. "She probably doesn't own one. I don't."

Jennifer was astonished. "What do you do when it rains?"

"Get wet," Camille answered. "This is North Queensland. The rain isn't cold and you sweat so much in a plastic raincoat you are usually better off without one," she replied.

Barbara could only agree with that. She stared at the dim shape of Chloe, and then blushed as she realised she was hoping to get a better look.

Am I gay? she wondered. *Do I prefer girls?*

At that moment a person wearing uniform, raincoat and hat came out of Chloe's tent and came running across to the hut. She was blocked at the bottom of the back steps by the crowd of girls on the small veranda. Barbara recognised her as a corporal named Maude.

"I need a lady officer," Maude called.

"Why?" Camille asked.

"Because that Chloe is being disgusting! She is out there with almost no clothes on where everybody can see her. Is there an officer in there?" Maude answered, her voice full of outrage and anger.

Just hearing her caused Barbara's stomach to turn over. *Oh dear! Chloe's offended this one!* she thought.

Maude went to come up the steps but Camille stepped across and blocked her, an action Barbara mentally applauded.

Camille put her hands on her hips. "No there isn't! And you can't come in here dripping water all through our hut," Camille replied. "Anyway, we can see she's wearing something."

"It... She... They are just those tiny, skimpy things," Maude answered. Again she moved to come up the steps.

Camille still blocked her. "There are no boys around. What's the big deal?"

"It... It's indecent!" Maude almost shouted, flapping her arms in her anger.

Maude bleated a few times and then ran off around the side of the hut, heading towards HQ. As she did she encountered Lt McEwen and Lt Curwen coming out of the darkness, both wrapped in raincoats. Maude at once grabbed at Lt McEwen's sleeve and pointed to where Chloe was still visible scooping mud.

Barbara only heard the word 'Chloe!' but it was enough to annoy her. *She doesn't have to be so self-righteous and bitchy about it,* she thought.

Sadly she watched Maude lead Lt McEwen over towards Chloe. As she did Lt Curwen came over to the bottom of the steps. "Into your beds girls. It's after lights out," Lt McEwen ordered.

Barbara really wanted to stay and see what happened to Chloe, but the officer was insistent and ordered them all inside, coming up the stairs to do so. As the girls moved back through the door of the hut Barbara cast a last glance towards where Maude and Lt McEwen were now standing over Chloe.

But Lt Curwen was obviously annoyed. "Inside|! Get to bed!"

Only then did Barbara realise that her folder and Verbal Orders were still in the lecture room. She wanted to go and get them. "Please Miss," she said.

"No Barbara. They'll be alright. Go to bed. You look very tired," Lt McEwen commanded.

Barbara turned and went to her bed. Only then did she realise she was cold and shivering. Quickly she snatched up her towel and again dried her face and hair. By then Lt Curwen had switched off the lights so Barbara turned her back on the others and peeled off her wet clothes and hung them up, hotly aware that she was also going to be naked where the others could see her. But she was too stubborn to go to the showers or toilets so she kept undressing, casting glances out the door from time to time as she did.

Many of the others did as well and there was a deal of speculation about what would happen to Chloe, ranging from the 'Serves the silly bitch right!' to sympathy. But to Barbara's frustration the darkness and rain hid the scene.

Quickly Barbara changed into flannel pyjamas and hung up her wet clothes then wriggled into her bed. Rain still drummed on the roof and gushed in the drains but the thunder and lightning had stopped. Jealous memories of Gordon and Monica then drove concern for Chloe from her mind.

For about ten minutes she lay shivering, aware that misery was her main emotion. Then she began to cry quietly. In her mind she went over the day's events and tried to sort out what was the truth and what she should do.

Sleep claimed her before she had half considered it.

It was a sound sleep, despite the rain which continued to pour. Barbara even slept through the confusion of a dozen drenched female Corporals dragging their sodden gear in out of the darkness and only woke when Wendy shook her at 0600.

Next to her on the floor, in a sleeping bag caked with red mud, was a tousle-headed Corporal with freckles who gave her a cheeky grin.

"Bit wet was it?" Barbara asked.

"Bit wet!" the girl shrieked. "We had to swim, well, not really, but the water flowed right through our tent."

Barbara got up. Rain still drummed on the roof. "What do we do for check parade?" the girl asked.

"Not sure. Wait and see. Come on you girls, up you get!"

Directly opposite Barbara was a sleeping bag which began to heave and writhe. Out of it wriggled another female Corporal with blonde hair. Fearing that she was about to be exposed to more nudity Barbara braced herself, having heard from others that Chloe normally wore nothing to bed. Camille, who had been Chloe's section corporal, had confirmed this. But it wasn't Chloe and the girl was dressed. She gave a friendly smile as she stood up.

"Talk about rain!" she giggled.

Barbara had to smile and made a friendly reply. *I wonder what happened to Chloe?* she thought, finding it hard to dislike someone who was so open.

For Check Parade they were ordered to their lecture rooms. This resulted in a giggling helter-skelter under raincoats. As soon as she got there Barbara remembered her Verbal Orders. Her folder was still on the table so she quickly picked it up and checked. To her relief they were still there. Outside it was still quite dark and there was a solid, low overcast.

Barbara felt cold and depressed. She sat at the back and didn't want to talk. Gordon was there but when she met his eye he looked away and they did not exchange greetings.

"This rain looks like it has set in for a while," Roger opined.

Lofty agreed. "Could be. There's a low in the gulf. That will be pulling this stuff in off the Coral Sea."

They all nodded and agreed. Being North Queenslanders they knew that there was nothing like a low-pressure system in the Gulf of Carpentaria to bring rain to the inland.

As they sat there during roll call Camille said, "I wonder what happened to Chloe?"

That led to a babble of speculation and then, as the boys did not know the story, to an explanation. Barbara watched the boy's faces, especially Gordon's, and pursed her lips at their obvious interest. *Bloody males! It's all they think about!*

Karen suddenly pointed out the door. "There she is now, over at HQ," she said.

There was a rush to peer through the doorway and louvres which Barbara resisted, even though she badly wanted to know. But she was soon told that Chloe had been marched over to the Colonel by Lt McEwen. *She will probably be marched out,* she thought.

Camille then summed up Barbara's thoughts by saying: "I don't see what all the fuss is about. If she wore that bikini on the beach no-one would take nay notice."

"It's just that Maude with a bee in her bonnet," Sharon suggested.

"She's a real prude," added a girl from Rockhampton.

Roll Call completed the girls hurried back to their hut through the drizzle. As they did Barbara saw Lt McEwen salute the Colonel and she and a very contrite looking Chloe turn away and head for the Corporals tents. Chloe marched, her head up and a slightly defiant look on her face. She was obviously aware everyone was staring at her and gossiping about her.

Once again, the girls offered a wide range of speculation, some hoping Chloe was off the course and others suggesting various punishments they would apply if they were in charge. Some of the comments seemed so tinged with vicious jealousy that Barbara could only shake her head and feel sorry for Chloe.

But when Mess Parade was called a few minutes later Barbara saw an unhappy looking Chloe join her platoon, mess gear in hand. The news quickly spread that she was still on the course but had been severely cautioned not to offend other people by her actions. This led to more bitchy and negative criticism by many others.

Then Barbara forgot about Chloe as she saw Gordon making his way from his tent to where the CUOs were forming up. She found she was so unsure that she avoided eye contact. And so did he. Nor did he sit with her at breakfast. He sat with people from his own unit, including Monica. Barbara felt a stab of pure misery. She wondered what she could do to repair the breach but was determined she wouldn't do any begging.

The next chore was cleaning up the hut. The female corporals began carrying their bedding back to their tent. "The water just kept getting higher," the blonde one cried.

"It was like a swimming pool!" another one added.

Barbara looked out at where the girl was pointing. It was the tent one along from Chloe's and she saw that those girls had made a mud wall outside their drain.

Sharon came and looked. "You noddies! The mud wall is to keep the water out, not in!" she exclaimed.

Camille laughed and agreed. "You dig the ditch right under the edge of the canvas and put all the soil inside to make a dyke. Storm drains only work on sloping ground when the water can flow away quickly."

Monica sneered. "You lot would know all about dykes," she commented.

There was a frozen silence as the double meaning sank in.

Chapter 13

DISTRESS

As the insulting meaning of the innuendo formed in Barbara's mind, she experienced a flash of anger so strong she momentarily lost control. She stepped towards Malone and her hand went back. But before she could swing it forward in the stinging slap she intended, her arm was grabbed by someone and she was held. Then she was shouldered aside.

Camille blocked her path and stood, hands on hips facing Malone. "Stop being a bitch Malone! We are just helping each other and being friends."

Barbara now glanced back and saw that Fiona had hold of her arm and that Wendy was hurrying to join her. "No Barbara," Fiona hissed in her ear. "She's not worth it."

Malone flashed a hostile glance at Fiona and then faced Camille, who had been joined by Karen, Sharon and Jennifer. "Stop stirring up ill-will!" Karen snapped. "The course is hard enough without us fighting among ourselves."

"That's right," Jennifer added. "Let's have some teamwork and coursemanship."

Monica looked from one to the other and Barbara saw a sulky and defiant look come over her face. But she also realised she was on the outer as she shrugged and turned to hurry away.

"Sour slut!" Camille muttered as Malone vanished through the door.

There was a sort of collective sigh of relief and the friends began to relax. Barbara muttered thanks to Fiona and then shuddered as the tension eased. She turned to look out the door.

Feeling more upset than she cared to admit, even to herself, Barbara watched as one of the female corporals flicked back a flap of her tent. Barbara saw that all their gear was piled on their stretchers and that the whole interior was still muddy and awash. Most of the water had gone because the mud wall had been breached, allowing it to flow away.

Then she glanced at the tent Chloe was in and saw that the interior was dry and all the girls there were busy tidying their bed spaces. "That's how you do it," she said, "Make a dam (she almost said 'or dyke' but stopped herself in time) to keep the water from flowing in."

Then her gaze lighted on Chloe. She was in full uniform and did not look happy but was busy straightening her webbing on the foot of the stretcher. She obviously wasn't going home. Barbara sighed with relief, half understanding Chloe's urge to be an exhibitionist.

Barbara turned away and set to work on her own bedspace, re-hanging her still damp clothes.

The morning inspection was a different affair as the hut was difficult to clean. The whole place was damp and damp clothing hung in every available space.

The rain had eased up to a steady drizzle by this. The concrete parade ground looked like one vast puddle.

"No parade this morning," Wendy said.

But she was wrong. The Colonel paraded the companies on the bitumen road in front of their tents with the Duty CSMs, Duty Sgts and Duty Pl Comds. It caused a bit of grumbling, but he stood out there in the drizzle with them.

The CUOs were then divided into their groups and sent with an instructor to whatever dry corner had been allocated to them, including in the huts and on the verandas. Barbara's group made their way to the back veranda of the canteen with Capt Royston.

Each then spent 20 minutes presenting their Patrol Orders as a formal 'Orders Group'. Barbara wished Gordon wasn't in her group as his presence made her feel very uncomfortable, but she managed to block her emotions when the time came for her to present.

Captain Royston nodded approval. "That was very good WO2 Brassington, a 'textbook' job," he complimented after she had finished. He gave her a mark of 39 out of 40. "Ok Sgt Farr, your go."

Barbara found herself hoping Gordon would do a good job. He set up his map board and shuffled nervously through his notes for a moment. He looked everywhere but at her. To Barbara's distress his opening was somewhat jerky but after a few sentences he settled down to give a confident presentation. As he spoke the deep timbre of his voice seemed to penetrate to Barbara's very bones, and again she thought how nice it sounded.

Just once their eyes met and she gave a faint smile of encouragement.

His voice faltered for a moment and he looked away. Barbara felt a rush of temper. *Well blow you then!* she thought in pique. Even so she was pleased when he got 35 out of 40.

Morning Tea was hot cocoa and biscuits. By then it had stopped raining except for a few sprinkles. Water still dripped but the worst of the puddles had soaked into the sandy soil.

After all had done their presentation the CUOs were given another 'Green': the narrative and orders for their next patrol planning exercise. This one was for assessment.

The Colonel said, "You've got four days to get this done. Your Verbal Orders Test will be on Monday night."

With something of a shock Barbara realised it was only the sixth day of the course. *We aren't quite half-way through the course,* she thought. It seemed much longer. On all her previous courses she had enjoyed every minute and hadn't wanted them to end but suddenly this one seemed to loom as a bit of an ordeal.

'How to command a Cenotaph Guard' took up the period after lunch. Capt Royston took the lesson. The CUOs were combined with the WOs and Sgts Courses. Capt Royston organised them into guards of four with a CUO in charge and talked a demo squad of WOs through the procedure. He had ten fire buckets spaced out on the concrete to represent memorials.

The rain held off most of the time and the surface water didn't bother Barbara as it just ran straight off her boots. It was only a few centimetres deep anyway. She found the wind cold though, cold enough to bring her out in goose bumps.

During lunch the weather began to clear a bit. There were anxious eyes cast at a few hopeful patches of blue. The anxiety was motivated by the knowledge that they were to go out map reading during the afternoon.

As soon as she had eaten Barbara followed the lead of several others and went and hung her damp uniforms on the clothes lines on the other side of the laundry. "I hope this rain holds off," she commented to Fiona as she did.

At 1400 they clambered into two minibuses and set off. Even Barbara was infected by the high spirits of the others. After six days in the camp even a short trip outside was a welcome break. The busses drove out to the highway and turned left. A five-minute drive had them on an open grassy ridge on the other side of the highway. From there they could look west down to the concrete highway bridge over the Bunyip River. To Barbara's relief the drizzle that had started while they were on the bus eased up and stopped.

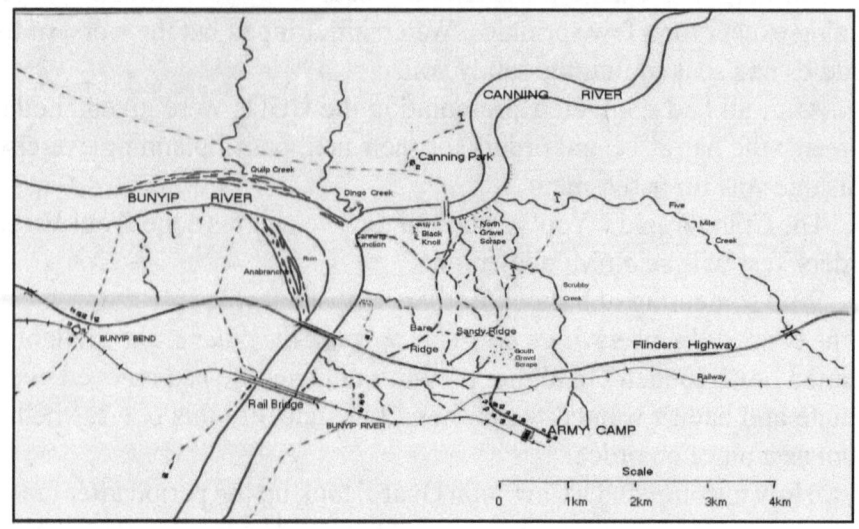

Bunyip River

As they climbed out Barbara felt a surge of excitement. All three of the annual camps she had attended had been in this area and she had many fond memories. Roger was infected by it too. He said, "This is where we had our annual camp in September. My platoon was bivouacked over there on 'Sandy Ridge'. This is 'Bare Ridge' and CUO Kirk found the girl down there in that little creek." He pointed the places out for an interested audience.

"Where were you Roger?" Karen asked.

"Me? I was over there at our bivouac. I was sending cadets down the creek one at a time at five-minute intervals."

The Colonel's voice interrupted them. "Move over here and stand in a single line," he called.

The fifty cadets moved up onto the highest part of the wide, flat spur. They were each issued a map and a compass.

"This is a practice at a Resection," the Colonel went on. "That is finding your position. We will do this one step at a time and an instructor will check each of you before we go on. That way you will understand it is not a difficult problem but only a series of very simple steps repeated three times. Now take out your notebooks."

He paused while they did that, then went on, his voice pitched against the wind. "Print the name WHALEBACK HILL in Block Letters. Print. No running writing."

Barbara did as she was told, then raised her eyes to look. From where they stood, they could see out for about 50 kilometres. They were facing west and looked down a long gentle slope to the big bend of the Bunyip about a kilometre away. On the horizon beyond, and just visible between curtains of rain, was the small grey silhouette of the hill. It was easy to pick as there were only three hills visible on an otherwise flat western horizon.

Then she dropped her gaze back to the bend of the Bunyip. She could make out the trees marking the junction with the Canning River. That was where the rest of the company had been camped when the crooks had caught up with them. Her eyes travelled right to the wooded slopes of Black Knoll. She had run up over that with Berzinski a hundred metres behind.

She had only lost him in the tangle of rubber vines where the road they were standing beside crossed the Canning. The memory caused her to shiver.

"You alright Barbara?" Capt Conkey asked.

"Yes sir. Just remembering."

"So was I," replied Captain Conkey, rubbing his cheek. "But the Colonel has told you to print the words MAG. BEARING. Do that like a good cadet."

Barbara nodded and concentrated on the task. They all took bearings with their compasses and wrote them down. Then they wrote GRID BEARING underneath and converted the bearing. Next, they printed GRID BACK BEARING below that and made the calculation. Using their protractors and rulers they pencilled this bearing on the map. It was a bit awkward kneeling on the short, damp grass with a mist of fine rain starting to drift in. Raincoats were pulled on or held to shield maps and notebooks.

Once that was done, they repeated the process for the near end of the huge steel girder rail bridge which spanned the Bunyip two kilometres to the South. Looking at the bridge gave Barbara other, fonder memories.

As a First Year cadet she had taken part in a night exercise in which their company had been the parachute raiders sent in to pretend to blow down the bridge.

That was a great exercise, she remembered. *We beat that Heatley mob, and St Michael's.*

Once the cadets had drawn their bearings on their maps the Colonel checked every one of them, then pointed behind them to the Southeast.

"If you look through that gap in the trees there you will see the highest point in the Tucker Box Range. Or you will when that rain shower passes. Print TUCKER BOX RANGE."

"Which hill sir? Is it that one?" A Sergeants Course student pointed.

"No. That's Hill 376. Look further to the right."

What an incredible ridge this is, Barbara thought as she set to work. *In the camp almost none of this was visible but from this low feature, barely marked on the map, you can see everything.*

She took her bearing on Point 509 in the Tucker Box Range, converted it and ruled it on her map. She looked at the result critically. There was a triangle of error of about 3mm, but two lines crossed exactly where they were.

"That's good," the Colonel commented as he went along the line.

He stopped to look at Monica's.

"Where do you think we are Cpl Malone?"

Monica pointed on her map.

The Colonel raised his eyebrows. "You are saying we are five hundred metres south of the railway? Where is the railway? No, not the railway on the map. The real thing!"

Monica pointed.

"Which direction is that?"

Monica shuffled. She turned her map around and finally stammered, "I don't know Sir."

"Don't know! Good heavens, you are training to be an officer. You must be able to navigate. You've got a compass. Use that!"

Barbara felt a dig in her ribs. It was Fiona. She winked and grinned. It rapidly became obvious to all that Monica did not know her basic compass directions. The Colonel gave up in exasperation.

"Capt Hamilton, explain the points of the compass to this corporal please," he said. Then he went on along the line.

The drizzle had eased off again, but a long grey wall of heavy rain could be seen coming in from the Northwest. The Colonel hurried them through another resection on a second map photocopy, this time using Hill 376, Bunyip River Railway Station (a little wooden shed at a siding) and TOWERS HILL in Charters Towers.

"I wish we could go into Charters Towers," Millet said. "I've never been there."

"You can if you go to church on Sunday," Roger replied.

"Church! I suppose you go to church?" Weismann sneered.

Roger blushed but looked him squarely in the eyes. "As a matter of fact I do."

"Church! What a load of crap! Anyway who needs to wait till Sunday? All the action's at night. We might go tonight eh Stevo?"

Weismann turned to Stephens, who nodded but not very enthusiastically.

Lofty shook his head. "You'd be fools if you did," he put in. "You know it's against Standing Orders to leave camp."

"So what? What are you going to do, tell on us?" Weismann replied, hooking his thumbs in his belt.

"I'm not a dobber Weismann," Lofty replied evenly.

Stephens then spoke up. "Aw! I just remembered. I'm on duty tonight as a Duty NCO."

Weismann looked at him and grinned. "All the better," he said.

Capt Conkey came over. "Stop gossiping you lot and get on with the job before the rain gets here."

As she worked Barbara remembered that the CUOs had no training that night. It was a free night, but there certainly wasn't leave. She was planning to finish her Patrol Orders and study. Now she found herself in a quandary. Was Weismann really going to sneak out, or was it just bravado?

Should I tell one of the officers? she wondered.

After agonizing over it for a while she then forgot about it in the rush to scramble back into the bus as more rain arrived. It was solid, drenching rain. The air temperature dropped so sharply Barbara went from sweating to shivering in a few minutes.

The cadets were driven back into camp in the tail-end of the shower. Barbara heaved a sigh of relief as they were dismissed.

"I'm glad we've got the night off. I'm getting very tired," she said to Fiona as she kicked wet sand off her boots on the steps.

"All those Corporals have moved back to their tents, thank heavens," Fiona noted.

"Teach them to dig proper storm drains," Camille said.

Barbara wanted to lie down, but as soon as she sat on her stretcher she remembered she was Duty Pl Comd of 4 Pl again. She groaned and got up to check the roster and find out who her Pl Sgt was. It was a boy from Townsville. She went to find him. As she looked, she remembered her washing. It was still hanging on the line, and soaked!

She was just wondering what to do when Gordon walked past.

"Bit damp," he said but with only a hint of a smile.

"Yes, it is," Barbara replied. She tried to smile but her facial muscles seemed to lock.

Gordon paused and met her eye. "I'm sorry about last night," he said.

Barbara shrugged but inside she was in a fluster of hope and anxiety. She struggled to find an appropriate answer. "That's alright. I had no right to speak to you the way I did. I..." She stopped, not wanting to admit she had been jealous.

There was an awkward silence as both tried to think what to say. At last Gordon spoke. "I didn't take your things."

"I didn't think you did. I thought it was Malone. But that isn't fair as I have no proof. It's just that she and I don't like each other," Barbara explained.

In both their minds the memory of Gordon talking to Monica was foremost. It made them both uncomfortable in different ways. In Barbara's mind it remained a niggling suspicion.

"I asked her about it last night," Gordon said. "She said she had nothing to do with it."

Barbara was surprised by this statement. It worried her a bit as she had only just considered the possibility. She shook her head but couldn't say outright that she didn't believe Monica.

She didn't need to. Gordon read her silence.

"She's not that bad you know," he said.

"Maybe. Sorry. I don't like her and I don't trust her," Barbara answered. Another horrible thought had just occurred to her. She had assumed Monica was sneaking out at night to meet Weismann. What if it was Gordon?

Gordon looked at her earnestly. "I didn't stop to talk about her anyway. It's you I like. Can we be friends again?"

Barbara looked into his clear blue eyes. He seemed so open and honest, his voice so sincere. She felt she did trust him. *I just hope my instincts are right,* she thought, *so that I don't get hurt again.*

"Yes, alright," she said. Then she smiled.

Gordon looked relieved and nodded. "I'd better go. I've got a lot of ironing to do."

"So have I. It's the only way I will get these clothes dry by tomorrow."

"See you in the laundry then," Gordon said, his face breaking into a smile. He turned and strode away, his shoulders squared and a whistle on his lips.

Barbara began unpegging her damp washing, humming happily to herself.

Chapter 14

FLAG PARTY DRILL

At Mess Parade, Barbara and Gordon stood next to each other in the queue. Then they sat to eat. Most of the girls positively beamed with relief, and even Roger was vaguely aware of a lightening of the mood. As people's spirits rose so did the level of conversation. Jokes began to fly and for the first time the room was full of laughter and happy faces. The officers on the other side of the room were drawn into the general mood.

After dinner Barbara made sure her platoon was at their night lectures on time, as the corporals were not having a free evening. Most of the course had changed into casual civilian clothes. Barbara decided to change as well. She told herself she could then wash and iron her other uniform, but she had to admit to a desire to let Gordon see her to better effect than in the relatively shapeless army clothing. To achieve this she chose some white shorts and a yellow cotton top. She put them on, then hesitated over the look of the top. It exposed a bit of her midriff and really emphasised her breasts.

Oh, is this what I want? she wondered. *I don't want to tease Gordon or appear to flaunt myself.* Unable to decide, she picked up a blue T-shirt and was holding it up when Fiona came in.

"That yellow top looks nice Barbara. He'll like that," she said.

Barbara looked from the T-shirt to her very prominent front and blushed. In her embarrassment she wanted to deny her motives for dressing as she had but couldn't think of an answer. She also realised she couldn't change the top without looking a bit silly to Fiona. So she dropped the T-shirt and scooped up her uniforms.

After that she made her way to the laundry. All the four ironing boards were in use, so she did some more washing and stood and gossiped while she waited. Gordon came in and she gave him a smile.

I wish I could give him a hug, she thought, and was then shocked at her own daring thoughts. *I'll be as bad as Chloe next,* she told herself. Then the idea that she might also be as bad as Monica flitted into her consciousness and she sternly suppressed any wild thoughts.

They chatted away together, Gordon describing his pet dog and how he had a part-time job in a workshop repairing heavy earth-moving equipment. As they talked Barbara was very conscious that Gordon was discreetly admiring her. She felt a warm twinge of pleasure and embarrassment as his eyes lingered on her bosom or ran up her legs. He made no comment but was obviously keenly appreciative.

I'm as bad as Monica, she reproached herself. At the same time she felt glad.

Barbara let Gordon do most of the talking, drawing him out with questions while she took her turn at the iron. Rain began to rattle on the roof again, but they barely noticed.

An hour later they ran through a lull in the downpour to take their ironing back to their accommodation, then to the lecture room. There Barbara found about half the course studying and writing plans or orders.

After about an hour they stopped work for supper. It was still raining quite heavily. The corporals had finished lessons as well and groups of them went splashing and scuttling past on their way to the canteen. Barbara went out onto the porch with Gordon and several of the others to watch the rain while they drank hot chocolate and munched on biscuits.

As the pair talked the white utility arrived. It swung past them to stop at the rear of the kitchen. Two men got out, a tall thin one in blue jeans and a blue singlet and a short thin one in blue jeans and black T-shirt. He wore glasses. The men began hoisting the garbage bins up and emptying them into 100-litre drums, swearing and cursing as they got wet. There was a third person still in the cab and Barbara idly wondered why he didn't get out to help them, particularly as the other two seemed to be having difficulty.

Gordon distracted her from these thoughts by murmuring in her ear. "I love the way your hair sparkles in the light. It looks like copper on fire. I get the urge to stroke it."

She turned to smile up at him, pressing lightly against his arm and side. "That would be nice. I wish we could," she murmured.

"Could what?" Gordon answered with a cheeky grin.

Barbara blushed when she realised what he meant and what her comment had possibly implied. "You know!" she whispered.

Gordon swallowed, then said, "Sorry, not at Cadets."

Hearing that really cheered Barbara. It told her that Gordon had real integrity and it also wiped away many of her doubts about him sneaking out to meet Monica. *If he won't try to sneak out to meet me then he won't be doing it for her either,* she told herself. Which raised the question of who Monica was sneaking out to meet?

Gordon then cheered her even more by saying, "When this course is over we can be together. Perhaps we could meet somehow during the holidays?"

Barbara nodded. "I'd like that but..." But she couldn't see an easy answer. Cairns and Broadsound were nearly 800 kilometres apart.

"Ah yuk!" Gordon cried. He pointed. "That fellow went to lift that scrap bin into the ute and it overflowed down his front."

Barbara looked to where the tall, thin man was cursing and flicking muck off his clothes. The cook and his offsider called ribald comments to him from the back porch of the kitchen where the short thin one was being given a cup of something.

The short thin man walked over to the ute and passed a cup through the window. *So there is someone inside,* Barbara decided. The tall, thin man was directed by the cook to a tap to wash himself.

Fiona came over and joined Barbara. "Bedtime in ten minutes, so drink up," she reminded.

Barbara turned and looked at Gordon while she drained her cup. He reached out to take it and their fingers met. His folded over hers and she was reluctant to release the cup. They both smiled and it was Roger who broke the spell.

"Come on you two! That's enough of that. You won't be able to sleep for hot dreams."

"That will be nice," Barbara quipped.

Roger snorted. "Not for me! Gordon's bed is next to mine. I don't want to be kept awake by his moaning and groaning, or worse," he replied.

Reluctantly they let go, aided by the appearance of two lady OOCs. After wishing each other sweet dreams the two separated and ran through the rain to their lines.

After changing and cleaning her teeth Barbara snuggled into her bed, her head swimming with happy thoughts. She noted with some surprise that Monica was already in bed and, apparently, asleep. Fiona and Wendy gave her cheerful 'goodnights' but she couldn't sleep as Karen, Sharon and Camille came in and proceeded to liven things up with singing and dancing.

Lt Curwen's voice abruptly terminated this and sent them scurrying to bed with giggles and laughter. The lights went out. Barbara lay back with a sigh of happiness and allowed her mind to wander into a pleasant fantasy of romance.

*****

The seventh day dawned clear and fresh, with not a cloud in the sky. Everything looked scrubbed clean and the bush looked very green but by the time the platoons marched down to the concrete parade ground, the sun had begun to suck up the moisture so that the humidity shot up. Sweat began to trickle down backs and foreheads and to form an uncomfortable slipperiness in armpits.

The morning parade was a practice for the platoons to march on from the side of the parade ground, then turn and face the front; thus forming a 'Company in Close Column of platoons'. This time the Platoon Commanders lined up along the right-hand side of the parade ground rather than the front. The concrete was still a mass of puddles, some several centimetres deep, which provided the wags with an excuse to stamp their boots much harder than they could normally be persuaded to do, even by WO1 Pryor.

That most military gentleman was not impressed by their first effort. He ordered them back to the west side of the parade ground, everyone calling aloud the timings to achieve unity of movement.

"One, two-three, one!"

As Barbara stood on the side of the parade ground 'at ease' she heard movement down to her left, and a gagging, splattering sound. She turned her head to look. It was Wilmot. He had turned and was bent over the drain vomiting. Looking at his pasty face with the eyes sunken and ringed by fatigue she felt some sympathy. But this evaporated into a turmoil of disgust and confusion when she overheard Weismann snicker and say, "Can't hold yer beer ya wimp!"

Wilmot looked at him resentfully and then heaved again. Weismann jeered a second time. Barbara overheard Hilditch asking Stephens, "What's wrong with Wilmot, is it the heat?"

"Nah!" Stephens sneered, "He just drank too much last night."

"Drank too much! Drank what?" Hilditch asked.

"Beer, ya git," Weismann laughed.

"Beer! Where'd you get that?" Hilditch asked in astonishment.

"In town of course."

"You did not."

"We did so. We went in last night," Weismann replied. His eyes met Barbara's horrified gaze. They narrowed and he curled his lip and spat.

Barbara looked away in disgust. Beer! Went to town! It was probably true. *What should I do?* she wondered. Should she dob? Did she have any proof!

Her thoughts were interrupted by WO1 Pryor shouting at them to take Wilmot to the side of the parade ground. Weismann and Stephens fell out and helped Wilmot off towards his tent.

Seething with anger that such people were on a course to become Cadet Under-Officers Barbara marched out to take over from her Platoon Sergeant. The business of the parade then claimed her attention.

After the parade the CUOs became Assistant Instructors. Either two together, or one with an officer, went to watch the corporals on their second attempt to teach a lesson to a squad. For two periods Barbara was rostered with Gordon to assess No 7 Section. The pair collected Assessment Forms to fill out and made their way to the shade of a tree just beyond the car park in front of the canteen and next to the guard tents.

Here they seated themselves side by side on folding chairs behind the squad. Each potential corporal had to teach a complete lesson of 20 minutes on a simple drill movement. The corporals were very nervous, but Barbara quickly found it fairly boring.

She also found it very hot, even in what little shade the straggly ironbark leaves cast. There was no breeze and the heat seemed like a fluid. Flies came to annoy. Unable to talk, lest they disturb the trainee instructors, the two sat and occasionally looked at each other, in between scribbling comments on the Assessment Form.

Gordon folded the form aside and scribbled something on a page on his clipboard. He held it across for Barbara to read. She took her eyes off the wretched cadet from Townsville who had got his lesson all out of sequence and mucked it up. The note read: I LOVE YOU.

She looked into Gordon's eyes and seemed to be swallowed up in their sparkle. The next ten minutes passed in a pleasant haze until the miserable cadet ended his lesson and they had to advise him on how to improve.

After morning tea Barbara was rostered to assess No 8 Section with Captain Carter from Rockhampton. This went on for two more boring and sweaty periods while four more hopefuls struggled through lessons on Drill. It was almost a relief to take the clipboard to her hut and to join the other CUOs and the WOs out on the concrete for Drill.

The puddles had shrunk noticeably since the morning and a haze of heat and evaporation shimmered in the middle-distance. Capt Royston and WO1 Pryor had them for Flag Drill. Lacking enough flag poles or carriers they were each issued a mop, broom or rake and stood in two ranks.

Captain Royston then explained the difference between flags, colours, guidons and banners and when they could be carried on ceremonial parades.

"Of course your units do not have proper colours and you need to remember that unit flags do not get accorded any honours," he said, looking hard at some of the cadets from southern units as he did. "You will mostly only carry the Australian National Flag, the ANF, and it has its own special rules. You may also get the honour of carrying the Duke of Edinburgh's Banner, which is the Army Cadet banner. It is a properly consecrated banner so gets treated like an army unit's regimental colours. We will assume you are training to carry the banner on a ceremonial parade," he explained.

Capt Royston then demonstrated how to move them to the 'Carry' and 'Order' in time with the commands by the parade commander to the troops with rifles. The cadets then practised 'General Salutes' and 'Royal Salutes' until the sweat dripped off them and their arms began to ache. The sun seemed to actually scorch their skin it was so fierce. Salt stung their eyes and tasted bitter on their lips.

There was a clatter and a crash. Wilmot had fainted, stretching himself headlong in a puddle on the concrete. Again Barbara wondered what to do. Captain Royston ordered Ying and Blackwood to carry him to the shade. The lesson went on.

The CUOs were given a break and then the Sergeants Course joined them. They were to be taught how Flag Parties with their escorts of Colour Sergeants manoeuvred on a Ceremonial Parade.

One group of five was talked through the sequence of moving on and off parade. When that was completed Capt Royston said, "Right, organise yourselves with two CUOs with flags and three Sergeants with rifles and practice that."

Barbara and Gordon at once went to each other. Wendy joined them and two other sergeants. They formed themselves up, three in line: flag, escort, flag, with two escorts 3 paces behind each flag. Barbara took the senior position on the right. Gordon smiled and shrugged. They began to practice.

After checking that the group were all in their correct positions Barbara called, "Attention! By the left, quick... March! Change Direction Left, Left... form!"

Up and down the concrete they went, wheeling and counter marching, halting and presenting arms.

"Ok Gordon. You have a go," Barbara said. They changed positions and began again.

As they marched along threading through a dozen other groups Barbara became aware of a group coming in at right angles on their left. Weismann was in charge and Stephens had the other flag. Barbara measured the distance out of the corner of her eye as they drew closer.

Weismann's group were slightly further back and Barbara saw that they could easily step short and pass behind them. She thought they would but at the last moment realised they weren't going to do that.

"Give way to the right!" Gordon called.

"Get out of our way!" Weismann replied.

"Look out you idiots," Stephens cried.

The two flag parties collided. Barbara narrowly missed Stephens but heard Gordon cry out. She looked and saw that Weismann had run into Wendy. Both went down in a tangle of legs and arms and his broom had come down to strike Gordon on the back and shoulder with an audible 'thwack'.

Stephens laughed.

Barbara snapped back, "Idiot!"

Wendy's angry voice sounded over them both. "Let me go! Get your filthy hands off me!" she cried. Barbara looked and saw that several buttons had come undone or been torn off Wendy's shirt, exposing her bra. Weismann appeared to be clutching one of her breasts as the two cadets rolled on the wet concrete.

"Let her go!" Barbara snapped.

Weismann actually pushed himself to his knees with one hand pressing on Wendy's left breast.

"Leave Wendy alone, I said!" Barbara cried angrily.

Wiesmann looked up at her and sneered. "Get stuffed moll!" he hissed. As he spoke his hand gave a definite squeeze to Wendy's front. Then he stood up, laughing as he did.

His sniggering leer sparked Barbara to explode. "You sexist pig!" she cried. In fury she lashed out. Her hand caught Weismann hard on the side of his face.

Slap!

It stung her hand.

Weismann sprang back and mouthed an obscenity. Then his fists came up and he sprang forward, his face contorted with rage. He snarled at her and swung a punch. Barbara saw it coming straight for her face and tried to shield herself with her arms.

A hand flashed out and caught the punch. Gordon grappled with Weismann and the two went down in a struggling heap. Weismann began to shout obscenities and struggled to his feet. He lashed out with his boot as Gordon went to regain his feet. Wendy saved him by pushing Weismann off balance. He turned to kick at her.

Gordon sprang up, fists clenched. Weismann recovered his balance and faced him, ready to fight.

"That's enough! Stop!" WO1 Pryor bawled. He stepped forward between Gordon and Weismann.

Captain Royston arrived. "What's going on here?"

They all spoke at once.

"Silence!" WO1 Pryor roared. "Stand fast!"

They all stood to attention. Wendy got up and pulled her shirt together to cover herself.

Captain Royston turned to her. "Are you alright Cpl Werribee?"

"Yes sir. I'm not injured," she replied.

"What happened?"

"Weismann's flag party ran into us," she said.

"We did not! You ran into us," Stephens shrilled.

"Silence! I didn't ask you Sergeant Stephens," Captain Royston reprimanded. He turned to Weismann. "So why were you going to punch Warrant Officer Brassington?"

"She slapped me!" Weismann muttered angrily.

That was obvious to all by this time. The red shape of a hand stood out clearly on his cheek. Captain Royston turned to Barbara. "Did you? Why?"

"He was molesting Wendy sir. He grabbed her by the ti... by the... by the breasts, and then he called me an insulting name."

Captain Royston arched an eyebrow and turned to Wendy.

Weismann cut in. "I did not sir. It was an accident. She tripped me and we fell down in a heap."

Captain Royston turned a fierce glare on Weismann. "Listen fellah, you keep your mouth shut and your heels together or I'll deal with you for insubordination. I'll tell you straight. If you had punched Warrant Officer Brassington we would be calling the police right now and you would be on your way home! I don't care what the provocation was. You learn some self-discipline."

Weismann swallowed and blinked. "What about Farr? He hit me!" he said angrily.

"Call me Sir! RSM! March this fellow to the Colonel," Captain Royston blazed.

For a moment it looked as though Weismann would completely lose control. WO1 Pryor stepped between him and Captain Royston and pointed towards the HQ, wisely making no attempt to touch the enraged cadet.

Muttering, Weismann turned and slouched off.

Chapter 15

SWEET AND SOUR

That was the end of the drill lesson for Barbara, Wendy and Gordon. Capt Royston added, "And anyone else who witnessed the incident." That added Fiona, Roger and Lofty to the group. Capt Royston ordered them to come with him and then told WO1 Pryor to resume the drill lesson. He then marched off towards the HQ. Barbara and her friends followed in an unhappy group. She understood that she could be marched off the course because she had assaulted Weismann, but she felt angrier than anything; and she could see Wendy was very upset.

"Do you want to fall out Wendy?" she asked.

Wendy shook her head. "No. I'll be alright."

Gordon looked at both. "He's lucky he didn't hit you Barb," he said. "Or I'd have smashed him to pulp."

Capt Royston looked back. "Stop talking! When we get to HQ sit on your own at least ten metres from your friends," he ordered.

They did so, sitting along the concrete drain outside HQ. One by one they were called in and questioned by the Colonel and Major Carroll, OC of Sarina. Wendy, Lofty, Roger and Gordon went first. They were then seated in a group under the mango tree near the canteen, supervised by Capt Buchan. As she waited Barbara saw Capt Conkey giving her anxious glances from over at the mess and that did not help. Obviously, the story had gone quickly round the camp.

I hope I don't get taken off the course, she thought, knowing that would hurt Capt Conkey and her unit as well. Those thoughts made her feel even more upset.

When it was her turn Barbara had to make a real effort to control her trembling limbs and emotions and tears threatened to shame her. With an effort of willpower she marched in and stamped to attention and gave her very best salute. At the Colonel's request she then gave her version of the incident.

As she did, she was aware that she was trembling slightly and her voice quavered with emotion a few times. Annoyance at her weakness helped steady her and she was able to get through the explanation without breaking down in tears.

The Colonel heard her through and then nodded. "That agrees with what I have been told. It appears that you were intervening to protect Cpl Werribee and that you were insulted and provoked. But having said that, technically you have actually assaulted Sgt Weismann. That is against both Cadet Regulations and Queensland State Law. I will deal with you under the regulations. It is up to Sgt Weismann if he wishes to take it further. Do you understand?"

Barbara swallowed and nodded, so upset she could not speak for a moment. Finally she nodded again and croaked, "Yes sir."

The Colonel looked hard at her. "I am now giving you a formal caution. Personally I approve of your actions but officially I must say that such actions are not allowed. Be careful in the future. You may go."

It took Barbara a moment to realise that was all. She nodded, muttered "sir!", stepped back, saluted, did an about turn and marched off, barely able to control her limbs for the rush of emotion. She joined her friends under the tree and there learned, to her immense relief, that Gordon had also only been given a warning as he had been defending Barbara and then himself.

By then the drill lesson was over and the platoons came marching back, the cadets giving them curious stares as they passed. They were then dismissed for lunch. Capt Buchan turned to the friends. "You lot can go as well," he instructed before walking back to HQ.

For a couple of minutes Barbara, Gordon, Wendy, Fiona, Roger and Lofty stayed in a group under the mango tree to discuss the incident. Barbara was really worried that Gordon would be taken off the course or punished in some way.

"Won't matter," he said, trying to act as though it was of no importance. "I'd do it anytime to protect you."

Barbara felt herself near to tears. She placed her hand on his forearm and gently squeezed.

Lofty gestured towards the HQ and said, "Weismann is still being spoken to by the Colonel."

"We'd better go to lunch, everyone else has," Roger added. They headed towards the Mess. As they passed the girls hut Wendy turned off. "I don't feel like eating," she said.

Barbara grabbed her sleeve. "Yes you do. You need to keep up your energy. Come on."

As they went past the HQ Barbara saw that Weismann was standing outside, but she pretended not to notice. When they entered the Mess Hall the atmosphere was heavy with rumour and gossip. They ignored most of this and sat in a group, keeping Wendy with them. Only half of the officers were there.

Suddenly Wilmot pointed out the door with his fork. "There he goes," he hissed. They all looked. Weismann marched off towards his tent and did not re-appear. The Colonel and a group of officers came out of the HQ and headed their way.

"They don't look very happy," Roger commented.

There was an awkward silence as the officers came in. The cadets busied themselves with eating and it was only slowly the level of talking rose. Barbara kept looking at Gordon. She expected to be summoned to an interview after lunch.

Instead the Colonel sat and ate his lunch and apparently ignored them. As soon as they could some of Weismann's pals, including Wilmot and Stephens, rushed off to the boys tents to find out his fate. The others sat and talked unhappily.

The to-and-fro of gossip via the uninvolved soon passed the news. Weismann had been cautioned and was still on the course.

The word was passed for all CUOs, WOs and Sergeants to assemble ten minutes early in the Sergeants Lecture Room. This was in a few minutes so there was a scattering to clean teeth, go to the toilet and collect things for the next lesson.

When all were seated and silent the RSM sent the Orderly Sergeant to report to the Colonel. Five minutes later he came in and proceeded to lecture them all on their attitude and behaviour. "In ten years I've never had a course like this. Start learning to co-operate. Stop your petty personality clashes and inter-unit bickering. Pull together as a team and help each other. I've had enough of this nonsense and the last warning has been given. Any more trouble and that person is off their course and can do Kitchen Duties for the rest of the camp."

The CUOs were then organised for the afternoon's work. Twelve, including Barbara and Weismann, were to go with the Corporals out to 'Bare Ridge' to help coach them through a Resection. The other eight, including Gordon were to help assess the Sergeants teaching Drill Lessons.

The two minibuses were busy shuttling the Corporals to Bare Ridge so they had a twenty minute wait before being moved. Barbara felt miserable and worried. There was an uneasy tension within the group which had split into two camps.

Barbara made sure she went on a different bus from Weismann and once out on Bare Ridge she went to the other end of the line of Corporals. She tried to concentrate on the work and for an hour so she was able to forget the unpleasantness.

Then the group of Corporals she was working with had to walk further along the ridge to get a clear view of the Tucker Box Range. Barbara went with them and this took her past Weismann. When she realised he was glaring at her, she turned her back and moved further away.

"You bitch!" he hissed close behind her.

Barbara jumped as though stung. She hadn't heard him walk up behind her. His face was a mask of hate and there was a bruise on his cheek.

"I'll get even with you," he grated. Then he spat near her boots, turned and walked off.

Barbara felt herself tremble. She took a few deep breaths to steady herself. *What a horrible person,* she thought. *Why can't he be nice? Why does he have to put people down all the time, or hurt them?* She considered whether she should report his threat but realised there were no witnesses.

Tears began to form. To hide them she walked across the road and behind a bus. By the time she had her handkerchief out the tears were dripping from her chin. She stood and dabbed her eyes and leaned on the bus.

Someone walked around the back of the bus. Barbara hastily turned away and pocketed her handkerchief.

It was Fiona. "You alright Babs?"

"Yes, (sniff)" Barbara muttered. She felt her bottom lip tremble and the tears just welled out again. Fiona passed her a hanky and put her arm around her shoulders.

After a few minutes Barbara stopped sobbing and dried her eyes.

"Sorry. I'm just being silly. It's just been so unpleasant. Weismann spoils things all the time."

"He's an objectionable turd, that's for sure," Fiona agreed.

The two girls talked for a few minutes, then walked back across the road to re-join the others. Luckily their absence had not been noticed amidst a hundred cadets all working out compass bearings. Barbara sought out her group and ignored their slightly puzzled looks.

A few minutes later there was another one of those little incidents that she so disliked. Standing near her group were Chloe, Jane and several hopeful boys. Chloe was taking compass bearings but with a lot of giggling and chatter, all the while wiggling her bottom and acting with what looked like flirting.

Barbara was kneeling down helping one of her squad with his protractor when she overheard two male cadets talking, obviously discussing Chloe.

"Who's that blonde sheila?" asked the first boy.

"Which one? Oh her, she's that Chloe," answered the second boy.

"Oh that's her eh? Geez, she good looking! She looks a real goer. I wonder if all those stories are true," commented Boy Number One.

"I reckon they are. She's probably the girl who supposed to be sneaking out after Lights Out. Why don't you ask her for a bit?" replied Boy Number Two.

"Aw, I..." At that moment the first boy caught sight of Barbara. He blushed and looked quickly away, bending back to his map.

Barbara felt upset. *Sneaking out! Oh, I hope not. What should I do?* But she knew she had to do something. *I'll have a word to Chloe first, and warn her,* she decided.

A few minutes later she beckoned Chloe aside. Chloe was smiling and obviously enjoying herself. "Yes Barbara, I mean Warrant Officer Brassington?"

"There's a rumour you are sneaking out at night. Are you?"

Chloe looked so hurt and surprised that Barbara felt sure she was telling the truth when she indignantly denied it. "No I am not! It took me a big effort to live down my past to get on this course. I'm not going to throw that away."

"I just thought I'd warn you," Barbara said.

"Well it's not me!" Chloe said. "I had a lot of trouble getting selected for this course and I want to pass. I can do without boys for ten days."

The matter of fact way she said that shocked Barbara, but she nodded and went back to her squad. *So which other girl is sneaking out?* she wondered. Monica's name floated on the top of her consciousness but, because she had no real proof, she then did not go and report the rumour to Lt McEwen. *It wouldn't be fair to let my personal dislikes enter into this. I'll wait till I've some facts,* she thought. But the incident lowered her mood even more and she felt tired and upset.

Two hours later they were shuttled back to the camp. WO1 Pryor and the WOs Course were busy measuring the grass parade ground and hammering in small coloured flags to mark it out for the Graduation Parade. Barbara realised she had completely forgotten her ambition to be top CUO because of the events of the last few days. It seemed like weeks ago they had first arrived. She gave a wry grin and tried to summon up her resolution.

Evening Mess Parade was an almost silent and uncomfortable meal. The gloomy mood pervaded the whole CUOs Course. Barbara wolfed her food down and bolted back to her hut. She didn't want to talk to Gordon in case she weakened and told him about Weismann's threat.

Then he would probably go and punch Weismann and that would end him on the course, she thought unhappily.

She had stood down from being Duty Platoon Commander, so she had no extra duties to attend to. Instead she tried to force herself to study.

She wasn't very successful and was easily diverted to talk to Karen and Sharon when they came in. It was almost a relief to pick up her folder and head off for evening lessons.

On the way she paused to check the notice board at the door of the lecture room. She had noted the previous day she was a Duty NCO the following night, but she hadn't bothered to check who else was on duty.

"Oh no!" she muttered.

Karen leaned over to look. "What's the matter?"

"I'm on duty with Stephens."

"You could ask to have the roster changed. It was made up before the incident today."

Barbara briefly considered this. "No," she replied, pursing her lips, "What reason could I give? That Stephens is a friend of Weismann? Or that I don't like him? No. It's only one night. I'll be alright."

They seated themselves in the lecture room. Gordon came in and Karen moved along to let him in next to Barbara. Barbara found his presence very comforting. She pressed her knee against his.

"Don't do that," Gordon whispered. "You set me on fire."

"Sorry."

"It's alright," Gordon whispered back. "It's just the wrong time and place."

The class was called to attention by Hilditch, who was Duty Student. He handed over to the Colonel who gave them a lesson on the Army Training System. This was followed by another by Major Wickham on Types of Exercises.

In the last lesson for the evening the Colonel talked about planning Training Programs. He introduced them to making up a Block Syllabus, then organizing the lessons in the correct sequence and gave them the task of planning a Detailed Daily Program for a two-day Bivouac. Once he was sure they understood the task he then left them to it.

As soon as he had gone Roger stood up. "Canteen anyone?" he asked.

The lecture room rapidly emptied. Barbara and Gordon went with a large group. They purchased chocolates and soft-drinks then went outside to escape the crush of Corporals. Here they seated themselves on a low concrete wall beside a storm-water drain. Gordon sat so close to Barbara, their bodies were touching.

They ate and talked but nobody felt like telling jokes or laughing. Barbara felt very tired, as though all her energy had been drained. To her surprise Gordon put his hand over hers. It was so dark none of the others would have seen the movement. For a moment Barbara stiffened. She sat quite still unsure what she wanted. Then Gordon gently squeezed her hand and her body reacted. There was a moment's fumbling and she took a firm grip on his hand.

For several minutes Barbara sat in silent wonder, all but oblivious to the conversation. All she was aware of was the power which seemed to flow through Gordon's hand into her. It was like an electrical connection had been made. Her emotions flew in two directions at once. The firm but gentle grip seemed wonderfully reassuring and she knew she was in love. This sent her pulses racing in a most delicious sensation.

No word was spoken between them and Gordon released her hand as soon as they stood up. It was a very reluctant Barbara who made her way to the girls hut. Her mind was full of yearning to stay out under the stars alone with Gordon. She constructed the wording of such a request, but it remained un-uttered. To her great relief Gordon also made no suggestions although she fancied his eyes mirrored her thoughts as they said goodnight under the streetlight.

It was a blissfully happy girl who changed into her cotton pyjamas, for it was hot and still. This drew comment from Wendy. "Look who's on cloud nine!"

"What? Were you talking to me?" Barbara asked as she absent-mindedly folded her uniform shirt. There was a ripple of good-natured laughter from most of the other girls.

"Look at the smile on her face. Talk about the cat that got the cream," Camille teased with a laugh.

Monica looked up from her bed with a sneer. "Maybe her pussy's had the cream," she suggested.

It took a moment for the innuendo to sink in. Barbara turned away with an effort. She managed not to reply but her mouth felt as though she had just tasted a rotten lemon peel.

Fiona wasn't so reticent. "What a coarse comment! Why do you have to spoil everything Malone? Are you jealous?"

"Jealous! Of Farr! He's not up to much when it comes to giving a girl what she wants," Monica jeered.

It was as though an icy hand had gripped Barbara's heart. Gordon did come from the same unit as Malone. Had he had sex with her? Her mind could barely frame the suspicion it hurt so much. She felt a pang of the most intense jealousy followed by a wave of nausea. She couldn't bring herself to speak. Instead she slumped down on her stretcher and tried to pretend nothing had happened.

Camille reacted though. "You talk like a cheap tart Malone. Shut your mouth and stop causing trouble."

Monica sat up, exposing her nakedness to the waist. "Don't call me a cheap tart!"

"If you act like one I bloody well will. And stop showing off your tits! We aren't interested and anyway, mine are twice as big as yours!" Camille retorted.

"Any more than a handful is a waste they say," Monica replied.

"That's enough all of you!" Barbara snapped. She stood up but it seemed to be a voice outside of herself. "No fights! No bickering! I've had enough of it. Now get to bed!" Blazing with anger she strode across to the light switch. The room was plunged into darkness and a strained silence settled as the girls crawled into their beds.

Barbara lay in hers with her back to Monica and felt herself overwhelmed by misery and suspicion. Tears trickled out and down into her pillow. With difficulty she prevented herself from sniffling or sobbing.

Bed-check came and went. Barbara lay mentally writhing in horrid fantasies of Gordon doing things to Monica. And she knew exactly what things. It would be the same disgusting things that repulsive man had been doing to her mother that day when she'd come home from school early and caught them.

The old wound of her mother's adultery added to her misery. She had to bite her knuckle to stop herself crying aloud. Thinking black thoughts, she drifted into a sleep of almost feverish exhaustion.

Chapter 16

DISGUSTING DISCOVERY

Barbara turned over in a restless sleep. A noise disturbed her. She opened her eyes and her tired brain registered the fact that Monica was just getting into bed.

Instantly she was awake. "Where have you been?" she hissed.

Monica paused halfway into her sleeping bag. "Mind your own business," she replied.

Barbara sat up. "Where have you been?"

"The toilet. Where do you think?" Monica answered.

"You have not. Where have you been?"

"Oh, out having a naughty with Gordon of course," came Monica's mocking answer.

Barbara struggled out of her sleeping bag, her emotions in a whirling turmoil of jealous misery. She gripped Monica's arm. "You have not!" she hissed.

Monica laughed. "I have so."

"That's a lie!" Barbara choked.

"Think what you like. And if you tell on me that is what I will say. Now let my arm go Brassington or I'll break your fingers."

A torch came on and Karen's voice came out of the darkness. "What's going on?" she called softly.

Before Barbara could speak Lt Curwen's voice called from the next room. "You girls be quiet and go to sleep," she said.

Barbara let go of Monica's arm but stayed crouched between the two stretchers. Her stomach churned and her skin seemed to crawl. Monica lay down and turned her back on Barbara.

Karen got out of her bed and padded over. "Are you alright Barbara?"

"I've got to go and look," Barbara replied, groping for her boots.

"What are you talking about? Look at what?" Karen hissed in a hoarse whisper. Other stretchers creaked in the darkness. Barbara began to pull on a boot. She gestured at Monica. "Malone just said she'd...she had...been with Gordon. I have to check."

There were murmurs. Fiona joined Karen and brushed long hair from her eyes. "Barbara, what is all this?"

"I have to go. I must!" Barbara muttered. She pulled on the other boot and felt for her torch.

"Go where?" hissed Fiona.

"To see Gordon."

"To see Gordon! Barb you can't go to the boys tents in the middle of the night!" Fiona replied in bewildered astonishment.

"I must," Barbara answered. She stood up.

Fiona grabbed her sleeve. "Barb, you mustn't! What's wrong?"

There were footsteps and another torch shone on them from the door. Lt McEwen's voice came to them. "What's going on? Why aren't you girls in bed? It's nearly one o'clock!"

"Yes Miss. It's Barbara... I... she. er... She isn't feeling well," Fiona replied.

Lt McEwen walked over and shone her torch on Barbara's face, then down at her boots. "Are you alright Barbara? Why are you wearing boots?"

"I. I can't sleep Miss. I had a bad dream and I felt sick," Barbara stammered. She shivered in misery and tears started.

Lt McEwen put out her hand to feel her forehead and then her cheek. "Yes. You feel a bit hot. Why, you're crying! What's the matter?"

"It's nothing Miss. I'll be alright."

"You get back into bed. I'll get you a warm drink. That will help you sleep."

The officer left the room. Barbara sat down and pulled off her boots. She couldn't help herself. Now she sobbed aloud. Almost as bad as the thought of Gordon with Monica was the thought that **she** was lying there silently gloating!

Karen and Fiona put their arms around her and tried to comfort her. Other girls woke up and there was muttering. Lt McEwen and Lt Curwen could be heard talking in the next room. Then the Lt McEwen returned with a cup of warm Milo.

"Now, you are sure it's not serious?" she asked.

"No Miss," Barbara replied with a sniffle.

"Then drink this and lie down."

Barbara did as she was told. Lt McEwen 'shooed' the other girls back to bed then sat and felt her pulse and her brow. When Barbara was calm, she gave her a re-assuring pat and went back to her own room.

Barbara lay in a torment but the warm drink, combined with her exhaustion, had its effect. She drifted into a deep sleep.

*****

A cool hand on her face woke her. The lights were on. Barbara blinked and looked up. Lt McEwen was kneeling beside her.

"Yes Miss?"

"It's check parade. I was just seeing how you were. You can stay in bed if you don't feel well."

Barbara saw the other girls pulling on shoes and clothes. Fiona and Wendy came over to talk to her.

"I'm alright Miss," Barbara replied. Despite feeling washed out she sat up. As she did, she remembered the incident from the night before. The sight of Monica's back departing through the door decided her.

I will go on parade. I'm not sick, she told herself.

Quickly she pulled on her boots and rushed out in her pyjamas. As she walked across the dewy lawn, she saw Gordon. He smiled at her, then turned and smiled at Monica who stood next to him in the front rank.

The bitch! Barbara thought.

Her jealous thoughts rose and seemed to choke her. By the time she arrived there was no space near Gordon and she had to stand near the end of the centre rank. For a few seconds she contemplated pushing in between Monica and Gordon but hesitated. She didn't want a scene.

Besides, if Gordon doesn't love me or isn't loyal then it would be pointless.

As Barbara stood at ease next to Ying, Monica spoke loud enough for all to hear.

"How are you Gordon? Did you enjoy last night?"

Barbara's blood seemed to freeze and there was a hiss of sharply indrawn air from several other girls. Barbara looked along at Gordon. He turned to smile at Monica but frowned. His voice echoed the frown. "Just another night I suppose."

"Did you sleep well?" Monica asked.

"As well as a man can with Roger snoring and Hilditch farting,"

Gordon replied with a laugh. He glanced up and saw Barbara. "Excuse me," he said to Monica. He stepped out of the ranks and walked around to push in next to Barbara. Barbara's heart fluttered.

Gordon looked at her anxiously. "What's the matter Barb. You look awful. I mean…I mean you look beautiful but upset."

Hilditch's voice cut in. "Righto you lot, be quiet so I can call the roll. Platoon. Attennn… shun! Stand at... Ease!"

Barbara responded mechanically to the orders, but she kept her eyes on Gordon's face.

"I didn't sleep very well. I had a terrible night," she whispered.

"Bad dream?"

"Worse." Barbara felt her throat constrict. *I'm going to cry,* she thought in alarm. Determined not to let her emotions show she battled to control the prickling tears.

Gordon frowned. "What happened?" he asked.

Barbara heard her name, but it didn't register. She struggled to find the right words to explain.

"Brassington!" Hilditch called loudly.

"Oh! Sir!" she replied, coming to attention. After standing at ease when the next name was called, she turned back to Gordon. "I'll tell you later."

When they were fallen-out they stood together for a minute. The others all headed off except Monica who came and stood next to Gordon. Barbara seethed. What a hide! She was about to snap at Monica when Gordon spoke.

"Excuse us Monica. This is private."

Monica sniffed. "Oh well, if that's how you feel!" she snapped. Angrily she turned and walked away.

Gordon frowned and turned back to Barbara. "Well?"

Barbara felt her heart hammering. Instinctively she knew this could be a make-or-break moment and out of fear hesitated. But she also knew she had to ask so she took a deep breath and spoke. "Her. She's the problem. She came in late last night and said she'd been with you."

"Oh did she!" Gordon replied. His mouth set in a hard line. "It's not true. Ignore her. She's just being catty."

Barbara was about to ask for more reassurance, but she checked herself. "Thanks. I'll see you at breakfast." She gave a weak smile.

"That's better. Breakfast then. Gee I'd like to kiss you!"

"You'd better not. Miss McEwen and Mrs Curwen are standing on the porch drinking coffee and watching us," Barbara said. Then she smiled.

Gordon looked around. Everyone else had gone indoors. "We are a bit conspicuous. See you later."

They went their separate ways. As Barbara entered the girls hut there were raised voices.

She heard Fiona shout, "Shut up Malone. You're just a bloody troublemaker." She pointed and added. "You sleep there from now on."

Barbara stopped. Five girls, hands on hips were facing Monica who now stood beside a heap of gear in the corner next to the wall of Miss McEwen's room. In Monica's old bed space was another pile of gear being sorted out by Karen.

Karen looked up at Barbara. "I'm sleeping beside you from now on," she explained.

Barbara nodded. She was glad. "Thanks. That will be nice."

Sharon laughed. "No it won't. She snores," she called.

"I do not!"

"You do!"

"Do not!"

Barbara felt happier when they went to breakfast, but she was still in a quandary. She knew she could cause Monica a lot of trouble by telling the officers she had been out last night. Then she was ashamed for having such a petty thought. Besides she had no proof. Malone may have only been to the toilet.

And she could really hurt Gordon with her lies, she mused.

The memory of her own behaviour made her blush with shame.

During breakfast she sat next to Gordon. He was his usual bright cheerful self. Barbara briefly wondered if it showed a clear conscience or whether he was just a good liar. Then she chided herself for such an unworthy thought.

After all I hardly know him, she considered.

The usual morning rush then over-ran them: Preparations for Inspection; Inspection; and Parade. They were then in the Lecture Room with Captain Conkey. He checked each person's calculations for the Navigation Exercise.

"Now each group will walk their planned route. You should always do this before sending cadets on a compass march. It's a safety measure. There may be hazards not shown on the map: steep-sided gullies, barbed wire fences, marshy ground, lantana, and so on. Remember the old army saying: 'Time spent on reconnaissance is seldom wasted.' You can then plan with greater certainty. Here are the compasses."

Captain Conkey issued the compasses and outlined the safety procedures for the activity, then said, "Give me a copy of your calculations before you go. Ensure you all have a map, compass, protractor, two full water bottles and a box of matches. Be back by 10:30. Action if Lost. If lost, backtrack if you are reasonably certain. If not sit and wait. Watch out for wild pigs."

Barbara's group comprised herself, Gordon, Karen and Cosgrove. After collecting their webbing, filling water bottles and having a big drink they set off. Their route took them almost due east for about half a kilometre. It was easy walking as the ground was bare red clay in many places and most of the grass was in short, spiky tufts. The sun was more of a problem.

Cosgrove wiped sweat from his face and said, "You wouldn't think we had all that rain a couple of days ago would you?"

"All soaked in," Gordon replied.

Barbara walked beside him content just to be with him. She found she was enjoying walking through the bush. The natural vegetation surrounding her home in Cairns was all dark green tropical rain forest so the lighter greens and browns of the more open savannah woodland was quite different. *But I like it,* she decided. After a bit of thought she decided that was because all three of her cadet annual camps and several weekend bivouacs had been in this type of country and they had been such rewarding or enjoyable activities that she was happy to be in such an environment.

The group came to a fence and changed direction southwards. They entered an area with waist high spear grass. It still wasn't continuous ground cover but it was scratchy and irritating.

"Pretty featureless," commented Gordon, looking around. The ground was almost flat, just a huge expanse of savannah woodland.

Barbara pointed off through the scattered ironbarks. "I got a glimpse of Hill 376 a few minutes ago," she commented.

"You sure?"

"Yes. Look, you can just make out part of the Tucker Box Range." She pointed. "Through there."

At three hundred paces they halted. The next leg took them Southwest for 450 paces. This ended near a line of paperbark trees along a small creek. Then they turned to head almost due West, walking parallel to the creek. They turned right and crossed the dry creek line, here just a gully with steep sides and a sandy bottom and 200 paces from the camp.

"That way," Gordon said, pointing then lining his compass up. The group tramped along into a thicket of spiky shrubs and stunted acacias.

In a small clearing a hundred or so paces from the tents they found an area of flattened grass. Several empty whisky bottles lay scattered around and there was a litter of cigarette butts, chocolate wrappers and food scraps.

"Someone's camp?" suggested Karen.

They stopped and looked around.

"Why camp here? It's only two hundred metres to the huts. There are our tents just ahead," Gordon replied. He bent down and picked up a bottle and sniffed it. "Fresh," he said frowning.

Karen bent down and studied the litter. "This stuff hasn't been here long. It wasn't here when it was raining. Look, those cigarette butts and that cigarette packet there are all muddy and soiled but these aren't." she agreed.

"What does it mean?" Cosgrove asked.

Gordon's mouth set in hard line. "Someone is sneaking out for a drink and a smoke," he replied.

"Corporals Course?" Karen suggested, indicating the rows of tents about a hundred metres away.

"No, I don't think so," Gordon replied. He tossed the whisky bottle down.

"I don't think so either," Barbara replied, swirling with suspicions.

Gordon bent to pick something up then abruptly changed his mind and put his boot on it.

"What is that Gordon?" she asked.

"What?" he replied.

"What you just put your boot on," Barbara replied, a bit nettled by his denial.

"Something I'd rather you didn't see."

"What?" Barbara queried.

"Nothing," Gordon replied, trying to sound disinterested.

This answer aroused Barbara's curiosity even more. She was also a bit annoyed as it was obvious Gordon was trying to hide something from her. "Show me please," she asked.

"I'd rather not. It's not very nice," Gordon replied firmly.

At that moment Cosgrove bent down and picked up a small plastic packet. It had been ripped open.

"What was in this I wonder? Oh!" he said, his voice changing as he realised what it was. Karen and Barbara looked. The printing was clear and they were able to read it before an embarrassed Cosgrove crumpled it in his hand.

A condom packet.

There had not only been drinking and smoking here but sex!

Barbara's mind whirled in surprise and the ugly spectre of suspicion intruded again. Who? Monica? Or perhaps Chloe? And who with? She couldn't help remembering what Monica had said and there was Gordon looking embarrassed (or was it guilty?).

She looked him directly in the eye.

"Is that a condom you are standing on?"

Gordon went crimson and nodded. "I didn't want you to be offended," he explained.

Karen wrinkled her nose in disgust. "I'm going. This place is filthy." She headed towards the camp. Feeling revolted and slightly nauseous Barbara wiped perspiration from her forehead and followed her. The two boys waited a moment then hastened to catch up.

"What will we do?" Cosgrove asked.

"Tell the officers of course," Gordon replied.

Barbara had been about to say the same thing. She was pleased at Gordon's decisiveness. But still the niggling doubts remained and she despised herself for having them.

As the group approached the Lecture Room Gordon said, "I'll go and tell the Colonel. There's no need for you people to come."

Barbara felt a bit relieved at that. She and Karen stopped in the shade and had a long drink while Gordon strode off down to the HQ. They watched him halt and salute and soon afterwards the Colonel and several other officers came out from under the shade roof putting on their hats. They followed Gordon off through the lines of CUOs tents and into the bush.

"We may as well finish writing this Navex," Barbara said. They went inside and settled around a table. There were two other groups there and Cosgrove at once went and sat beside Millet and Wilmot and told them what they had found.

Karen frowned. "I don't think we should talk about this," she said.

Barbara nodded. "I agree but it is too late to keep it a secret now," she replied. Feeling annoyed and upset she had another drink and sat looking through the louvres into the harsh glare. A faint breeze cooled her slightly but most of the sweat just dripped off. Suddenly she felt very tired and drained.

One more unpleasantness to spoil the camp! she thought unhappily. There seemed to be just one thing after another!

As they waited another group came in. It was Roger with Jones, Ying and Monica. Barbara pretended to work on her writing but carefully watched Monica's face as the gossip reached them. Monica looked immediately in the direction of the 'camp' and seemed to look a bit worried. Then she sneered and made some sarcastic comment Barbara couldn't catch before bending to study a map.

Was Monica guilty? Barbara couldn't tell. She turned back to her work and began helping Karen check their calculations.

When Weismann's group came back twenty minutes later Barbara again carefully watched to see his reactions. Monica made no move to tell him but seemed absorbed in her work. It was Wilmot who moved from one table to another to tell Weismann. He appeared unmoved by the news but Stephens appeared agitated and worried. He looked nervously around, fidgeted and licked his lips.

Was he the culprit?

Again Barbara was puzzled by the problem of where Stephens fitted into the picture. He was clearly a crony of Weismann but that wouldn't account for his actions in accusing Gordon of theft.

He must have some powerful motive to have done that, she reasoned. *Does Weismann have some hold over him?*

She had seen the ugly facts of blackmail in her own family a few years before. Was this another face of that courage crippling coercion?

Fiona, Sharon and Camille joined her and Karen relayed the gossip to them. Their reaction was sour disapproval and obvious disgust. Barbara was further dismayed and annoyed to overhear Stephens mutter to some boys, "Probably that Chloe bitch."

Poor Chloe! Barbara thought.

But there was nothing she could do and she had to admit that Chloe's name had flitted across her own list of possible suspects. They did not have time to discuss it however as Capt Conkey came in with a face like thunder, followed by Gordon.

Capt Conkey made no comment about the find but at once began a lesson on planning a Night Navex. In answer to Barbara's querying glance Gordon gave a shake of his head. Later he remained tight-lipped.

"I can't say. Please don't ask me," was all he said.

By the end of the lesson the tension in the room was like an invisible web. Barbara expected something to be said but Capt Conkey merely told them to get on with planning a night navex which they would run on Sunday night and left them to it.

Nor were they given much time to speculate as the Colonel arrived and cut short their break. Again Barbara expected something to be said but the Colonel simply began the next lesson, on 'How to Control an Exercise.' After 40 minutes on the need for clear orders, for checkpoints, boundaries and alternate routes; and on planning radio nets for friendly forces, opposing forces and umpires, the tension had eased somewhat.

The training grind continued to overlay itself on the sordid personality sidelights as Lt Buchan lectured them about 'How to Communicate with helicopters'; on how to mark Helo LZs; how large LZs needed to be; how to pin down Helicopter Marker Panels (strips of orange material) and on the codes used to convey information by the panel arrangement.

As they worked Millet muttered angrily. "Why do we need all this crap! We are never going to work with helicopters. We don't even see them!"

"We do," Camille commented. "There is a squadron of 'MRH 90s' based at Garbutt RAAF Base near our school. They fly over all the time."

"Yeah, but do you as cadets ever get to fly in them?" Millet queried with a sneer.

Camille had to admit they didn't. The groups lapsed into silence and resumed work. By lunch-time the discovery in the scrub had faded to relative insignificance and had already been forgotten by most. Barbara found herself absorbed by the need to assimilate all this new information and by sorting it into her notes and 'Clue Book'.

She was also feeling very tired. At Mess Parade she asked Gordon what had happened.

He made a face then answered, "The Colonel and some of the officers came with me and had a look. He then sent me away and told me not to talk about it. He was pretty annoyed. I could tell. I don't know what they are going to do about it."

"It must be a real nuisance," Fiona commented. "I mean they have all the problems of planning and running four courses at one time and they all teach nearly every other lesson."

"It must certainly be a worry," Sharon agreed.

"I just think it's such a shame," Barbara said. "It spoils the atmosphere of the whole Course."

"What spoils the atmosphere?" Roger asked as he joined the group.

"You do when you don't wash your socks," Gordon replied good-naturedly.

After lunch the CUOs were rostered to help assess and advise the Corporals and Sergeants teaching lessons. Barbara found herself allocated to No 18 Section with Lt Hope, Monica's OC.

She had never worked with him before and had an instinctive dislike of the man. He was in his thirties, was pudgy in build and with a big bum and shifty eyes. He also had a sort of false friendliness she found a bit trying.

She seated herself in the folding chair beside him and opened her folder.

I'm just being silly, she thought. *It's probably because I associate him with Malone.*

All in all she found the afternoon a bit of a tedious trial. The heat, combined with her fatigue, made it hard to concentrate and stay awake. On top of that most of the lessons were mediocre to say the least. She found it painful to watch some of the elementary mistakes being made.

Lt Hope didn't make it any easier. He kept interrupting. This tended to throw already nervous and unsure cadets into a fluster. The lieutenant was also sarcastic and reduced one boy from Townsville to tears. Barbara resented the officer's methods but could do little except offer some words of helpful advice and praise for their good points when she had the opportunity to speak.

She was heartily glad when it was over. Thankfully she went to join the other CUOs on the edge of the grass parade ground. The last period was a 'talk-through' practice for the Graduation Parade. Even though it was 1600hrs the sun still seemed to hang in the sky like a malevolent blow-torch. There was no breeze. The heat-haze shimmered and the eucalyptus leaves dripped and drooped.

Capt Royston took charge of the CUOs while WO1 Pryor organised the remainder.

"There are twenty-four of you. Only one can be top CUO. We don't know who that will be till the day before, so we have to have two practices just picking people at random for the jobs. We will swap you around from day to day and from job to job. That will give you training and experience," he explained.

He paused and ran his eyes over them. Barbara remembered her own high resolve on arrival as their eyes met. Capt Royston went on, "For the parade we are going to organise you as a small battalion of four companies. That will create more opportunities for you all to have an officer's job to do on the parade. You CUOs will command. There will be no adult staff on parade except the Reviewing Officer and band master. Thus we will have the following: a Parade Commander, who will be the top CUO; the Flag ensign, 2nd on the Course; the battalion 2IC, 3rd; four Company Commanders, 4th, 5th, 6th and 7th; an Adjutant, 8th; four Company 2ICs, 9th, 10th, 11th and 12th. The remainder of you will be Platoon Commanders."

He held up a cardboard box and said, "In this box are twenty-four pieces of paper with a job written on it. Take a lucky dip and that is your position on the parade today."

They filed past and each took a slip of paper. Barbara ended up as OC B Company. She was disappointed not to be Parade Commander but happy she had a job with a sword. Gordon became OC A Company. This made them smile at each other. Weismann became 2IC and Monica got to be Adjutant. Jones from Sarina was Parade Commander.

The practice then went for 45 sweaty minutes but only two cadets fell out in the 40-degree heat. They had all started to toughen up and acclimatise and the humidity was very low. Barbara enjoyed the practice and was in a happier frame of mind when she was dismissed. She returned the sword she had been using to Capt Royston and marched briskly away. Because she was rostered for duty, she had to hurry to have a shower and change into her DPCU ceremonial uniform in time for Guard Mount at 1730.

Chapter 17

PIQUET DUTY

By 1730 hours Barbara stood at attention on the parade ground in front of a section of the Sergeants Course. She was perspiring freely from the rush to change into a clean uniform, polish the brass on her black belt and get the duty section on parade in time.

She handed over to Sgt Watts, a cadet from Townsville who was the new Orderly Sergeant. Barbara cordially detested him, believing him to be an arrogant and abrasive person, but she kept her features neutral as he made a critical inspection of the eight Sergeants Course cadets who made up the guard. Barbara took post at the flagpole while the Orderly Sergeant handed over to the new Duty Officer, Lt Hope.

His appearance and manner caused her opinion of him to go down even more. Every other Duty Officer had been in their ceremonial uniform with Sam Browne belt and badges but Lt Hope still wore camouflage work dress and had obviously made no attempt to clean up after the day's training. But that did not stop him berating one of the Guard for having mud on his boots.

What a pompous twit! Barbara thought.

The Guard 'Presented Arms' to the officer's feeble orders and the flag was lowered by Sgt Wilmot who was the other Duty NCO. Barbara stood to attention and saluted until the 'carry on'. Lt Hope ordered the Guard back to attention and then called the Orderly Sergeant. But instead of waiting to hand over to the Orderly Sergeant to march off the guard Lt Hope just turned and sauntered off with the Orderly Sergeant, leaving the Guard standing on the parade ground.

By then Barbara had begun to help Wilmot to fold the flag. Then she noticed the Guard standing there, obviously wondering what to do next. For a moment Barbara stood in surprise but she quickly recovered.

The Guard should have marched off and given the Duty Officer an 'Eyes Right' as they did, she thought.

Handing the flag to Sgt Wilmot she marched across to the front of the Guard. As she did, she noted they were all males.

"You, last cadet, go and help Sgt Wilmot roll up the flag. Fall out!" she snapped. She saw that Wilmot was allowing the flag to drape on the ground, but she forbore from calling his attention to the lapse in front of the squad.

In her best 'parade ground' voice Barbara called, "Guard. Atten... shun! Move to the right in single file, Right....turn. Quick March!" She marched them over to the four tents which were diagonally across from the canteen near the bitumen car park. One tent was allocated to the Duty Officer, another for the female members of the piquet. The other two tents were the sleeping accommodation for the male members.

After ordering the Guard to fall out and telling them to wait Barbara marched over to the canteen. In the front room of the canteen, which doubled as Guardroom, a cadet from the 'Old Guard' sat reading a comic behind a table on which lay a telephone, and various books.

Barbara was aware the Orderly Sergeant should have organised a roster for the 'New Guard' but a quick search revealed nothing. Watt's strident bellow in the distance told her he was busy calling Mess Parade. With him was Stephens, the third Duty NCO. Barbara knew his job was to supervise the hot water and washing up area. So she made some quick decisions. She knew the Quarter Guard was organised, so there was always someone on Telephone Piquet in the 'Guard Room', with one of the three rostered CUOs Course members who acted as Duty NCOs. The Duty NCOs also had the task of changing the two sentries every hour.

Barbara returned to the waiting Guard. Pointing at a cadet she said, "You, take over as Telephone Piquet. The rest of you, under the command of the last corporal, march up to your lines, have your meal and bring your sleeping gear back here. Then wait here till time for evening lessons." She then pointed at another cadet. "Last Cadet, you eat quickly and hurry back to relieve your mate as phone piquet so he can eat. Carry on!"

Wilmot arrived with the flag as they marched off. Barbara said, "You go and eat. I'll stay on duty till you get back. Make sure you remind the kitchen to save two late meals please."

Wilmot shrugged and tossed the flag on the table. "Suit yourself," he said and walked off.

Barbara sat on one of the folding chairs and made conversation with the cadet on duty. He was a nice kid from Mackay and very keen. He was happy to talk 'Cadets'.

Time passed and nobody came. Barbara checked her watch. 1830. *More than enough time for Wilmot to eat,* she thought. Despite her growing annoyance she decided to wait a bit longer. Footsteps on the road made her get up in anticipation but it was only the cadet she had detailed to hurry back.

Barbara felt a surge of irritation. "Have you seen Sgt Wilmot or the Orderly Sergeant?" she asked.

"No Ma'am," the corporal replied.

"Never mind. You take over here." She turned to the one sitting down. "You go and eat."

Barbara then spent a few minutes explaining what the boy should do if a vehicle came and what to say and do if there was a telephone call. By this the trees in the distance had taken on the ruddy hue of sunset.

Barbara began to feel both hungry and annoyed. She looked at her watch. 1845. Wilmot had been gone nearly an hour. There were only fifteen minutes till training began and she was part of a demonstration squad to show the Corporals how to give an 'O' Group.

I might just have time to eat if I hurry, she thought.

She turned to the cadet on telephone duty. "I'll have to leave you while I go and get Sgt Wilmot. I've got a lesson," she explained to the new boy, who looked nervous at the prospect of being left in sole responsibility.

Barbara marched briskly along past the girls hut. Apart from feeling tired and a bit peckish she felt well and relatively content. She enjoyed the evening hush settling on the surrounding bush. On the way she passed a couple of members of the piquet heading for the Guard Tents with their sleeping gear so felt a bit easier.

"Don't be late for your lessons," she cautioned them.

As she entered the Mess Hall, Barbara saw Wilmot sitting with Weismann and Monica. Wilmot was talking and laughing and did not look at all concerned. Rather than provoke an incident, Barbara went through into the kitchen. The Duty Section was hard at work washing up, scrubbing tables and cleaning. The army cook and his civilian offsider, Old Jim, were eating their dinner at a table in the Sergeants Mess Hall.

"What do you want?" the cook snapped as Barbara stopped at the end of the table.

"My tea please."

"Tea! You're a bit late aren't you? Mess Parade was an hour ago," the cook replied testily.

"I'm on piquet. There should be a late meal left for me," she said.

The cook snorted. "Well there ain't. Nobody told me."

Barbara stood her ground and met his gaze. Her annoyance at Wilmot turned to anger. Old Jim gave her a sympathetic smile. "I'll rustle up somethin' for you," he said.

Barbara looked at her watch. Only seven minutes.

"Thanks, but there isn't time. I have to go to a lesson. I'll just grab a drink."

"Come back after that and I'll see you get a feed," Old Jim replied.

"Thank you."

Barbara walked over to the table with the tea and coffee urns on it. Finding a cup she poured herself a drink. While she was stirring in the sugar Wilmot came in with his unwashed plates and utensils and dropped them on the bench with a clatter.

"Wash them," he ordered the corporal wiping the bench.

Barbara took a sip, then said, "Thanks for organising my late meal and hurrying back to relieve me." Wilmot flushed and made no reply. He turned to walk away. That angered Barbara even more. "Wilmot! You had better get back to the Guard Room. I have to go to a lesson."

"Don't tell me what to do. I'll go when I'm ready. Besides what's it matter? It's only a pretend guard," Wilmot replied.

"It is not!" Barbara flared. "We need someone on the phone for personal emergencies, like that one two days ago where that kid from Rockhampton had to go home because his grandmother was dying. And we need someone awake to watch for fire with all those tents."

Wilmot shrugged. He picked up an apple and sauntered out. Shouted orders indicated the platoons were moving to their night lessons. Barbara scowled, gulped down the still too hot tea, and doubled over to her hut to grab her folder.

She was just in time to join the Demo Squad before the Colonel called for them. Her part in the demo was acting as the Company Signals Corporal and she had to issue and explain a set of Signals Operating Instructions for a company search exercise. Otherwise she had only to sit and write the orders and look at the map as the Colonel did the presentation.

Directly the lesson was over Barbara buttonholed the Orderly Sergeant. "Sgt Watts, have you worked out a roster for the piquet yet?"

"No. Not yet. I'll get 'round it. There's plenty of time," he replied.

"Nonsense!" Barbara exploded. "We've been the guard for two hours. Some of those corporals have already done an hour and so have I."

"So what are you worrying about? It'll work itself out."

"That's a poor attitude. It's your job," Barbara said.

"If you're so worried you go and do it," Watts replied.

"I can't. I have to give a lesson to some Sergeants."

Watts curled his lip. "Well run along and do it like a good little girl."

"Don't patronise me you male chauvinist!" Barbara snapped. Seething with annoyance she turned on her heel and strode off.

She found her squad waiting in the laundry: eight cadets from the Sergeants Course, including Wendy. There was no officer present to assess, which Barbara found a relief. Barbara quickly made up a simple blanket board, seated her class and proceeded to teach them section patrol formations. To show the actual formations she used 1:35 scale model soldiers with different coloured helmets to identify the groups. The name of each formation and its advantages and disadvantages she had printed on strips of white cardboard which she now placed on her blanket board as required.

It was a subject she knew well, and she was in full flight when Major Wickham came in the back door. He returned her salute and told her to continue. After assessing for about fifteen minutes he left. Barbara enjoyed the lesson but by the end of it was perspiring freely as it was still very hot and with little breeze, even though the sun had been gone for two hours.

Before returning to duty she gulped a drink and, very conscious of grumbles in her empty stomach, headed for her hut. Quickly she packed away her gear, collected her sleeping bag and pillow and headed for the guard tents.

Barbara dropped her bedding on a spare stretcher in the tent allocated for girls on duty, noting that hers was the only bedding there. *That's because all the others on duty are males,* she thought. She next went to the Guard Hut. Seated in it were Wilmot, Weismann, Stephens and a corporal. There was no sign of the Duty Officer or Orderly Sergeant.

Barbara hesitated at the sight of Weismann. He had his boots up on the table and was reading a glossy 'Girlie' magazine full of large colour photos of naked women. Several similar magazines lay on the table. She pointed to these and said coldly, "Excuse me. I'd prefer you took that objectionable literature somewhere else."

Weismann sneered. "Why, don't you like looking at naked women? Look at the boobs on this one." He held the magazine in front of her face and laughed coarsely.

Barbara saw the glossy photo with all its intimate detail and blushed. With an effort she held her hands to her side. Through clenched teeth she replied, "I object! I will not be subjected to sexual harassment or intimidation by you. Nor will I allow the girls who come in here to be subjected to such objectionable treatment. Now, get that disgusting filth out of here or I shall complain to the Colonel."

"Aw, keep your shirt on," Wilmot sneered.

"Maybe she'd rather take it off," Weismann suggested with a snigger.

"Right, that does it!" Barbara cried. She swung around and began to march towards the door.

Weismann sprang to his feet and called after her, "OK! OK! We'll get rid of them."

Barbara halted. Knowing that the sort of harassment she had just been subjected to was specifically forbidden by the regulations made her pause. She was still tempted to go and complain but decided not to stir up more unpleasantness. Instead she spoke to Wilmot as he came out of the door. "Did the Orderly Sergeant make up a roster?"

"Haven't seen one."

"Where are you going now?"

"For a break. I've been here two hours. You take over for a while," Wilmot replied.

"But I haven't had tea yet and I've just done two lessons," Barbara expostulated.

"Tough! See you later," Wilmot said as he swaggered off. Weismann and Stephens stood up and followed him.

Barbara was really angry by this time. "Stephens, you are a Duty NCO too. You can stay here for half an hour while I have something to eat."

"Get stuffed!" Stephens retorted. "You can't tell me what to do. We are all on the CUOs Course." With that he pushed past her to join his cronies. All three vanished into the darkness while uttering teasing chuckles and singing a ribald song.

Barbara fumed and considered finding the Orderly Sergeant or Duty Officer. Instead she seated herself in the Guard Hut near the embarrassed corporal who had also been reading an erotic magazine but had tried to hide it under his chair.

She spent twenty minutes compiling a roster for the piquet. Once she had done that she made a copy and stuck it to the tabletop beside the telephone with sticky tape. Then she made up one for herself and Wilmot and put it beside the other one.

That done she tried to relax. She talked to the cadet on telephone piquet but he was poor company. She had nothing to read so she sat and pondered the events of the last few days.

The cheerful babble of many voices approaching the canteen indicated that lessons were finished for the night. The thought of that made Barbara realise just how hungry she felt. The canteen soon filled with hungry cadets. A few minutes later Sgt Watts arrived, followed by Wilmot, who dumped his bedding and produced a chocolate.

Barbara pointed to the rosters. "I've done them. You are on from 2300 to 0100. I will then do from 0100 until 0300 and Stephens can do from 0300 to 0500."

Wilmot grumbled but accepted it. He said, "I'm going to bed now. I'm tired," he said. He finished his chocolate and licked his fingers.

"But I haven't had any tea yet," Barbara pointed out.

"Tough!" Wilmot replied.

"Well, where is Stephens?"

Wilmot shrugged. "No idea. In bed probably."

"Can't you wait a few minutes please?" Barbara asked.

"No," Wilmot said as he walked away.

Barbara turned to Sgt Watts. "Can you wait a few minutes while I go and get something to eat?"

Watts just shrugged. "Yeah, alright, but you can put all those corporals to bed as well," he called.

Wilmot's response was to shake his head and keep walking. Watts swore, further angering Barbara.

"Lights Out is your job," Barbara pointed out.

"You do it. I'm tired. I'm going to bed too."

"Where is the Duty Officer?"

"Lt Hope? He's asleep in his tent. Can't you hear him snoring?" Watts answered, jerking his thumb in that direction. He then looked at the cadet on telephone piquet and said, "If you need me I will be in my tent." With that he turned and walked out into the darkness towards the guard tents.

Barbara was astonished. She rose and went to the front door. "You said you would stay."

Watts called back, "I'll be just over here."

"What about Lights Out and the Bed Check?" she called after him.

"You do it if it bothers you," Watts replied.

"It's your duty, and the Duty Officer's. It says so in Standing Orders."

"Just a load of crap! Nobody's ever been missing yet," Watts replied from the darkness.

"It's your job," Barbara insisted.

"You wake the Duty Officer then. I've delegated it to you," Watts replied. There was the sound of a stretcher creaking as Watts lay down.

Barbara stood for a moment in silent disgust. A glance at her watch showed it was already five minutes past 'Lights-Out'. She turned back into the Guard Hut and spoke to the male cadet there, pointing to two names on the roster as she did.

"You find these two cadets. It is time to change. You change over with them now. Tell the cadet rostered on sentry to wait in front of the officer's mess. I will go and supervise 'Lights-Out'. I will be half an hour or so," she instructed. The whole arrangement annoyed her as she knew it was sloppy but she also knew things had to be made happen, so she picked up her torch and the Duty NCO clipboard.

Using her best 'Sergeant Major's' voice she cleared the canteen of customers and told the two cadets behind the counter to close up and get to bed. Then she marched out and along the road towards the tent lines. She was pleased to note the girls hut was in darkness.

But the female corporals tents still had lights on. "Lights-Out! Get to bed!" Barbara ordered.

Female corporals scuttled into their tents. Barbara walked along, shining a torch on each bed. In particular she checked that Chloe was in her bed. She was. Barbara then walked to the girls hut and turned off the porch lights. Then laughter and splashing from the male S.A.L. block attracted her attention. She stamped angrily over and bellowed in the door, "Get out of the shower and get to bed you people!"

"Or what?" called a cheeky male voice, adding, "Will you come in and get us?" Several ribald comments were added by the boy's friends, suggesting he would like that, or Barbara might. The boy was obviously having a shower and Barbara could only fume. She looked around for a male with rank but none was visible. Feeling frustrated and angry she went and chased more people out of the laundry.

By then she was deeply annoyed. The Duty CSMs had done their jobs, but she knew the Duty Officer and Orderly sergeant should now be conducting a complete bed check. She sent Sgt Barker to chase the boys out of the showers. He did this swiftly and returned to report.

For ten minutes Barbara walked up and down making sure the Duty CSMs were stamping out any muttering or joke telling. Silence eventually settled over the camp.

Barbara found the cadet who was rostered as the sentry. He was waiting outside the CUOs lecture room. She gave him his orders. These were printed on one of the sheets on the Duty NCO clipboard she had so all she had to do was read them. He was to march up and down the road from the girls hut to the far end of the boy's tent lines, halting in front of the CUOs lecture room.

Having posted the sentry, Barbara rejoined the Duty CSMs and walked up and down the lines of tents and stamped on any muttering or joke telling. Silence settled over the camp.

Next, Barbara went through the lecture rooms and tents, turning out lights as she went. In the kitchen she encountered Old Jim having a cup of tea. He looked up.

"I was just about to turn these lights out and lock-up," he said, then added, "Would you like a cup of tea?"

"I'd love one. I still haven't had dinner."

The old man's face creased in a frown. "Oh! That's no good. I'll get you a feed. You just wait here."

Barbara gave him a smile. "Thanks very much. But I'll just do another walk around to check they are all in bed. Those boys on the Sergeants Course are a bit restless."

She walked around the tent lines once more. The odd whisper indicated a few still awake. They were silenced. This time she shone her torch into every tent as a bed-check, hoping she didn't see anyone undressed and silently cursing Lt Hope and Sgt Watts.

Back at the kitchen ten minutes later she found that Old Jim had prepared a plate of cold meat and salad. "I'll put you on the back porch," he explained. "I've just hosed the floor in here and it's all wet. I'll just mop it out then take myself to bed."

Barbara took the plate to a table under the light on the back porch.

"Still want a cup of tea?" Old Jim asked.

"Yes please. I'll just check these girls tents first," Barbara replied. The sound of whispering and giggling had just come from them.

Old Jim nodded. "OK. When you finish just put the plates in the kitchen and pull this door shut from the outside. I'll go out the other end."

Barbara walked over to the girls tents. But all was now quiet. To check that they were all in bed Barbara shone her torch into each bed. Once again she was anxious she might find someone in a state of undress (Chloe!). But none were, not even Chloe. To Barbara's amusement she saw that Chloe was lying on her side clutching a teddy bear and was sucking her thumb.

She is truly beautiful, she thought. Then she shook her head. *How can she look so innocent if even half of those stories are true?* she wondered. Then another thought came to her: *Monica!*

The name came to her like a stab of pain.

Barbara quietly made her way up into the darkened girls hut. She shone her torch from stretcher to stretcher. Her own was the only empty one. Monica lay in hers, sound asleep. Barbara walked through as quietly as her boots allowed on the wooden floor and made a quick visit to the toilet. As she came out, she saw a cadet wandering past. It was the sentry. From 2200 till 0600 there were two on duty, plus an Orderly Sergeant or Duty NCO. One cadet sat by the phone. The other patrolled the middle of the camp. The Duty NCO also patrolled the camp and changed the sentries. Barbara spoke to the sentry and he marched off towards the corporals tents.

Satisfied she had done all she could for the moment Barbara returned to the back porch of the kitchen and seated herself at the table. With a sigh of relief she put down her torch and clipboard and took off her KFF. To her delight she saw that Old Jim had not only left a cup of tea but also a bowl of jelly and ice-cream.

Bless him, she thought. *But bother these insects!*

Flying ants and moths had come out of the surrounding darkness to swarm around the light.

Noting that she had only fifteen more minutes of duty to do before she woke Wilmot, Barbara began to eat. She felt pleasantly relaxed. From in the sergeants dining room came the sounds of Old Jim mopping the floor. Otherwise the camp and surrounding bush were very quiet.

She finished her main meal and scooped a flying ant out of her tea. Then she brushed several out of her hair while she had a drink. Next, she extracted a wriggling moth from her ice-cream.

The sound of a vehicle made her look up. Headlights were coming from the main gate. She took no particular notice but began to eat. Another insect plummeted into her ice-cream. She picked it out and flicked it away just as the vehicle swung around the girls hut, half-blinding her with the glare of its headlights. It pulled up beside her and she saw it was the white utility that collected the food scraps.

The ute's engine died. At that moment something fell in the pantry, which was just inside the kitchen door. Curious as to what had made the noise Barbara rose from her chair, barely noticing the man getting out of the ute beside the garbage bins. She turned and walked 2 paces to the back door of the kitchen.

A man walked into the light near her and grabbed a garbage bin. Another moved around the vehicle to help him. Barbara was about to walk through the door when there were rapid footsteps behind her.

Before alarm could register, a massively strong arm encircled her throat and a smelly hand clamped over her face.

Chapter 18

THE NIGHTMARE BEGINS

For a moment Barbara froze in surprise and shock. Her first thought was that it was some sort of prank. But then the awful smell of stale sweat and the size and strength of the person registered in her brain. Then instinct warned her that she was in deadly peril and she began to struggle. She tried to scream but the nicotine-tasting hand over her face stifled her attempt. The smell made her gag. She clawed at the arm around her throat as a wave of fear swept over her.

With it came cold sweat and cold thought. She knew she had to get free. She stopped struggling and tried to kick. It was no good. She wasn't strong enough. An almost paralysing feeling of helplessness gripped her insides. To her dismay she found herself being lifted and carried backwards off the porch.

Pain streaked up her neck and into the top of her skull. Dots danced before her eyes. Barbara squirmed in desperation. Her racing brain told her that this could be the fight of her life. As the terror built towards panic, she perceived it could be her very life which was at stake.

When first she had been grabbed, the name 'Weismann' had flashed into her mind, to be instantly ejected as the smell and the feel of the man who gripped her registered. It was someone worse than Weismann, far worse.

A voice confirmed her thoughts. "Christ Lenny. Wot ya doin'?"

"Shut up Wally!" snarled another voice in her ear.

A stab of pure terror lanced through Barbara. It was Lenny the Pig Hunter!

And there was Weismann's face!

As Barbara struggled, she saw his head look around the pantry door. His eyes bulged in astonishment and then his head vanished.

By this time Barbara had been dragged off the porch and into the semi-dark behind the ute. *I must get help,* she thought. *I must cry out. Weismann is just there. Old Jim is somewhere in the Sergeants Dining Hall.*

Through her frightened mind flashed other hopes: there was a cadet patrolling on piquet somewhere. Just behind her, not ten metres away, was a hut with four lady officers and twenty girls asleep in it.

If I can only call out, or scream, she thought.

She managed to open her mouth and bit. Her teeth crunched into a thick fold of flesh in the man's hand.

"Aah! Bitch!" he swore.

Quicker than she could imagine possible Lenny's right hand released her mouth and returned a stunning blow to the side of her face. Barbara tried to cry out but the arm around her throat restricted her effort to a gurgle. Again he punched her, harder this time. She tasted blood from split lips and her right eye lost its vision and went numb.

Wally, the Pig Hunter's crony, hissed: "Christ Lenny! Stop it!"

Lenny grunted as he hauled Barbara around beside the ute. "Shut up Wally or I'll pulp you too. Just get that garbage loaded," he snarled.

On the verge of blacking out Barbara felt his arm go between her thighs and next moment she was lifted and dumped hard on her back on the filthy floor of the utility's tray. Lenny's hand stayed at her throat, half strangling her. Quickly he changed his grip and hauled Barbara's face up. A stinking rag was shoved into her mouth so hard several teeth were loosened.

The smell of rotting food scraps and the stench of the rag combined to make Barbara gag. She felt her stomach heave and tried to stop it. But she couldn't. She vomited, even as Lenny vaulted into the ute and sat on her. Blocked at her mouth the vomit forced its stinging path out through both nostrils. Some of this obviously squirted onto Lenny as he swore and punched her again. Muttering coarse obscenities he rolled her over, so she was face down and again sat on her. His hand went to the back of her head and her face was ground into the muck and grit on the metal floor.

Stunned and nauseated Barbara spewed again. As she struggled to breathe, she was terrified she would drown in her own vomit. She felt her wrists being seized and her arms were twisted up behind her back. Feebly she tried to heave Lenny off her back, but he was too heavy. In desperation she kicked up with her boots. Her left heel connected with something, possibly his elbow. He grunted and pounded the back of her head with his fist.

The blow smashed Barbara's face so hard on the floor she was stunned for a minute. Her whole head seemed to explode and throb, and she was sure her nose and left cheekbone were broken. She was only half-conscious as wet garbage spilled onto her.

Lenny swore at Wally. "Watch what ya doin', shit-head! Hurry up!"

"You're mad, Lenny. Let her go. We're in enough trouble already," Wally whined, fear making his voice tremble.

"Belt up, ya little runt! Get in and drive, nice and slow. Act normal," Lenny ordered.

Barbara heard the car door slam and the engine start.

They are going to take me away! she thought, panic rising to grip her.

To do what?

Her mind recoiled from the nightmare thoughts which crowded it.

The motor roared and the vehicle moved, to jerk and stall. A garbage bin fell with a clatter on her legs. Lenny uttered a stream of filth. "Hand brake, ya stupid drongo," he snarled.

Barbara heard Wally mutter an explanation which was drowned as the engine restarted. It revved twice. Then the vehicle began to move. Lenny remained in the back sitting on her and gripping her wrists. Again her stomach heaved. The warm liquid streamed out onto her face and solid lumps seemed to clog the back of her nostrils. The bitter taste of bile became all-pervading and she had to struggle for breath. The weight of the man on her back made this even more difficult. The terror of drowning built until she was gasping frantically.

For a fleeting moment she half-hoped she would black-out. It was too awful to face. But she didn't. The vehicle swung around the girls hut onto the bitumen. Wild hope surged. Perhaps the cadets at the guard tents would notice something?

They didn't. The vehicle drove past the canteen and guard tents and into the darkness without stopping. *Perhaps the civilian caretaker at the front gate will see me?* she thought. It was a straw to clutch at, but she knew after a couple of minutes that the hope was vain as the lights at the caretaker's hut registered in the corner of her eye.

Then hope welled again. The car was stopping! It pulled up and Lenny thumped on the roof telling Wally to open the gate. Barbara's half-formed wild plan of escape was dashed. In another minute they were

C.R. Cummings

through the front gate and running down the long driveway. Barbara felt the vehicle shudder over a cattle-grid, then the railway, then another grid. She was able to note that they turned right when they reached the highway. This surprised her as she had expected it to turn left towards Charters Towers.

Then her stomach churned again. She again had to struggle for breath, the mucousy liquid gurgling in her nostrils. Her senses swam and she closed her eyes and went limp. She could see nothing anyway.

It became a ride of terror, her imagination filling it with the disgusting defilements she feared were to come. And worse, she knew with terrifying certainty that once they had sated their bestial passions on her they would kill her.

They will have to, she reasoned.

The fear of death almost swamped her sense of reasoning and she sobbed (or tried to, the revolting rag in her mouth making it a painful grunt.).

Then her will re-asserted itself. *I want to live! I must escape!* she told herself. But how? Should she meekly submit to rape while waiting for a chance to run? Or should she fight tooth and nail regardless?

It was a topic she and her friends had discussed and had not been able to agree on. And that was then and this was now! She was a prisoner of a terrifying reality, of a brute stronger than she would ever have believed possible.

Oh God, please! she prayed.

That steadied her. She resolved she would beg for help from the Almighty. But not for any mercy from the monsters who held her!

Barbara's mind was such a turmoil of thoughts that she lost track of time. She was only aware that the utility was speeding along the highway. When it suddenly slowed and turned right onto a dirt road, she realised with a guilty start she had no idea how far they had come. Had they been driving for five minutes? Ten? Fifteen?

Dust billowed into the open back. Lenny coughed and swore. The dust coated the slime on Barbara's face and made her sneeze. The vehicle hit a bump. Barbara's face hammered onto the floor. A second later Lenny's bulk landed back on her with a bruising thud. It felt as though all the air were forced out of her lungs. She feared her ribs would splinter under his weight or that her heart or lungs would burst.

165

Another bump. Pain lanced through her. Her senses swam. She began to dry retch, cough and gasp all at once. It seemed she would die sooner than she expected.

More bumps, more pain. More dust, more coughing. Her ribs seemed like bands of hot iron. *Stop! Stop!* her mind cried. Bump! Her nose began to bleed. The side of her face was numb.

An even bigger bump tipped a garbage bin over with a crash. Lenny yelled and swore. Then the vehicle braked suddenly, shuddering on corrugations. Lenny rolled over her shoulders and head, crashing against the back of the cab. Barbara felt searing pain in her neck and right shoulder. She felt sure her neck was broken.

Lenny struggled to get up, only to be bounced back as the vehicle struck a washout with a jarring crash. Another garbage bin tipped. The lid came off. Barbara and Lenny were engulfed in rotting cabbage leaves and swill. Barbara had to arch her head up for fear she would drown in the tide of muck.

Lenny struggled to his knees yelling obscenities. He pounded on the roof of the cab. "Slow down, ya stupid bastard!"

The brakes came on again hard and the ute began to slow. Again Lenny lost his balance and fell amongst the garbage cans and muck. As he did Barbara realised he was not sitting on her and not holding her. *Is this my chance?* she wondered, terror momentarily paralysing her but then urging her to action. Fear of such a disgusting death got her moving.

In desperation she struggled to her hands and knees and went to fling herself over the side. The fear that jumping from a moving vehicle could injure her and would certainly hurt flashed across her mind but the alternative was much worse, so she grabbed the side and went to jump.

But Lenny was quick. His hand flashed out and he grabbed her sleeve. "Oh no ya don't!" he shouted. Barbara found herself dragged back and again flung on the tray of the ute on her back, squelching in the muck as she did. Lenny moved to grab both her wrists as she hit at him and screamed. Nearly beside herself with disappointment and fear Barbara screamed again. Lenny began slapping and punching her face and head.

For a few seconds Barbara was stunned by the blows and by the turn of events then fear spurred her to move. Spitting out the filthy rag and rotting garbage and ignoring the pain she squirmed and threshed around in a frantic attempt to break free.

But she wasn't strong enough and Lenny began to chuckle, obviously enjoying himself. Then the ute suddenly accelerated again. This caught Lenny off balance as he had been trying to get up. Shouting and swearing he rolled over on his back, still gripping Barbara's left wrist. She saw he was struggling to get up and knew it was her only hope and she at once seized the opportunity. As Lenny tried to roll back she lashed out with her right boot. It smacked hard into the side of Lenny's face.

"Aaaugh!" he cried, flinching back. In desperation Barbara kicked again. He moved to block her kick with his right hand, but the shock and pain of her blow made him let go of her wrist and he clutched at his face. Frantic to escape Barbara kicked wildly with both boots. This time her right boot struck his jaw, snapping it shut with an audible 'chunk!' Lenny rolled away, knocking over more garbage cans as he did. Rage and pain made him scream obscenities and threats.

Yelling obscenities Lenny struggled to get up. Still half on his back and off balance he pounded on the roof of the cab. "Stop ya bloody drongo! Stop!"

The ute's brakes again came hard on and it began to rapidly slow. Again Lenny lost his balance and fell amongst the garbage cans and muck. As he did Barbara realised she had to move. In desperation she struggled to her hands and knees and then flung herself over the side as the ute shuddered to a stop. She landed hard on gravel and dust. For a few seconds she was stunned by the hard landing, but fear spurred her to move.

Spitting out dirt and ignoring the pain from sharp little rocks and prickles she again got to her hands and knees. Billowing dust engulfed her and set her coughing. Tears of pain and misery went gritty in Barbara's eyes as she struggled painfully to get up. To her dismay the ute had stopped only ten metres further on.

As it did, she heard Wally call out: "What did ya say?"

Lenny coughed, then shouted, "You stupid bastard! You bounced us all over the place and the bitch has got away. Get after her!"

"Got away?" Wally replied.

"She just jumped out. Get after her!" Lenny shrieked.

To Barbara he sounded like he was still on his back and tangled up among the garbage. She did not hesitate. As she scrambled to her feet Barbara glimpsed the dark shapes of Lenny and Wally. Lenny was on his feet but as he moved he slipped. He fell with a clatter and a crash among the garbage cans, sparking a spurt of malicious satisfaction in Barbara as she started running. Wally appeared at the back of the ute but sounded confused and obviously had not grasped what was happening.

Lenny struggled up and slid over the side of the ute and shoved Wally hard. "Get after her you bloody fool!" he screamed.

Barbara ran, heading away from the ute and directly into the darkness. There wasn't a light to be seen, just dark bush. Barbara bolted into it. There was no moon but her eyes had adjusted to the dark. She dodged a tree and entered short grass. Behind her she heard Lenny shouting angrily and the sound made her emotions boil to utter fear. She sensed that he was no so enraged that he would just kill her. Terror spurred her legs.

But part of her mind was still functioning. Fence! Miss McEwen had run into a fence! Barbara's frantic gaze took in the post just in time for her to check her run. She hurled herself flat and rolled under the bottom strand. Barbs tore at her trousers and nicked her buttocks and she was very aware of sticks, burs and spear grass scratching and prickling her bare skin.

Scrambling to her feet she fled. As she ran Barbara realised that there was something revolting still stuck in her mouth. It was hampering her breathing. Desperate to get away she stuck her fingers in her mouth and fished out more of the revolting muck which was choking her. Ah! Cool air was sucked in. She fled.

Wally finally moved, dashing after her.

Twang!

"Yaaah! Ah, bloody hell!" Wally howled in pain as he ran full tilt into the barbed wire fence.

Barbara couldn't help it. She uttered a malicious whoop. Still running she dodged the black-trunked ironbarks easily. A glance behind her showed Wally still at the fence. Lenny was just a dark bulk struggling to follow.

Barbara ran as fast as she could, thankful she had her boots. Fear and desperation lent her strength and made her oblivious to her physical condition. Then she stumbled on a log in the grass. She sprawled in the dust, skinning her knees and knuckles on deadfall. Her ankle hurt but the boot had saved it from a sprain. Instantly she sprang up and started running again.

Her eyes detected the shadow. A washout. She jumped it but miscalculated and went sprawling again. A quick study showed her that the washout was far too small to hide in. Picking herself up and dusting knees and hands that smarted with pain she glanced back. Through eyes blurred by terror she saw that she was 50 paces from her pursuers.

At the fence there was yelling. Two dark forms could just be seen. It appeared that Lenny had snagged himself on the barbed wire and was yelling for Wally to unhook him.

Gasping great gulps of air Barbara paused and crouched in the washout. She needed to recover her breath and get her bearings. *I can probably outrun Lenny but not Wally,* she thought. Anxiously she watched the dark shapes of the two men stand up. They started walking in her direction but not directly toward her.

"Where'd she go?" Wally bleated.

"Shut up and stand still," Lenny ordered.

"But she's gettin' away."

"Shut up, ya dill. We gotta listen to see which way she went," Lenny snapped. The two men paused. Barbara crouched lower among the prickly grass. The men were so close she could hear them breathing heavily.

Wally said, "Why did you want to stop here? We're only just past the Saltpan Turnoff."

"I didn't want to stop till we got back to the hut," Lenny snarled. "You were driving so bloody fast over the bumps we were bouncing all over the place and I got tossed off."

"By why did ya grab her? What were ya gunna do?" Wally replied.

Lenny swore. "What do ya think, ya stupid nong? Do you think I snatched this red-headed bitch just to talk about old times?"

Wally shook his head. "You're mad, Lenny! I knew I shouldn't have told ya I seen her that first night when I went to help Johnno. You've been crazy ever since."

Lenny leaned on a tree and peered into the darkness. He was breathing fast and wheezing. "You would be too if she'd shot you. I'm gunna make her feel as much pain as she made me. She's gunna pay for what she done," he snarled

"What ya gunna do Lenny? Christ mate, we gotta let her go and get out of here."

"Shut up ya fool. We can't let her go. Not now. She'd dob us straight into the coppers. Besides, we got the big job to pull off tomorrow night."

"What will you do with her?"

Lenny gave an evil chuckle. "What d'ya think?"

"Christ Lenny. We're in enough trouble already. That'll be rape. You'll go to jail for years," Wally replied.

"They gotta catch me first," Lenny snarled. "Now help me find the bitch."

Wally started again. "Stop it Lenny! Let her go. We're already in the shit. You'll just make it worse. She'll talk."

"No she won't," Lenny replied. "I'll make sure she doesn't."

"Christ Lenny, what'dya mean? How ya gunna stop her talking?" Wally asked.

Barbara could tell he was really scared and wondered how she could turn it to her advantage.

Lenny snapped, "Stop whining, ya little shit! I'll tie her up and leave her in the hut. By the time they find her we'll be clear away."

No he won't, Barbara told herself. *He will kill me. I've got to get away.*

Lenny started forward. "Come on, let's find her. She's just here somewhere."

Barbara crouched even lower, ignoring the irritation from the sharp ends of the tuft of grass. She turned, ready to run. The two men came closer but still not directly toward her. She heard Wally stumble and swear. Her heart hammered wildly and she was worried they would hear her breathing. To her it sounded like a wire brush in a drainpipe.

There was a scuttling, thumping noise off to her right.

"There she is!" Wally yelled. He began to run. Lenny started running too. But he stopped about 10 paces from her.

"Stop Wally. It's only a bloody wallaby, ya Wally!"

There was a crash and oaths from Wally. He had tripped over a log in the grass. Lenny went towards him. The wallaby thudded off into the night.

"Shut up Wally and listen," Lenny snarled.

"How we gunna find her in the dark?" Wally whined.

"Shut up I said. She's only a girl. She won't go far. She'll be just here somewhere hidin'."

Barbara's spirits jumped. *Only a girl eh!* she thought angrily. *They are forgetting I am a cadet. I'll show them!*

It dawned on her that they thought she would be scared of the bush at night and would not be able to go far. Now she remembered all those night fieldcraft and navigation exercises over the last three years and gave a thin smile of satisfaction. They had made her quite familiar with bush at night. In a flash of insight she realised she was probably more experienced in that environment than either of the two men.

Lenny was now about 15 paces to her right. He stopped moving. "Is there a torch in the ute Wally?" he asked. Barbara's heart sank.

"Yeah. In the glove box," Wally replied.

"Go and get it," Lenny ordered.

Wally started walking. Barbara took the risk and began crawling along the washout away from Lenny. This was back towards the road but that seemed like a good plan. She saw Lenny turn and look in her direction. Fear gripped her and she paused and held her breath.

Wally stumbled and swore, his boots crackling on dead leaves and twigs. Lenny looked the other way and then walked a few more paces away. Barbara estimated that he was at least 30 paces distant now. When Barbara heard Wally swearing as he negotiated the barbed wire fence she considered running.

She had half formed an impression and now, as she watched, it was confirmed. Lenny was limping. Then the fear clutched at her throat as Lenny turned and started limping towards her.

Has he seen me? she wondered.

Her heart hammered furiously as adrenaline prepared her to flee. She heard Wally open the car door. That decided her. By then Lenny was only 20 paces away, looming like a great ape in the starlight, muttering to himself.

Barbara sprang into a sprint. Lenny yelled and flung out an arm. She went sideways across his front. He broke into a run. Barbara ran as she had never run before. She dodged trees and anthills, skirted a bush and jumped a log.

Anxiously she glanced back. Lenny was crashing through the scrub in pursuit. He was cursing and breathing hard, and he was obviously limping. Already he was at least 15 or 20 paces behind. Spurred by desperation Barbara ran on.

She jumped a log. The sharp pain of a stitch began in her side. She ignored it and ran. By now she was starting to pant and sweat by this.

A single stumble and I am doomed! she thought anxiously.

Her whole being swamped by desperation Barbara ran on, skirting a patch of low bush as she went. Lenny tore through it and swore. Barbara glanced back again and saw that Lenny was further behind, at least 20 or 30 paces.

I am winning! she thought. A glimmer of hope sparked in her mind.

A light flickered. It was Wally with the torch. He was nearly a hundred paces behind but might still catch her. Barbara cast about for a plan other than simple flight as she knew her strength was going. She could feel her heart thudding heavily. Her breath was now great sucking hot gasps and the stitch grew worse to hot needles.

Then Lenny tripped. He fell heavily and cursed loudly. Barbara at once eased her pace to a walk and turned sharp left. She knew she had to conserve her strength or she was done. Off to her left rear she could see Wally's torch now probing in her direction, but it was too weak to reach her.

Lenny struggled to his feet and started running again. Barbara halted behind a tree, leaning on its rough bark. Lenny ran only about 10 paces then stopped, looking in all directions. It looked as though he had temporarily lost her. He yelled, "Wally! Git that bloody torch over here! The bitch has gone to ground again. Come on! Bloody well run!"

Barbara could hear his breath sucking in great gasps. He was unfit alright.

Wally began running. Barbara knew she could not wait so she began walking away, keeping the tree between her and Lenny. She was hoping the sound of Wally's running would hide the sound of her own progress.

Lenny swore again. "Hurry up Wally, run ya bloody slug! Jeez, is she gunna pay for this. My leg hurts like hell," he yelled.

"You wanta be (puff) careful. You've only had the plaster off for a week. The doctor said it was a nasty break," Wally replied as he puffed over to join him.

Barbara stopped behind another iron bark as Wally reached Lenny. Despite her fear she managed a thin smile.

Broke his leg did I! Serve the bastard right! she thought with grim satisfaction.

Wally swung the torch around, the beam shining out through the bush. "Which way did she go?" he asked.

Barbara turned and peeked around the tree, tensed to run. Her whole body was trembling and sweating, and she tried not to gasp in air. She became aware of the rough bark of the tree scraping the skin of her hands and realised that the tickling sensation was caused by ants running over her body.

An ant bit her painfully. She stifled a yelp and stepped back from the tree, her attention still on the two men as she used both hands to brush the ants off. Several more bit her hands while she did this.

To her immense relief Lenny pointed away to her left. "Over here I think," he said. Wally shone his torch that way and they both began walking slowly in that direction. Soon they were a good 30 paces off. Barbara at once began 'Ghost walking' away from them.

Frequent glances behind showed her that the men were moving even further away. She began to hope she might escape. Carefully she continued to walk in exactly the opposite direction, and this caused her to circle back to the left as the men cast back in the direction she had actually gone.

Then she trod on a dry stick which snapped noisily. She froze but the men were making so much noise themselves they hadn't heard her. By this time she was a good 50 or more paces from them.

Something ahead made her pause. She puzzled for a moment over what she was looking at and then realised it was the white utility showing through the trees. It was only 50 paces to her left-front.

An idea sprang into her mind. *The car! Maybe I can immobilize it?* she thought.

She was sure the crooks would use it to search for her. Biting her lip with anxiety she looked back. The two men seemed to be even further away. They were muttering angrily but she couldn't hear what they were saying.

As quickly as she dared Barbara walked towards the vehicle. Just in time she remembered the fence. Cautiously she went down on her bottom and then edged herself under it diagonally feet first as she had been taught, holding the bottom strand to keep it clear of her clothes. Anxiety over the barbed wire tearing her tender flesh overrode the discomfort of stones, sticks and prickles on her buttocks and back. On the other side she moved into a crouch and looked back. To her relief the men were still searching and were at least a hundred paces away.

A few steps took Barbara to the dirt road. Quickly she walked to the vehicle and began looking around. A light flickered in the corner of her eye. To her dismay she saw that the torch was shining in her direction!

The men were heading back!

They weren't running though so she didn't think they had seen her. From the angry muttering they were having some sort of argument. Barbara hesitated. She did not know much about cars and wasn't sure if she could damage it enough.

Should I just start running again? she wondered. And if so, which way? She decided that she would have to use the road as a navigation guide. *But I will have to keep clear of it because the men will use the car to search for me,* she thought.

The car!

Can I use the car to escape? she wondered.

Chapter 19

INTO THE FIRE

B arbara had never driven a car. She had only turned 17 a few weeks before and had not felt the need to get a learner driver's licence. Nor was she very interested in machines. But she had an idea of what to do and her need was urgent.

If I can get the car started perhaps I will be able to outdistance the men and reach safety, she thought.

For a few seconds she flustered. A glance showed that the men were heading back towards the utility. *No time,* she thought, her body quivering with anxiety. Forcing herself to concentrate she reached in the driver's door and felt around the steering column.

Yes! She was in luck. The key was still in the ignition.

There wasn't a moment to lose. Barbara opened the door, swung it wide and slipped into the driver's seat. She left the door open so as to avoid making a noise.

A glance through the side window showed the torch much closer. *Oh! I must do something!* she flustered.

But what? She fluttered her fingertips together in nervous frustration. Cold sweat broke out all over her and she began to gulp air as though she was running again.

Oh help! What do I do? Which pedal is which? she worried.

Frantically cudgelling her memory she went through what an overenthusiastic boyfriend had bored her with: accelerator on the right, (She could hardly feel it through the thick sole of her army boot), clutch on the left (What the hell is a clutch?) and brake in the middle. She gave the clutch a tentative push with her left boot.

Oh help! The men were much closer. She considered jumping out and running then steadied herself. *They will hear me anyway and chase me,* she thought. She realised that she had left it too late and now had few choices.

Gears?

What was a gear? Her clothes she called 'gear'. Did it matter? Yes it did. The car had to be in the correct gear to start. She felt around next to her and found the gear lever!

More fumbling. No. It wasn't an automatic. Her quick hope died. Tentatively she pushed at the gear lever and felt it move. Hoping it was in the correct setting she bit her lip and again experienced a few seconds of fluster. *I will have to risk it,* she thought in desperation. The torch was nearly at the fence.

To Barbara she seemed to be all fingers and thumbs and her palms were slippery with sweat. She wiped them on her shirt. Then, with a sudden spurt of resolve, she turned the ignition key. Red lights came on in the dashboard and there was a whining noise. The car convulsed and jumped. She let the key go. The noises stopped but two red lights stayed on.

"Hey!" came Lenny's voice, yelling in alarm.

The men were at the fence! Clutch! She realised that she had started the car in gear and stalled the motor. *Get out and run! They are getting through the fence! No! Try again!*

Almost beside herself with desperation Barbara pushed in the clutch and turned the key. The motor whirred, then roared into life.

The men were through the fence!

Too late to run! But the car wouldn't move! *Oh yes! Handbrake. Wally forgot that,* she remembered. Luckily she knew where that was, thanks to having one dig into her when her boyfriend had been trying to kiss her one day. Quickly she fumbled and undid it.

Barbara remembered the clutch had to be let out slowly or the motor would stall. But how slowly? She had no idea but began easing it up. But her right boot was on the accelerator and the engine roared into a screaming whine which drowned out the men's voices.

The car wouldn't move!

And there was Lenny, clawing at the passenger door. A hand reached in on her right and grabbed at her sleeve – Wally.

Barbara forgot about the clutch. Her left boot came off and the engine, howling at almost maximum revolutions, was suddenly connected to the transmission. The wheels spun and gripped. The utility gave a mighty leap and the driver's door swung closed with a ferocious jerk. There was a *thud!*, a *whack!*, and a scream. Wally's hand let go. The vehicle skidded forward.

Then it all happened too fast. Barbara saw that Lenny had lost his grip on the other door. But in her terror the car began to go faster and faster until the noise of the overdriven gears became a terrifying howl.

Lights! I need lights! she realised in panic.

She could barely make out the road in the starlight. Shocked by the speed at which things were happening (and going wrong) she gripped the shuddering wheel, bemused by the noise and movement. With her left hand she began pulling and pushing the knobs on the dashboard.

Orange hazard lights flickered, confusing her more. Then she remembered that in many cars the lights were on a little lever on the steering column. With her right hand she groped and found one. A bump made it go down and orange lights began to flick on and off, confusing her even more.

But it was too late. The front wheels hit a washout. The steering wheel flicked, striking her left hand so hard it went numb and she let go. The utility slewed sharply to the right. Its wheels struck the earth drain and the vehicle bounced. Barbara was flung up and forward, striking her face on the steering wheel.

The utility leaped like a horse stung by a wasp. It bounced and clattered over the drain at an angle, throwing Barbara violently from side to side. Garbage bins clattered and rattled in the back.

Crash!

Barbara again hit the steering wheel. Her face and body felt numb. Her head throbbed and her vision went blurred.

No it wasn't. It was dust. She coughed and rubbed at her battered face. As she did she became aware that her skin was covered in grit which was stuck on by the wet garbage. But that was trivial physical discomfort and fear got her moving.

The engine stopped and in the silence she heard shouted obscenities.

The men! *Oh no!* she thought. *They are still after me and they will be madder than ever!*

Desperately she fumbled with the door. It swung open and she slid out onto unsteady legs. She had no idea how far she had come but thought it must have been a hundred metres or so. In the starlight she glimpsed Lenny's massive bulk hobbling rapidly towards her along the road.

He was about 50 metres away. There was no sign of Wally. Barbara turned and took to the bush again, this time on the other side of the road.

Barbara forgot about the fence. She only remembered it when she had run about 30 paces. Then she slowed down but could see no sign of one. As she did she looked back. Lenny was nearly at the utility. From his language and tone of voice he was almost beside himself with rage.

Barbara also became aware of a flickering glow. For a moment she puzzled. Then she realised it came from a vehicle's headlights. Someone was coming!

Can I flag them down and get them to help? she wondered.

She paused as the vehicle came into view from the same direction they had come. In the beam of its headlights she saw Lenny waving it down. The sight made her pause.

The ugly suspicion was confirmed. The vehicle, a 4 Wheel Drive light truck, shuddered to a halt in a cloud of dust. A voice yelled from it. "What's up Lenny? Ya had a prang?"

"Nah! Quick Johnno. We gotta catch a girl. Let me in."

Johnno!

The name connected. A mate of theirs. *Another one of the mongrels!* Barbara swore to herself and turned. Sobbing with fear she began running into the bush.

As she ran, she heard the vehicle's door slam. Its engine roared and it swung off the road and into the bush. Its headlights swept up and down as it bounced over the drain, but then they lit up a great swathe of bush— and Barbara. She considered throwing herself flat in the grass but guessed that was futile. This was an entirely different problem. The vehicle was designed to be driven through the bush and with its headlights on she had nowhere to hide. All she could do was run.

Out of the frying pan, she thought. Even as the words flitted across her mind a savage *crack!* beside her made her realise there were still depths of terror to be plumbed.

Lenny had fired a rifle at her!

Barbara glanced back as she ran. The vehicle was only thirty or forty metres back and catching up quickly. In desperation she swerved and ran between two trees too close together for the vehicle.

Crack! Bang!

She knew what it was. Cadets had taught her that. The crack was the sound of a bullet breaking the sound barrier near her; the 'thump' the sound of the gun going off.

Lenny means to murder me! she thought, the fear welling up to grip her with a new intensity of terror.

She knew she was in trouble with a vengeance. In a frantic effort to escape she dodged around more trees. The vehicle hit a log with an audible crunch. It bounced and she heard the gun go off followed by angry swearing. It gave her a few paces lead.

But the vehicle came on, going more slowly as it weaved around the trees and other obstacles. Barbara went off sideways.

To her horror and dismay a spotlight came on. Its beam wavered and then pinned her. She knew what was coming and dodged frantically sideways.

Crack!

The bullet struck the ground ahead of her in a skitter of tiny sparks. Her bowels almost voided themselves. She swerved, jumped a log, then tore through some spiky bushes which scratched her thighs even through her trousers.

A terrible feeling of helplessness began to creep in. It was like a cat playing with a mouse. Wherever she ran the crucifying beam went also. The vehicle, a 'Landcruiser' she recognised, had only to keep her in sight until she was exhausted.

And that isn't far off! she told herself grimly.

A painful 'stitch' had developed in her right side. She seemed to be gasping air from a fire and her legs felt like lead. In her heart she knew she couldn't last much longer.

The grass was longer here too, nearly waist high, and it impeded her running. Several times she stumbled but desperation kept her going.

Ahead in the beam of the headlights she detected a shadow, a washout or gully of some sort. It was angling in from her right. It led towards a wall of thicker timber. *That must be a creek line,* she reasoned.

That offered her hope. It would be somewhere to hide. It might even stop the terrible machine with its lights. She felt so exposed in them.

She swerved away from the gully and ran parallel to it towards the creek: 50 paces, 30, 20...

Crack!

Her left arm stung like fury. A wave of cold followed by hot swept over her.

That bullet grazed my arm! she thought in shock.

It was all too horrible to be true, but she knew with sickening certainty that it was. Now the vehicle was only about 10 paces behind. It was rapidly catching up. She swerved left around a tree and ran on. Shadows ahead indicated a steep drop.

She went over the bank at full speed, skidding down an almost vertical earth bank onto a grassy flat beside the trees lining the creek. Behind her the vehicle stopped on top.

Barbara checked in her stride. The vehicle's lights weren't on her here. *I am in 'dead ground',* she thought.

So which way? Right, left or across the creek? The spotlight shone over her head into the creek bed. That decided her. She turned and ran right.

About 10 paces along, she saw the dark cleft of the gully she had run beside. It led back almost beside the vehicle. Quickly she scrambled up it on hands and knees.

As she did, she heard the vehicle's doors slam but its engine and headlights stayed on. Ignoring the dust and small stones which dug into her knees and hands Barbara lay flat in the metre-deep runnel and peered through the grass.

A man ran past only two metres from her and went down into the creek. She realised that he must be Johnno when she heard Lenny's voice further to her right. Then she saw him, rifle in hand, as he limped into the headlights.

"Which way did she go?" Lenny yelled.

"Dunno. There's somethin' behind this tree," Johnno replied.

"Only a bloody possum. You got your torch?"

"Yeah."

"Start lookin' fer tracks."

Barbara felt her sweating body freeze. Tracks! Of course! These men hunted animals, whether for sport or a living she did not know.

They will find me in minutes! she thought. She had to act.

It was no good just running. Even in this extremity of fear she could still reason that. The vehicle would just run her to earth again. So the vehicle or its lights must be her target. She began crawling up the washout, very conscious of the voices in the creek behind her.

"What you tryin' to kill this sheila for?" Johnno asked.

"So she won't talk. She knows too much," Lenny replied.

"Jeez! The boss is gunna be cranky when he hears about it, what with the big job termorrow night," Johnno answered.

"Don't tell the bastard," Lenny growled.

"Do we have to shoot her? Can't we have some fun with her first?" Johnno asked.

Lenny swore. Barbara was so appalled at the man's callousness she thought she would be sick again.

By this time she was only three metres from the vehicle. She crawled out of the washout and across to it, her head half-turned to watch the creek bank. Blood pounded in her ears and she feared she was going to black out.

The vehicle's door was open. Shaking with stress she stood up and looked in. It took a moment for her eyes to adjust to the semi-darkness. *Can I drive this one, or will they just shoot me while I am trying to turn it?* she thought.

She was going over options in her head when she spied the packet of cigarettes and box of matches on the seat. That sight changed her plan.

Instantly an idea came to her and she snatched up the matchbox. The old saying 'into the fire' flitted across her mind again. *Fire! I'll show them,* she thought as she slid the box open.

Amazingly, her hands didn't shake. Gripped by fierce determination she crouched low in the grass. A quick glance. The men were still in the creek. She struck the match. It flared up. Carefully she held it into the base of a tuft of grass.

Smoke curled. Individual stalks caught fire, then burned through, then fell off. *Is the grass too wet?* she wondered. In desperation she tried again.

Even as she struck the second match, she heard Johnno call, "There's her tracks!"

No more time!

Barbara dropped the burning match into the grass, stood up and reached in. Taking a great gulp of air to stiffen her resolve she turned the key. At once the motor stopped.

"Hey!" Johnno yelled.

"The bitch! She's at the truck!" Lenny cried.

Barbara paused to pull the key out. As she did smoke made her cough and her eyes watered. *Enough! Run!*

She turned and fled, fearing she had left her run too late. Out of the corner of her eye she saw Johnno scramble up out of the washout with his torch. He shone it after her. "There she goes!" he yelled.

"Where?" came Lenny's voice. He was still climbing the creek bank. "Hey! Fire!"

"I can't fire. I can't see her. Where is she?" retorted Lenny.

"No! Here! A fire! Put it out!" Johnno cried in alarm.

Barbara glanced back and saw a red flame flare up under the vehicle. Johnno began stamping at it with his boot.

Lenny yelled, "Where'd she go? Johnno! Shine your torch!"

"Bugger her! Help me put this fire out," Johnno replied in an agitated voice.

Barbara stopped running and began walking in a big circle to the left, keeping her eye on them. By then she was fifty metres away and thought that the light of the growing fire would blind them.

She saw Lenny run past the vehicle, looking for her. "Where'd she go, Johnno? Give me your torch."

"Never mind her! Help me put out this fire!" wailed Johnno

Johnno beat at the flames, but they grew and spread under the vehicle out of his reach. Barbara saw fire lick up around the front wheels.

Johnno began to scream, "Lenny! Never mind her. Help me push the truck out of this fire."

Barbara paused behind a large gum tree to watch. She was gasping for breath and sweat streamed off her. She wiped her mouth and found it covered with dust and blood from her nose. Her body seemed to quiver and sting all over.

Johnno climbed in to put the vehicle out of gear and to take the handbrake off, but Lenny backed away as sparks flared up. Smoke billowed up. Johnno jumped out and ran around to the front of his vehicle. Leaning on it in the flames he screamed again, "Push Lenny! Push!"

"Too late! The engine's on fire," Lenny cried.

"Ah shit! Bugger it!" Johnno wailed.

Chapter 20

NIGHT NAVIGATION

Gripped by feelings of fierce exultation Barbara watched the growing flames. *Serve the mongrels right!* she thought.

She saw that the grass fire was spreading out in a wide semi-circle, leaving the burning vehicle in the midst of a black, smoking void. The flames spread quickly along under the vehicle until it was ablaze from end to end.

Lenny shouted, "Back off Johnno! The petrol tank will blow in a minute!"

"Petrol! Bloody hell! There's a 'forty-four' of petrol in the back. Bugger you Lenny. I'm gunna kill that bitch!" Johnno screamed.

"Which way did she go?" Lenny asked.

Barbara could clearly see them. The fire was halfway to her, spreading slowing in an ever-widening curve. She turned and began walking away, keeping a big tree between her and them and hoping the flickering shadows and smoke would hide her.

Off to her left rear she heard a voice. "Hey Lenny, what's goin' on?"

It was Wally. Barbara had forgotten Wally. With her heart hammering with anxiety she crouched in the grass and saw him go past only twenty metres away.

"Lenny! What's goin' on? Answer me for Christ sake! I'm hurt. I got a broken arm," he wailed.

Whoomph!

A huge fireball soared up, causing all the men to cry out. The flames reached the leaves of the trees and these began to burn and crackle. Barbara saw an open-mouthed Wally stagger back on the edge of the grass-fire. As she looked there was an even bigger fireball as the 44-gallon drum of petrol exploded.

The drum hurled itself into the air in a terrifying scythe of liquid fire. Barbara glimpsed Lenny and Johnno running off in the opposite direction. Within seconds there seemed to be fire everywhere. The vehicle was a blazing wreck. Barbara was delighted yet appalled by what she had done.

She decided to put some distance between herself and vengeful pursuit. It was the men she was worried about, not the bushfire. There was not enough grass and very little wind. She knew it was unusual for bushfires to be serious in North Queensland. Already the grass fire had become patchy and it did not look as though the tree canopy would catch fire. Even the leaves over the 4WD had now burnt themselves out without spreading flames to neighbouring trees.

Barbara's eyes smarted from the smoke and the fire had temporarily ruined her night vision, so she stumbled a bit as she walked. She had to suppress several sneezes by squeezing up on the base of her nose. That was a trick she had learned at cadets. But this reminded her of just how sore it was. It felt like a huge ripe tomato and pressing on it caused her to wince at the pain.

"I must look a sight," she muttered to herself, clutching the torn shirt across her front. She was vaguely conscious of other bodily discomforts: skin coated in grit and muck, clothes too, prickles, scratches and bruises. But they were not important. Pushing her physical condition to the back of her mind she concentrated on getting away.

After a few more minutes, she arrived on the bank of the creek and carefully made her way down the grassy slope. It was only a small creek, its bed just dry sand. Using one hand to shield her eyes, she picked her way through the bent and twisted paperbarks which lined its course.

"God I'm thirsty! I wish there was some water," she murmured, her eyes searching the sand.

With a regretful sigh she crossed and climbed up the far bank. Here she paused and looked around. The glow of the fires showed dull red under the smoke a couple of hundred metres to her left. For the first time she felt fairly safe from pursuit.

"Now, where am I and how do I get home?" she asked herself. For a minute she scanned the bush. Not a light to be seen. Nor did any high ground show against the stars.

Just flat savannah woodland, she decided.

"I must be east of the camp because we didn't cross the Bunyip or the Burdekin," she reasoned. "So the question is, do I go north or south to the highway?" After a moment's thought she muttered, "We turned right onto the dirt road so I must be south of it. But should I go near the highway? They are sure to search along it."

Still trembling from reaction she stood and pondered the problem. Her heart rate had slowed to normal, but she was feeling distinctly anxious and knew she was stressed and hurting. It took a couple of minute's reasoning before the idea came to her that walking west back to camp might be the safest option.

It can't be too far, she decided. *Less than 30 kilometres because we didn't pass through the township of Mingela.* It seemed the best idea and the safest. *The danger of treading on a snake in the dark will be much less than being seen by those men in daylight,* she told herself.

"I wish I hadn't thought of snakes," she said, remembering a deadly Western Taipan which had slid through their camp when she was a corporal: two metres of honey-coloured death.

Then she thought of wild pigs and bulls. "Stop being a silly little girl!" she reproved herself. "Now, which way is west?"

There was no moon. Barbara searched the heavens for the Southern Cross. It was nowhere to be seen. Exasperated she searched again, then remembered a lesson on 'Navigation by the Stars' that reminded her that in December the Southern Cross was not up at night, was not visible to people in North Queensland.

Oh help! I wish I'd paid more attention in those lessons on finding direction by the stars, she thought.

Her gaze travelled hopefully from constellation to constellation. To her consternation there were so many, like a brilliant scatter of jewels on black silk.

Then a line of three bright stars side by side caught her eye. *Ah! Yes. That bright star is Sirius. And there is the Constellation of Orion,* she told herself. Barbara felt unreasonably cheered by the discovery. But then frustration set in. How did she use it?

"Those three stars are Orion's belt," she said, pointing with her right hand. "Now how do I use it? What's the name of those stupid stars at the top end? Ooh!" she groaned in frustration.

She stood for a couple of minutes silently cursing herself for not having learned. Then a distant shout brought her back to earth.

It was the men calling out over at the fire. She listened. They seemed a long way away. *What are they shouting about?* she wondered. The breeze had blown the fire away from her. She could see a few tiny flickers of flame through the trees, but they seemed a long way off.

"I'd better get going. I'll just put a bit more distance between those men and me," she whispered.

So saying she turned her back on the glow and began tramping through the scrub. It was easy going physically although the grass was scratchy and irritating when the spear grass seeds stuck through the cloth of her trousers. It was only the fear of snakes which made it hard to put one foot in front of another. She wished she had a stick.

After five minutes she came to another small creek running at right angles to her direction of travel. It was dry as well.

"Oh blast! God, I'm thirsty! Perhaps I should follow this creek? Maybe I'll find a pool of water?" she wondered.

Then she remembered that snakes were more prevalent along creek lines. Also it would be slow and difficult going with all the rocks, logs and bent trees. She tried to visualise the map to get an idea of the general trend of the creeks.

"I think they mostly flow south on the southern side of the highway. But then, Five Mile Creek and Scrubby Creek flow north. Oh blow!" In her distress and frustration she stamped her foot. She could tell by the way the trees were bent and by where the dry grass and other flood debris was caught which way the creek ran.

Then she slapped her forehead.

"Oh, I'm a fool! I don't need to know the names of those stupid stars to be able to navigate by them," she said aloud.

The sound of her voice caused some small creature to scuttle away a bit further up the creek. It frightened her. *Pig? No. Too small. Oh help! Can I hear something slithering?* she thought. She strained her eyes to peer into the gloom.

Summoning up her resolve not to panic she forced herself to walk the few paces up out of the creek bed onto the grassy flat. It was much more open there, the grass very short and in isolated clumps. Suppressing a fit of shivering Barbara looked up at the stars. What was bothering her was remembering a heated argument after a lesson on navigation by the stars. Capt Conkey had pointed out that the person teaching the lesson had used a diagram drawn for the northern hemisphere and which was therefore upside down for Australia.

After a moment's thought Barbara considered she had the thing correct in her head. Pointing at the stars she told herself, "Now, there's

Orion and those three stars are his belt. The three in line going away from the belt are his sword and it hangs down. So those two are his knees and feet. That means those are his arms, or are they his shoulders? Anyway, a line joining them is approximately East-West."

Her gaze travelled across the sky. Having worked that out Barbara felt an immense sense of relief. "Knowledge certainly is power," she muttered. She then selected a bright star to the West. "I'll walk towards that, but I must remember it will sink and set as the earth revolves. So then I'll pick that one."

Despite feeling sick and battered she began to stride confidently through the dark bush.

Twenty minutes later she came to another small creek. It ran diagonally across her course. Again she made her way carefully down the steep bank and this time was even sufficiently aware to make sure she left no tracks in the dry sand by stepping from stone to stone but when she scrambled up the far bank she was temporarily disoriented. She had to pause to relocate her star.

"Where is it? Oh blast!"

She checked from Orion but couldn't see that particular star. A tree was hiding it. After moving sideways 5 paces she located it. It was now low to the west, just above the treetops. She selected another star that was well above it.

The halt made her realise just how distressed, sick and sore she felt. "God, I'm thirsty," she muttered again. She felt her face. It was very dry and flushed. "I was cold from sweat a while ago. I'm not sweating. That's bad. I must be dehydrating. I'll get heat exhaustion if I'm not careful," she told herself.

It took an effort to force her tired muscles into motion. "Ouch! That hurts! I must have pulled a muscle when I was running," she grumbled. With her right hand she massaged the sore thigh as she walked, hoping it would ease up with use.

Despite feeling that she just wanted to lie down and cry she went doggedly on. There didn't seem to be another living creature. Not a sound or a light. Her eyes grew weary of straining in the dark. Her attention started to wander. She easily avoided the trees but more and more frequently ploughed into small bushes or stumbled on logs.

She plodded through another dense patch of spear grass and the long, twisted seeds scratched at her thighs. Irritated by the pin-pricks she stopped and gingerly extracted all she could find by feel.

Was that a sound? she thought. She cupped her hand to her ear. *I thought I heard a car.*

Anxiously she searched the dark skyline to the north. The highway was somewhere in that direction and she hoped to see the loom of headlights. A gentle breeze rustled the leaves and caressed her heated face, making her aware that her temperature was well above normal. She felt slightly feverish and had a bad headache.

After checking her direction she started walking west again.

I wonder what time it is? It must be well after midnight.

Gritting her teeth she resumed walking. It soon became a real plod. Her legs grew more tired and the army boots felt heavier and heavier. Her head began to hang as fatigue set in. She lost track of time and was hardly conscious of distance. Sore muscles became more and more of a problem. Her mouth felt very dry. Her bruised and battered head throbbed and ached.

She stumbled on an ant hill and nearly fell. "Gosh! I was nearly asleep. I'm not going west at all. I'm going south. I'd better keep my wits about me," she told herself.

After checking the stars Barbara corrected her direction and went on. The walk developed all the qualities of a nightmare: hazy vision, vague shadows, never-ending and monotonous bush, her boots walking on what felt like chewing gum.

A meteorite flashed briefly. Barbara tried to make a wish but confused two. She realised that she just wanted to get safely back to camp more than she wanted to see Gordon.

That made her remember Weismann. *The bastard! He was stealing food from the pantry,* she thought. A spurt of white-hot rage suffused her blood. *He saw Lenny grab me but did nothing! He didn't even call out!* she thought angrily.

The anger helped her. She tramped on for a good ten minutes, seething with indignation. Then she began to relive the abduction but that was too upsetting to think about, so she forced the memories from her mind.

I've got enough to deal with, she told herself.

Something moved ahead.

She stopped. Thudding and snorting. Something large and black. Pig? No. Cattle. She half relaxed. *They won't be wild cattle. They will just be ordinary beef cattle,* she told herself in an attempt to steady suddenly fluttering nerves. *But there might be a bull.*

With an effort of willpower she resumed walking, moving slowly ahead until she saw more cattle. The animals were mostly lying down. Alarm spread among them and they rose, shuffling and snorting. Barbara kept walking determinedly. The cattle were off to one side. There was a sudden rush of hooves. Her heart leapt in alarm. Then she breathed out and relaxed. She wasn't being attacked. The animals had taken fright and bolted. They only went 50 or a hundred paces before stopping in a milling, dusty throng to watch her; black and grey shapes in the gloom.

Barbara came to a fence with an obvious vehicle track inside it. *A fence. That must lead somewhere. Perhaps to a station homestead? Which way?* she wondered.

North! Barbara began walking along the wheel ruts, feeling a sense of relief. *With a bit of luck it won't be long, and I will be safe,* she thought.

Black patches on the grey ribbon of sand puzzled her. Then she realised what they were: cow turds. At that she even managed a smile. She had nearly stepped in one.

There were more cattle. They scattered ahead of her to her right. Drifting dust made her sneeze and she tasted grit in her teeth.

Something large bulked ahead. It stood in a grey wasteland vacated by the cattle. Against the stars Barbara made out the silhouette of a wind pump. The large thing was a water tank.

Water!

Barbara walked eagerly to the base of the tank. The ground was thickly spattered with cow pats, but she ignored them. A quick search failed to discover a tap on either the corrugated iron tank, or the steel frame of the windmill. Leading out along the other side was a long drinking trough.

Barbara stopped and put her hand down into it. The trough was full of water. It felt surprisingly cold. Despite her thirst she hesitated over drinking. She had memories of similar troughs, all lined with green slime and murky brown sediment.

But I need the water. And there isn't a house in sight. It might make me a bit sick but that will take hours and I should be safe by then.

She leaned over the trough and gently scooped up water in her cupped hands. Gingerly she sipped at it. It tasted alright but smelt horrible. Only after the first handful did she realise just how thirsty she really was.

Forcing herself to ignore the smell and thoughts of the cow poo and muck that must be in it she drank and drank; deep gulping draughts which seemed to flow in a cool stream right down into her thighs. Within a minute she broke out in perspiration and shivered. Once she had drunk her fill she carefully washed her battered face.

"I must look terrible," she told herself as she gingerly rinsed dried blood from her nostrils. "I hope I'm not scarred for life."

It was hard to tell. Her whole face felt bruised and numb. Shivering and trembling with reaction and fatigue she peeled off her shirt and sluiced water over her body.

"Oh, that's good!" she murmured.

Then she shivered again as her skin came out in goose bumps. Next, she washed her shirt to try to remove the coating of muck and sour smell of rotting food. After allowing the cool breeze to caress her bare skin for a few minutes she pulled the wet shirt back on. That took some time as her ribs and body really hurt. But the wet cloth on her skin was very refreshing.

Her almost numb nose told her that her trousers needed the same treatment but there was absolutely no way she was going to risk taking off her boots and trousers just to try to remove the muck and odours.

As Barbara stood there a fit of trembling shook her and she felt the need to lie down. *But not in all this filth,* she thought, looking around in the starlight at the mud, dust and cow manure. It took an effort of will not to break down into sobbing or hysteria.

After a few minutes, when she had calmed down slightly, Barbara had another drink. She then stood leaning on the trough to take stock of the situation. Nearby she saw a wire gate. Groaning at the stiff muscles and various aches she bobbled over to it and looked around. Not a light anywhere. The only sounds were a faint breeze rattling the mill and the snuffle of the cattle. She found her legs were trembling almost uncontrollably.

"I'll keep following this track. It must lead somewhere. It's going more or less the way I want to go," she told herself.

Having made the decision she baulked. After just washing herself she didn't want to roll in the grass and dust to get under the fence. She considered climbing over as easier than opening the gate, which was one of those made of barbed wire and held in tension by a straining latch.

So she put her hand on top of the post and her right boot on the second strand. Then she hoisted herself up so her right boot was on the top strand. For a moment she wobbled unsteadily and knew she had made a mistake. Fearing a fall she sprang forward. As she dropped the back of her shirt snagged on the top wire, which snatched it taut.

Rip!

"Oh blast! That was silly. I should have known better. It's always safer and easier to go under," she berated herself. She examined the tear, then shrugged. "Could be worse. It could have been my bum."

The dirt track meandered off through the trees in a roughly westerly direction. With an effort of will she forced her aching legs into motion.

"Won't be long now."

Chapter 21

TWO MEN IN A HUT

After only a couple of hundred paces, Barbara encountered more cattle. At first there were only a few. As she got closer these scrambled to their feet in alarm and scampered away. More cattle were then disturbed by them. This time however there weren't twenty or thirty beasts. There seemed to be hundreds.

She realised this from the noise. It made her stop in alarm. Ahead of her the whole paddock seemed to seethe. Snorting black objects bobbed and swayed before her eyes in a rising mist of grey dust. A bull let out a loud trumpeting bellow.

Suddenly the nearest beasts took fright. They turned and ran. The pounding of their hooves became a drumming thunder. Barbara felt a real clutch of fear. Afraid that she might be trampled she scurried quickly to the nearest tree and looked around. To her relief she saw that the stampede was heading away from her. But she stayed at the tree until the noise died away in the distance.

What should I do? she wondered. Following the track still seemed the best option.

She walked back to the track and considered it. It seemed to head a bit north of where the cattle had gone to. That decided her to keep going along it, but to try to skirt around any more herds of cattle.

Barbara had only gone 10 paces when she stopped again. Not far ahead a dog had begun to bark. A second joined it and then a man's voice called out.

About a hundred metres ahead, slightly to the right a dim yellow light came on. It outlined a window.

A house!

"Thank God! People. I'm safe," Barbara cried aloud. She uttered a prayer of thanks and began walking towards the building. As she did she saw that a fence had come angling in on her right and now ran beside the track. The house was beyond the fence.

The dogs kept barking. They had gone racing off into the night in the direction of the cattle and the owner was whistling and calling. Then a second man spoke.

Barbara reached a gate just to the rear of the house. From there she could see it quite clearly in the starlight. It was a corrugated iron hut with grey dust all around it. A truck stood nearby.

The owner of the dogs whistled again. It sounded very loud in the stillness that had settled. The men were at the front of the hut and not visible. Barbara paused.

I wonder if there is a woman here? she thought.

Barbara crawled under the fence and walked to the back corner of the hut, her boots stirring up dust but making no sound. Now she could hear the men quite clearly.

"I wonder where the hell Johnno got to," one of the men said.

Johnno!

Barbara had just walked around the side of the hut and could see the man, about five metres away. She froze in her tracks.

Johnno was the man driving the 4WD. He was a friend of Lenny. Were these men also friends of Lenny?

Barbara stepped back around the corner and stood with beating heart. *What should I do?* she wondered.

The other man spoke. "Never mind Johnno, Sharkey. You're just grumpy cause ya ran outa grog."

"Yeah, well, it's alright for you, Stevo. You got plenty of that rot-gut whisky."

"Johnno probably decided to spend his last night in town havin' a good time. After termorrow night it'll be a long time fore he sees the old 'Towers' again."

"Yeah, well. I wouldn't mind a good night in town meself. Strewth, we bin hidin' in this stinkin' hut for nearly three months now!"

Barbara was puzzled. Hiding from what? Or from whom? Who were these men? And there was this reference to tomorrow night. Was that just a coincidence? She had been about to withdraw but now stayed to listen.

The man named Stevo said, "Stop whingin' Sharkey. It's been better than rottin in Stuart Prison. And termorrow, after the Big Job, we'll be away to New South with a bag of dough."

"'Bout time. I hope that bloody Castledine's got things organised. I don't trust that bastard," Sharkey replied.

A piercing whistle made Barbara jump. The owner of the dogs, Stevo, called them again. "Bloody dogs! I wonder what spooked them cattle. They ain't never took orf all in a mob like that before."

"Dingo?"

"Nah! Ain't heard one," Stevo snarled. He emitted another piercing whistle.

Dogs! Barbara made her decision. *These men are up to no good and they are mates of Johnno's, if not Lenny,* she thought. She didn't feel inclined to trust herself to them.

Immediately she turned and walked back to the gate and rolled under the fence. As she stood up and dusted herself she got an awful shock.

A massive, grey Brahman Bull was standing not ten metres away!

Barbara swallowed and decided to bluff it out. She didn't dare risk staying as the man was whistling the dogs again and a bark indicated they were returning. She started walking directly away from the hut while keeping her eyes on the bull. It turned its head to watch her.

"Stay there bull," Barbara murmured. With her heart hammering in her mouth she covered 10 paces, 15, 20. She began to relax and cast a glance in the direction she was heading. It was just flat open bush and scattered ironbarks.

A sound made her look sharply back. It was what she feared: the bull had begun walking towards her. Then it gave a snort and pawed the ground.

Just like in the cartoons! Oh help, Barbara thought.

She went cold with fright for it was a truly enormous beast and she imagined she could see malevolence in its beady eyes even in the dark.

In the hopes of finding safety she looked ahead. No more than 5 paces to the left front was a large ironbark tree. As quickly as she could without running, she walked to it and slipped behind it.

To her dismay, the bull kept coming at a slow walk. It then stopped and let out a trumpeting bellow that made Barbara's hair stand on end. *It is going to attack!* she thought. It didn't have horns that she could see but she was sure that its sheer bulk would trample and crush her.

In desperation she looked at the tree. It was about half a metre thick. The rough bark was harsh on tender skin and there were no branches anywhere near the ground. She knew she would never climb it. The bull snorted and bellowed again.

Barbara looked frantically around for another tree but there were none within 50 paces. She measured the distance back to the barbed wire fence.

If I can dodge its first rush, I might just make it! she thought.

The bull suddenly broke into a charge. It was so sudden and so much faster than Barbara would have believed possible for such a bulky animal that surprise and fear caused her to momentarily freeze.

Then she crouched behind the tree. The enraged animal put its head down and rushed towards her. Barbara tensed, ready to spring aside.

A small grey object moving so fast it could have been an optical illusion darted across behind the bull. The animal suddenly swerved and bellowed in pain. It spun very fast, throwing up a cloud of dust as it did. It bellowed again. A dog began barking furiously.

"The dogs! Thank God," Barbara gasped.

Another dog joined in. It also flashed in to nip the heel of the bull, which whirled to face this new tormentor. Snorting and barking filled the air. Dust billowed up.

Over this came Stevo's piercing whistle. Then he shouted, "Come behind you bloody dogs or I'll take a whip to you! Come be-bloody hind I say!"

"What's goin' on Stevo?" Sharkey called.

"Bloody dogs have found that big bull we was lookin' for yesterday, that mean bastard wot chased you," Stevo replied. He whistled again. "Come behind Bluey! Snapper, come here you mongrels or I'll shoot yer!"

"Let em bite the bugger. Do him good."

"Don't be a dill, Sharkey. That beast be worth a heap of money. If we're gunna sell these cattle we want 'em in good condition. Here! Bluey! Come behind! Christ, Sharkey, do somethin' useful. Go and get me bloody stockwhip and a chain."

The dogs had backed off at their master's call but crouched growling and barking at the bull. The bull snorted and made short rushes first at one, then at the other. The dogs easily evaded these. Barbara remained behind the tree. She was afraid to move in case she was seen but fearful that if she stayed one of the dogs would scent her.

At last Stevo got his whip. He cracked it with a sound like a pistol shot. The bull spun and lumbered off twenty metres. The dogs obviously knew what to expect as both now slunk over under the fence to their master. He clipped chains on their collars. "Bloody disobedient mongrels!" he called.

Barbara didn't see what he did, but one of the dogs yelped in pain. There was the sound of several kicks and the dogs were dragged whining back to the house. Barbara leaned on the tree feeling drained. She found she was wet with perspiration and shaking with fright. She also badly needed to go to the toilet.

It's time I took myself away from this place, she thought. She looked around for the bull. It was nowhere in sight.

Barbara was astonished. How could such a large animal move so silently? She peered into the gloom, straining her eyes for any white patch which might indicate which way it had gone. She was afraid to move till she had some idea of where it was.

Then the bull bellowed. The sound was so loud and unexpected that Barbara jumped. Then she sighed with relief. The animal had gone off in the same direction as the other cattle and was fifty or a hundred metres off.

"Whew! Nearly wet myself then," she sighed.

That reminded her of her urgent need. She set trembling legs into motion and walked briskly away from the hut. After about a hundred paces it occurred to her that she must be going roughly south, which was not the preferred direction.

As she walked, she reasoned with herself. "I wonder how far I've come?" Thinking to check the time she felt in her pocket for her watch, but it was not there. "It must have fallen out. Pity! Anyway, I must have walked ten kilometres at least."

She mulled this over. "Normal marching pace is five kilometres per hour in flat, easy going. I must have been walking two or three hours."

Then she had to admit she was trying to raise her own spirits be being too optimistic. She halved the figure to 5, then decided that was the most she could have walked.

Probably I have only walked three or four kilometres, she told herself.

Next, she tried to reason out how far she had to go and put it at 20 kilometres. She found that a depressing prospect. Her legs suddenly felt tired and all her aches and scratches irritated.

To ensure she avoided the cattle, she counted out a dogged 750 paces southwards. Logic told her there must be a road from the hut either to the highway or to the road where Lenny and Wally had attempted to rape her. She rejected that as an option.

"I don't think I'll like anyone I meet on that road. I am safer walking through the bush. I wonder who these men at the hut are? They all seem to know each other. No, that's silly. In the bush people do know all the other people in the district. But these all seem to have something in common. They've all got a 'Big Job' tomorrow night. I wonder what it is?"

Turning west once more she began a weary trudge through the flat, featureless bush. She tried counting paces to keep some track of time and distance, but her thoughts kept wandering. After she had lost count for the third time, she gave it up.

Instead she settled down to a determined plod. But now her boots seemed to drag and scrape. Her toes began to pinch and blisters started to form on her heels and under the front edge of the 'balls' of her feet. The grass scratched at her legs and itched. Leg muscles began to ache. Her mind seemed to go dull with fatigue and fear.

Thirst began to develop again. The exertion of walking caused Barbara to perspire so that she felt hot inside but had a faint clammy chill on her skin from the night air. Several times she lost her guiding star among the trees. She stumbled frequently and tripped and fell once.

"God, there must be an end to this!" she muttered crossly.

For some time Barbara had been aware of a change in the light, with all sense of perspective and tone being lost in the area ahead of her. She realised there were now distinct shadows being cast on either side and saw that she was also throwing a shadow ahead. Puzzled, she paused and glanced back. The yellow sickle of a new moon was just rising above the treetops.

"I wonder what time it is? It can't be long till morning."

She ran her tongue over dry lips and rubbed eyes which had begun to ache and scratch in their sockets. With an effort of will she resumed her dreary plodding.

"People must be getting worried about me by this," she thought. She imagined the consternation that must be going on back in camp. She knew that Capt Conkey and Miss McEwen would turn the camp upside down once they realised she was missing.

"They will find my hat, clipboard and the plates," she reasoned. But how would they know what had happened?

Of course! Weismann saw Lenny dragging me to the ute. A police search at daybreak will soon find the ute, she decided. *Or will it? How badly is it damaged? Ah! The burnt 4WD. It will still be smouldering and should attract attention!*

She came to a creek larger than any she had yet encountered. Carefully she made her way down the bank and through the bordering trees. To her intense disappointment the bed was flat, dry sand with no trace of water.

"I must have a drink," she told herself. She plodded up the creek bed, hoping to find a pool. A fallen tree blocked her path. She scrambled painfully over it, dislodging a shower of dry leaves, twigs and other flood debris.

"Ouch!"

It felt as though something red-hot had touched the edge of her left hand. Barbara sprang clear and rubbed her hands together. The sharp stab of pain persisted.

"Something bit me!" she cried. But what? Snake? No, too small. Spider or Scorpion possibly? *Oh I hope I don't get sick!*

Barbara had a horrible vision of slumping down in agony; of crows plucking her eyes out; of ants and other disgusting beetles devouring her rotting flesh. "The next flood will scatter my skeleton down the creek," she said aloud. Then she sobbed in self-pity.

Close to hysteria she scrambled through the line of trees and up the bank. There she stopped, gasping in great gulps of air. *Slow down you fool,* she told herself. *You'll spread the poison faster.* Besides, the pain had already subsided to a dull ache. It did throb right up her arm though. She stood for a moment going through 'Bites and Stings' in her head.

I should bandage my arm. But what with? I could rip my shirt up I suppose! she thought. She jibbed at that. An unreasonable sense of modesty made her decide that she would rather die.

After another couple of minutes a lump formed under her arm. She felt a bit dizzy, but the pain went away almost completely. "I must not go to sleep," she told herself. "I'll have to walk." She looked up at the stars to check her direction, then slapped her forehead. "Oh! I'm a fool. I've run back out on the same side of the creek."

She didn't want to go back into the dark shadows amongst the trees, but she forced herself to do so. As quickly as she could she pushed her way through the trees and bushes and a minute later was in the open bush on the other side.

Once she had her bearings, she commenced trudging west again, wondering how long it would take the poison to take effect. "Won't be long. I'm ready to collapse anyway just from exhaustion," she muttered.

Ten minutes later she was still doggedly putting one foot in front of another. The bush had subtly changed. There were patches of bare grey clay, small clusters of thin trees and clumps of waist-high bush. She knew these were prickly and avoided them carefully.

From time to time she felt under her arm. To her relief the lump had subsided. It hurt to touch but less than before. *Perhaps it wasn't a really poisonous one, whatever it was,* she decided.

Still she made herself keep walking. Another ten or fifteen minutes of flat scrub passed behind her heavy boots. Ahead the bush seemed to open up. Abruptly she came to a barbed wire fence with a faint track beyond it. Exhausted by the ordeal she paused and leaned on a fence post. Her mind seemed to spin. She seemed to have trouble focusing her eyes. With difficulty she crawled under the fence.

As soon as she stood up she felt giddy. A wave of nausea made her alternately sweat and shiver. "I'd better sit down before I fall down," she muttered thickly.

She looked around for a place to sit. *There isn't a log anywhere and besides,* she thought, *it would be sure to have a few metres of slithering horror lurking in it.* The best she could find was a patch of bare clay beside a fence post.

Very gingerly she sat down. With a sigh of relief, she leaned back against the fence post and closed her eyes.

Chapter 22

THE DROVER'S DOG

Several times Barbara stirred in her exhausted slumber as the lancing pains of cramps seized her leg muscles. Then she became restless as flies and ants began to crawl over her body and face. Sounds penetrated dimly into her dreams.

Something wet touched her face and there was snuffling in her car. She opened red-rimmed, sleep-gummed eyes into the glare of full daylight to find a dog's nose only centimetres from her face. She woke with a start and went to sit up. Her shirt snagged on the barbed-wire and held her.

The dog stuck out a long pink tongue and slobbered at her face. Barbara put up her hands to push it away and became aware that a thin faced, unshaven man sat on a horse not five metres away looking at her.

Then she remembered unbuttoning her shirt to cool herself during the night. Fierce shame flamed through her and she hastily pulled at her shirt to cover herself. Surprise and shock held her speechless for a moment.

The dog wagged its tail and licked her again. It was a 'blue-heeler' with one brown eye, one yellow eye and a comical frown.

A fly crawled around Barbara's left nostril. Irritably she slapped at it. The man licked the paper of a cigarette he was rolling, inserted one end in his lips and reached into a pocket in his greasy grey trousers for his matches. "G'day," he said.

"Er. Hello! Er. Good morning. Who are you? Where am I?" Barbara stammered. Her gaze took in dozens of reddish-brown beef cattle ambling past.

"I was gunna ask you that Miss. You look like you've had a rough trot. I'm Frank and I'm a drover, see," he explained, pointing at the cattle. "I'm just gettin' this mob down to the Saltpan Outstation before it gets too hot. Be no joke movin' em in the heat of the day. Besides, they'd lose too much condition do ya see?"

Barbara nodded. She found it hard to think and her tongue felt so swollen she could hardly speak. "I suppose so," she mumbled. "Please. I need to get back to the army camp at Bunyip River. Is there a telephone at your station?"

"No Missy, it's only an outstation like. Come away Spinner!" (That directed at the dog which had begun to sniff at Barbara in an embarrassing way.)

"Can you help me please? I've been attacked by some men and, and... and I need help," Barbara said. She felt very weak and her eyes prickled with painful, salty tears.

"You bin raped 'ave yer?" the man asked in a sad voice.

"No. No. They tried to. But I got away."

"Aw yeah? Lucky fer you! When was that?"

"Late last night," Barbara replied. She licked dry lips. Was it only last night? She spied a canvas water bag on the man's saddle. Fierce thirst gripped her. "Please, can I have a drink?"

"Drink? Aw, yeah. Sorry. I'm fergettin' meself." The drover dismounted and unhooked the bag. The dog sat, tongue out and tail wagging. The drover walked over to Barbara and knelt down. He fondled the dog's ears. "Not fer you old feller. Yer can ave some in a minute."

Barbara gulped at the water. Some spilled down her chin and onto her chest. She realised her shirt was probably gaping open as she had forgotten to hold it. By the way the man was pretending to be interested in the dog she guessed it had. Hotly ashamed she gripped the shirt closed and passed the water bag back. "Thanks. Can you take me to the station please?"

The drover nodded. "Yeah. Righto. Look, I'll go get me car or you'll ave ter ride the horse with me. I won't be long. It's only a coupla 'k's' that way," he said. He pointed down the track to the south. "I'll just leave old 'Spinner' here with ya. E'll make sure the cattle don't wander back."

He turned to the dog and ruffled his ears. "Ya got that old fella? You keep these cattle 'ere. An' keep an eye on young Missy 'ere too."

The dog wagged his tail and gave Barbara a quizzical glance. It made her smile. That hurt as her split lip cracked but she felt better. *I'm safe now,* she thought.

The drover held out the water bag and said, "You keep the water bag. I won't be long." He then strode to his horse, swung into the saddle and set off at a canter.

Barbara had another drink as she watched man and horse vanish in the distant haze of heat and dust. Then she noticed the dog watching her hopefully. His tail wagged. "You want a drink boy?" she asked. The dog seemed to nod and wagged his tail again. Barbara rose painfully to her feet and squatted to make a cup with one hand.

Into this she poured a little water which the dog thankfully lapped. She repeated the process three more times. The dog then lay down beside her. He began to pant, his mouth open and tongue lolling out.

Barbara straightened up, groaning in pain as stiff muscles reacted. She dabbed some water in her eyes and had another long drink. A hot wind blew her shirt wide, revealing her battered condition. Ruefully she looked down at her body. "Heavens! No wonder I hurt," she muttered, seeing the dozens of scratches, bruises and red splotches on her skin.

After examining herself she buttoned the shirt up and tucked it back in then looked around. The surrounding country was just flat, hot, dry bush. On her side of the fence it was more open with fewer small trees, just large eucalypts every fifty or so metres. To the south it looked even more open.

The herd of cattle had stopped moving and were slowly spreading out. One of the beasts began ambling back the way it had come. The dog rose and trotted across the dusty track to emit a low growl. The bullock stopped and hastily turned around. The dog padded back and flopped down. Barbara smiled again. To her he looked just as though he was laughing.

"You enjoyed that didn't you?" she said as he made himself comfortable in the shade of the fence post. The dog looked at her and panted. It looked so like a grin that Barbara's face broke into a painful little smile.

Shimmering movement and billowing dust away down the track caught her eye. It was a vehicle heading her way. Barbara felt a momentary twinge of fear, then relaxed. *That was quick,* she thought. *I will soon be safe.* She stood up and leaned painfully on the fence post.

A battered blue panel van drew up with the drover at the wheel. He grinned at her and beckoned. "Here, hop in. Spinner, you stay 'ere boy. I'll be back. You watch them bullocks like a good dog."

Barbara opened the door and painfully climbed in. The old leather bench seat was broken and springs poked through. One stuck into her backside in a painful way. Despite the pain, discomfort and embarrassment she did not care.

On my way, she thought.

The car started up again and the drover began to do a U-turn. That surprised Barbara as it wasn't what she wanted. "Could you take me straight to the army camp please?" she called above the roar of the unmuffled motor.

"Yeah. I will. This is the shortest way," the drover replied. His half-smoked cigarette was stuck to his lower lip.

The track was rough, but the drover took it at high speed, swerving around the worst potholes and tree trunks. The car rattled and banged. Barbara tried to relax and badly wanted to close her eyes, but the speed had her on the edge of being frightened.

A grassy paddock dotted with dozens of cattle swept by. Through the trees ahead appeared a scattering of wooden-railed cattle pens and several corrugated iron and timber buildings. These were set in a wasteland of bare ground—whitish dust marked by hoof prints and hundreds of cattle droppings.On the left were several steel mesh cages with black pigs penned in them and another with half a dozen large dogs. The largest building had a small front veranda, a water tank and wind pump beside it and several curved sections of corrugated iron forming more dog kennels. The drover's horse stood tied to a hitching rail at the front of the house.

The drover braked to a standstill in front of the house. He then swore as the following dust engulfed them. "Bugger! Always forget that. Give me a bloody horse any day," he coughed.

Barbara bit her lip. "Why have we stopped? Please, just take me to the army camp."

The man switched off the motor. "Thought you'd like a wash and clean up. You look a sight, I can tell ya."

"I suppose I do," Barbara said. She felt uneasy but could think of no reason to refuse the offer of hospitality.

The drover hopped out and pocketed the car keys, then gestured towards the door. "Only be a coupla minutes. Come on. I'll make a cuppa tea while you freshen up."

Without waiting for an answer, he walked up onto the low wooden veranda. Reluctantly Barbara opened the car door and eased her stiff legs out. Slowly she hobbled up onto the veranda and in through the doorway.

The interior of the house was dark after the harsh glare outside and it took her eyes a moment to adjust.

A little thrill of alarm ran through her as she realised there was another man standing beside the drover. He was solidly built, with short hair and brown eyes. Both hands and one arm were bandaged.

"Hello," he said. "I've bin lookin' forward to meetin' you. I'm Johnno and you owe me."

Johnno!

Barbara reeled in shock. As realisation exploded in her mind she reacted. In desperation she turned and went to run.

"Git 'er Brute!" the drover yelled.

Barbara had only taken 5 or 6 paces when she was pulled down. A huge dog came out of the shadows in a brown flash and latched onto her ankle. She fell heavily and kicked furiously but the dog hung on. He was a big brown dog, some sort of bulldog mongrel with yellow eyes. The dog clamped its jaws into the leather of her boot and worried her.

Barbara screamed and lashed out with her right boot at its head. The animal shut one eye and uttered a slobbering growl from deep in its throat but did not let go. Nails and splinters from the rough floor boards tore at Barbara's skin. The dog scratched at her.

Then rough hands seized her by the arms and legs.

Thud!

A fist punched Barbara in the side of the head, making her senses reel.

Johnno snarled savagely in her ear, "Stop kicking my dawg, yer bitch or I'll tell 'im ter really bite yer!"

Barbara was held flat by the drover. The cigarette was still stuck to his bottom lip. Sweaty hands grabbed at Barbara's body but she found her struggles to no avail. To her utter horror she found that she lacked the strength to break free. The dog 'worried' her ankle again and she cried out in fear and pain.

Johnno spoke near her head. "Mind them boots of hers Frank. She clobbered Lenny a beauty with 'em. That's how she got away. Now hold her down."

He put one hand to her throat and with the other ripped her already torn shirt open, the buttons popping off or tearing undone. Then he paused and groaned. "Jeez, that hurt!" He held a bandaged hand in front of Barbara's face. "You done that you bitch. You burnt my truck and boy, are you gunna pay! Oh yeah! Are you gunna pay!"

The drover knelt down and gripped Barbara's legs. "What ya gunna do Johnno?" he queried.

Johnno grunted with lust and then croaked in a curious sounding voice, "I'm gunna have her now." Barbara saw him start unbuckling his trousers and she began to struggle frantically, her mind filled with awful thoughts.

The drover tightened his grip and managed to hold her down. "Better tie her up first," he warned.

"Yeah. Hold them legs tight. We'll stick her on the bed," Johnno agreed.

In desperation Barbara began to hit at him with both fists. At the same time she squirmed and writhed with all her strength. *I may as well go down fighting,* she told herself. The word 'die' had been there in her thoughts but she had shied away from using it.

Johnno swore and tightened his grip until she began to gasp and choke. Black dots danced in her vision and she began to lose consciousness. "Stop strugglin' ya bitch!" he shouted.

But Barbara didn't, despite being slapped again. Johnno grabbed her left wrist with his bandaged left hand and then let go of her throat and after a few attempts managed to grab her right wrist with his right. Barbara had the satisfaction of seeing him wince with pain as he had to use his burnt hands to do this.

And she was not strong enough. To her dismay and despair she felt herself being lifted. The two men gripped Barbara's legs and arms tightly then picked her up and carried her into the hut. In a side room was an old iron-framed bed with a coarse grey blanket on it and a yellowish-stained pillow. The place stank of stale urine, sweat, dog and horse. Barbara was dumped on the bed, Johnno still holding both her wrists and the drover gripping her legs together.

Again Barbara went into a frenzy of twitching and squirming and the men had to use all their strength to hold her. Johnno got more and more angry. "Stop struggling ya bitch or we'll really hurt ya!" he shouted.

Barbara ignored that, certain that the men would kill her anyway.

But she had to stop because she was exhausted. She lay back gasping and sobbing, glaring hate at the two men.

The drover kept his tight grip on her legs. "You keep hold of her hands Johnno while I tie her legs for a minute. Then we can tie her wrists to the bed frame."

Barbara arched her back to look and saw the drover reach down to pick up a leather stockwhip that was coiled around the bottom bedpost. Sensing that once her legs were firmly tied she was doomed Barbara again began struggling, but to no avail. The drover held her legs with one arm while uncoiling the whip and then wrapping it tightly around her ankles. He then secured the end to the bed frame.

"Now missie, get out of that!" the drover taunted as he let go of her legs and turned to help Johnno. "Keep hold, Johnno, while I get some rope."

Johnno did, managing to keep Barbara held down despite her frantic struggles to break free. The drover returned and it was painfully obvious to Barbara that he knew what he was doing. He leaned over and slipped a length of rope around Barbara's left wrist. Then he put a clove hitch on her right wrist using a short length of sisal rope.

"Keep holdin' her, Johnno," the drover said. He then leaned across and secured the rope around Barbara's right wrist to the far bedpost.

That done the drover stood up. "You tie her left arm to the bed post, Johnno," he said. "I'll find some more rope for her legs."

Johnno did as he was told, working with evident difficulty and pain because of his bandaged hands. Barbara continued to struggle, hoping to at least force a knot to be loose but it seemed to no avail. Gasping and momentarily exhausted she slumped back and began to cry.

And all too soon the drover was back with two more lengths of rope. The drover handed a length to Johnno and said, "Hold her tight while I get them boots off."

Johnno took the rope and nodded. "Watch her. She kicked Lenny a coupla beauties last night with them army boots."

The drover nodded and sat on the edge of the bed to gip Barbara's legs while he unwrapped the whip. This was again hung over the bottom bed post and he then set to work to unlace and remove Barbara's boots. Again she struggled, arching her back and bending her legs and body, but to no avail.

Johnno chuckled at this and said, "Better get them duds off her while you are at it."

The drover nodded. "I was gunna," he replied.

He continued unlacing and tugging off both boots. These were tossed aside behind the door. Her socks followed and then what Barbara really feared began. The drover bent to unbuckle her belt. Being in ceremonial DPCU she had her black web belt on and for a few seconds the unusual buckle arrangement baffled the drover.

"What the f...?" he muttered. "How does this bastard of a belt buckle work?" But then he mastered it and he set to work unbuttoning her waistband and then unzipped the trousers. "Gawd, these stink!"

"Yeah, Lenny put her in the back of his ute and they got garbage all over them," Johnno said, chuckling as he did. "Lenny wasn't happy."

"Now the tricky bit," the drover said. "You come and hold this leg while I pull these duds off the other one."

Johnno did as he was instructed. Barbara sensed that once her legs were tied she was doomed. Sobbing with fear and outrage she writhed her hips and tried to break her legs free but was unable. First one trouser leg and then the other were slid off, leaving her lying in her knickers with both men staring down at her with lustful eyes.

Her knickers were then just torn off by the drover who tossed them on the floor near the trousers. Again the men stared. Barbara flamed with embarrassment mixed with outrage.

The drover then again demonstrated that he knew his knots when he slipped a clove hitch around her right leg and quickly and expertly tied it to the far bed post. He then stepped back off the bed. "OK Johnno, now her other leg."

Johnno held Barbara's left leg firmly while the drover tied it to the bottom bed post, spreadeagling her legs in the process. Then he stepped back and ran his eyes over her and chuckled. At the sight of his lust-filled eyes and almost dribbling mouth Barbara felt nauseous. She averted her gaze and stared at the corrugated iron wall. In all her life she had never felt so helpless, humiliated or terrified.

And there was more to come! To Barbara's dismay Johnno took out a pocketknife from a small leather pouch on his belt. Barbara recognised it as the sort of knife stockmen used for castrating bulls and the thought flashed across her mind that she would like to use it on the men for that purpose. But fear of what he was going to use the knife for swamped that and she found she was sobbing again.

That the knife was very sharp was instantly obvious as Johnno slid the blade in under the cloth of her shirt and then slit the right sleeve all the way to the cuffs so that the sleeve just fell off. Seeing her horrified look he laughed and then proceeded to cut away the left sleeve as well, leaving her wearing only her bra. Not wanting to be thus exposed Barbara tried to struggle but found she was now so tightly bound she could only squirm a bit.

And what she feared now happed. Johnno just used the blade to cut the front of her bra and then the bra straps, exposing her breasts to the men's lascivious gaze. Now stark naked all she could do was pray and sob, her emotions aflame with fear and shame.

To Barbara's disgust Johnno ran the un-bandaged finger tips of his left hand around the nipple of her left breast. Horror and revulsion flooded through her. She squirmed and felt sick with fear and disgust but was helpless. The man prodded at both her breasts with the bandaged hand, making them quiver.

The slack-jawed lust evident on his face made Barbara want to vomit again. Her mind swirled with panic and dismay.

Oh God! This is worse than before! What sort of animals are they? How can I escape? Oh, please God, don't make it hurt too much!

She felt a rough hand crawling between her thighs like a monstrous spider. Johnno reached across to fondle her other breast. Barbara sobbed and turned away. But the stench from the pillow was so vile that she gagged and then vomited. Some of it went on Johnno's shirt and arm.

Johnno wiped his arm on the blanket and kneed her head. "Stop pukin', ya troll. This is gunna be the best one ya ever had."

Barbara was revolted. She wanted to plead that she had never 'had' any; that she was a virgin, but she didn't. Instead she bit her lip and prayed for it to be quick and not too painful.

Her disgust and revulsion then went up another notch when Johnno stood up and unzipped his trousers. As he did he snarled, "Piss orf Frankie. You can have a go later. Go and bring them cattle in."

"What about Lenny? He mightn't like that," whined the drover.

Johnno uttered an obscenity. "Stuff Lenny. He owes me too. Now get!"

The drover reluctantly backed out of the room. Barbara heard the creak and jingle of harness as he mounted, then the thud of horse's hooves.

Her mind raced. *I am now alone with Johnno. Can I somehow escape?*

She met Johnno's eyes and knew she could expect no pity from him. He swore as he tried to pull his trousers down with his bandaged hands. Then he realised he needed to take off his boots first.

Barbara lay there, sweating and trembling, while the man wrestled off his elastic-sided riding boots. Then he paused and padded out of the room. Frantically she cast around for a means of escape. She pulled and twisted but the knots all seemed tight and she could not get loose.

From the sounds she deduced that Johnno was having a drink. Then he padded back in, the smell of his socks overpowering even the reek of the pillow. He peeled off his trousers and hung them on the bed post next to her left hand. Then he peeled off the dirty underpants and tossed them aside before standing to look at her. Not wanting to see his horrible maleness Barbara again turned her head away and closed her eyes. Her thigh and pelvic muscles began clenching and contracting in futile protective spasms.

Johnno began running the tips of his bandaged fingers over her legs and body.

Get it over with! Barbara's mind screamed. Her mouth she kept grimly clamped.

Then she heard the sound of a vehicle's engine. Someone was coming!

Perhaps they will save me? she thought hopefully.

Chapter 23

NAKED LUST

Barbara listened to the sound of the vehicle. Would it just drive past? No. It was stopping! Hope and fear jangled inextricably in her.

Who is it? Will they help me? she wondered.

The vehicle's brakes squealed. Johnno swore and stood up. The motor died. A car door slammed and boots sounded on the veranda.

Barbara turned her head to face the door, then emitted a muffled cry of disappointment. Her worst fears were realised. The huge bulk of Lenny filled the doorway. The side of his face was all yellow and black from a massive bruise. He stood there like a monstrous ape clenching and unclenching his hands.

"Frankie told me yer got her! Bloody good! Now back off, Johnno. She's mine. I'm first. Ow!"

The howl of pain was so unexpected they all jumped. The brown dog had come from somewhere and clamped onto Lenny's leg. "Ah! Ow! Get this bloody dog off me! Call the bugger off or I'll kill him Johnno!" Lenny swore and howled.

"Down Brute! Let go boy! Let go!" Johnno ordered.

Reluctantly the animal opened its jaws, but it kept snarling and showed its yellow fangs.

"Chain the bastard up Johnno," Lenny ordered.

Johnno was reluctant to go. His eyes kept flicking to Barbara. He was obviously embarrassed to be there standing without his trousers. But he was also obviously scared of Lenny. Muttering and grumbling he moved to seize the dog's collar. The dog resisted but after a short tussle it was dragged out towards the back of the house.

Barbara would have cringed had she been able to when Lenny walked over. First he ran his leering eyes over her. Then he ran his hands down her body and back up, giving both breasts a bruising squeeze.

"Ah yes! That's nice," he muttered thickly. "We won't be interrupted this time."

Barbara cringed and wrinkled her nose in disgust. He smelt of beer and sweat and she decided he was at least half drunk. Lenny undid his trousers and then, like Johnno, realised that his boots must come off first. Swearing with frustration he sat on the bed to pull them off.

Barbara's mind reeled in shock. The nightmare not only seemed to have no end. It was getting worse! *They are all going to rape me!* she thought. Terror and disgust made her whole being squirm.

Johnno came back just as Lenny stripped off his trousers. Lenny pointed towards the back of the house. "Get me a beer, Johnno. I'm bloody thirsty," he ordered. He hung his trousers on the bed post on top of Johnno's.

"Get it yourself. I'm first," Johnno replied. He was plainly in the grip of lust.

Lenny stood up and shook his fist. "Do what yer told," he snarled.

Johnno muttered but turned away. Lenny peeled off soiled underpants and tossed them aside. Barbara looked away, her whole being in shock. To her horror he gripped her cheeks and turned her head. Still she kept her eyes tight shut. He smacked her so hard, and so unexpectedly, that she gasped in shock.

She opened her eyes, to be confronted by his ugly, rampant maleness. Instantly she shut them tight again and kept them that way in spite of more vicious whacks.

Lenny chuckled. "I thought you'd like to see what ya gunna get."

Barbara said nothing but tears came. Her whole face smarted and stung. It was all too revolting for thought.

The bed then creaked and Lenny climbed up over her right leg and lay on her. His weight seemed to crush the breath out of her. His foul body odours nauseated her. She felt fumbling and prodding and tensed herself for the stabbing pain.

Then Lenny levered his bulk up off her. "This is no bloody good. I can't get in," he muttered. He turned and fumbled at the knots holding Barbara's right ankle. Then he grabbed her leg and hauled it up and out so that she was totally open to his assaults.

"Here's your beer," came Johnno's voice.

Barbara waited, trembling in fright and anticipation. Lenny put her leg down and held it with one hand. Barbara opened her eyes and looked. Lenny was crouched, guzzling the beer from a bottle.

Disgust and hatred flamed in Barbara. She suddenly jerked her leg free and lashed out. Her foot caught Lenny's jaw, driving his teeth together with a loud snap. The beer bottle flew from his grasp and burst on the floor.

"You bitch!" Lenny raged.

Desperately Barbara kicked again and again, her foot smacking into his face, forearm and beer belly. Lenny smacked back and grabbed at her but lost his balance. He slid off the bed feet first, then screamed, "Aah! Ooh, you fucken moll!" He hopped aside and grabbed at his left foot, plucking broken glass from it.

Then he seemed to go insane. Spotting the stockwhip he snatched it up and flicked it out to lie across Barbara's stomach.

"You bitch! I'm gunna teach you a bloody lesson you'll never forget!" he shouted. He pulled the whip back and swung it with all the strength of his arm.

"Aaah!" Johnno yelled. "Aaargh! Watch what yer doin', ya bloody moron!"

The whip had curled back and caught around Johnno's neck. The vicious return flick had then jerked him hard forward. He fell heavily then sprang up, punching and swearing.

Lenny let go of the whip in surprise and turned to grapple with him. Both men fell in a swearing, struggling heap.

For a moment Barbara gaped at the disgusting spectacle. Then her mind leaped. *This is my chance!* she thought.

But how?

She looked frantically around. Driven by absolute desperation she struggled. Suddenly she felt her left hand come free. Gaping in astonishment, she saw that Johnno's knot had come undone. Whether he wasn't as skilled at knot tying as the drover or whether he had trouble with his bandaged hands she didn't care. It was undone.

A glance showed that both men were on their feet now, circling warily and lashing out with punches. Both were sweating and swearing and made the most disgusting spectacle Barbara had ever seen. They paid no attention to her but continued their fight. Lenny rushed in. Blows smacked on sweaty flesh. The men grappled and crashed against the door frame and went down again.

Barbara turned her attention to the knot holding her right hand. It had been properly tied but she instantly recognised a clove hitch and the words of her OC flashed across her mind: 'One of the qualities of a good knot it that it is easy to untie.' And Barbara had been properly taught. Her left hand flashed across and began tugging at the rope in the right place. As she did she let out a gasp of triumph. Sweat trickled into her eyes and her heart beat wildly but she concentrated on her task. Near her the two men still gouged and punched and swore.

Yes! Barbara saw the knot loosen. She tried even harder. A whole strand came loose. Then another. The entire binding began to come loose. In desperation she pulled. Suddenly she had her right hand free!

She darted a fearful glance at the two men. Had they noticed?

They weren't looking. Johnno had broken free and fled into the main room where he picked up a chair to defend himself. Lenny went at him bellowing horrible threats and obscenities.

Barbara at once sat up and began untying her right leg. She was able to work the rope loose. Within seconds she slipped her leg free and was about to sit up when a bottle burst beside her head.

She looked in alarm and saw that Johnno was backing into the room pushing at a broom handle. Lenny had the other end. He landed a punch and Johnno went down. Lenny jumped in and kicked him. Johnno grabbed his leg and pulled him down.

Now or never! Barbara thought.

She sat up and pulled her legs under her. Beside her the two men were now in a wrestling lock on the floor. Lenny was on top and was winning.

Run!

Barbara sprang off the bed behind Lenny and went through the door. As she did she heard him bellow.

"Let go ya stupid bastard! Let go! She's getting' away!"

Barbara didn't stop to think. She ran through into a kitchen and straight out the back door. The glare half-blinded her. A few metres away the brown dog barked viciously. It sprang forward, teeth bared. Barbara croaked in fear and jumped back, heart leaping into her dry throat. But the dog did not reach her and she saw that it was chained up. For a moment she paused, feeling extraordinarily exposed and vulnerable in her naked state.

Which way?

With her heart hammering wildly Barbara turned left and ran around the back of the house. A medley of sensations and emotions flooded her, among them the awareness that the sand was so hot it hurt her bare feet.

From inside she could hear both men yelling. To her dismay she saw that there was almost nowhere to hide; only an old outside dunny 25 metres away and, about 50 metres away, some sort of stables or shed. She heard the men running inside.

No time to reach the shed!

Almost jibbering with terror, she scuttled around the corner and dodged around the low tank stand with its corrugated iron water tank. *Can I hide there?* she wondered, rising panic threatening to cloud her thinking. *No. Not good enough,* she reasoned.

She kept going along the side of the house, horribly aware that she was utterly naked. This took her past the steel framework of the windmill and the window of the room she had just fled from. In a few more racing strides she reached the front of the house.

A sound warned her and she skidded to a stop and peeked around the corner.

The drover was there on his horse and with his dog. Barbara turned and looked frantically in all directions.

Where can I hide? she thought. She knew she couldn't outrun a horse. Next to her was the ladder of the windmill. It seemed her only hope. *Perhaps I can get onto the roof?*

It was a slim hope but seemed her only one so she sprang onto the ladder and began climbing. But she was only level with the roof when voices warned her. She froze, clinging to the metal and totally exposed to anyone who glanced up.

Johnno came running around the water tank. His face was covered in blood and he was holding one eye. To Barbara's disgust he wore only a shirt. He looked in behind the water tank where Barbara had thought to hide.

She tensed ready to fight as he turned but to her intense relief he kept running towards the front of the house. He dodged around the windmill supports so close she could almost have kicked him, but luckily he didn't look up. A moment later he went around to the front of the house.

Barbara didn't wait. She scuttled up another five rungs then swung out along a crossbar and reached across to the corrugated iron roof.

"Ah!" The sudden pain was so bad she let out an involuntary cry.

The roof iron was so hot it burned to the touch. *Too bad!* she told herself.

Gritting her teeth to ignore the pain she stepped across onto the roof and lowered herself flat. The heat seemed to sizzle her naked flesh. It hurt her breasts so much she had to lie half on her side. Her right foot and hand held the guttering to stop her slipping off.

Shouting at the front of the house told her the three men were there. Lenny was loudest. "Where's the bitch gone? Did you see her Frankie?" he yelled.

"Didn't see her come this way," replied Frankie.

"Out the back then. Johnno, you check the dunny and dog kennels. Frankie you come with me," Lenny ordered.

There were thudding footsteps below. Barbara lay still but saw them run past. It made her smile with grim satisfaction to see the two men without their trousers or boots. Lenny hobbled with a painful limp. They went out of sight and her mind raced.

What do I do now?

Chapter 24

BARBARA'S BOOTS

Watching Lenny limping on sore feet in the dust and dung caused Barbara a grim smile. She remembered just how hot that sand was. Then it hit her.

Boots!

If I am going to escape I have to run through the bush. I can't do that in bare feet, she thought.

Nor could she stay on the roof. Even if she wasn't seen the heat would cook her. She was in agony from the scorching hot corrugated iron roof and sweating profusely. The sun was already hot on her bare skin.

Squirming with pain and anxiety she watched Lenny, Frankie and his dog run across to the stables. As they went inside she moved. The heat was so bad that she couldn't wait another second. Whimpering softly from the pain she rose and almost sprang onto the windmill.

Her haste was almost her undoing as her sweaty hands slipped and she nearly fell. But another of Capt Conkey's lessons saved her: Never grip the treads of a ladder with your hands, only the uprights. She whacked her forearm painfully but managed to cling to the two sides. Luckily her feet found the treads of the ladder and she slid down, knowing she was in full view if the men came out of the shed.

Heart in mouth she turned and ran around to the front of the house. A quick glance around the corner showed no-one on the veranda. At once she ran up onto the veranda and along to the open front door. There she paused to listen, her heart beating wildly. The horse looked at her with large brown eyes.

No sound came from inside. Barbara slipped through the doorway and stumbled on an overturned armchair. Her eyes had to adjust to the semi-dark again. With her heart hammering wildly she made her way across to the hated bedroom.

It was a place of such trauma she hesitated to enter. Steeling herself she stepped in and began a frantic search. Almost at once she stepped on a shard of broken glass and that caused her to pause and look more carefully where she was putting her feet. Luckily it was only a small cut and she plucked the piece of glass out and then ignored the wound.

There was one boot. She snatched it up. There was a sock. Hastily she sat on the hateful bed and pulled it on then bent to scoop up the second sock. That was pulled on as well. But where was the other boot?

It was under the bed. She knelt on the filthy floor and broken glass and reached under. As she did she heard voices approaching.

Oh no! The men are coming back. I am too late! she thought as panic welled up to make her feel utterly frantic with fear. There was a louvred window but a glance showed that she couldn't escape through that. She heard hasty footsteps in the kitchen. *Did they see me?* she worried.

She grabbed the other boot and stood up, uncertain what to do. A splintered broom handle lay nearby. It could be a weapon. She was about to drop her boots and pick it up when the men's voices made her pause.

"Where the hell could the bitch have gone?" Lenny snarled.

"Beats me. She didn't go out the front or Frankie would'a seen her," Johnno snarled.

Frankie the drover joined in. "She couldn't 'ave reached the bush in time. It's too far ter run," he added.

The men came into the lounge room. With her mouth dry with fear Barbara tip-toed over behind the door.

Perhaps they won't come in? she thought. After all it was the last place they'd expect her to be. With an effort of will she silenced her gasping breathing.

Lenny snarled again, "I'm gunna kill the bitch when I get her."

Hearing that threat sent a tremor of mortal dread through Barbara. She tensed, ready for a desperate fight to the finish. *They might kill me but they will pay for it,* she vowed.

Johnno spoke next. "Where the hell did she go?" he asked.

"Which way did she turn when she went out the back door?" Frankie asked.

"Dunno," Lenny replied.

"She musta left tracks in the dust," Frankie pointed out, scorn clear in his voice.

"Tracks!" Johnno echoed foolishly.

Barbara realised she would soon be found. She leaned on the wall, put her boots down and, with trembling hands began fumbling on her left boot.

Frankie spoke again. "What about Spinner. He'll soon sniff her out," he suggested.

"Yeah! Good idea," Lenny agreed.

Spinner! Oh no! Barbara groaned at the thought of the nice dog tracking her by her scent. With shaking hands she struggled with her second boot.

Johnno spoke. "There's her shirt on the bed. Give him a sniff of that," he said.

The men were only a couple of metres away. Barbara edged further in behind the half open door. To her horror Johnno stepped into the room and scooped up her shirt. It seemed that she must be seen but he turned away from her and went back out, calling the dog as he did.

For a few moments Barbara trembled uncontrollably with relief and shock. Knowing she had only seconds she knelt to lace up her right boot. She heard Spinner come padding into the other room and Johnno telling her to go find.

And there was Spinner!

The dog had put his head around the door and was looking at her! Her heart seemed to stand still. She sucked in her breath in fright. The dog cocked his head and looked at her in that quizzical way she had previously thought amusing.

Frankie spoke, so close that Barbara thought he had come into the room. "Spinner! Come 'ere dawg!"

The dog turned its head and looked at its master, then wagged its tail and looked back at Barbara with a happy grin.

Barbara felt black despair.

Frankie called again. "Come 'ere ya stupid dawg!"

Spinner turned and padded out. Barbara almost collapsed with relief. She heard the men holding her torn shirt for the dog to smell. Then she heard them turn and walk back. *I can't possibly hide from a dog!* she thought in despair. She slumped against the wall in defeat.

The dog padded straight into the bedroom and looked at her and barked.

She was discovered!

Lenny snapped at it in exasperation. "Not in there ya stupid mutt!"

Frankie tramped into the room and bent down. He was so close Barbara could have hit him. He grabbed Spinner's collar and dragged him out.

"Come on dawg. We know she was in there. Show us which way the bitch went."

Barbara couldn't believe her ears. The dog barked but was hauled to the back door. She heard Lenny giving orders at the back door. "There's her footprints. Come on!"

Unable to believe her luck Barbara did up her right boot. What should she do now? She heard the men go out the back door and around the side of the hut. Gasping with anxiety she pulled on the laces of the left boot. But was there time to lace it up?

No, she decided, tucking the laces in with shaking fingers. She straightened up and glanced around, trying to decide what to do next..

Clothes! Her shirt was gone and she couldn't see her trousers. She didn't like the idea of running through the bush stark naked. Then she saw Lenny's trousers still hanging on the bed. In three steps she had them. As she lifted them off the bedpost she heard the men right outside the window. They were already half way round the house!

Frankie called, "There's her footprints. She went up the windmill."

"Johnno, you useless bastard! You came this way," Lenny yelled. "Get up and see if she's on the roof, quick!"

Barbara hesitated. She had thought of heading for the front where there were vehicles but that was where the men were headed. *Should I just run out the back door and make for the bush?* she wondered. In her heart she knew it was a forlorn hope.

She went to the bedroom door and paused. The iron roof creaked as Johnno stepped onto it.

"Yaah! Bloody hell! This is bloody hot!" he called, hopping up and down in a jig which made the old house shake.

"Is she up there, ya fool?" Lenny snarled.

"Can't see her."

"Look over the other side."

Barbara heard Johnno walk across the roof, cursing the heat. Frankie interrupted. "Here's her footprints. She went round the front."

From overhead came angry obscenities and the sound of Johnno hurrying back across the roof, swearing the whole time. She heard him step across from the roof to the top of the ladder.

Barbara knew she had to move. She walked quickly to the back door. Again she paused as an idea came to her. In her right hand she carried Lenny's trousers. But there was no time to put them on.

Once outside Barbara turned left and walked quickly along the back of the house. *I'll follow them,* she reasoned. *They won't expect that.*

After a quick glance which showed no sign of the three men, she went around the corner to the tank stand. The brown mongrel began barking furiously and jerking at its chain. She had forgotten it. Then she saw that Johnno was still climbing down the ladder. He was facing her way but was on the other side of the water tank.

From the front of the hut came Lenny's voice. "The cunning bitch!" he shouted.

"What?" Johnno shouted, jumping down and running towards the front of the house. Barbara crouched and looked under the tank stand.

Frankie answered in a high pitched yell from inside. "She's run around the house and gone in the front door."

There were crashing noises. Johnno vanished onto the front veranda. Now driven by absolute desperation to take extreme risks Barbara rose and ran around the tank stand and windmill after him. As she passed the louvres, she heard Lenny yell.

"She's bin in 'ere. She's got my bloody duds. The bitch!"

"Listen ter Brute," Frankie cried. "She's gorn out the back."

"Quick!"

Barbara heard the men running towards the back door. *This will be my last chance,* she thought. *I must get away from here.'* Fear clutched at her throat and drove her to run. She fled around to the front, avoiding the veranda as her boots would make too much noise.

She ran to the blue panel van and looked in. No keys! A vivid memory of Frankie putting them in his pocket came to her. Almost beside herself with panic she ran to the brown Toyota Landcruiser parked next to it. Lenny's, she assumed. It had bull bars, spotlights and the steel cage of a pig-hunter.

A glance showed her no keys there either. Then she heard voices yelling at the side of the house. *No more time!* They were hot on her heels. She turned to run, panic grabbing at her.

The horse!

She skidded to a halt, pulled the reins loose and went to fumble at the left stirrup. It was a year since she had ridden a horse and she was no expert. As she hauled herself up she heard a shout.

"There she is!" Lenny cried.

Barbara cast a terrified glance over her shoulder as she swung her leg over the saddle. The men were running onto the veranda. The dog was barking at their feet.

"My horse! Get orf my horse!" Frankie yelled.

Barbara didn't wait to get her right boot in the stirrup. She wrenched the horse's head round and kicked hard. The shouting and barking did the rest. For a moment Barbara thought the horse was going to buck and she clutched desperately at the saddle and its mane. Then the horse kicked up its heels and bolted, just as Lenny's huge hand reached for her.

Barbara looked back and saw Lenny running after her. To her horror she saw that he was almost within arm's reach. Still gripping the saddle with her left hand she swung Lenny's trousers above her head to flail at him. Even as she swung them down she realised it could be a mistake as he could grab them. She checked the swing just in time and nearly lost her balance.

It was enough though. Lenny looked up and raised his left arm to protect himself and suddenly down he went. He had slipped in a wet cow pat. Barbara saw him sprawl in the dust, his right hand splattering in another pile of wet dung. In her relief she emitted a whoop of exultant laughter.

Lenny rose to his feet, flicking the manure off. Some of it splattered on his dust-covered face and shirt. He hobbled a few paces, waving his arms and mouthing a stream of gutter language. To Barbara he looked a truly obscene figure dancing in the dust without his trousers but she laughed again. The sound of it seemed to drive him into a frenzy of rage.

As Barbara looked back she saw both Johnno and the drover stop running just past Lenny. They had obviously realised they couldn't catch the horse. The drover was screaming for her to 'git orf his horse'. Of more concern was Spinner.

The dog came racing after them, his paws pounding up little puffs of dust.

The horse suddenly swerved. Barbara almost fell off. She was sure she would have except that her sweaty bare thighs stuck to the leather of the saddle. *If I had been wearing trousers I would have slipped off for sure,* she thought. But even so it gave her a shock that sent her heart palpitating again. It also made her glance ahead.

The horse was now heading past the dog kennels and pig-pens. It was also slowing down from a gallop to a canter. Ahead was the dirt road Barbara had been driven down. Aware that she was only just clinging on she tried to find the right stirrup but couldn't get her boot in. By this time she was a hundred metres from the men.

Again she glanced back again. The dog was running alongside, barking with excitement but making no attempt to interfere with the horse. The men were still yelling but Lenny was pointing and hobbling towards his Landcruiser.

Barbara's wildly thumping heart seemed to leap up her throat before settling in despair. *The horse can't possibly outrun a car,* she thought. Then she shook her head. *Yes it can! Off the road.*

A moment's thought told her that the horse would make better time cross country. But there was a barbed wire fence on either side. Barbara knew it couldn't be jumped. She was no horsewoman and she didn't know the horse.

But it is a stockhorse, not a show pony. It has probably never jumped a fence in its life. I need a gate, she thought.

Looking anxiously ahead she saw one, not twenty metres away on her left. Driven by the urgency of the situation she snatched at the reins and pulled back. She must have pulled too hard and hurt the horse as it swung its head and whinnied. But it did slow down.

Dare I stop? What will the dog do? Will it latch onto me? What were the men doing? she wondered. She was now so anxious she was having trouble thinking straight and her vision kept going blurry.

Barbara looked back. She was a couple of hundred metres away now. Even as she looked she saw Lenny slam the door of his Landcruiser and go hobbling around the front, waving his arms and shouting.

Why didn't he get in? The answer came instantly and made Barbara smile. He could not start it. *The keys are probably here in the pocket of his trousers.* But she didn't dare waste time checking.

That decided her. She pulled the horse to a stop at the gate. It led into the grassy paddock full of beef cattle. It was a wire gate with a straining latch. She realised she would have to dismount to open it. There was the risk the dog might attack her, or that she might not be able to remount.

A single glance told her the dog wouldn't do anything. He had stopped barking and was standing panting, tongue out.

"You're enjoying this, aren't you Spinner?" she said.

The dog looked up and wagged his tail. Barbara draped Lenny's trousers over the saddle, causing a minor cascade of coins into the dust. Taking a firm grip on the reins she climbed down.

She kept her boot in the stirrup ready to spring back up in case Spinner bit her. Instead the dog came and licked at her legs and sniffed at her behind which made her flame with embarrassment. Satisfied she was safe she stepped down and walked over to the gate. As she took hold of the loop of wire holding the straining bar she heard a car engine roar to life.

The drover's blue van!

Barbara felt a fierce surge of hate for the false friend and his treachery. Then she moved fast. As quickly as her fumbling fingers could work it she eased off the latch. The gate sagged. She lifted the end post out of the wire loop holding its bottom end and cast the gate in a tangle.

As she led the horse through the opening she saw the blue van back out, turn and accelerate in her direction.

"Oh my God! Here they come!" she cried.

Gasping with anxiety she fumbled with the stirrup and got her boot into it. The horse turned to look resentfully at her but luckily stood still.

By the time she had hoisted herself astride the saddle the blue van had covered half the distance. In near panic Barbara kicked with her heels without waiting to get her right boot in the stirrup.

The horse started moving but only at a fast walk.

"Go horse, go!" she cried, flicking the reins and kicking again.

By then the blue car was slowing down to turn through the gate. Reluctantly the horse broke into a trot. Mouth dry with fear she looked back. The car swung through the gate in a cloud of dust. Within seconds it was only twenty or thirty metres back.

How can I possibly escape? she thought in despair.

Suddenly the car slewed to a stop. The engine roared. The car surged forward and stopped again with a jerk. There was a loud, metallic *twang!* Barbara saw that the drover had turned too fast and the car had snagged on the wire gate which hadn't been properly pulled aside. This had wrenched the whole gate off its post, making an even bigger tangle.

Barbara heard loud swearing and saw the drover's head lean out to look down. Lenny was in the passenger's seat. The car engine roared and the vehicle surged forward, dragging the tangle of wire and star pickets with it.

The incident had gained Barbara another twenty metres of lead. In desperation she tried to kick the horse into greater speed, if only because the trotting was causing her breasts to jerk and bounce in a most painful way. To stop this she held them with her right hand while keeping the reins in her left.

The horse broke into a canter which was easier. Then it jumped a log. Barbara cried out in fright as she nearly fell off. Next the horse dodged some trees and she almost slid off sideways. Alarmed beef cattle began scattering ahead of them.

The car followed but didn't seem to be gaining. No doubt the drover wasn't too keen on driving fast in long grass. Barbara began to hope. *Perhaps I will get away?*

Behind her there was a crunch and loud bangs. The blue car bounced over some obstruction which had been hidden in the grass. Barbara heard yells and swearing over the roar of its engine. Then the car stopped with a vicious jerk. She saw Lenny's face almost hit the windscreen. The remains of the wire gate had snagged on a log.

The car engine roared as it tried to pull free. Then it reversed and tried again. Barbara drew further ahead. "Come on horse, run!" she yelled, kicking at him again.

This time the horse broke into a gallop. Barbara found it very difficult to stay on. She tried to get her right boot into the stirrup but couldn't. The iron was jerking and flailing, hitting her and the horse.

Again she looked back. The car was at least a hundred metres behind. Ahead of her cattle were running off to each side, parting before their progress like the Red Sea parting for Moses. Spinner began barking furiously and nipped several of the slower beasts. These bellowed in pain. This caused the animals to flee in panic, stampeding in all directions.

Barbara looked behind to see if the blue van was catching up. It wasn't. It was still stopped and the drover had opened his door and stepped out. Lenny opened his door as well.

At that moment the horse swerved sharply. Barbara cried out in fright. She grabbed at the saddle to hold on. Instead her fingers closed on Lenny's trousers. She experienced a sickening series of images, each spelling failure: the horse's side, the horse's underbelly, the horse's hooves in long grass.

Instinctively she put out her hands as the ground rose to hit her. She tumbled heavily. Her head struck something and the world seemed to go black and red.

Chapter 25

LENNY'S PLEASURE

Barbara lay on her back in the long grass and shook her head. Spinner appeared and licked her face. Her senses swam, then returned. Half stunned she looked up. Above her were the strands of a barbed wire fence.

That is why the horse swerved, she thought. Lenny's trousers were tangled around the wires. Her head had struck the fence post.

Men's voices jerked her back to her peril.

They were coming!

Quickly, Barbara rolled under the fence and sat up. About fifty metres away she saw Lenny. He was hobbling rapidly towards her. The drover was still back at his car, bending down beside it.

The horse?

It had stopped ten metres away but Barbara was now on the other side of the fence. A quick estimation decided her that she didn't have time to crawl under and mount before Lenny arrived. She scrambled to her feet.

Lenny saw her and yelled for her to stop. Barbara turned to run, then had an idea. The trousers. She needed them and Lenny obviously wasn't enjoying running through the long grass without them either, by the way he was holding himself.

Barbara pulled at the trousers but they were firmly hooked. The fence twanged and more money and a set of keys tinkled out of the pockets. So did a box of matches.

Matches! Fire! *Can I use it again?* she thought.

Lenny was only fifty metres away but he was gasping and sweating. Barbara snatched up the box, opened it and took out a match and struck it. She was amazed her hand didn't tremble. In a flash of decision she would later marvel at she put the burning match down on the sulphur heads of the other matches in the box.

There was a sharp hissing as they all flared up. Then she dropped the box in a shower of flaming droplets and ran. By then Lenny was almost at the fence. He swerved to avoid the small fires which sprang up in the long grass. At the fence he hesitated as to whether to climb over or under. He went under. Barbara looked back as she ran. She had already gained ten metres. Lenny was red in the face and puffing as he rose to his feet. He ran a few paces in a painful hobble then stopped, looking first at her, then back at the fire.

He hasn't got any boots on, Barbara realised. *Thank God for my own boots.* She kept running, confident she could outrun Lenny.

Barbara glanced back and felt a surge of relief. Lenny had stopped chasing her and gone back to try to get his trousers. He then appeared to hop and dance around the edges of the rapidly spreading flames. His trousers were on fire. Barbara heard the drover yelling in alarm. Already panting she slowed down and looked back again.

Smoke was billowing up in a thick white cloud. Barbara could hear Spinner barking. The horse had taken fright and was trotting off along the fence. The flames spread quickly in the long grass. A gentle breeze took it away from her.

A sudden stab of worry struck her. The cattle. Would they be burnt? She hoped not. *The gate is open,* she reasoned.

The drover was yelling the same thing. "Lenny, catch that bloody horse. We gotta get these cattle out of this paddock."

"You do it," Lenny screamed. He was dancing with rage as he backed away from the fire. He shook his fist at Barbara.

The drover yelled back, "You get the cattle Lenny. I gotta get me car untangled."

Barbara kept running but she was now gasping for breath and her head seemed to spin. Feeling she was safe for the moment she stopped and crouched to quickly tie the laces of the left boot. Then she set off at a slow walk until she reached a belt of thicker scrub. Behind her she could only see leaping flames and smoke spreading. There was no sign of Lenny. Wiping sweat from her eyes she walked steadily on.

As her breathing steadied Barbara started to shiver and shake from delayed shock. Trembling with reaction she hugged herself. What a predicament! Here she was tramping through the bush in the middle of nowhere and stark naked to boot! Or at least not quite.

I do have my boots. Thank God for that, she thought. She knew she would have been in a hopeless situation in tender bare feet. Suddenly overcome by emotion she dissolved into sobs and shaking.

"Get a grip on yourself kid. You aren't out of the woods yet," Barbara told herself.

Another look behind showed just bush and an amazing amount of smoke billowing into a cloudless blue sky. The sun seemed to hang in it like a white ball of agony. She could feel its rays burning her bare back and shoulders.

"I daren't stop to rest in the shade. I must put as much distance as I can between me and those men," she told herself. She hoped they wouldn't chase her but feared they might. To make it easier she knelt and relaced her boots and then stood up and continued walking.

After hurrying through the bush for about ten minutes she stopped for a moment to regain her breath and to orientate herself. She guessed it must be near midday as the sun was overhead. That made it very difficult for her to work out which direction was which.

Remembering Cadet Navigation lessons helped. "It's December. That means the sun will be south of me, down near Rockhampton on the Tropic of Capricorn. So the other direction must be north. And the dirt road is behind me. I went left off it so I must have gone west. Oh no! I've been running southwest."

Satisfied she was correct she began walking in the direction she believed was west. The sun blazing down on her left side gave her a guide, as did the huge column of smoke behind her. She pushed her tired body to maintain a fast walk.

The grass thinned out and gave way to sparse clumps of a different type of grass amidst areas of bare soil and leaf-litter. The dominant tree type remained the monotonous ironbarks but closer together.

While she walked Barbara looked down at herself. Her whole body seemed covered in scratches and bruises. She had a splitting headache and her stomach was starting to grumble from lack of food. "God, I look a sight! I hope I don't meet anyone," she muttered. Never in her life had she imagined she would end up striding through the bush wearing nothing but a pair of boots!

"Isn't it hot! Oh, am I going to get sunburnt!" she told herself.

By this time she was feeling calmer and safer but the heat made her realise just how thirsty she was. Perspiration was trickling uncomfortably down her face and body. It dripped from her nose and chin and even from her fingertips.

"That looks like a creek line down there to the left. I wonder if there's water in it?" she muttered on observing a line of thicker timber. Hopefully she angled towards the creek which seemed to run roughly East-West. It was the first creek she had come to which had run that way and that made her try to visualise the map again to pick which it might be.

As she got closer Barbara saw it was a larger creek than any she had so far seen. Its banks were lined with clumps of lantana and rubber vines. Huge River Gums with their smooth, white trunks, along with a mixture of paperbarks and she-oaks, lined its bed. The creek bed was at least 20 metres wide and was flat, clean sand. Barbara followed an animal pad down between the masses of lantana into the thankful shade.

"Water!"

To her great relief there was flowing water. It wasn't much; just a trickle against the bank on her side. The water was only a couple of paces wide and a couple of centimetres deep but it was flowing; obviously a legacy of the recent rain. There were even a few small pools.

Barbara crouched and drank. Next she rinsed the sweat from her body as well as she could. This made many of the scratches sting but she felt much better. Then she drank some more. Her spirits rose.

"That's better. Now all I have to do is find my way back to camp. It can't be that far. If I keep going west I must at least come to the Bunyip," she said.

Then a sound shattered her composure: distant barking down the creek.

"Dogs! They're still after me! Oh no!"

Barbara remembered the pig-dogs locked in the cages; big, vicious brutes, some sort of bull-terrier breed. The fear returned with almost paralysing force. Instantly she fled.

She ran west along the creek bed. It was very hard going on the soft sand. Then she cursed.

"Oh you fool!" she upbraided herself. "Get off the sand."

She swerved up through a gap in the lantana and out into the open grass. As she did she was annoyed with herself again. Her boots would have left clear tracks in the damp sand.

"Too bad! It's done now. I don't have time to go back," she told herself. She cast a fearful glance behind her but there was no-one in sight. Keeping just on the edge of the belt of lantana and rubber vine she hurried on. As she pushed herself through another pain barrier she tried to decide whether it would be better to strike off at a tangent into the featureless bush or to stay near the creek which at least offered some thick cover.

In her heart she guessed that trying to hide from dogs would be futile but she kept on. The creek at least ran in the right direction. She skirted a large clump of lantana and was able to run along under the trees close to the bank for about fifty metres.

Barbara was soon gasping for breath. A stitch began to develop. She found the effort of running while holding her breasts very tiring but the alternative too painful and irritating. Dread clutched at her as she knew she was weakening.

There was a fresh outburst of barking and a man's shout a couple of hundred metres back. She guessed they had found her tracks. Her stomach seemed to knot itself into a ball of sickening despair. The thought of what the men would do to her made her feel giddy and nauseous, or was that from the heat and exertion? She knew she was near the end of her run.

A branch of lantana gave her ribs a painful scraping slash as she ran into it. Then she ran through a large spider web. So overwrought had she become that she just brushed the creature and the sticky mess off as she ran. A fallen tree and matt of flood debris blocked her path. Baulked and desperate she cast around for a way of escape and then had to back-track. But that was also a dead-end and she had to force her way between two clumps of lantana, getting more scratches on her thighs and hips.

The fear kept mounting until she was on the edge of hysterical panic. Her vision became blurred and sweat trickled into her eyes, stinging them and adding to the problem. Her breath began to come in hot, rasping gaps and her throat felt as though it was on fire and closing up.

Terrified but still determined Barbara forced herself to run another hundred metres and wondered when her heart would burst as it was beating so wildly. Breathing was a rasping, painful effort. Her legs were just dull, numb extensions of aching buttocks. Her boots felt like lead. Black spots began to dance before her eyes.

The dogs barked again, this time much closer!

"They must have the scent. They've let them go!" she croaked. She knew she could never outrun a dog. But she kept on trying. Terrifying images of 'Brute' flashed across her mind.

"Ah! Pig!" she cried.

Barbara swerved and skidded to a stop at the base of a large paperbark. Just ahead of her the most enormous black pig she had ever seen was rooting in the leaf mould.

And it had seen her! It was a boar, a monster Razorback. Barbara's vision seemed to focus on its vicious curved tusks even as it turned its beady eyes on her. To her added horror the pig snorted ferociously and began to charge. Barbara was momentarily mesmerised by the sheer speed of its movement. It was unbelievable that such a large animal could move so fast!

Then she fled. Just near her was another large paperbark, its trunk bent by the annual floods. Fuelled by frantic desperation she ran up the sloping trunk even as the pig reached her. It scrabbled on the bark behind her and the bristles on its snout actually touched her ankles. Driven by utter terror, she scrabbled frantically for a handhold.

Somehow Barbara made it up to the first branch. She was dimly aware that the boar had slithered back down. Shaking with reaction and effort she hauled herself into a fork about four metres up. Sobbing with fear she sucked in great wracking gulps of air then coughed as dust from the paperbark lodged in her throat.

The pig circled the base of the tree, snorting in rage and tearing up the leaf-litter. Barbara was appalled. *I'm trapped!* she thought, the terror ripping her with what felt like physical force.

Dogs barking brought Barbara back to an even worse reality. The men were far more to be feared than a wild pig and they were close!

The boar heard the barking. It turned in that direction and swung its head from side to side. It uttered a series of primeval grunts, which the dogs answered with ferocious yelps and growls.

Next instant, the pig was off. It ran out onto the open sand of the creek bed. As it did there were more high-pitched pig squeals. Twenty metres further up the creek a large sow erupted from the lantana. Four or five piglets, Barbara couldn't be sure how many they moved so fast, scampered out as well, running in all directions.

Bang!

A rifle shot made Barbara jerk in surprise. By then the pig was almost across the creek. The sow and three suckers followed it.

Bang!

"Reeek! Reeek! Qweeek!" the sow screamed in pain and stumbled. It rose instantly and tried to keep running but one of its hind legs had been broken by the bullet. The piglets milled in shrieking fear.

Then the dogs arrived: five of them, including Brute. With snarls and growls which made Barbara's blood run chill they bounded across the sand with terrifying speed.

The piglets scattered in panic. Two ran back the way they had come. One made it but the other was caught by Brute almost at the base of Barbara's tree. She heard the dog's slavering jaws clamp onto the little animal which squealed in pain and fear.

Out in the creek bed a terrible battle erupted. A dog grabbed the third piglet. The others began attacking the wounded sow, rushing in to tear at its legs and hindquarters. The barking and grunting was appalling. Barbara shook with fear and revulsion as she stared in horror at the primitive scene.

Men's shouts reminded her of her own desperate peril. She looked up the tree and wondered if she should climb higher. Even as she thought this Johnno appeared. He was fully dressed and carried a stock whip.

Barbara froze as he ran towards her. Luckily he was looking at the fighting animals so he did not glance up but he passed so close she could have kicked him in the head. His attention stayed on the revolting spectacle at the base of the tree where Brute was literally tearing the piglet to pieces while it was still alive.

Lenny's voice sent another stab of fear through Barbara. She looked in the direction of the sound. He appeared out in the creek bed. Barbara saw that he was also fully dressed and carried a rifle. He stopped to watch the dogs attacking the pig and to Barbara's horror began to urge them on and to shout with laughter.

Barbara tried to remain still and to calm her gulping breathing. But then she had to move her right arm. Dust from the powdery paperbark was making her sneeze. Just in time she pressed hard on the base of her nose, another skill she had learnt at Cadets. It made her eyes water and darts of agony shot up through her face but no sneeze came. Sweat poured down her back and felt horribly sticky.

And the ants had found her. Green ants. Dozens of them. They began to nip in the most tender and painful places. Barbara bit her lip and tried to ignore them. Into her misted vision appeared a bobbing, shimmering pattern of movement which she saw were hundreds more coming down the trunk in a hurrying, pale-green swarm.

Just below her Johnno kicked hard at Brute. "Let go, ya mongrel!" he yelled. He uncoiled his stockwhip but had trouble holding it with his bandaged hands. The dog ignored him in its frenzy as it ripped the piglet's stomach open. Johnno lashed at the dog. "Let go Brute. Get on. We gotta find that bloody girl. Lenny! Shoot that bloody pig!" he yelled.

"Why? This is real good," Lenny replied.

Barbara was so sick she would have vomited if there had been anything in her stomach. The look of slack-jawed pleasure on Lenny's face was the ugliest thing she had ever seen.

Johnno yelled again, "Lenny, don't be a fool! We gotta find that girl. If she gets away we're in deep shit!"

At that moment, Johnno was right behind Barbara and she felt her flesh crawl at the thought of him seeing her naked from that angle. *If he looks up!* she thought. She felt horribly exposed and fierce shame coursed through her.

Then she began to shake as the terror overwhelmed her. Through her mind flooded images of the attempted rape of two years before when she was a First Year cadet. It had been in a creek bed very like this one and memories of the terror and disgust of that incident caused her to shudder and feel ill.

I was naked then, she remembered. Her whole body began shivering and trembling and she thought she was going to black out and lose her grip. *Keep still! Hang on! Don't let go!* she told herself. For a few seconds she feared she had failed but bit by bit she regained control and the trembling subsided and clarity returned.

Loud shrieks of pleasure from Lenny drew her gaze back to the creek bed. Lenny screamed in a voice raw with delight, "Rip him, Jaws! Rip him!" He danced with excitement.

Johnno again yelled angrily, "Lenny, shoot the bloody pig! We ain't here to hunt pigs. We gotta catch that girl."

He stepped down onto the sand and walked towards Lenny. As soon as he passed below her Barbara had to move. Dozens of ants were swarming on her face and several had bitten at the edge of her eyelids. Hundreds more were swarming over her body, exploring and nipping. She shuddered and gritted her teeth as they bit her.

Lenny and Johnno argued for several minutes while the dogs continued their savage attacks. Then, with obvious reluctance, Lenny raised the rifle. Johnno used his whip and voice to force the dogs back.

Bang!

"Aw, that's good! Look at all that blood and guts!" Lenny exulted.

Barbara found she had to look. The bullet had punched through the sow's stomach, spattering bloody flesh onto the sand. The dogs darted in, four of them now. One seized the pig's throat. Another tore at its entrails. Barbara saw what looked like a string of bloody pork sausages stretch out in the dog's jaws. The images nauseated and terrified her and she retched and looked away.

Shivering with fear she closed her eyes and clung to the tree. More ants swarmed onto her. They were in her ears and her nostrils and everywhere. What a nightmare! If only it would end.

Bang!

Another gunshot made her flick her eyes open in fright. Lenny had walked up and shot the sow in the head. The dogs again leapt in despite Johnno using his whip and kicking at them.

Then the third piglet, which Barbara had supposed was dead, suddenly rose groggily to its feet, shook its head and skittered off across the sand. One dog saw it and gave chase, emitting a volley of excited barks as it did. The other dogs then saw it and followed, even one that was streaming blood down its side. The mutilated carcase of the sow was left in the sand.

"Come back here you bloody dogs!" Johnno screamed.

He ran after them uttering shrill whistles and calling their names. They all vanished into the tangle of lantana on the far bank. Lenny was left standing in the creek bed. He looked around. A horrible grin spread across his face. For a moment Barbara thought he had seen her because he started limping across the sand towards her.

But he was looking down. Barbara screwed her eyes around, ignoring an ant which bit painfully at the lower lid of her right eye. The second piglet lay twitching at the base of the tree, blood and mucous trickling from its mouth.

Lenny walked behind Barbara and she heard a thud and the piglet grunted in pain. Almost overcome by terror she swivelled her head to see what Lenny was doing. To her dismay she saw that his head was only a metre from her bare backside. Then, to her horror and disgust, Lenny kicked the piglet in the head as though it was a football. It rolled and spun in the dust. Muttering with pleasure he walked over to it and kicked it several more times. As he did he chuckled, a chilling, evil chuckle that almost paralysed Barbara with terror. He then crushed his boot heel down on its skull.

Almost beyond feeling by then, Barbara watched wide-eyed as Lenny again kicked the piglet, this time in the stomach. It hurtled up and into a clump of lantana. Lenny chuckled again, then swore, then chuckled again. Then, to Barbara's intense relief, he walked out of sight along an animal pad in the lantana.

Barbara waited half a minute but then she had to move. Her muscles could not hold on any longer, nor could she endure the ants. Trembling with fright and squirming at the prickling sensation of the ants on her skin she slid to the ground and brushed at them with her hands, all the while darting fearful glances around. From over on the other bank of the creek she could hear Johnno and the dogs, but they were some distance away.

Good! she thought.

But it was Lenny she was most terrified of.

Where is he? she worried.

Chapter 26

FEARFUL RISKS

Almost beside herself with hysteria, Barbara plucked and scraped off the last few ants. Her whole body seemed to tingle and burn. Fear almost paralysed her. She felt utterly drained and just wanted to collapse but knew she must move. Forcing herself into movement she began walking. Creeping cautiously from tree to tree and from bush to bush she continued on along the bank of the creek.

Where had Lenny gone? At any moment she expected to encounter him. Johnno and the dogs she could still hear but every step took her further away from them.

For twenty minutes or so Barbara crept along the creek bank, every nerve a-quiver. In this way she covered only a couple of hundred metres. The sounds of Johnno and the dogs receded to occasional distant barks or shouts.

"That's a vehicle track," she murmured. She had first taken the eroded marks ahead on the far bank to be just an animal pad but as she got closer she saw it was a definite formed road. As she got closer she observed that it came down a shallow cutting and crossed the creek via a concrete floodway. But which road, and where did it lead? She tried to visualise the map.

Barbara crept closer to the road, moving at a crouch or on hands and knees. In this manner she reached a small washout which led down to the creek bed near the concrete crossing. Very carefully she slid into the washout and crawled up it to the top of the bank. Once there she carefully raised her head behind a clump of grass and looked around.

Almost immediately she subsided, her heart thumping wildly. *Thank God I was careful!* she thought. Lenny was there. He was standing just across the road at the top of the bank where he could see along the road in both directions and also all of the creek bed.

Barbara lay flat in the ditch. It was less than a metre deep and right beside the road. There were tiny black ants here. They began to nip with a sting out of all proportion to their size. The sun seemed to scorch her whole back. Sweat trickled and the dust stuck to her. Fear held her there. Trembling grew as the terror again gripped her. Then the searing pain of a cramp in her right calf muscle stabbed through her. To stop herself whimpering or calling out she bit her lip. She tasted blood and felt the stinging sensation that told her she had re-opened the scab on her already split lower lip. Grimly she struggled to stay in control, digging her nails into her palms to counter the agony of the cramp.

Slowly the pain eased and she was able to relax her muscles while lying prone in the dirt and dry grass. Then flies came to land on her split lip. And more ants found her. The irritation helped her to start thinking rationally again.

I can't stay here, she thought. She decided she must move back down the washout again and try circling well away from this point. *If Lenny walks to this side of the road he will see me.*

Ignoring the pain from sharp stones and sticks she started moving slowly but it was much harder going backwards and even the faintest crackle of a dead leaf or twig under her boots or knees made her freeze in fear. Her heart thumped so loudly she was sure he must hear it and her breath seemed to choke and rasp.

To add to her feeling of being trapped between the Devil and the deep blue sea she heard the dogs begin to bark back along the creek. They were closer and on the same bank.

Have they picked up my scent? she wondered fearfully. Her heart sank. *I'm trapped!* she told herself. Then she cocked her head. What was that noise? Ah! A vehicle was coming along the road. *Can I scuttle across in its dust?* she wondered. Then she shook her head. *Only if I got well past Lenny further along the road.*

With this in mind she began to crawl back up the ditch. The vehicle noises grew louder. At the top of the slope Barbara paused to take another cautious look. What she saw sent her hopes crashing. Only a few metres past Lenny the washout became a shallow drain beside the road. With a sinking heart she realised that she would never be able to crawl along it unseen. The situation made her want to scream in frustration.

Wild thoughts of jumping out to wave down the vehicle in the hope that the driver might stop and help her formed in her mind as a last desperate plan. She tensed herself ready.

But just as she was about to spring out Lenny walked out onto the road and put his arm up. The vehicle, a truck made to carry cattle, began slowing down. Lenny's actions indicated he knew the driver. Barbara tasted bitter defeat as her hopes were dashed.

The truck rattled and shuddered to a stop with its motor running. The cab ended up just past Barbara. Above her were the rear wheels and the timber framework. There were cattle in the back. She heard an angry man's voice.

"What the bloody hell are you doing here, Lenny?"

"Aw, lookin' for a girl Mister Castledine."

"Looking for a girl! Funny place to look," replied the driver with sarcasm. "I'd go to town meself. What bloody girl? Why aren't you helping Frankie move those cattle from Saltpan down to Box Flat like I told you? Where is Wally?"

Castledine! *That was the name mentioned by one of the men at the hut with the bull,* Barbara remembered. *He must be one of this gang.* She crouched listening, trying to decide what to do.

"What happened to yer face?" Castledine queried.

"The bitch kicked me with her boots," Lenny answered, the anger evident in his tone. "She's gunna regret that.

"Serves ya bloody right! What happened?"

Lenny gave a halting explanation. "It was that red-headed bitch wot shot me in the leg boss. I snatched her last night from the army camp. I was gunna teach her a lesson."

"You what! You bloody moron! We've got the big lift on tonight. The trucks are on their way. There's more than a million bucks riding on this job and you have to kidnap a girl!" Castledine yelled incredulously.

"Yeah. Sorry boss. I just seen her and couldn't help meself," Lenny mumbled.

"You bloody fool! So where is she? What happened?" Castledine shouted.

"Aw! She got away."

"Got away! Which way? What's all that smoke over near the saltpan?"

"She done that. She took orf on Frankie's horse an' she lit a fire."

Castledine swore. "Lit a fire! Bloody hell!"

"Yeah. It burnt Frankie's van. He's real cranky about that," Lenny replied.

"Serves him bloody right if he had a hand in this," snapped Castledine, a sentiment Barbara heartily agreed with. "So where is he?"

Lenny shuffled his boots in the dust. "He's roundin' up the cattle. They all stampeded and broke the fences. Johnno and me is lookin' for the girl," he explained.

"Johnno!" Castledine expostulated. "What's he doing here? He should be at Emu Pump."

"Yeah well, when she first got away she burnt his truck," Lenny said.

"First got away! Burnt his truck!" Castledine exploded. "What the bloody hell's been going on?"

Lenny gave a halting and disorganised explanation. Listening to it gave Barbara a fierce feeling of satisfaction. Castledine was livid. "You bloody drongos! So Johnno is tracking her with dogs. What are you doing?"

"Makin' sure she don't cross this road. She ain't far away. We seen her tracks back there and the dogs got her scent but some pigs sidetracked 'em. You can hear Johnno comin' now."

Barbara could. The dogs sounded horribly close. *I can't stay here. I have to act,* she told herself.

As she looked desperately around seeking a way to escape, the cattle in the back of the truck jostled each other, rattling the frame. She saw their eyes peering at her.

At that moment an idea came to her. It was a mad idea but it seemed her only chance. A quick glance assured her that neither Lenny nor the driver could see her. She stood up and in two steps was at the back wheels. Her heart beat so furiously she felt giddy. Things seemed to happen in a blur of slow motion.

The cattle bellowed and jostled away from her. She feared it would attract the men's attention but the driver was angrily berating Lenny. Barbara began to climb the side of the truck. As she did Lenny spoke. "It's OK Boss. We'll catch her an' she won't talk," he said.

"She'd better not!" Castledine hissed venomously.

"She won't. I'll shoot the bitch the moment I lay eyes on her," Lenny replied.

Barbara seemed to freeze. She could actually glimpse Lenny down through the opposite slats in the framework. With an effort of willpower she forced herself to keep climbing.

"Don't be a mug Lenny," Castledine yelled. "Don't add murder to kidnapping. Christ! Just tie her up and leave her for the cops to find."

"Yeah Boss. But this is personal. I got a score to settle."

"Listen Lenny, if this job comes unstuck because of this girl you'll bloody well regret it," threatened Castledine.

By this time Barbara had reached the top. The float had a roof on it but, like the sides, this only comprised boards bolted to a steel frame. Very carefully she slid onto the top. This made the float shake and rattle but the cattle kept moving as well. With a wildly hammering heart she lay flat.

I've made it! she thought. But she also knew with sickening finality that she was absolutely committed.

Castledine was still speaking. "What's she look like this girl? What's she wearing?"

"Red-headed. Real well stacked. An' she ain't wearin' nothin'," Lenny replied.

"Nothing?"

"Well, she's got boots on."

"Boots! How did she get that way? Oh, don't tell me. I can guess. Bloody Hell! Stay here. I'll go and get Wallis and Norton and help search," Castledine said. He swore foully and Barbara heard the truck's gears crunch.

The motor roared and the truck began to move. As it did Barbara could see Lenny through the gaps between the slats. She realised that when the truck dipped into the creek bed and went up the other bank he would be able to see her if he looked.

Knowing she had no choice she gripped the frame with her fingers and braced her boots against a steel bar as the truck ground down onto the concrete floodway. As it did she turned her head to look back. Lenny was still standing there but luckily he was not looking.

And there was a dog on the road! Two more dogs arrived a moment later, running up the ditch and then around in circles. Lenny was yelling at them. She saw Johnno appear in the creek bed as the truck climbed the other bank. *Oh hurry up truck!* she silently urged.

The truck roared up onto the flat and began to accelerate. Barbara saw Johnno run up to join Lenny but the scene was then thankfully blotted out by the dust kicked up by the truck.

Would they guess? She didn't care. By the time they could act she would be a long way away.

But how far? *Where is the truck going?* she wondered.

She found it extremely difficult to hold on. The truck seemed to be a huge vibrating mass as it roared heavily over the rough dirt track. Her body kept lifting and thudding down, bruising kneecaps, hips and elbows. A series of corrugations almost shook her loose. Then a low branch threatened to scrape her off.

She raised her head to get warning of any more branches. As the truck drove away from the creek she felt a spasm of intense relief. Then she began to look around to try to plan her next move. There were hills off to the right she saw, rocky hills covered with stunted scrub. They weren't more than a kilometre away.

That's the Tucker Box Range, she told herself.

Relief flooded through her. From memory she had been roughly able to locate in her mind the Salt Pan Outstation and Emu Pump but now she knew exactly where she was.

The hills drew closer and closer until the truck actually skirted the base of the nearest one. Barbara found this a bit disconcerting as it meant she was now being rapidly transported south, away from the army camp. She thought about climbing over the back and jumping off but the truck was now travelling at such a speed she was afraid she would end up lying on the road with a broken leg or back. She decided to wait.

The truck's brakes suddenly squealed and it shuddered to a stop at a gate right at the bottom of a steep rocky slope. Castledine climbed down and walked forward to open the gate.

Is this my chance? she wondered.

She wriggled over to the left side of the truck ready to climb down. But there was nowhere to hide within 50 paces. The ground was bare. The grass had been eaten or trampled and there were no trees, logs or ant hills. Besides, the man was too quick. It was a steel gate on hinges and it swung open easily. Castledine climbed back in and the truck drove through and stopped again. Castledine got out again to close the gate. Barbara could hear him muttering and swearing but she did not dare lift her head to look. The vehicle lurched into motion.

Only a couple of minutes later it came to a fork in the road. The left-hand road ran on to vanish into a creek line. The truck took the right-hand branch which ran between the hills and the creek. There were several small dry gullies leading down from the hills which the driver had to negotiate slowly.

I'll jump off at the next one, Barbara decided.

But there wasn't another one. Instead the truck ran up a spur of the hill. There were hills closing in from the south now and Barbara looked over the edge and got a real fright. The road clung to the top of a steep drop. Below was the creek in a small gorge. The bottom was a jumble of black rocks and a few trees. Several times she caught the gleam of water.

The truck gave a vicious bump on the rough surface. Barbara was nearly catapulted over the edge. She hung on grimly and braced herself.

As the truck topped the crest and began its descent on the other side she had a good view ahead. She was so surprised at what she saw that she actually gaped. On later reflection she realised she should have expected it because she had noted it on the map a dozen times.

Ahead was an open valley almost bare of trees and completely surrounded by the rugged hills. It wasn't circular, more rectangular, about two kilometres long and one wide. Several small gullies and creeks led down to join the main creek which 'flowed' out through the little gorge.

"Centripetal drainage," she murmured, remembering a geography lesson by Capt Conkey. *Of course. That's why they call it the Tucker Box Range. The early pioneers probably used it to keep their cattle in before they had their properties fenced.*

And it was being used to keep cattle in now, hundreds of them. The whole valley was dotted with them, more than Barbara had ever seen in her life.

The dusty road led down and across the north side of the valley to a couple of buildings and a set of cattle yards with a wind pump. From there another road went on to climb over a saddle at the South-West corner.

Deadman's Gap, Barbara remembered. Then the realisation that she was being rapidly transported into another dangerous situation dawned on her. *I think it's time I got off,* she decided.

But the truck had picked up speed and was out on the open flat. Barbara could only hang on and hope. Anxiously she peered ahead seeking an opportunity, like another gate or a creek but there were none. Worse still she could see clouds of dust from cattle milling in the yards.

That indicated at least one man was working there. *If he looks this way, he might see me,* she worried.

The truck rattled over a cattle grid and screeched to a halt in the dusty front yard of another corrugated iron and timber outstation. There was a dunny behind it and a shed further on. A battered grey Land Rover was parked nearby. The nearest bush was fifty metres away and the bottom of the hills nearly twice as far.

Barbara lay flat and prayed she wouldn't be seen. Castledine tooted the horn, making her heart leap into her mouth. Then he switched off the motor and climbed out, slamming the door. The cattle surged and trampled. He began yelling towards the hut, "Wallis! Norton!"

There was no answer but a cattle dog yapped from somewhere behind the hut. Castledine swore and turned to walk around the front of the truck. Barbara saw his face clearly, red with heat and anger. He re-appeared on the other side, walking towards the cattle yards. Barbara swivelled her head to watch and was appalled to see a man on a horse in amongst the cattle and another sitting on the top rail at a gate.

If they look this way they could easily see me, she thought with dismay. She knew she had to move and risk there being a third person in the hut.

Without further thought she slithered across to the right hand side and lowered her legs over, just as Castledine began yelling to the two men. Barbara scrabbled to get a foothold but decided she dare not wait. Ignoring scraped skin and bruising to her breasts she slid over the side and lowered herself with her arms so that the truck hid her. Then she dropped.

The fall jarred her and she fell backwards to sprawl in the dust. She was up in an instant, crouched against the back wheels. Sand and dust coated her bottom and back, stuck to her by sweat. She ignored the irritation and peered under the truck.

By then Castledine was nearly at the yards, still calling to attract the men's attention. Luckily they were yelling at the cattle but she saw there was at least one dog there. "Oh well, nothing for it," she muttered. She looked anxiously at the hut. "No sign of life. So run."

Holding her breasts with her arms both from instinctive modesty and to stop them bouncing she sprinted across the dusty yard, keeping the truck between her and the men. Then she ran past the side of the hut, fearful someone might be there. As she reached the rear she had to swerve to avoid a clutter of rusty machinery and dog's dishes. She glanced left and saw an open back door and window.

Barbara kept running. She swerved again and ducked under some washing on a clothes line. Every few paces she looked back to ensure she had the truck and hut between her and the men. The stunted scrub and bushes drew closer and closer as she thudded over the bare, stony ground.

Thankfully she hurled herself behind the first large bush she came to, and instantly regretted it. It was spiky and the ground was hard and covered with burrs. She let out an involuntary yelp and scrambled into a crouch. Her heart thumped so hard she felt dizzy. A black haze seemed to lower across the top half of her vision.

While plucking prickles from her hands and knees and whimpering with pain she peered back towards the hut. It was only 50 paces away. There was no-one in sight but she could hear the men yelling down at the cattle yards. From under cover Barbara looked around to choose her route.

The ground behind her started to slope up steeply. It rapidly became a rugged jumble of rocks varying in size from footballs to huge boulders. Clumps of spiky grass, grass trees and the prickly bushes covered it but there were almost no trees. Amongst the boulders on the upper slopes grew some sort of dark green bushes.

Barbara's fieldcraft training told her that to go straight up the hill would expose her to the risk of being seen. *Expose is the right word,* she told herself ruefully, taking in the scratched and bruised state of her grimy and sunburnt body. She had never felt so sore and worn out in all her life.

Having recovered her breath she began working her way sideways along the foot of the hill, moving carefully from bush to bush. This brought her to a position where she could see the cattle yards beyond the hut. She crouched low and peered through a bush.

"Oh blast! Here they come," she murmured. Three men had come into view walking from the cattle yards towards the hut. Then her heart seemed to falter and tighten. A 'blue-heeler' cattle dog came bounding past the men to sniff around the truck before vanishing from view.

Another thought struck Barbara like ice water. *My boot tracks will be plain to see if the men look!* A glance showed that all three men wore elastic-sided riding boots which left a completely different mark from the rubber soles of her army boots.

The men seemed to be having an argument but she could only pick up odd words. "That bloody drongo Lenny. He... ....." one man said.

"... stupid bastards... should be..." agreed another.

"Would have.... ..... if he had a.... rifle and..." Castledine replied.

"What a... ... ... cattle?"

"Bugger the cattle!" Castledine exploded. "If we don't find this bloody girl we're all up shit creek."

The men went out of sight at the front of the hut. Barbara half rose to run then froze. The dog had appeared at the back of the hut! It sniffed around then looked up. Barbara sank back behind the bush with her heart thumping wildly.

Even as she did she knew she had made a mistake in moving as the dog saw her and broke into furious barking. Then it bounded forward.

Barbara could only stare through the bush in horror as a man appeared at the back door of the hut. The dog stopped only ten metres away from her and began growling. Barbara tensed, ready to run.

The man looked towards her. Then he shouted. "Come here you stupid dog! Come behind!"

Castledine appeared. "What is it?"

"Stupid dog chasin' somethin'. Come here 'Devil'. Get behind I say!" the man yelled.

The dog hesitated but from the way its tail went down it obviously knew what would happen if it didn't obey. It turned and padded back a dozen paces then paused and turned to bark again.

"Come on! Let's move!" Castledine snapped. He vanished inside the hut. The man took a couple of paces forward and pushed some washing aside to scan the hillside before calling the dog again. "Get here you mongrel or I'll belt ya," he said.

The dog now turned and scurried back past the man. He let the washing drop and gave the cringing animal a kick before vanishing inside. The dog followed.

Barbara realised she had been holding her breath. She expelled it and gasped in several big gulps. For a minute or so she trembled violently. Then her muscles began to cramp and she had to change position. While she did her eyes remained fixed on the hut. But the washing half obscured her view of the window and back door.

Washing. Barbara licked her cracked lips and looked longingly at the clothes hanging there. *If only I could steal some,* she thought.

Then the dog re-appeared at the back door and barked again. The man called out and Barbara again tensed ready to run. The three men appeared at the front of the hut. This time they carried guns and Barbara felt a new spasm of fear.

The men walked over to the battered Land Rover and the dog was called and reluctantly jumped in the back, still looking in Barbara's direction and barking.

"What's that bloody dog barking at?" Castledine asked again turning to look.

"Dunno. Wallaby probably. Saw one up there a while ago," the man replied.

To Barbara's intense relief the men climbed into the vehicle. It was started up, backed out, then turned and driven back the way the truck had come.

Get out of here! Barbara told herself.

Chapter 27

THIRSTY WORK

"Thank God!" Barbara whispered. She eased her cramped legs but remained crouched behind the bush until she saw the vehicle vanish over the crest of the spur which blocked the eastern end of the valley.

Only then did she stand and stretch her legs. Sweat trickled and dripped off her. Little rivulets of grime streaked her body. The afternoon sun seemed to scorch her exposed skin. She was painfully conscious of the heat and her thirst.

I must have a drink or I will collapse from heat exhaustion, she thought. *There is a windmill down there at those cattle yards,* she noted.

It looked to be only about 200 metres. But it was very open ground, just dust and short grass. Temptation warred with prudence. What if there was someone else there? Or if another vehicle came?

She bit her lip in indecision. That made her run her tongue over them as they were dry and cracked. "I need a drink. Oh, what will I do?" she cried. Every instinct told her to run, to get away while she had time, but her brain said she needed water.

Swallowing in attempt to moisten her dry throat she blinked and stared at the windmill and surrounding country through eyes that felt hot and gritty. A heat shimmer made it hard to see properly. She was acutely conscious of the heated air. It seemed to her that the encircling stony hills were radiating heat at her.

I need water, she told herself. *I'll collapse from heat exhaustion if I don't drink. I wonder if there is any water in that hut?*

For a few more seconds she stood there dithering. Once again she looked at the clothes on the line.

Can I spare the time? Is it worth the risk? Is there anyone else around? she wondered. There were no women's clothes visible so she guessed there were only stockmen living in the hut. *I will do better with clothes on, so they might be worth the risk,* she reasoned.

But the instinct to flee remained dominant. *Get away from here,* her mind kept telling her. In her mind's eye she visualized the Land Rover pulling up where she had climbed onto the truck. Johnno's dogs would have lost her scent there but the men would have seen her tracks. *I left at least two boot prints on that road before I climbed up onto the truck,* she remembered.

Dogs... tracks...

Barbara stopped in indecision. *I should just start running to cover as much distance as I can could before they come back to track me. I might be able to find more water along the way,* she thought. A simple calculation told her that the men could return in a few minutes. That decided her but then another plan came to her.

"I had better hide my tracks or they will instantly know and be on my trail. It might delay them a bit," she told herself.

So she turned and walked to a small leafy tree and snapped off a branch. Then she quickly walked back past the hut, carefully following her boot prints and brushing them out as she went.

At the clothes line she paused to listen then looked in the window. It was a single room. There was no-one there. She went to the clothes and went to unpeg a pair of trousers.

As she did she paused and shook her head. "This is no good. Why wipe out my tracks if I then steal something obvious. Perhaps they won't notice for a time. Yes they will. I'm being silly," she argued with herself.

She bit her lip in indecision. Thirst made her run her tongue over her lips as they were dry and cracked. "I do need a drink. Oh, what will I do?" she cried. Her heart hammering with anxiety, she pegged the trousers up again and walked to the back door of the hut.

Inside on a bench stood a larger plastic water container. Using a dirty enamel mug Barbara drank until she was full, all the while standing at the side window to keep her eyes on the road.

"That's better! Now, let's see," she muttered as she turned and looked around.

There were two bunks with blankets on them, a litter of tools, saddles, boxes and tins, a kerosene fridge, table and two packing cases for seats. Beside one bunk was a suitcase. Barbara quickly knelt to open it. As she did her eyes fell on a heap of dirty washing on the concrete floor beside the case. Yes! They wouldn't notice that as soon. She pulled out a shirt and trousers. The shirt was a brown 'ringers' shirt with little silver press studs instead of buttons. It was yellowed under the arms and stunk of stale sweat. The trousers, made of thick material, had once been grey but were now almost black with grime and grease. They reeked of horse.

Barbara wrinkled her nose in disgust but knew it was the best she would get. She stood up and went to pull on the trousers.

Then she gave a wry smile. *I have to take off my boots to do that,* she told herself.

It also made her aware she was coated with grit that was clinging to her sweat-soaked skin. "I need a wash. Oh, get a move on silly girl. They'll be back any minute with Johnno and his dogs. Oh bugger!"

A glance showed her nowhere to wash other than a washbasin. She looked outside but apart from the outhouse and shed there was nothing. Her eye fell on the windmill down at the cattle yards.

For a moment she dithered. Then she shook her head. *I'm being stupid. I must get away from here and quickly.* Through her mind flitted images of the section of road back to where she had climbed on the truck. *They must be there by now and could be back here at any moment. Get moving and never mind modesty!*

Dropping the clothes back on the pile of dirty washing she picked up her leafy branch and backed out of the hut, brushing out her tracks as she went. *I need to brush out my tracks from the truck as well,* she reminded herself. So she backed across to the truck.

As she passed the front of the truck she paused. How to brush out her second set of tracks? It meant going round in a circle. She knew she was wasting a lot of time. *I could have been a kilometre away by this.*

But then she shrugged. *Either do it properly or accept the consequences,* she rationalized. So she hastily brushed out her boot prints from the truck to the base of the hill.

Barbara had passed the hut and was half way to the foot of the hill when she remembered one of the men had been on a horse. Where was it? She couldn't see it, only the milling herd of cattle at the yards.

Too bad! I'll just have to walk, she decided.

"Be safer and it's only about ten or twelve kilometres from the Tucker Box Range back to camp. I should be able to do that in ..." She tried to calculate it but lost concentration as she dusted out the last tracks she could see.

It was obvious to her that there had been dusting done but it wasn't as obvious as her boot prints had been. *Might gain me a few minutes,* she told herself. At the edge of the scrub she stopped for a last look around.

The stony hills were radiating heat like a reflector fireplace. Barbara found she was sweating profusely. She wiped her brow. "I should have looked for a hat."

Anxiety made her abandon that idea. She began walking quickly westwards along the foot of the hill, angling up onto the grassy slope. But climbing the steep, rocky slope was hard going. The grass here was of a different kind, being quite stiff and prickly and the ends kept giving her sharp little jabs on her legs and lower body as she pushed through it. After three minutes climbing she came to a shallow re-entrant.

This will give me a bit of cover, she thought, knowing that she would be very exposed if she went straight up a bare ridge. *And exposed is the word!* she thought, glancing at her sunburnt and scratched nakedness.

After another look behind Barbara turned and began climbing up the hill. Again she tried to calculate when she might reach the army camp. "Three or four hours if I push it. I wonder what time it is now?"

She squinted towards the sun and decided it must be about mid-afternoon. "I might make it by dark. If nothing else goes wrong, that is."

That thought made her glance fearfully back to where the road entered the valley. She could hardly believe her good luck and consciously suppressed any sense of exultation at having won free, warning herself there was a long way to go yet.

The effort of clambering up the scorching rocks soon had her breathing hard. Sweat poured from her, and after only a few minutes she stopped to allow her rapidly thumping heart to slow down. Her stomach rumbled from hunger and a wave of dizziness made her pause. From up on the hillside she had a good view back over the valley and she was able to study the road out to the east. There was still no sign of any vehicle or dust and all she could do was hope that they hadn't worked out yet how she had escaped.

After only a minute or so, as soon as she had recovered some breath, Barbara started upward again. It was hard going as her muscles were so strained and sore. Sharp pains stabbed through her legs and buttocks at each upward step. She looked hopefully upward but was depressed to see she had barely begun to climb.

"What was the highest point? Was it Hill 450? Or 560? No, 509 I think. That's no use. What's the height of the surrounding country? It's not sea level because we come up the Mingela Range to get here. That must be one or two hundred metres."

After some thought she decided she probably had to climb somewhat over 200 metres. Again she stopped briefly to get her breath. She looked back and down trying to guess how high she had come. It was a pleasant surprise to see the whole valley laid out below her. The buildings and yards were so far away they looked like a model.

"Still no sign of the men," Barbara muttered.

But strewth! Isn't it hot! I wish there was a breeze, she thought as she looked around. The far side of the valley and the hills forming its south wall were distorted in the heat shimmer.

Again she turned to plod wearily upward. There wasn't a cloud in the sky and the sun seemed merciless in its white intensity. Already she could feel herself drying out. Several hawks began circling high overhead.

"Bloody vultures! Well, you won't get me," she muttered between clenched teeth. Deciding she was now far enough away she tossed her branch aside.

After a few minutes she stopped for another breather. She was close to one of the piles of boulders with small dark green trees growing out of them. The shade looked inviting so she made her way across to the bushes.

Finding the shadiest spot Barbara carefully settled her tender bottom on a rock. It was uncomfortably warm to the touch but it was a relief to be out of the sun. For a minute or so she sat. A pleasant torpor began to creep over her.

"I'd better not nod off. Ouch!"

Barbara sprang up and detached a green ant from her hand. "Rotten little horrors! Oh, look at them all!" The rock appeared to have dozens more of them crawling over it. The nice little tree suddenly wasn't so nice anymore. It was swarming with green ants and she saw one of their nests of gummed-together leaves just above her head.

"Oh well. It was nice while it lasted. So much for the rest!"

Groaning with the effort she plodded on upwards, skirting another similar patch of boulders and bushes. The top seemed as far away as ever as she heaved herself up to one false crest after another. She knew that was an illusion though because she could gauge her progress by the hills on either side.

Then she stopped, chest heaving, and smacked her forehead. "What a fool I am! I don't have to climb this stupid hill. I should be aiming for the lowest point, the saddle between this hill and the next."

Having reasoned that she turned left and began walking around the side of the slope. This led her into a steep re-entrant choked with boulders and scrub but with relief she saw the crest of a saddle not far above. After another short rest she skirted up beside the steep gully and, with a gasp of relief, walked onto the crest line.

Ahead of her opened a vast vista of rolling bushland. Even in her distress she found it an amazing spectacle. She calculated that she could see for an enormous distance, about 50 or 100 kilometres she estimated. From the angle of the sun she knew she was looking Northwest. Her eyes eagerly searched for the camp. To her intense disappointment she couldn't see it but she at once picked out other landmarks she knew.

There is Hill 376 only four or five kilometres away, she noted.

In the middle-distance a long shadowy crestline marked the line of the Bunyip River and, right on the horizon, she made out the tiny blue silhouette of Whaleback Hill in the haze.

Then something caught her eye. It was the silver roof of the big shed. It was almost hidden behind Hill 376.

"There's the Camp! Now I am alright," she cried.

Her spirits soared. There was even a faint breeze to cool her feverish skin. The end of the nightmare was in sight.

She stood there for another couple of minutes while she carefully scanned the terrain ahead. There was a 'divide' between her and Hill 376, a wide flat area from which creek lines ran either east into the area she had been (Emu Creek?) or west into the Bunyip. It was all open savannah woodland without a single trace of human settlement, other than just a hint of a dirt road a few kilometres to the north.

Back to the east her eye registered a gently drifting column of smoke. *That is my handiwork, the grassfire at the Saltpan Outstation,* she thought. Her mouth registered a grim smile of satisfaction. *Burnt the drover's blue van did it? Serve the deceitful mongrel right! And he had such a nice dog too!*

Barbara had cooled down by this to just mild perspiration. Her legs still shivered and trembled from the effort though. They were, she noted, now coming out in a red rash. *Allergy to the grass,* she wondered. She glanced at the sun. It was getting well down to the west, although it was as hot as ever.

Biting her lip she shook her head. "I'd better move. I've still got ten k's to go and if I waste time it will get dark."

The thought of a second night alone in the bush spurred her into motion. With several groans she forced her tired muscles into motion.

If anything, it was harder going down. Her calf and thigh muscles pulled in hot stabs at each step as she lowered her weight from rock to rock. Several times she slipped, bruising herself and skinning her bare buttocks. The pain and unhappiness caused tears to prickle in her eyes.

As she descended the slope the silver shed vanished from sight. By then Hill 376 was skylined and gave her a clear marker but soon it also was hidden from view as she came level with the forest crown.

Barbara came down the hill with only one rest-stop. She guessed it had taken her twenty minutes or so. Ahead of her stretched more of the everlasting ironbarks. Luckily there was very little ground cover so it was easy walking.

Without any visual reference in front to keep direction she had to use the sun and the hills behind her to help her navigate. Walking soon became a mechanical plod. She was so tired and sore the urge to just lie down was all but overwhelming.

"Keep going weakling! You've got to make it by sundown... Ooh!" she cried in fright, but it was only a grey kangaroo. It sprang up from where it had been resting in the shade and bounded away. Several other kangaroos became visible, hopping away in the distance.

Her route took her across the top end of several small gullies. She was too tired to detour the hundred or so metres to avoid them but found the effort of crossing each one very painful on her overstrained muscles. But she still had sufficient focus to note that their direction of flow was west or southwest.

For a while the going was easier, a wide, grassy expanse dotted with large iron barks. In a few places the grass was waist high but most of it was cropped short.

"There's been a lot of cattle here," she told herself observing the manure pats scattered thickly over a wide area.

Flies buzzed up from them as she passed, to crawl on her skin and annoy her. She had to beat at them continually to keep them away from her face and out of the open scratches in her skin. Hundreds settled on her back but there was little she could do.

"In fact there seem to be cattle everywhere, more than normal," she considered.

She couldn't be sure. After all she lived most of her life in Cairns, which was a city. The only time she went into the country was on picnics or with Cadets and that was often to sugar cane farms and tropical rainforest.

Another ten minutes plodding brought her to a fence. It ran off in both directions as far as she could see. She decided it ran approximately north-south.

Should I follow it? It probably goes to the highway. That can't be more than five or six kilometres, she calculated. She thought about it and discarded the idea. *The Camp should be only seven or eight,* she reasoned. Besides, she didn't feel like flagging down vehicles. *Especially in the all-together,* she thought, *and there is no guarantee Lenny and his mates won't be patrolling the highway.*

Before crawling under the fence she carefully scraped away burrs on the ground with her boot. As she slithered under she was again very conscious of not wearing any clothes. To avoid dragging her bare skin on the hot sand she tried to keep herself as high as she could but when her bare back scraped the barbs on the bottom strand she had to lower herself. While doing that her breasts dragged on the ground and she winced as her knees were again pressed hard onto small stones and prickles.

After standing up Barbara dusted herself, muttering with annoyance. There were also a few small prickles in her hands and knees. Once again tears were close.

Tired, hot and grumpy she resumed her trudge. There was a lot less grass now and the tree type included thickets of stunted acacias. Here and there were patches of bare grey clay.

At least the flies aren't so bad but I wish that sun would go away. God, I'm thirsty again. She felt her skin with the back of her hand. It was dry and hot, and she realised she had stopped sweating. *That's a bad sign. It's not just sunburn. I'm getting heat exhaustion.* she told herself. She looked at the cherry-red flush of her sunburn and winced.

I must be cooked. Should I stop until it cools down? I can walk in the cool of the evening, she reasoned.

Ahead of her through the trees she noted what looked like a clearing. Anxiety at blundering into more of the men made her slow down and she covered the last 50 metres sneaking from tree to tree while carefully searching the area ahead. Crouching behind a bush she noted that it was a clearing, perhaps a hundred metres across and in the middle stood a set of timber cattle yards with a windmill and drink trough. The yards were crowded with cattle.

Is there anyone here? Barbara wondered, anxiously scanning the clearing and bush in every direction. To her relief she could see no-one.

"There's water there and I need water," she told herself, again passing her tongue over her dry lips.

Once again temptation warred with prudence and for a minute or so she dithered, picturing the men back at the hut starting the dog after her. Then she shook her head.

If I don't drink, I don't make it so I have to risk it, she told herself.

Noting the bare ground she remembered her tracks and once again broke off a leafy branch. Then, walking backwards and brushing out her tracks as she went, she began making her way out across the open ground towards the yards. As she walked she kept her head swivelling to look in every direction. The yards appeared to have at least a hundred cattle penned in them in a shuffling, bellowing mass. The place stank of dung and urine. Dust billowed up to hang in the still air.

The drinking trough was in the yard. Barbara stopped at the rails and looked anxiously around, feeling absurdly exposed. Then she climbed up the rails going carefully on the dry and splintered old timber. At the top she paused for another careful look in all directions. Seeing no-one she swung her leg over, scraping the smooth skin on the inside of her thighs as she did. Then she hesitated again and anxiously eyed the cattle. In her nude state their horns made her feel particularly vulnerable. Absurdly she blushed at having no clothes on in front of all the animals. Her stomach churned with fear of being gored but she bit her lip and shook her head and forced herself to climb down inside the yard. *I must have water,* she told herself.

The beasts backed away in fright. They rolled their eyes and jostled into a mass in the far corner. Keeping a wary eye on them she quickly picked her way through the splatterings of dung to the long, black drinking trough.

Looking into it Barbara wrinkled her nose in disgust. The water was filthy. Wet manure dribbled off the edges into it. Mud, dung and green slime floated in it. The thought that she must have drunk just such a mixture the previous night made her stomach turn.

Luckily clear water was trickling from a pipe at the end of the trough. She went to that and cupped hands under it. The water smelt and tasted stale but it was water so she began gulping down handfuls of it. She drank until she felt she could drink no more. Then she splashed water on her face.

"Oh! That's nice!" she cried.

She was surprised how cool it felt and it made her conscious just how hot and sore she was. Sighing with relief she quickly plunged her head and shoulders in then splashed water down her back. As she rinsed her body the scratches all began to itch and burn but it felt very good.

Having washed off the worst of the grime Barbara examined herself and noted that large parts of her body were lobster pink from sunburn. Her shoulders were dark red and burned. But other than splashing more water on her smarting skin there was nothing she could do about it.

Grimacing with revulsion she forced herself to drink some more and then turned to go. As she did a malicious thought struck her. A quick glance around showed her what she sought. With rapid strides she walked across to the end of the yards. There she unlatched the yard gate and swung it open. Then she hesitated. She had been going to open the gate and leave it open so that the cattle could escape. Then prudence made her abandon that plan.

The men might see my tracks if they look, she reasoned. She shrugged and closed the gate behind her. Suddenly it seemed very petty to want to cause the men that sort of annoyance. *It is justice I want, not revenge,* she told herself. So she began backing across to the other side of the clearing, brushing out her tracks as she went.

It took her two more minutes to reach the edge of the timber on the western side of the clearing. Here she paused for another look around and to orientate herself. Feeling much refreshed she strode off into the scrub.

For another half hour or so Barbara plodded steadily on through the bush. As she did she sweated profusely. Her skin became slippery with perspiration. Salt trickled into her eyes, causing them to sting and she muttered with annoyance as she brushed away flies and tried to blink her vision clear. All too soon she felt thirsty again and she began to hate the searing rays of the afternoon sun. These seemed to just focus on her and she knew she was more sunburnt that at any other time in her life. The air felt superheated. She began to wilt and plod.

She came to another fence. This also ran north-south and the grass on the other side was more eaten out. Wondering if it was the property boundary Barbara looked carefully along it in both direction and then again crawled carefully under the bottom strand. This time there was dry grass with no burrs so she was able to wriggle under on her back while holding the bottom strand clear of her body. Then she resumed her walk.

Ahead she saw a wide eroded patch of clay with a belt of small trees and bushes beyond. They offered some shade.

"I'd better stop for a rest. If I don't sit down, I'll fall down," she told herself.

She lowered herself onto the bare clay in the best patch of shade. It felt cool and smooth. Spots seemed to dance in her eyes. She closed them and lay back, carefully stretching out her trembling legs.

Exhaustion claimed her. She was asleep in moments.

The flies woke her, rather than the noise but she was simultaneously aware of both. Flies were crawling in her nose and her open mouth. Her eyelids were gummed together with grime and mucous. She rubbed them gently and forced them open.

Where am I? Barbara wondered. *Oh, on the claypan in the bush.*

She sat up, then cried aloud as a calf muscle cramped. Groaning in agony she pummelled and massaged it. Once the spasm had eased she looked around.

With a shock she saw that the sun was right down among the treetops. The bush was still and quiet. There was no breeze and the sky was still clear. "I must have been asleep for an hour or more. I'd better move, or it'll be dark," she told herself.

Groaning at the stiff muscles and numerous aches and pains she stood up and looked around. She could hear cattle. Then a crow uttered its mournful croak.

She crouched behind some bushes and looked. A hundred metres or so beyond the bushes was an earthen mound which she recognised as being part of a 'dam' or 'tank'. Beyond that was a herd of cattle. A barbed wire fence enclosed both dam and cattle. There was no sign of any buildings or yards.

"Claypan Dam," Barbara muttered. The name came to her at once. "Dams mean water and there must be water or those cattle wouldn't be here," she reasoned.

Barbara felt her burning skin and realised her tongue was swollen and lips cracked. She felt quite giddy as she stood up. "I'd better have a drink," she murmured as she started walking.

But her muscles had gone stiff and the effort of moving them made her cry out in pain. Stiffly she hobbled forward to the fence and crawled under it.

The edges of the pond impounded by the earth wall were all churned up mud and cow dung. The water looked filthy with mud and weeds. The look of it made her stomach turn.

"I'd better drink it. It doesn't matter if I'm sick tomorrow if I make camp tonight."

She made her way to where the mound of the dam met the sloping muddy ground. But there was no way she could reach the water without getting mud on her boots. It was sticky clay which sucked and clung, doubling their weight. Slowly she made her way to the water at a spot where the dam was too steep for cattle. Even so she had to stand in the water to get enough depth.

"Oh blast!" she complained as her left foot sank into the ooze too far so that water slopped over the top of her boot, wetting her sock. She quickly pulled it out but the effort made her right foot slip and she fell heavily on her backside.

"Oh bugger, blast!" she cried.

Annoyed and so emotionally fragile that she felt like either shrieking or laughing she hauled her boots clear. Luckily not much water had got in.

"I won't walk far with wet socks," she muttered.

Gingerly she edged down again and scooped up water in her hand. "I shouldn't have looked at it," she said, screwing up her face at the sight of the solids suspended in it. There was even something wriggling. She flung that handful aside and scooped up more water and made herself drink it. It stank and tasted foul.

Barbara drank again, then again, each gulp a mental effort but a physical relief. Then one of the cattle standing on the far side unburdened itself of a gushing yellow stream which trickled into the water.

Barbara nearly threw up. "There must be a hundred cattle here and I'll bet they've all done that. Aw, yuk!"

She couldn't make herself drink any more but it was reviving to splash water on her sunburnt skin.

"I'd better get on. The sun's going fast," she told herself. She crawled back up to the top of the dam wall and hobbled across it. As she did the cattle on the far side began to edge away. She found it unnerving how all their eyes followed her and how all their heads turned at once.

She had just reached the middle of the dam wall when she got a shock which made her stop in her tracks.

There was a man there!

Chapter 28

THE FIRE IN THE CREEK

A stockman was squatting at a campfire under the trees about a hundred metres away. Luckily, he had his back to Barbara and was stirring a cooking pot over a small fire.

Has he seen me? Barbara wondered. She didn't think so. As she stood watching, he straightened up and began picking up sticks for his fire. *Hide!* Barbara thought.

Heedless of the dung and prickles, she dropped flat and wriggled under the fence which ran along the top of the dam. Quickly and silently she slid down behind the mound, at that point about two metres high. She didn't care whether he was a nice man who might help her or not.

I've had enough of strange men, she told herself. She was hotly aware of her lack of clothes and her heart was now hammering from anxiety. Risking a careful peek through the weeds, she studied the man as she plucked out several bindis from her hands and knees. *Come to think of it, this patch of bush seems to be crawling with strange men and cattle,* she decided. *It all sounds mighty fishy. This 'Big Job', is it cattle duffing?* she wondered.

For several minutes Barbara lay in the long grass and considered her next move. The creek line below the dam was the obvious escape route but it was so small it barely warranted the name.

It will have to do, she decided.

She was about to move when another sound came to her: a heavy vehicle engine. Cautiously she again peeked over the dam. Her initial thoughts were that it was Lenny and her being was almost swamped by paralysing fear. But then she saw it was a truck. It was coming along a track from the north, trailing a cloud of dust.

Is it that man Castledine? she wondered. But then she saw that it was much bigger, a proper road-train.

There wasn't enough cover to risk moving so Barbara lay motionless until the massive truck ground to a halt where the man stood waiting. It was a big yellow and black prime-mover hauling three trailers to move cattle, all painted the usual alternate red and white timber on a steel frame. On the door of the truck it read:

R.G. MORTON
LIVESTOCK TRANSPORT
MOORABBIN, NSW.

The engine was switched off. The driver spoke for a moment on the truck's CB Radio then climbed out, greeting the man beside the fire. They shook hands and the first man offered the driver a cup of tea.

That would be lovely, thought Barbara. She realised she was not only thirsty but very hungry. Her stomach suddenly 'grumbled' so loudly she was afraid the men would hear it.

Time I was gone.

She turned and began crawling away from the dam on hands and knees.

"Aah!" She stifled the cry and had to bite at her thumb to counter the agony in her left knee. Tears came to her eyes. She had crawled onto some 'Bull Heads', the pea-sized burrs with three vicious thorns. One had dug right in at her left knee cap.

Gingerly Barbara pulled it out. A trickle of blood followed. She paused to rub it, then sniffled and wiped her tears. God it hurt!

Fearful lest the men had heard her she raised her head behind a tuft of grass to look. To her relief it was obvious they had not. They were standing beside the fire drinking tea.

Being more careful where she put her hands and knees, Barbara started crawling again. It was painful on her knees just from the small stones and grit. She also found it very undignified and embarrassing as she knew she must present quite a spectacle from behind. To her shame she was acutely conscious of her bare buttocks and rear view.

Oh, I hope they don't look! she thought, worried as much by the embarrassment as by the probable deadly and violent consequences.

The creek line was a bit better. It was deep enough to move along at a crouch. Cautiously she backed from tree to tree and bush to bush until, about fifty metres further downstream, she reached a large bare expanse of clay. Feeling stiff and sore in every muscle and joint Barbara straightened up behind a large iron bark.

Through the trees and bushes she could still see the truck and get glimpses of the men. Their fire was more obvious as the evening shadows settled. The sun was now amongst the tree trunks and the Western sky was a mass of crimson and gold. Barbara decided she could risk walking.

Almost whimpering with pain she hobbled like a crone to begin with until her muscles warmed up and loosened. To begin with she made sure she had the tree between her and the men. But to get well away from the men she had to go south for several hundred metres. This brought her to a dusty vehicle track heading in the same direction. The track snaked through the scrub so she was in no danger of being seen by the men as she crossed it. She even remembered to take care not to leave boot prints in the dust.

The bush was now extensive belts of low bushes amongst mostly small trees. It offered plenty of cover but she had to wend her way around the clumps. Within minutes she covered enough ground to be confident the men could not see her. Now she circled northwards for a while before turning Northwest again.

Ahead of her, the bulk of Hill 376 appeared as a shadowy mass among the trees, the sun just bathing its upper side in a russet tinge. That cheered her up. *Only five or six kilometres to go,* she told herself. *I can walk that in two hours.* So she gritted her teeth and trudged on, conscious that the sun was rapidly sinking.

Soon it was gone altogether, and the twilight gloom made it hard to see where she was putting her feet. Fear of snakes welled up.

"They come out at night to hunt. Oh, aren't people contrary creatures. All day I've cursed the sun and wished I could get out of it. Now it's gone and I wish it wasn't!" she muttered.

Exhausted she tramped on. The red glow to the West lasted for half an hour after the sun had set but it too slowly faded and shrank till blackness took its place. By then Barbara was at the base of Hill 376. For a moment she considered climbing it to see if she could see the camp.

No. That's silly. I can keep direction by the stars. I'm heading into a 'V'. Bunyip River runs across my left front and the railway across my right front. Even if I miss the actual camp I must come to either one of them and they will lead me to it, she reasoned.

Feeling happier she started walking again.

"Aaaargh!" she cried, stifling with difficulty the involuntary scream.

Barbara jumped back and brushed frantically at her face with her hands. She had walked into a spider web between two trees. The spider had felt enormous, as big as her hand across its legs. The repulsive creature had scuttled over her face and onto her chest. Quivering with fright she flicked it off.

For the next few moments she stood and fought down hysteria. Her flesh 'crawled' and she hugged herself. For a minute she considered camping for the rest of the night. Then she shook her head. "Don't be a coward. You can be safe in a couple of hours. There must be a lot of people worrying about you. Keep going."

She imagined Captain Conkey and Miss McEwen searching. Then images of Gordon filled her mind. "I wish I'd thought to get a good walking stick while it was still light," she told herself crossly.

To find one she cast carefully around in the dark bush, afraid she might be bitten on the hand by a spider or a snake. After a few minutes she found a suitable stick. It was only deadfall and it was a bit crooked but it was long enough and the right thickness.

She set off again, placing the stick ahead of her on every second step. Her direction was again taken from the stars.

Perversely she now felt cold. She shivered and knew it was from sunburn and over-exertion. Her whole body felt so sore that her progress was little more than a shuffling hobble. For at least an hour she forced herself on. The dark bush seemed monotonous and never-ending. Only the mournful cries of curlews broke the silence. There wasn't even enough breeze to rustle the leaves.

A large bird, an owl perhaps, flapped low overhead, sending Barbara's heart up into her throat. *I've had enough for a while. I need a rest,* she decided. She stopped and carefully cleared a space to sit down. Very carefully she stretched out her aching legs. *I must not drift off to sleep,* she told herself, but try as she might her eyelids slid down and she dimly perceived that, temporarily at least, she was at the end of her tether.

Fierce cramps woke her. The muscles of her left foot and calf were knotted into seemingly solid lumps. Whimpering in agony she pummelled them and tried to ease into another position. The pain was like white-hot needles and she cried out. Tears came, but only a few. Her body was too dry for more.

At last the pain eased. She lay panting and looking up at the stars. "I wonder how long I've been asleep? I'd better get up and push on," she muttered. A glance at the stars suggested it had really only been a few minutes but it felt longer.

But she lay there resting for a few more minutes, getting colder and more uncomfortable by the minute. Then the noise of some animal caused her to sit up, senses groggily alert. What was it? Wallaby? No, too heavy in its movements. Pig? Cow? Horse?

Whatever it was it was some way off. Barbara struggled to her feet using her stick but was at once seized by more cramps. She bit her lip and clung to the stick, trying to keep her balance. By the time the pain eased she had lost track of the animal. Not knowing what it was spurred her into movement. She checked her direction from Orion, selected a star and resumed her limping progress. As she warmed up several more cramps seized her but she punched at them and kept on.

She lost all count of time and distance. It was all just dark bush; varied only by the odd log, anthill, clump of scrub or notable large tree. There was a fence but it ran diagonally across her route so she had to crawl under it. Dusting her hands and buttocks she plodded on, aware that her whole body was hurting.

An impression of paleness ahead puzzled her. She kept on till it became clear what it was caused by. It was a large area with no trees. She kept moving, expecting to come to a fence or a road.

There was an overgrown track. Barbara paused and looked both ways along it. The clearing ran from starlit horizon to starlit horizon. Puzzled over the size of the clearing she looked around and saw an apparent spider web of straight lines. It took her a minute to realise it was a large steel pylon.

"A power line clearing!" she said. When she realised what it was, she let out a little whoop of delight.

I remember seeing it on the map. It runs roughly east-west only a couple of kilometres south of the camp, she thought.

Thus cheered, Barbara continued on across the clearing and into more monotonous bush, trudging through waist high grass and too tired to care about snakes. But the spear grass seeds she could not ignore. Again and again she had to stop to pick out the sharp little seeds. She was also very aware of the tingling pain from her dry and sunburnt skin. Chafing also began to bother her. This was mostly under her arm pits. Gritting her teeth she continued on.

It was when she stumbled on the log that Barbara realised she was starting to hallucinate. Her eyes were starting to play tricks on her. Things seemed to move, grow large, then shrink. Several times she became disoriented and found she had been wandering south or north instead of northwest. She found herself back close to the power line.

Exhausted and disappointed, she stopped to rest again. Her eyes felt hot and gritty and wouldn't water. Alternately shivering and flushed with heat, she stood in silent misery.

"Come on old girl! Can't be far now. Half an hour should see us there," she muttered.

Gritting her teeth, she forced her aching body into painful motion. Mosquitoes helped. They had begun to buzz annoyingly and now began to bite.

"Bloody things!" she swore, slapping at them. They were biting her all over. Of course they had to bite between her shoulder blades where she could only scrape at them with her stick!

For about twenty minutes Barbara plodded on, going down a distinct slope, across a small dry creek, then up a long gentle rise. Then some instinct caused her to stop.

What is it? she wondered.

She blinked and shook her head to clear her thoughts then looked around. Suddenly it came to her. Just to her left, within arm's reach, was a thin black vertical object.

A steel post, not a tree stump, Barbara's tired brain reasoned. And that meant a fence. Gingerly she reached out. Her fingers encountered cold and rusty barbed wire. *Bloody hell! I nearly walked straight into that!* she thought.

Shuddering at the thought of the barbs ripping her soft skin, she carefully crawled under the bottom strand. Then it took an effort to stand as cramps began to assail her.

After relaxing and massaging her thighs and calves, Barbara forced herself back into motion. The ground sloped gently upwards and was covered with more savannah woodland. After another ten minutes steady plodding, the scrub ahead of her seemed to open out and she found herself on the edge of another clearing, only much wider. Checking her direction, she set off across it.

The clearing was much longer than it was wide. She could see the dark line of timber on the other side and at the end to her right. Suddenly, her boots crunched on gravel. *What is this?* she wondered.

"The airstrip! The Camp is only a kilometre away!" she cried.

Her spirits soared and she felt a new surge of energy. As she came off the other side of the gravel she saw lights twinkling through the trees to her right front.

"The Camp! Oh, thank God! I'm a bit off line but not much," she told herself. Offering up a silent prayer of thanks Barbara strode into the bush on the long down slope beyond the airstrip. She knew exactly where she was now and aimed for the cluster of lights at the eastern end of the Camp.

It was a long 500 metres down to the creek line on the southern boundary of the camp. There was another fence to negotiate and she went under this one on her back as there was only bare dirt and no prickles.

As she stood up on the other side she shuddered as relief flooded through her. *Safe!* she thought, doubting very much that the men would come into the army camp to chase her. The lights now looked to be only a few hundred paces away and she sighed as the tension seemed to drain out of her.

"Nearly there! Let's get this over with," she said.

A large clump of rubber vines barred her way so she skirted them and reached the bank of the creek. Having walked beside it in daylight when planning the Navigation Exercise she knew it had steeply eroded banks two or three metres high. Stopping on top of the bank to look for a safe way across she glanced towards the camp again and noted that it was now only a couple of hundred paces away. *Nearly there!* she told herself.

I just have to cross this creek and plod through a bit of flat bush and I will be at the first tents, she thought. But to cross it safely she had to walk along to her left 20 paces to find a slope she could easily descend.

As she was about to slither down into the gully a glow caught her eye. It was a small fire in the bed of the creek just at the next bend to her left, perhaps twenty metres away. It puzzled her but she had set her mind on reaching the camp. Carefully she slid down to the sandy bed of the creek. She was searching for a way up the other bank when a sound reached her that made her freeze in alarm.

It was a girl sobbing in pain!

Barbara hesitated. The crying sound came again and then a mutter of voices followed the distinct 'thud' of a blow. The girl whimpered and Barbara heard her cry, "No!"

Intense emotion welled up to grip Barbara. She turned and trudged along the sandy bed of the creek towards the fire. Fearing the worst she moved carefully, gripping her stick across her bosom and hunching, but what she saw as she got closer so enraged her she cast caution to the wind. Completely forgetting her own nakedness she hurried forward.

Three naked people stood beside the fire, two men and a woman, or rather a girl. As the girl turned her tearstained face upwards, the firelight illuminated it and Barbara gasped. Monica Malone! Weismann was twisting her arm and pulling her head back by the hair. He and the other fellow, Barbara couldn't place him, were most obviously ready for sex.

Weismann twisted Monica's arm again. "Shut up Malone! Now get down and do it," he snarled.

"Ouch! Let me go. No! I don't want to," Monica sobbed.

"Do it or else! It's part of the deal, now get down," Weismann ordered. He twisted her arm again.

"I don't want to. Not with him. Ouch! Let go. I'll scream," Monica wailed.

"You do and I'll shut you up for good, now get down you moll. Quick or I..." Weismann stopped speaking and turned to look into the darkness as he heard Barbara's footsteps.

"Let her go, Weismann!" Barbara snapped.

Weismann released Monica instantly and sprang back, eyes wide with surprise. "Brassington!" he gasped in disbelief.

"Get dressed Malone," Barbara ordered.

Weismann recovered himself. "Where the hell did you spring from, you bitch? You can't be here! I saw that man take you. I..."

Barbara stood grim-faced while Monica looked fearfully from one to the other. There was a stunned silence which Barbara broke. "Get dressed you animals!" she spat.

"Don't tell me what to do, you bitch!" Weismann retorted. Fear and dismay chased each other across his face as the implications of the situation dawned on him.

Fists on hips and only partly aware that their eyes were goggling at her own nude form, Barbara noted the erect penises of Weismann and the other man. The sight roused her own fear and it dawned on her that she might again be subjected to possible rape. But it also angered her and she gritted her teeth.

Weismann swallowed and looked frightened. "Grab her Benson. She'll dob us in!" he croaked. But the other man just looked horrified and stared at her in shock.

Weismann suddenly lunged forward. Barbara was just in time to dodge. She swung up her walking stick. It struck him hard on the hip and broke. But she was able to jump aside.

"Help me, Malone," she cried, painfully aware of her weakness when confronted by Weismann's strength. "Help! Help!" she yelled at the top of her voice.

"Shut up slut! Grab her Benson. Grab her! Shut her up!" Weismann shouted.

But Monica just cowered against the creek bank. Barbara skipped to one side, narrowly avoiding another rush. To ward Weismann off she hold the broken stick with its jagged end towards him. Barbara now recognised the other man. He was one of the army drivers. The soldier hopped about in indecision.

Weismann charged in again. Barbara hurled the stick into his face then jumped sideways and snatched up a blazing stick from the fire.

Desperately she waved this at the two men. They circled warily. Barbara called again, screaming at the top of her voice, "Malone! Get going. Go and get help. Help! Help!"

The sight of the two naked men, their arousal rapidly subsiding, roused Barbara's fury even more. *Men! Disgusting creatures!*

Blazing with anger Barbara lunged forward, swinging the flaming brand at him. Weismann jumped back and then charged in, shouting obscenities. Barbara had guessed he might. Instead of swinging her arm up and down again she flicked the stick downwards with her wrist in a fiery arc.

Weismann's grasping hands missed the burning stick. It came up between his legs, striking him hard in the genitals. There was the sizzle of scorching flesh and the pungent reek of burning hair. Weismann uttered a shrill scream and sprang back, clutching at his scrotum. The stick snapped, scattering hot coals on the sand.

Barbara swung the still burning remnants of the stick back towards the soldier and yelled again at the top of her lungs, "Help! Help!"

The soldier backed off and began scrabbling for his trousers amongst a pile of clothing. Monica stayed crouching wide-eyed. Barbara turned to face Weismann. For a minute or so he crouched, clutching himself in obvious agony. Then the pain and fear seemed to drive him berserk. He ranted and shouted.

"I'm gunna kill you, ya bitch! You're gunna die for that."

His face twisted with rage he rushed forward. Barbara swung the foreshortened firebrand but he just smashed it aside and punched her. The blow took Barbara in the left eye and knocked her down. Then Weismann began to kick her, luckily with only bare feet. Barely able to see Barbara lashed out with her boots in a last desperate defence.

Weismann dodged the boots but in doing so put one of his feet in the fire.

"Aaaah!" he screamed in agony.

Swearing and screaming abuse he danced around for a few moments and then began to kick at Barbara with his bare feet. Barbara was stunned by one of the kicks which took her in the side of the head. She sprawled on the sand, aware that she must move but was unable to do so.

Weismann snatched up another burning stick. He raised it above his head with both hands like a Japanese executioner. Hate and pain contorted his face in the flickering firelight. Monica screamed.

Voices shouted. Down came the burning club. With a desperate heave Barbara managed to roll away. She felt the wind of the blow. Twitching violently to get clear of another blow Barbara collided with Monica who screamed again. At that crucial moment Barbara's left leg was seized by cramp. Unable to move she looked up, raising her right arm to shield herself as Weismann swung the club up for another murderous blow.

There were more shouts and the thud of running feet. A figure hurtled from the creek bank and thudded into Weismann's side. The two fell in a tangle of arms and legs. The newcomer, in uniform, sprang to his feet, fists raised.

It was Gordon!

Chapter 29

Weismann scrambled to his feet, grunting and screaming obscenities. Gordon stepped back and waited. Weismann snarled and rushed at him, fists flailing.

Smack! Gordon dodged his furious blows and punched him hard in the solar plexus. Weismann gasped and doubled up.

Thud! Gordon's right took him on the jaw. Weismann went down and stayed down, a sobbing heap on the sand. He began to whimper and clutched at himself.

More people arrived at the run: Lofty, Roger, and a dozen other male CUOs. Barbara staggered to her feet, quite forgetting her nakedness.

Gordon turned to look. His eyes opened wide in surprise. Then he goggled. "Barbara! It was you. You are safe!"

Barbara could only nod. She was trembling with shock but stepped towards him. As she did, Gordon's face changed to dismay and puzzlement as he took in the nudity of the others. "Barbara, what are you doing here? Are you... Are you with...?" He could not finish the horrible question.

Barbara felt indignation flare through her relief that he should doubt her. Angrily, she checked in her steps and gestured at her naked but scratched, blotched and sunburnt body.

"Oh Gordon! How could you think that?" she cried.

Bafflement and happiness mixed on his face. This quickly changed to embarrassment as he ran his gaze down her body. He evidently liked what he saw but then realised what he was doing.

"Oh, Barbara I... er... you are here with these people and have nothing on," he stammered in confusion. Then he blinked, licked his lips and shook his head. "You're safe!" he cried.

Barbara stepped forward. Gordon opened his arms and hugged her. She gripped him fiercely and buried her head in his shoulder. At that moment she was near to hysteria and collapse and she didn't want him to see that. Tears came but mercifully not many. She was too dehydrated. It felt wonderfully comforting to be held in his strong arms, despite the pain from her sunburn.

There more voices and Barbara was dimly aware that Lofty and a couple of the other CUOs were ordering the cadets on the Corporals Course and Sergeants Course to keep back.

Then more voices sounded and Barbara noted torches. The Colonel, Major Wickham and Captains Conkey and Royston raced down into the creek.

"What the Devil's going on here?" demanded the Colonel. He swung his torch from one to the other, taking in Lofty standing over Weismann's huddled form, Gordon embracing a naked Barbara, a nude Monica crouched and sobbing, the fire, the blankets, the whisky bottles and the half-dressed soldier. The Colonel's face registered shock and amazement.

"What the blazes! You people are supposed to be studying for an exam. What is going on?" he queried.

Capt Conkey shone his torch on Barbara's battered face and then down. He stepped forward. "Barbara! You're here! Where have you been? What have you done to her?" This last directed at Gordon.

Barbara found her voice. "He's been rescuing me," she croaked.

Capt Conkey frowned. "Rescuing you! From whom? From these?" he asked in astonishment.

Barbara was so emotional she had to pause and swallow before answering. "I was kidnapped by two pig hunters," she said shakily before giving Gordon a tight squeeze of gratitude.

"But.. but where are your clothes?" Capt Conkey cried. His eyes kept flicking to her and away and he was obviously embarrassed but puzzled.

"The pig hunters stripped me and tried to rape me sir," Barbara replied. The saying of that brought a flood of horrible memories and she began to tremble and cry. Gordon held her tighter.

"Stand still you!" the Colonel rasped at the soldier, who had begun to sidle out of the firelight. "You are under close arrest Private Benson." The Colonel then looked up. "RSM! Move all those cadets back to their lecture rooms. Only CUOs Course to stay here."

"Sir!" came WO1 Pryor's voice, followed by bellowed orders, quickly seconded by Captain Royston.

The Colonel turned and pointed with his torch at several more CUOs and OOCs who had arrived. "Major Ross, Captain Buchan, guard this soldier. You two CUOs, keep an eye on Weismann. Get dressed Malone, cover yourself! Farr, were you part of this?"

"No sir. I was in my tent. We ran down here when we heard the screaming. I found Weismann belting into Barbara so I..."

The Colonel cut him off. "Explanations in a minute. Barbara, are you alright?"

Barbara nodded. "Yes sir," she managed to croak. She clung to Gordon.

Capt Royston picked up the blanket and tossed it over Monica. "Wrap yourself in that girl. Are you alright? What's your part in this?"

Monica made no answer, just sobbed.

Barbara hugged Gordon fiercely. His muscular shoulders and back felt so good. She felt a wave of comfort from his strong arms. Relief flooded through her. She closed her eyes. Suddenly she just seemed to sag at the knees.

"Hey!" Gordon cried. He grabbed at her but she slumped to the ground.

The Colonel rapped out more orders, pointing to cadets and staff who had arrived and were staring down from the bank above. "You two, run and get the stretcher and the medic from HQ, and a blanket. You two, get Weismann dressed and take him up to HQ. Malone! Get dressed!"

Weismann remained curled up, whimpering as the pain of his burnt skin became the dominant thing in his life. Gordon stared down at Barbara, his face a mixture of wonder and concern. Then he realised he was staring, and he blushed. Quickly he began to unbutton his shirt, his fingers fumbling in his anxiety and embarrassment. Hurriedly peeling the shirt off he draped it over her. Then he sat and cradled her head on his lap, stroking her hair and staring at her in wonder.

From time to time he reached down to adjust the shirt but from the coolness around her buttocks Barbara guessed the shirt was just too short. To her own surprise she realised she did not mind if he saw her. She lay there curled up and shivering with reaction and overexertion but feeling intensely relieved and safe. Without thinking she reached up and tenderly stroked Gordon's cheek.

The officers had a good look around. They were plainly mystified about what had been going on, or at least Barbara's part in it. Barbara lay on the sand and trembled. Gordon cradled her tenderly but firmly.

"Sorry for thinking you were with them, Barbara. I was so glad to see you and it came as such a shock," he said.

Barbara smiled, grimacing as her dry lips cracked. "That's alright. It must have looked suspicious."

Gordon nodded. "It did; two naked men with two naked girls," he replied.

Barbara nodded, then reached up and grabbed his head and pulled it down, lifting herself to kiss him on the lips. "Thank you for saving me… ow!" she gasped.

"What's wrong?" Gordon asked.

"Cramp!" Barbara cried between gritted teeth. Her left thigh had seized into an agonising ball. She pummelled at it. Gordon waved his hands, obviously not sure whether he should touch her or not. "Ow! Help me!" she groaned.

Gordon began to massage her leg with reluctant pleasure. As he did Barbara became aware that the shirt had half slipped off and had ridden up so that most of her lower body was exposed. Quickly, she reached down and adjusted it to cover herself.

Gordon blushed. "Sorry," he croaked.

"That's alright, I don't mind," Barbara murmured.

It dawned on her that she would happily let Gordon see her naked any time. Then she realised what she was thinking and blushed fiercely.

Capt Royston gave a chuckle before grabbing the blanket still lying on the sand beside Monica. He draped it over Barbara. "Keep it up son. You're what she needs right now," he said.

The Colonel snapped at Monica. "For God's sake Malone, get your clothes and get dressed!"

Monica reluctantly stood, snatched up her clothes and retreated along the creek into the darkness. Capt Conkey and the Colonel both came and knelt beside Barbara, who was crying. Capt Conkey reached down and gently stroked her brow in a fatherly way.

"It's alright, Barbara. You are safe now," he said. After her trembling stopped, he asked, "What happened? Where have you been? We've been worried sick. Did Weismann and that soldier abduct you?"

Barbara shook her head. She sniffled and wiped her eyes. "Sorry. I'm just so glad to be back. No. Not Weismann. The Pig Hunters, Lenny and Wally."

She started to tell her tale. After a minute the Colonel stopped her. "Alright Barbara, just give us an outline. We can get the details later. Do you need a doctor?"

"No sir. I'm just a bit sore. They didn't, er… didn't do anything to me," Barbara replied.

"Thank God for that! We might get one anyway. Capt Royston, go and phone the police, and for a doctor, and the Military Police."

More voices and torches appeared. It was the boys with the stretcher. With them were Lt McEwen, Lt Curwen, and nearly all the older girls. The Colonel stood up and spoke to Lt McEwen, "We will leave you to it. Malone's somewhere there too. Bring them up to camp as quick as you can." He turned. "Get up Weismann. Why isn't he dressed?"

Lofty stood over the shuddering form. "He's been hurt sir. Had his almonds scorched."

"Almonds scorched?" queried the Colonel.

"Barbara roasted his nuts, Sir."

"Ahumpf! Yes. That will do. There are ladies present, Sergeant Ward," the Colonel replied. Despite his rebuke, a titter ran through the group. "The stretcher can come back for him. Major Wickham, you and these two CUOs stay and watch him."

The ladies now took over. Gordon was shooed away and Fiona took over tending Barbara. She was helped gently onto the stretcher by Sharon, Camille, Karen, and Jennifer. They were agog with interest when they realised that Barbara had no clothes on. The girls were all full of questions but were hushed.

Lt McEwen said, "She can tell you later. Now take hold of the stretcher you girls and let's get her up to the camp. Prepare to lift. Lift!"

Two hours later, Barbara lay in Lt McEwen's bed. By then she had been showered and shampooed, her cuts and scratches doctored and she had drunk several cups of cold cordial and hot soup. Now, with hair combed and in clean pyjamas, she was propped up by pillows between clean sheets. She was very tired but had refused a sedative from the doctor as she wanted to tell her story to the police.

She had just finished doing that. Gathered in the little room listening were the Colonel, Captain Conkey, Lt McEwen, a Police Inspector and his Senior Sergeant. The Colonel shook his head in amazement.

"You have done exceedingly well, Warrant Officer Brassington."

The Inspector nodded. "She's certainly been damn lucky," he added.

Barbara bristled. "It wasn't just luck, sir. It was training too. If I hadn't been trained as a Cadet I couldn't have done it!"

"Er, yes. Quite so," the Inspector conceded.

Barbara turned on him. "Well, what are you going to do? You can't just let these crooks get away. They're obviously up to something. Tonight's the night. The 'Big Job'. I'll bet they are stealing cattle. Twelve road trains the man said. How many cattle is that?"

The Inspector looked uncomfortable. He paused before answering. "Possibly as many as nine hundred to a thousand head roughly."

"That's a lot isn't it? Aren't you going to do something?" Barbara demanded angrily.

"Yes, we are. But it's not that simple. We've heard rumours but the Stock Squad are out at 'Acacia Plains'. We got a whisper that that was where the job was."

The Colonel snorted. "Looks like you've been sold a pup," he observed dryly.

The policeman looked uncomfortable. "Yes. It looks like it. It will take three or four hours to round my men up. Blast!"

Barbara was puzzled. "But there must be something you can do? You can't let them get away."

The Inspector turned to her. "Now don't you worry your pretty little head over them. We will do what we can."

Barbara flared up. "Don't patronise me! I'm not a child. And don't be sexist. Can't you just stop them on the highway? There aren't that many roads."

"It's not that easy Miss," replied the embarrassed Inspector. "Yes we can set up roadblocks and we will but if the cattle aren't branded or correctly tagged and earmarked then we haven't got a leg to stand on. We really need to catch them in the act."

"Won't the cattle be branded and tagged?" Barbara queried.

"Probably not. Castledine has been the manager of Emu Plains for a year now. The owner and his family are away. Their daughter needed specialist treatment and they could only get that in London. What I mean is that, if he was planning to lift the stock, he wouldn't brand and he's had plenty of time to doctor the computer records."

Barbara was puzzled. "Computer records?"

The Inspector nodded. "Yes, every beast has to have, by law, a computer record on a microchip on its ear tag. Part of the national stock identification scheme. It's to try to stop this sort of thing."

The Colonel added, "But they can be falsified if you have enough time, like several years and a lot of false records set up."

Lt McEwen said, "There seem to be an awful lot of men involved. Won't they talk?"

The Inspector shook his head. "Once we've arrested them maybe, but people like the truck drivers wouldn't know the whole story. They might suspect it but it would be just another job for most of them. As long as the paperwork appears to be in order they shouldn't question things."

"Does this go on much, cattle stealing I mean," Lt McEwen asked.

The Inspector sighed. "Yes it does. Not as much as it used to. But it's *the* major criminal activity in Western Queensland. That's why the police have a special Stock Squad. It's a multi-million dollar industry."

Barbara's temper boiled. "Well here's your chance!" she cried.

"Yes, but I haven't got the men," answered the Inspector.

"Why?"

"Too many roads. Too many places to watch. We don't have the information to act with certainty. If we try driving in there they will just vanish, or have a plausible excuse."

"There can't be that many roads," Barbara said.

The Inspector made a face. "There are. Have you got that map?" He turned to the Colonel, who passed him the map Barbara had used to describe her story with.

"Look, there is a whole web of dirt roads. There are four going south from the Flinders Highway: one from the Bunyip River Railway Siding, one here going to Claypan Dam, one beside Pandanus Creek, that's a Stock Route, and another going to Emu Plains homestead. Then there is one going south from Deadmans Gap to Brownlows Crossing and across to the Burdekin and one going south from Rocky Mill to near Ravenswood and another from Emu Plains homestead going east to Kirk River area. That's seven roads and I've only got two detectives, seven uniformed men and four in the Stock Squad."

"Surely you can get more from Townsville. It's only an hour's drive," Capt Conkey asked.

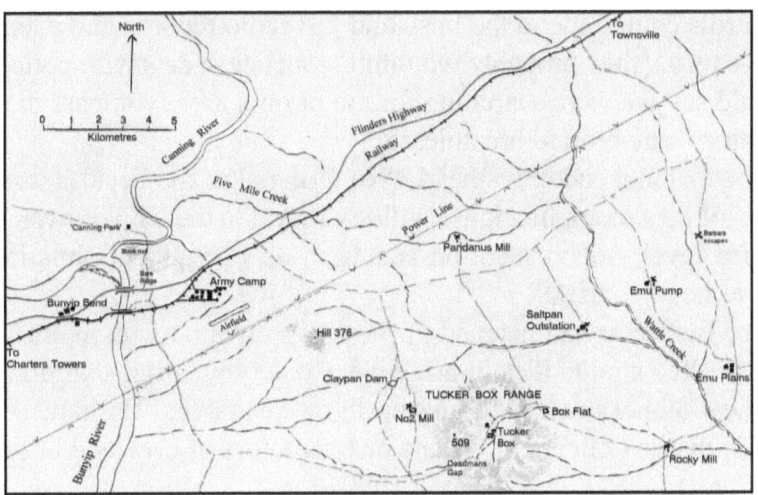

7 Roads

"Yes, and I will, but it will be two or three hours to even get them up here and even longer to get them in position," the Inspector explained. "To act properly, to really catch these crooks, I need people in position to give me detailed info to plan on. There are a dozen places I need to have people quickly, with radios here, here, here at the road junction, here." He jabbed at the map.

Barbara looked at the web of tracks and roads on the map. She felt cheated and baffled. *I walked right across that, even crossed three of the roads,* she thought angrily. A feeling of disappointment made her feel tired and down. Then she sat up with a jerk.

"We can do that!" she blurted out.

The adults looked at her mystified.

"Do what?" the Colonel asked.

"We can provide the information. But we must move quickly," Barbara cried. Excitement made her voice rise.

"What? How?" the Colonel asked.

"Sir! The Inspector needs people with radios at all these places to give him information. Then he can swoop. We've got a dozen radios and the CUOs and Sergeants could sneak in as recon patrols and report and…"

The Colonel held up his hand. "Just a minute young lady."

"But sir! We could do it. There wouldn't be any danger, or not much.

277

The patrols could hide in the bush and just radio reports, and even if the crooks saw us, they probably wouldn't associate cadets with police. And we could say we were searching for me or on a night compass march or something," she blurted breathlessly.

The Colonel shook his head. "No. Too risky, and besides, there are all sorts of legal complications. Military in Aid to the Civil Power. That's Canberra level, not to mention cadets in an operational situation. No cadets to be put at risk."

The Inspector had listened to Barbara's outburst with interest. Now he spoke. "It's a good idea in principle. Could your adult staff do it?"

The Colonel mused, adding up those available. "Hmmm. I've got 17 ACS, that is Officers of Cadets or Instructors of Cadets, but four are ladies."

Barbara cut in. "Oh Sir! Don't be sexist!"

The Colonel turned on her. "That will do young lady. This is 'operations' and while government policy might allow females in an operational area, I will only risk people who volunteer and are fit. That probably gives us two of the four, which gives us 15. But I must keep a couple here to supervise the cadets so take out at least two. Then there's Warrant Officer Pryor, the two drivers... no, one driver. Benson's under arrest, plus the cook. That's... um, eighteen."

"There are the two ARA Staff," Capt Conkey reminded.

The Colonel tugged thoughtfully at his chin. "Yes. That's twenty. Hmm. That's probably only two people per radio. And we'd need at least one at HQ here for control. How many places do we need to watch? Lt McEwen, please pass me one of those map photocopies we use for the Nav. Test."

Using a 'highlighter' pen the Colonel quickly marked all the roads in the area. Then he placed a sheet of tracing paper over the map and with a pencil numbered all the road junctions, outstations, windmills and other likely spots.

"Twenty nine points to watch," he said.

"That's a lot. Can we reduce it somehow?" Capt Conkey asked.

The Colonel nodded. "Let's see. These ones along the Flinders Highway and at Kirk River, Ravenswood and Brownlows Crossing, they would be best watched by the police. Could you do that Inspector?" he asked.

The Inspector nodded. "Yes I could but it won't leave me anyone to move in. I'll have to call in the Torrens Creek and Ayr police to help as well as reinforcements from Townsville."

The Colonel bent back to the map. "Now, let's see which places we must watch and which we can leave." In a few moments he had crossed off three road junctions because OPs on either side could monitor any traffic through them. He looked at the Inspector and asked, "I take it it's more important to watch the actual loading of the trucks than their later movement?"

The Inspector agreed. "Yes. We need detailed eye witness accounts: times, places, names, and vehicle registration numbers for it to be any use in court."

"Ok. So we would need to watch all these yards, dams, mills, outstations and so on. Let's see… Hmmm." The Colonel bent back to the map.

Capt Conkey leaned over to watch. He pointed and said, "You could chop out that road junction there, the one you called '14'. The people at '11', '21' and '17' would still catch them," he suggested.

"Right. That's eleven places. We can just do it. If all the radios work, and if we get approval," the Colonel said.

Once again Barbara interjected. "But sir, that means some OOCs will be on their own."

"Yes. I know it is a risk," the Colonel replied.

Barbara said, "If you send CUOs with them they will be safer. If there is an accident the CUOs can give First Aid. And they can carry the radios and operate them from well back under cover where they won't be heard. And they could carry food and water and even stand guard while the OOC eats and rests and so on."

The Colonel thought hard for several minutes then nodded. "If they do it that way there is minimal risk. But I do not want a situation where any cadet is placed at risk. I will see what headquarters says."

The Inspector looked pleased. "We will have to move fast. I'll get on the radio," he said.

Barbara was horrified. "Oh sir! Don't use your radio. The crooks have got CB radios in their trucks. They could be listening."

"Quite right. Telephone it is. Senior, start rounding up all our men." The Inspector gave the senior sergeant rapid instructions.

Barbara turned to the Colonel. "Sir, if speed is important how will you get the officers into position without being seen?"

"I was just going to drive them in and drop them off and take the risk," the Colonel said.

Barbara shook her head. "That will give the game away sir. It will be too obvious."

"Do you have a better idea Barbara?"

"Yes sir. There's a vehicle track along this power line. Drop them off along it and they can walk in, at least some of them. It's only a few kilometres."

The Colonel shook his head. "Take too long. We need these lookouts in position in an hour or two. We may be too late as it is."

The Inspector joined in. "I like her idea. I'd prefer to not raise their suspicions if I could."

Barbara spoke again. "With respect sir, some of the OOCs aren't all that fit. If you sent the CUOs they could run in. They'd be alright."

Capt Conkey patted his chubby stomach. "She's right sir. I can't see me or old Major Burnside or tubby Major Ross or Captain Carter running through the bush in the dark, and I doubt if Lieutenant Hope or the cook or the driver are good enough navigators."

"Don't talk to me about Lt Hope!" snapped the Colonel angrily. He chewed his lip. "That only leaves about six, including me."

"Use the CUOs Sir," Barbara urged again.

The Colonel turned to the Inspector. "What do we know about these crooks?"

"A fair bit actually. Castledine, the manager of Emu Plains, he's got no record, but we've had some suspicions about him. As far as we know there are eight others and all of them are in the category of being 'known to police'. The pair of animals that abducted Miss Brassington: Leonard Boyer and Wally Wescott, are already awaiting trial. The two at Emu Pump: Nigel Costigan alias 'Sharkey' and Steven O'Reilly, are both escapees from Stuart Prison. They were serving three years for, you guessed it, cattle duffing."

They all laughed at this. The Inspector went on. "The two at Salt Pan Outstation have both done time for a number of minor offences, that's Johnno Johnson and I guess Frank Lehman. The other two at Tucker Box, Wallis and Norton, we are checking on. The Senior says he remembers reading a bulletin on them. The New South Wales police want them for questioning over the armed hold-up of a motel at Gunnedah."

"Are they dangerous?" the Colonel asked.

"Probably. Lenny and Wally certainly. I am going to ask for a Tactical Response Group."

"What exactly is that?" Capt Conkey asked.

"A dozen heavily armed officers with bullet-proof vests. They are police who are specially trained to deal with armed criminals," the Inspector explained.

"I don't want any of my people hurt, that's all," the Colonel said.

"But how are you actually going to catch them?" Lt McEwen asked.

The Inspector frowned and shook his head. "I can't decide yet. I need more info, then I'll make a plan and we can swoop."

"Swoop!" interjected Barbara.

"Eh?"

"Swoop. From the air," she explained. "By helicopter."

"You're not just a pretty face are you?" the policeman said. "That's a great idea, but I don't have a helicopter. The nearest police chopper at the moment is in Cairns."

"By Jove she's right!" the Colonel put in. "The army's got a dozen or more sitting at the RAAF Base at Garbutt, Black Hawks and MRH90s. They can easily lift a dozen men each. You could group your strike force or tactical group or whatever you call them there and whistle them up when you need them, day or night. They have night vision equipment."

"What an excellent idea. I'll ask for them. Let's get on the phone and get cracking," the Inspector exclaimed.

The Colonel turned to Capt Conkey. "It's just on 2300 hours. Let's see if we can be moving within the hour. Call all the staff, plus the CUOs and Warrant Officers Courses to the CUOs lecture room. I'll go and ring the relevant authorities while you organise them and issue maps and radios. Let's move."

Chapter 30

PATROL PREPARATION

The room became a bustle of excitement. Barbara threw off the sheet and swung her legs out of bed.

Lt McEwen held up her hand. "Where do you think you are going young Miss?" she enquired.

"To join the CUOs Miss."

"Oh no you don't! You need a good rest. You lie down."

"But Miss! Aw! I'm too excited to sleep and I'm not all that tired."

"No. You are overtired; and over-excited. You probably should be in hospital. You lie down," Lt McEwen ordered.

"Please Miss. I only missed one night's sleep and I'll get back to bed once the CUOs go out. Please!" Barbara pleaded. Her face felt numb and every part of her body was sore but she was animated by a burning passion to see justice done. "Please Miss! I've been there. I can advise the patrols and draw them sketch maps. It doesn't matter if I collapse or if I'm exhausted tomorrow," she pointed out.

Lt McEwen considered this. "You have a point. Alright. But you take it easy. I'll get a couple of the others to help you across."

Fiona and Karen were quickly beside her bed. Slippers were eased onto her blistered feet and her dressing gown wrapped around her. With an arm around each friend's shoulder she hobbled painfully down the hallway, limped and hopped down the stairs and was almost carried across to the lecture room.

Outside was a milling group all abuzz with rumour and excitement. Most were dressed in uniform even though it was an hour after 'Lights Out'. Barbara was carried inside and settled in a chair at the front. She was at once besieged by almost the entire course wanting to know what had happened.

Major Ross looked up from where he was working on a map with Major Wickham and Captain Conkey. His voice blared out. "Silence! Time for that later. Sergeants Course, Corporals Course, get to bed! Who is the Orderly Sergeant?"

Melissa O'Toole, a girl on the WOs Course, stepped forward shamefaced. "I am sir."

"Who are your Duty NCOs?" the Major asked.

"Sharon Whalley, Fiona Davies and Jason Hilditch Sir."

"Who is next girl on the roster, tomorrow?"

Camille put her hand up. "I am sir."

"Take over from Sgt Hilditch tonight. Now listen. CUOs Course and WOs Course, Warning Order. Type of activity: Recon Patrol. No move before... um," Major Ross looked at his watch. "Within the hour. O Group, this location in twenty minutes. Admin, Dress, Patrol Order with full water bottles. Stores: compasses, protractors, map, radios. We will issue food in a minute, torches. Probable duration, I'm guessing but plan on all night and all day tomorrow. Warning, this is real. Volunteers only."

He paused to let that sink in. "Girls, you will not be going."

There were groans of disappointment and cries of indignation. "But sir," Fiona began.

"No 'buts'. Colonel's orders. This is an operation to support the police, not an exercise. Now all you girls, go and get all the radios out of the Q Store, set them up with fresh batteries and check them. Use the frequency they were on for the Navex this afternoon. Move it! We want to be gone within the hour. Not you Barbara. You help us plan."

There was a rush of excited cadets into the night. Grey haired old Major Burnside came in wearing his dressing gown followed by Capt Royston, Captain Carter, Capt Hamilton and Capt Buchan. Other officers joined them. Barbara was beckoned forward to the front table where the map was laid out. The cook and Old Jim came in from the kitchen.

Major Ross turned to them. "Get some of the Sergeants Course to help, the piquet will do. We want... let's see... umm, about 25 cut lunches and 25 tins people can use for a single meal, ready to issue in 40 minutes time. It's an emergency. Move!"

Major Ross then turned to Capt Hamilton. "Get the duty driver to drive you to the front gate. Get the ARA Sergeant and his offsider back here within 20 minutes. Tell the driver to have his truck and the Land Rover outside, fuelled and ready, within 30 minutes."

Major Ross then turned back to planning. Barbara sat herself against the wall beside him, conscious of the curious and sympathetic glances the staff gave her. She saw that Major Ross had drawn two vehicle routes on the map overlay in pencil.

"These are the routes least likely to attract notice. Now, let's measure the closest distances to each patrol objective from it. Write these down Cyril (this to Capt Conkey) under the headings one to eleven."

Major Ross then used a ruler to rapidly measure the distances, calling them out as he did. At that moment the Colonel came bustling in with WO1 Pryor and the Inspector in tow.

"It's a 'goer'. Canberra has said yes. Where are we up to?" he said.

There was a surge of excitement and an exchange of significant glances. The Colonel listened and nodded. He sat opposite Major Ross and began scribbling in his notebook.

"Eleven groups we need," the Colonel said. "Now, who is to lead which? I will go to the 'Tucker Box' with Roy. The next most dangerous place we know of is the Salt Pan Outstation. I'll send you there RSM, with the ARA Sergeant. Is that ok?"

WO1 Pryor nodded. "Suits me sir."

Barbara put her hand up. "There are savage dogs there," she warned.

"We can handle them Warrant Officer Brassington. Don't worry about us," the RSM replied with a grim smile.

The Colonel looked up. "Now, Cyril, you are a good navigator. I want you to watch this junction just east of the hills and check out this 'Box Flat Mill'. Ok? Good. Major Burnside, I will get the Land Rover to drop you at this junction where the road from Deadmans Gap joins this road coming up to near the Camp. That will save you any walking. Alright?"

The 65 year old Major, who'd been an OOC more than half a lifetime, nodded. "Yes, I can do that."

Major Ross, as the army staff officer who was camp commandant had to stay at the camp and would be in the Command Post with the Inspector. He then allocated all the other officers to a patrol. In this way all the adult staff, including the female OOCs, were given a job.

Major Wickham then made a suggestion. "We could have real trouble with 'coms' over those distances. What about a relay station?"

The Colonel looked thoughtful. "You're right. But we would have to drop one of the patrols. Which one?"

The Inspector leaned forward. "There's no need to watch this junction north of Emu Plains homestead. The patrol at Emu Plains can cover the road at one end and my people will watch the junction with the Flinders Highway."

"Ok. The best place for a relay would be on Hill 509, here, on the highest point of the Tucker Box Range. They can come in with Capt Royston and I and we will drop them off along the way. Which CUO is best with a radio?" The Colonel turned to Barbara.

"Millett sir," she replied without hesitation.

"Now, this is the tricky bit. The two patrols that have the furthest to go must be made up of the fittest – the one to watch Emu Plains homestead and one to Rocky Mill. Rocky Mill is thirteen or fourteen kilometres from the drop-off point. Who are the fittest? I will want them to run in. Capt Hamilton can lead one and Capt Zimmermann and Lt Hansen the other."

"Run sir?" Captain Carter asked.

"Yes run. A 19 year old soldier is expected to run five kilometres in 25 minutes. These young chaps should manage six in an hour in patrol order. But who? I want three fit cadets."

Barbara ticked off the names. "Gordon Farr." She met the Colonel's eyes and blushed. "Lofty Ward, and Oakwood from Mackay."

The Colonel pencilled their names. Having given all the officers a job he looked at them and said, "Good. Now, let's share the rest of the male CUOs around. Who wants who?"

Very quickly all the male CUOs names were added to patrols. By then the boys were back on the porch, dressed in field order and talking in excited murmurs.

The Colonel looked up. "Capt Royston, would you organise the O Group in the Sergeants Mess Hall. I want them sitting in their eleven groups, in order."

The Colonel wrote rapidly, continually checking his watch. Sounds from the kitchen and outside indicated hurried preparations. The Land Rover returned. The puzzled ARA Sergeant and his Corporal came in and the RSM met them and quickly briefed them.

Again the Colonel checked his watch. "Bloody hell! 2340 already. We'd better start. I want this thing moving by midnight. Have all the staff in, including those staying in camp. Have the girls bring the radios in. They need to listen as well. Let's go!"

The Colonel rose and picked up his notebook then walked into the Sergeants Mess Hall. Barbara hobbled after him and found a seat at one side. She had never seen such an air of excitement in a group. It reminded her of the time when Chloe and her friend had gone missing during the exercise along the coast north of Flying Fish Point when she was only a corporal.

When everyone was present, all the older girls crowding in at the rear next to the servery, the RSM called them to attention and handed over to the Colonel.

For a moment the Colonel stood, hands on hips, surveying their faces. "These are Verbal Orders for an Operation in support of the police. I stress the word 'operation'. It is not, I repeat not, an exercise. Only volunteers are to go. If you do not wish to take part say so now." He paused and looked at them again. No-one moved.

"Good. Let us begin. One, Situation. Alpha, Ground. You all have a map photocopy and every patrol leader has the 1:100,000 Scale Map. Look at the map and note the following."

He turned to copies of the map hastily stuck on the blackboard. One by one he named all the main features, gave nicknames to roads and had everyone present mark in pencil the number of each patrol's objective.

"Bravo. Enemy. Real enemy, not a cadet Opposing Force. Number uncertain but at least nine plus up to a dozen truck drivers. The nine are all criminals wanted by the police. At least two are escapees from Stuart Prison. Two are wanted for armed hold-up in New South Wales. Two are the mongrels who abducted Warrant Officer Brassington and tried to rape her. They are a vicious pair of thugs. They are armed and very dangerous."

The mention of Barbara drew her many glances and there was some growling and muttering.

"We'll get the bastards," Lofty murmured.

"Charlie. Friendly Forces: Police and eleven Observation Posts and one radio relay station." The Colonel explained that the police road blocks even now moving into position. Then he mentioned the helicopters and Tactical Response Group to be inserted later. This caused a real ripple of excitement and grins.

He went on, "Two. Mission. We are to provide the police with detailed intelligence."

Roger murmured to Pat Sheehan behind his hand. "I'd heard the police needed some."

The Colonel glared. "Be quiet Sgt Dunning. If you have something to say, say it later."

"Yes sir," Roger replied abashed.

The Colonel resumed. "I will repeat the Mission. We are recon patrols. I stress reconnaissance. Once in position as Observation Posts we must not be seen or heard. We are to provide the police with detailed information. Three. Execution. Alpha. General Outline."

Pens and pencils scribbled in notebooks as the Colonel described how the Land Rover would go down the south road to drop off Patrols 1 and 2, while the truck would go along the power line dropping off Patrols 3 to 11. He then listed who was in each patrol and went on.

"The information is required in exact detail, as things happen, or as soon thereafter as possible, of all sightings and movement of people, vehicles and cattle. Try to get vehicle makes and, if possible, number plates. I'm not sure how to do that but I want no risks taken. Remember patrol commanders, only the adults are to take any risks. The cadets are to stay well back in a safe place and do the radio work."

Roger put his hand up. "Sir, we could drop a small tree over the road and while the driver gets out to drag it aside we could note the vehicle's number."

"Good idea. As long as you aren't seen. Now, is everyone clear on what is needed? Likewise negative info, if there are no people, vehicles or cattle at your objective. We want a constant flow of info back to the CP that the girls are to run so that the Inspector can plan his ops."

The Colonel bent back to his notebook. "Time Out, as soon as we finish here. Time in. We will call you in or pick you up but here we must be flexible. It might be tomorrow morning but plan on being out all tomorrow as well. Now. Delta, Movement. By vehicle to a drop-off point. I then want you to move as quickly as you can. I mean run. Doesn't matter if you get tired. Follow roads or tracks if you can, but with care near your objectives. If you see a vehicle's lights take to the bush and hide. Don't be seen."

He looked around the room to be sure he had their undivided attention. "Now. Echo. Action on Contact. I don't want any contact. You are not armed. They may be. Keep hidden. Don't be seen. Don't be heard while talking on your radio. Remember what I said earlier; all cadets to be well back and in a safe place."

The Colonel paused to make sure they got the message, then continued, "If you are seen just walk away. If you are confronted tell them you are searching for Barbara and have got lost and could they show you the way home. That is our deception plan. No bluff. No risks. I want NO Casualties. Got it!"

"Sir!" they chorused.

"Good. Foxtrot. Routes In and Out." The Colonel went to each patrol in turn and showed them their route. While he was doing this Barbara met Gordon's eye. He smiled happily. His face was aglow with excitement.

The Colonel then covered 'Golf, Action if Lost' before going on to 'Four, Administration and Logistics'. After another glance at his watch he ran quickly through paragraphs on dress, water, medical, rations; then checked they all had a torch, a map, matches, toilet paper (several smacked foreheads) "In a plastic bag too you dumbos!" protractor, notebook, pencil.

"Now radios. Five. Command and Signals. First, Inspector Frazer is in charge. He gives the orders. Subject to his concurrence I will direct the patrols. He will be here with Major Ross at a CP to be set up in the Guard Hut."

Capt Buchan, who was to command the relay station on Hill 509, caught the Colonel's eye. "Sir, what if we can't get radio reception to here, even with the rod antenna?"

Major Wickham answered, "Throw a vertical aerial up over a tree. The CP can do the same."

"What if we lose Coms altogether sir?" Lt Curwen asked.

The Colonel mulled it over for a moment. "When the truck comes back move another team, you and three girls head to Hill 376 and try from there."

The Radio Net Diagram was then drawn on the blackboard and copied into notebooks. Cosgrove put his hand up. "Sir, shouldn't we use nicknames or codes? If the crooks hear us they will know what we are talking about."

The Colonel shook his head. "No. They can listen in to the police frequency on CB sets but it's unlikely they can pick up military frequencies. It's not a problem. Besides we are more liable to confuse ourselves. Ok, there's the frequency and alternate frequency and we have an air frequency: 66.50. Net Call Sign is November Quebec Zulu. Password is PIG, Countersign: HUNT. Synchronise watches."

Once that was done the Colonel took several questions. Hillditch put his hand up. "Sir, we were supposed to do our exams tomorrow. What will happen now?"

"Don't worry about them. On Tuesday you were rostered to help assess the Corporals and Sergeants. I will reschedule things so you do your tests on the same day. Any other questions? No? Now, it's just after midnight. Are all those radios tested? Good. Each patrol collect one and sign for it. Grab some food from those boxes and get on the vehicles. Let's move!"

There was an organised rush and in five minutes they were scrambling onto the vehicles. Barbara hobbled out with the other girls to watch. It suddenly dawned on her that the boys were doing something potentially very dangerous. She saw Gordon walk to the back of the truck stuffing his lunch in his basic pouch. A terrible feeling of dread clutched at her heart.

She ran over to him.

"Gordon."

He turned. Not caring who was watching she hugged him and gave him a kiss, a proper one, full on the lips. No-one seemed to think it odd. "Take care," she said, her worried eyes searching his, and her feminine intuition sensing the emotion that this young warrior was more in the grip of the thrill of battle than of love for her. It nettled her, but tears still came.

"I'll be okay," he grinned.

She gave him a squeeze and stepped back. The Colonel came along to hurry them aboard.

"He'll be alright," the Colonel said as Gordon scrambled up into the back of the truck. "Only the good die young."

The tailgate was slammed up and latched, drivers ran to their cabs, doors slammed, engines roared to life, headlights flicked on and they were off. The boys gave a cheer and their laughter and high-spirits could be heard as the vehicles roared off into the night.

The girls were left standing in a mixture of excitement and regret, coming to terms with the reality of life… and possible death.

Chapter 31

NIGHTMARE

Fiona walked over and put her arm around Barbara's shoulders. "Come on Babs! He will be alright. It's the traditional way of the world. Men must fight and women must weep."

Barbara felt a surge of resentment at the unfairness of gender. Then she felt herself choke up with emotion. *I am responsible for all this,* she thought. The idea filled her with guilt and she shivered.

Lt McEwen came to her. "It'll be alright Barbara. The Colonel wouldn't let them go if there was any risk. Now come and have a cup of Milo and we will put you to bed."

They walked back into the mess hall. Camille was bursting with indignation. "Boys! They get all the fun. It's not fair!"

"They could get shot too," Jennifer pointed out. Then she saw Barbara's tear streaked face. "Oh, sorry Barbara."

Barbara sniffled and wiped her cheeks. "It's alright. Stupid creatures! I hate them all."

The girls smiled, instinctively understanding the contradiction.

Barbara turned to Lt McEwen. "Miss, what happened back at camp when you found I was missing?"

"Oh Barbara, you should have seen it! We didn't know until this morning. Apparently Lt Hope and Watts, the Orderly Sergeant, were already asleep. Stephens apparently went to bed too. And Weismann just went to bed as well, though God knows how he could sleep if he saw you being abducted. That only left the piquet on duty. They kept up their roster alright but their duty statement said nothing about waking cooks or Duty CSMs or whatever. That was the Orderly Sergeant's job."

She passed Barbara a cup of hot Milo as they sat down. "Here, have this. Well, the result was that, in the morning, the cooks weren't woken so breakfast was an hour late. Reveille was late and when the Colonel found out he was livid. He tore strips off the Duty Officer and Orderly Sergeant and it was only then that we discovered you were missing. We ran round like chooks with their heads cut off when we couldn't find you."

Lt McEwen shook her head in dismay. "Weismann told the Colonel that he'd seen you at about 2300 and said that you told him you were sick of it all and had had enough and that you were going to hitch-hike home. He said he thought you were joking and had gone to bed. We rushed to the hut but all your gear was gone, every bit."

Barbara was appalled. "But I was eating desert on the back porch here. My hat, torch and clipboard were on the table."

"Gone. Not a trace of you. Well, we never dreamed you had been kidnapped. We were all very worried but more disappointed than anything. I was very hurt. I just couldn't believe you would do such a thing. Anyway we searched the whole camp for an hour and sent vehicles along the Flinders Highway both ways. The Colonel phoned the police and asked them to look out for you. Captain Conkey phoned your father and he was absolutely shocked."

"Oh Miss! My father! I must call him."

"It's alright. I did it as soon as you were back. You can call him in the morning," Lt McEwen reassured her. "So you see we just went on with training. It was a miserable day."

"Sorry Miss," Barbara said. She sipped at her Milo.

"Oh, it wasn't your fault. We are just so glad you are back safely," Lt McEwen replied, patting her wrist. "Anyway, bed for you young lady."

All the other girls were sitting or standing listening. Old Jim came over. "Excuse me, Lt McEwen. I just brought Barbara some ice-cream." He held out the bowl.

"Oh, alright," Lt McEwen relented.

"Don't eat it, Barbara!" Camille cried. "Remember what happened last time he gave you ice-cream."

That brought a much needed laugh.

"What about us. Don't we get any?" Jennifer asked.

Old Jim smiled. "No. Only good girls get ice-cream."

"I like that!"

Barbara looked up. "Speaking of good girls; where's Monica Miss?"

"Sleeping in the Guard Tent next to Lt Curwen. Don't worry about her. She's getting her just deserts."

Barbara nodded but felt sad. Her mind crowded with conflicting thoughts as she spooned ice-cream into her mouth.

Sharon leaned forward. "What happened down the creek, Miss?"

Lt McEwen shook her head. "You don't need to know. It wasn't very nice," she replied.

"Oh Miss! Please! We hear things that aren't very nice all day, every day at school," Camille responded.

Lt McEwen shook her head firmly. "You might, but I don't have all the facts and it is not fair to destroy people's reputations by gossip. The subject is closed. You will have to wait till it is all fully investigated."

"Aw Miss!"

"Enough. Now go and get this CP set up. Barbara, you go to bed."

"I'm not tired Miss. I couldn't possibly sleep."

"Don't argue. Karen, Fiona, put her to bed. Stay with her till she is asleep. You others, come with me."

A few minutes later Barbara thanked Old Jim and was helped over to the hut. Karen pointed to the room she had been in earlier. "You are to sleep in Miss McEwen's bed. She will sleep on this stretcher next to you," she explained.

The girls tucked her in and turned the light out, then sat with her. Barbara found her thoughts centred on Gordon. *He will be bouncing along through the dark bush in the back of a truck,* she thought. What worried her was that she seemed to have a terrible sense of foreboding.

"I'm worried," she said.

Fiona smoothed her hair. "Sssh! Don't talk. Go to sleep."

Barbara lay quietly but her mind raced on. Now that she was still, every bruise, bite and scratch seemed to throb, itch or ache. Her sunburnt skin felt sore and dry. She became aware of just how sore and drained she was.

Sleep came within minutes, the deep sleep of exhaustion. Barbara muttered and groaned. Sharp pains stabbed through her. She felt a nameless dread. *I have to run, have to get away!* her mind cried.

It was coming! It was catching her! She tried to run but couldn't. She turned her head and saw it—large and black, blacker even than the night. It loomed up, rearing on its hind legs. Great black bat-like wings spread out then swooped to enfold her.

She screamed. Horrible talons closed around her throat. She couldn't breathe. Desperately she clawed at the choking grasp. She screamed again. Her hands felt wet. She took them away and saw it was blood— red blood spurting out. She...

"Barbara, wake up!" It was Fiona.

Barbara groaned and opened her eyes. Fiona was holding her. Karen joined her, with hair rumpled from sleep. "You were having a bad dream."

Was it only a dream, or a premonition? *Angel of Death* fluttered through her imagination. She realised she was sweating and that her body was rigid with fear. The muscles began to cramp. She cried out in pain. The girls flung off the bedclothes and pummelled her tormented muscles. Wendy appeared with a glass of water.

Barbara took the glass and sipped the cool water gratefully. "Thanks. I'm sorry I woke you. I'm alright now," she whispered hoarsely.

Fiona stroked her hair. "Go back to sleep then. You need the rest," she said.

"No. I couldn't. I'm wide awake now. How are the patrols going? Are they in position yet?"

"Some of them are. I'm not sure," Karen replied.

"What's the time?"

"Nearly four o'clock. You've had a good three hours sleep," Fiona replied.

"I need to go to the toilet."

They helped her up. Afterwards she didn't want to lie down. The image of the monstrous black bat still hovered in the back of her mind, overlaying the image of Gordon. The thought of him out there in that dark bush full of evil men impelled her to check.

"I'm going to the CP to see how things are going. I can't sleep for a while yet."

"We'll come with you then," Karen said.

The three girls made their way slowly along the road. It was very quiet and peaceful but as they got closer to the Guard Hut they heard a radio give its distinctive crackle and a voice answer it. A police car with a young constable in it was parked in the lamp light just in front of the building. Major Ross and Lt Curwen sat at the radio with Melissa, Camille and the Police Inspector. Sharon lay sleeping on a stretcher. At the back of the room, curled up asleep and looking very young and helpless was Monica.

"Poor Monica," Barbara said.

"Hello Barbara," Lt Curwen said. "You should be asleep. Don't worry about her. She'll get her just deserts."

"She can't help herself, Ma'am. It's the way she is," Barbara replied.

Karen nodded. "We're all like that, if it's the right man," she commented.

"Yes. The right man," Barbara agreed. She shivered again at the thought of Gordon. "Is Gordon in position Ma'am? He is Patrol Number Ten."

Lt Curwen smiled. "Yes. They reached their position about 02:30. He radioed to report there is a hut, a dunny, a windmill and a pig-pen with three feral pigs in it and no sign of people, vehicles or cattle."

"Are they still there?"

"Yes. They will stay there till this is over. Don't worry. He will be alright. It will all be over in a few hours. You should be asleep."

"I had a bad dream Ma'am. I'm wide awake now. Where's Weismann Ma'am?"

"He and that soldier are in police custody – don't worry about him," she replied.

Barbara nodded and moved to join Fiona, standing behind Melissa. She peered at the map. "How's it going?" she asked.

"Pretty good. All our patrols are in position," Melissa replied.

"Can I tell her sir?" Karen asked. She looked at the Inspector.

"Sure," he replied, stuffing tobacco into a pipe.

"You shouldn't smoke sir. It's bad for your health," Fiona pointed out.

Lt Curwen spoke up, "And it is against Cadet Regulations to smoke in view of cadets."

The Inspector raised an eyebrow and looked grumpy. The match in his hand remained unstruck. With a surly grunt he thrust the unlit pipe in his coat pocket. "Undoubtedly. Being a policeman is often bad for your health too," he said.

Camille pointed at the map and checked the Signal Log, then said to Barbara. "All the police roadblocks were in position by 0055. They report five road-trains moving into the area – one here, another here and three here. They've stopped one coming out loaded with cattle here, at Kirk River, and have arrested the driver."

Barbara nodded. Camille went on: "Patrol 1 reported the three road trains passing them going east only ten minutes ago. Patrol 2 is moving down into the Tucker Box area now and have left Patrol 11 on top. That's

Capt Buchan, Millett and Ying. Patrol 3, that's Major Wickham with Wilmot and Stephens, is at Claypan Dam. They report no sign of any people, cattle or vehicles."

The Inspector interrupted. "Your Mr Morton must have loaded early and be on his way back to New South Wales already. Never mind. We'll get him."

Camille resumed speaking, "Patrol 4, Major Lavis with Tolput and Banaboos, have seen nothing. Patrol 5, that's Major Carroll and Blackwood are at Pandanus Mill and say there are no buildings, just a mill and trough and a lot of cow pats. Sorry Miss. Patrol 9, Capt Conkey with Roger and Lofty, are near the Box Flat Mill but say the place is swarming with hundreds of cattle and they are having difficulty moving without disturbing them."

Barbara pointed at Salt Pan Outstation. Even thinking about the place made her stomach turn over. Camille checked the notes. "Patrol 8 is there. That's RSM Pryor and the regular army sergeant. They report a vehicle at the house, dogs in the yard and a lot of cattle. Hang on."

The radio had crackled to life. "Zero Alpha this is Six. A road train has just passed this location heading west along Pandanus Road, over," came Captain Carter's voice.

"Six, this is Zero Alpha, roger, over," Camille answered. She began to write the message into the Signals Log. Major Ross marked it on the map overlay with a green felt pen.

"Six, out."

The Inspector leaned over to look. "That's the fellow who turned south off the highway a few minutes before. He came from Townsville."

"Barbara, you'd better go back to bed," Lt Curwen said.

"Please Ma'am. This is exciting. I'm alright for a while. May I sit and watch?" Barbara asked. It suddenly seemed desperately important to follow the action, even at a distance.

Karen spoke up. "We will get some more chairs Ma'am. Would you like some coffee or Milo?"

"Milo please," Camille said at once.

Lt Curwen nodded. "Oh, alright. Coffee for me, and one for Major Ross," she said.

Karen went out. Barbara sat on the corner of the table.

Camille looked at her and shook her head. "God, you are a sight

Barb. You should see your black eye. It's the best I've ever seen," she said.

Barbara gingerly felt her cheek. "It should be. That bastard Lenny punched me real hard a couple of times and so did Weismann." She paused as the memories flooded back. They made her tremble and her voice choked up. "I … I'd rather not talk about it."

"Sorry mate .. Ooh! Here we go again."

Again the radio hummed and crackled. "Zero Alpha, this is Ten, message, over." Gordon's voice came clearly through the night air. Barbara felt her heart skip a beat.

"Ten, this is Zero Alpha, send, over."

"This is Ten. A cattle truck with a trailer has just passed us. It came from the south on the Ravenswood Road and has stopped. The driver is studying a map. Over."

"Ten. Roger, over."

"This is Ten. He's moving again, turning left onto the road towards Box Flat. Over."

"Roger Ten."

"Ten, Out."

Barbara realised she had been holding her breath. She relaxed. A shiver ran through her.

The Inspector looked puzzled. "That fellow must have come up the road before our fellows from Ayr got to Ravenswood," he commented.

Barbara looked at the clock on the table. "It's twenty past four. It will be light in another hour. I would have thought these fellows would want to be well away by first light," she said.

The Inspector nodded. "I would have thought so. Perhaps something's thrown their timetable out. You must have caused some delay by your actions yesterday."

"But wouldn't the trucks just arrive on time?"

"That's how I'd do it but trucks break-down, they get flat tyres. They're driving on strange bush roads at night. They get lost." The Inspector waved his hands in the air.

"Zero Alpha this is Seven, message, over," came a faint voice.

"Ssh!" Camille picked up the handset. "Seven, this is Zero Alpha, send, over."

"A road-train has just pulled up here. There are two men at the hut with horses and two dogs. They have a large herd of cattle penned in a yard but we can't see any details."

The Inspector stuck a green pin in the map next to a red one. "That is the truck Six reported a minute ago. This is getting interesting. If my figures are right, we've now got six road-trains in the area, one caught and one got away. Nearly time to pounce."

At that moment Karen and Fiona returned with a tray loaded with coffee, Milo, milk, sugar and biscuits and three chairs. They settled to enjoy them.

"Aah! That's nice," the Inspector said. Then he held up his hand for silence. The radio had crackled. The sound of the carrier-wave reached them.

"Someone transmitting. Couldn't hear what they said," Camille added.

Then the radio squeaked loud and clear. "Zero Alpha, this is One One. Message, over."

"One One, this is Zero Alpha, send, over."

"Zero Alpha, this is One One. Message from One. They are in position and report there are five road-trains there. One has just arrived. The others are loading cattle. They can't get close to be sure but think there are five or six people there. There is a Land Rover and a Toyota Landcruiser parked near the hut."

The Inspector beamed and smacked his right fist into his left-palm. "That's it. Time to move." He turned to Barbara. "Now, Miss, can you show me suitable areas for helicopters to land?" He indicated the map.

Barbara brightened. "Oh yes. We learned about Helicopter Landing Zones and how big they need to be." She took a pencil and began to ring the areas she remembered as being fairly open. As she did Major Ross picked up the phone and began talking to Garbutt RAAF Base.

A minute later he put down the phone and looked at his watch. "4:25. We might do it. The choppers will be here in about 20 minutes. Warrant Officer Brassington, I'd like you to show Major Hammer these LZs. He will land here."

"Won't the crooks hear the helicopters sir?" Karen asked.

The Inspector shook his head. "No. They will come in low along the Bunyip from the north and land on the parade ground," he replied.

"Oh dear. I'd better put a uniform on," Barbara said.

"Yes. I was going to ask you to do that actually," the Inspector replied. He turned to Major Ross and Lt Curwen. "I'd like to take Miss Brassington with me. That way if we can't hold anyone on cattle duffing we can still catch whose who assaulted and abducted her. She could point them out."

Lt Curwen looked very doubtful. "I don't know.."

Major Ross said, "Only if you guarantee that she will not be in any danger."

"It will be quite safe I assure you. We will be in the Command helicopter and will only land when all the crooks have been disarmed and rounded up. I'll call the Colonel if you like. Anyway it's up to her if she feels up to it," the Inspector said.

Barbara felt a rush of adrenalin and a fierce urge to be 'in at the death'. She was very aware of the other girls casting envious glances at her. "Please Ma'am. I'll go. I'll get dressed."

She didn't wait for permission but hurried out the door and hobbled along the road. Karen and Fiona ran after her.

"Oh you lucky thing!" Fiona said.

"Getting a ride in a helicopter," Karen breathed.

"I have earned it," Barbara laughed. Her spirits seemed to soar. *Oh, vengeance is sweet!* Then she remembered. "Where's all my gear?"

"I don't know. We couldn't find it," Karen replied.

"It's ok. I'll lend you a shirt and trousers," Fiona added.

Back in the hut Fiona and Karen dug out clothes and panties for Barbara. She then got all shy and insisted they turn their backs while she dressed, even though the lights were off. Unfortunately none of the other girls had a bra that would fit her. In the end Barbara went without. Pulling on the clothes hurt and made her aware of just how abused her skin was. She could barely tolerate the shirt rubbing on her sunburn.

That not only hurt a bit but Fiona's shirt was a bit too small. After straining to do the buttons up Barbara studied the way the cloth was stretched over her bosom. For a few moments she hesitated and then shrugged.

It will have to do, she decided. She sat to pull on her socks and boots.

Barbara was still lacing up her boots when the vibrations of approaching helicopters made her pause. "Here they come. Oh, where's my hat?"

"You don't need a hat. You can't wear one near a helicopter," Karen pointed out.

Their talking had disturbed the girls on the Sergeants Course. Several looked out of their blankets and muttered. Wendy sat up and asked, "Barbara, where are you going? What's that noise?"

"Helicopters. I'm going with the police to arrest the crooks," Barbara replied.

"Ooooh! Lucky you. Be careful," Wendy replied. There was a buzz of excited conversation. More girls woke up and sat up. Barbara, Karen and Fiona walked to the steps.

"Ah! Ouch! Oooh!" Barbara cried as pains stabbed through her legs.

"Serves you right," said Fiona with a laugh.

As they made their way past the canteen the darkness was filled with an increasing roar. Suddenly it swelled in volume and a huge black shape swung overhead, the swish of its rotors as they sliced the air making the girls duck, even though it was well above the tree tops. Barbara looked up and shivered. It reminded her of her nightmare.

Or was it a premonition?

Chapter 32

DAWN SWOOP

When the girls reached the Guard Hut they found everyone there standing out on the road looking up into the darkness, including a sleepy Sharon and a miserable Monica.

Lt Curwen turned to Barbara as she limped breathlessly up. "The Colonel has said you can go Barbara but you are to stay with the Inspector. Wait here while they land."

Another army helicopter roared over, and another and another. All were completely blacked out.

"How many are there?" yelled Fiona.

"Five at least!" Karen shrieked excitedly.

One by one the machines and came in to land on the concrete parade ground and the grass field beyond. They still did not turn on any lights.

"Isn't that dangerous?" Sharon called. "Flying without lights?"

Lt Curwen, who was also an Army Reserve officer, shook her head. "No, they have Night Vision equipment," she replied.

The roar of the helicopter's motors now dominated everything, echoing from the big shed and making the air and leaves tremble. The lead machine settled on the concrete parade ground. A mini tempest engulfed the girls from the rotor wash. Dust and leaves billowed making them cry out and shield their eyes. The nearby tents flapped and strained at their lashings.

One after another the other helicopters landed. Out of the darkness came the Inspector with two men. One, in a flying suit and with major's rank was the commander of the squadron. The other was a policeman dressed in black and wearing a black bullet-proof vest and hung about with a pistol, radio and various pouches. Barbara thought he was the hardest looking man she had ever seen.

The Inspector led them into the hut. "Excuse the introductions. Major Ross, Lt Curwen, this is Major Hammer and Senior Sergeant Crowe. This is Cadet Brassington. Now, here is the map. Here are copies for your pilots and your team. The girls have marked LZs in yellow and objectives in red." He handed over a bundle of maps. "While you've been on your way there has been one change. The truck reported going Northwest from Number 10, that's Rocky Mill, is now stopped at Number 9, Box Flat, loading cattle."

"That gives us three locations with cattle?" the TRG sergeant asked.

"That's right. Now, this is the known location of the men and vehicles: Tucker Box: five or six men, five trucks plus their drivers and two other vehicles. Box Flat: two men, one truck plus driver. Emu Pump: two men, one truck plus driver." The Inspector pointed to the locations.

"Two men not accounted for then," the TRG sergeant commented sourly.

The Inspector shrugged. "They're probably at one of those places. It's hard to tell in the dark. Now, here's my plan."

Barbara stood respectfully beside the Inspector while he explained. Camille stayed at the radio while Lt Curwen hustled all the others away. Major Ross made notes and marked the map.

"A simple plan is best," explained the Inspector. "We need to be flexible. We can always change. We've got five choppers. Sgt Crowe, your TRG people are to be in three of them. As well two uniformed constables with cameras go in each. One chopper is to land on either side of the Tucker Box Outstation on the road, or as close to it as you safely can. Spread out. The group to the West is to be a roadblock. The main group, led by you, is to spread out in extended line then close in. The choppers will probably put the cattle in a state so wait till the helicopters have lifted off before you move."

"We could lose them in the dust and confusion," the Senior Sergeant pointed out.

The Inspector nodded. "I know. We will go in just after first light. I'll circle overhead and keep an eye on things. Your third chopper can come down at Box Flat and round those people up. The other chopper, with Sgt White and his four uniformed constables can go to Emu Pump. They shouldn't have any trouble from Costigan and O'Reilly." He looked at his watch and out into the darkness. "Let's see. It's nearly 5am. We've got about fifteen minutes. The flight time should be only a couple of minutes?" He glanced at Major Hammer who nodded. "It's just getting light now so we've got ten minutes to redistribute people and give them instructions. Get cracking!" He turned to Barbara. "You stick with me. We go in the Major's chopper."

Barbara nodded and bit her lip. Now action was so close she was scared. She felt very light-headed and her body seemed to be just a vague ache.

The constable in the car called out. "Sir, call from Smith at Bunyip River. A road-train has just crossed the bridge coming from Charters Towers and has gone on along the highway heading east."

"Good. That might be another one. He's a bit late."

"Won't he hear the helicopters?" Barbara asked.

"Possibly not. His own engine noise will drown them. Besides he won't associate army helicopters in an army camp with himself. Come on, let's walk out to the chopper," the Inspector said.

"Good luck Barbara. Take care," Camille said.

"Thanks." Barbara started walking, feeling the original 'butterflies' in the stomach. She wished she had gone to the toilet.

It was still quite dark but there was a definite fading to the stars and a streak of grey showed among the tree tops to the east. It would soon be dawn. Out on the parade ground the helicopters sat in two rows, like huge ugly black insects, their engines throbbing and rotors swishing round. Co-pilots sat in each cockpit, dimly illuminated by the glow from the instrument panels. A cluster of pilots stood on the edge of the grass while the major explained their tasks with a torch. Men ran from one helicopter to another.

Barbara kept walking with the Inspector. Her heart thumped wildly and her legs seemed to move of their own volition. She was very scared but also very excited. Her face felt cold and numb.

Then they were under the rotors and the wind whipped up her hair. A crewman in flying helmet, flying suit and gloves, who was hooked to the machine by a microphone lead, flashed her a brief glimpse of teeth under his visor and took her arm. She was helped up and sat on a seat on the port side just behind the cockpit. From there she could see up and into the cockpit and she was at once impressed by the array of screens and dials and the way the co-pilot's gloved hand was tapping at buttons.

The co-pilot then turned to look at her. He grinned under his visor and gave her a thumbs-up. The Inspector climbed past and sat on the other side of the door. Barbara was confused by the multitude of new impressions, sounds and smells. A gloved hand took her arm. She looked around into the grinning teeth and shining plastic visor of the crewman. He pointed to the end of a seat belt in his hand and then down beside her. She groped and found the thick nylon strap but could only fumble as she had no idea how to do it up.

The crewman took it and clipped it together, then tugged the end to make it firm. As he did Barbara met the eyes of three soldiers smiling at her from the opposite seat. The stretcher at their feet and satchels she recognised as First Aid Kits proclaimed them to be medics. A nudge on her shoulder made her look up. The crewman held a pair of headphones.

He helped her adjust these then held up the small button on the cord. "Crack... Crackle... p-sh to talk," came his voice.

She nodded and gave a wooden smile. When he was sure she was ready he went past her to help the Inspector. Barbara adjusted her seat and looked out the open side doors.

It was now the grey half-light before the dawn. In the next helicopter she could see a row of black clad men clutching automatic rifles and grenade launchers. They looked so grim and business like she shivered in trepidation. She saw the pilot clamber into the machine. There was a crackle of voices in her headset.

She fumbled for the talk button then realised whoever it was speaking was not talking to her. Hoping no-one had noticed, she toyed with the button and looked around. The headphones chattered to life again. A head poked around right beside her; Major Hammer was in his seat.

"Everyone strapped in?" he asked, his voice sounding distorted but deep.

The crewman answered. Then the Major's voice came again. "Townsville, this is Victor Whisky November. Request permission to proceed with our Mission."

Barbara realised she could hear the Air Traffic Control radio as well as an intercom. She heard a voice buzz and crackle. The Major spoke again. "Roger, Townsville, Out. Victor Whiskey November proceed."

Barbara felt rather than heard the engines rise in pitch. She had the most peculiar sensation that her mind was floating free while her body was too heavy to lift. For a second she wondered if she was having an attack of hallucinations or vertigo. Then she looked out and saw that everything had moved.

They were off the ground, winding straight up. The other helicopters seemed to sink. Then the world tilted and she had a horrible sensation of swooping. The concrete started to rush beneath them, getting closer and then sharply receding. The bitumen road and rows of tents, grey in the dawn light, swept beneath them. Below her she saw the lights at the guard hut and tiny figures waving.

The upper branches of a large tree went past so close underneath she sucked in her breath in fright. Then more treetops flashed past. The helicopter seemed to skim so close to them she felt real fear. She looked out the other door, starboard she remembered, and saw the long grey strip of the airfield.

The radio crackled again, Major Hammer. "Victor Whiskey November. Watch out for the power line. Just ahead."

Barbara looked out and could see the darker shadow in the tree canopy which marked its line. How glad she had been to reach it last night. She returned a nervous smile to a grin from one of the medics. She realised a cold wind was sucking in the open doors and she blessed the fact that her hair was cropped short as it was blown around.

What was that? She strained to understand. It was a girl's voice. The girl spoke again and Major Hammer responded. "Send, One Five."

"This is One Five. The police checkpoint at Echidna reports a cattle truck turning south off the Flinders Highway onto Pandanus Road, over."

"Roger that One Five. Did you hear that Inspector?"

The Inspector nodded, looking through the door at the Major. "Yes. That will be the chap that crossed the Bunyip just before we took off."

"More the merrier," Major Hammer commented.

Barbara tried to visualise the map. She twisted in her seat and looked into the cockpit. For a moment she studied the numerous dials and switches, then looked at the co-pilot's gloved hand pointing to a large map display on the control panel. The co-pilot then reached up and adjusted something above him. It all looked very professional and reassuring.

Out through the windscreen Barbara could see the dark treetops and the first pink flush of dawn spreading across the sky. They were rushing over the trees at an alarming speed.

Major Hammer turned his head. "Been in a helicopter before Miss?"

Barbara realised he was speaking to her. She fumbled for the switch.

It made crackling noises. She cleared her throat and spoke. "No. This is my first time."

"First time for everything," Major Hammer chuckled.

"I wish it had been this easy last night. I was the other side of Hill 376 when it got dark and it took me four hours to travel back to camp," she said. Ahead she could see the dark bulk of Hill 376.

Major Hammer replied in astonishment. "You walked that distance in the dark! Were you alone?"

"Yes, I was." For a few seconds Barbara relived that awful trek as they raced past the hill. Its upper slope was just taking on a pinkish glow.

"From what I've heard it sounds like quite a..." the Major began. He cut off as the radio crackled.

It was One Five again, Camille from the sound of it. "Our Patrol Number One reports one of the road-trains at the Tucker Box has departed heading east."

The Inspector looked at the map photocopy he was clutching. Major Hammer replied, "Got that One Five. Over."

The Inspector spoke, "It doesn't matter. There should still be four there and every road out of the area is still covered."

"We are just passing over Claypan Dam now," Major Hammer said. Barbara saw the grey ribbon of the vehicle track flash underneath and about half a kilometre to the north the grey patches of clay and the narrow streak of the dam wall. Out on either side she could now see two of the helicopters. It was rapidly getting lighter. Things were more grey than black and there was even a hint of reflection from the Perspex windshield of the next helicopter.

By this time Barbara was beginning to relax and enjoy herself. Even the treetops flashing by just underneath ceased to alarm her. She tried to pick out the route she had followed.

One Five called again. "Our Patrol Number Eight at Saltpan Outstation reports there are two men there. One is on a horse rounding up cattle and the other is at the house with bandaged hands."

"The drover and Johnno!" Barbara said.

The Inspector nodded. "They are the missing two. Major, could you call Senior Sergeant Crowe and let him know? Tell him to proceed as planned but then have one of your helicopters go to watch them as soon as they have unloaded their men."

"Roger," Major Hammer replied. "Victor Delta Charlie this is Victor Delta Alpha. Did you monitor that transmission from One Five about two men at Saltpan Outstation?"

An affirmative reply crackled over the radio. Major Hammer went on, "Make sure Sgt Crowe knows. Victor Delta Echo this is Victor Delta Alpha. As soon as you have landed and unloaded proceed to Saltpan Outstation, Objective Eight. Circle. Do not land. Observe and report, Over."

The other helicopter had no sooner replied than the engine note changed. Barbara looked through the front and gasped in alarm. The dark mass of the Tucker Box Range filled the windscreen. It looked so close and so high it seemed they must fly headlong into it.

Then, as this alarming thought crossed her mind, the trees seemed to sink. The helicopter rose with that peculiar motion so devoid of the expected sensations. They didn't go over the top. Instead they went up a re-entrant so close to the ground that Barbara was sure the tips of the rotors must strike the trees and rocks. She gripped her seat in fear. A glance out the side showed a dark hillside. Movement caught her eye. She had a fleeting glimpse of two rock wallabies bounding in terror around the spur. The other helicopters were nowhere to be seen.

With a clatter of rotors they zoomed through a saddle. The ground dropped away so sharply Barbara's stomach fell even though the helicopter continued to climb. Out to her right she glimpsed another helicopter come around through the next saddle. It was diving down the slope, its rotor looking like a disk of silver in the dawn light. This side of the hills was much lighter, tinged with pink.

Major Hammer cried out, "Got the bastards! There they are!" Barbara knew they were now over 'Tucker Box' but despite craning her neck to try to see she found that the bottom of the valley was out of sight. Then the helicopter tilted sharply to the left and the scene rolled into view.

There are the shed and hut, Barbara noted.

Near them was a line of big trucks and their trailers. In the first flush of dawn they stood out clearly next to the yards which were black with cattle. There was rapid radio chatter as the two accompanying helicopters swooped and landed. Barbara only saw one of them as her chopper continued to bank in a wide circle.

She saw the helicopter settle just to the west of the shed. A little circle of dust blew out and tiny ant-like figures spilled out both sides and ran out to form a line. The helicopter at once lifted off and banked sharply off to the right. This caused cattle in the paddock next to the yards to run helter-skelter in all directions. Tiny figures could be seen running around at the yards. Barbara distinctly noticed the pale blobs of faces looking up.

Fierce excitement surged through her.

Got them!

The Inspector was now using his own portable radio to talk to the men on the ground. Major Hammer spoke to him. "All helicopters have unloaded. All groups are now moving on their objectives. Victor Delta Echo is on his way to watch the Saltpan Outstation."

The command helicopter continued to circle. Barbara clenched her fists and cried out with delight as she saw the line of black-clad police close in, moving from tree to tree with weapons at the ready. One truck started up but was quickly stopped on the road. The driver was hustled back to join the others.

Surprise had been complete. The only confusion on the ground was among the thieves. The cattle in the yards seethed in fright. Barbara couldn't hear what the Inspector was saying but he then switched on the intercom.

"There's no resistance there. Let's do a quick check on the others."

"Roger that."

The machine tilted and dropped so sharply Barbara cried out in fright. She found herself looking at pale sky. Then she was pressed into her seat as they pulled out of their dive, swooping low over the eastern ridge of the valley to clatter around what she decided must be the Box Flat Mill.

Cattle ran in all directions. Dust billowed. Three men in civilian clothes stood with hands up beside a road-train. Five police were searching them. Three figures in army camouflage could be seen walking across the dusty flat from the nearby creek line. The lead one waved up at them.

Barbara recognised Captain Conkey and waved back. The helicopter levelled out and zoomed past.

Victor Delta Echo came on to report. "The man at Saltpan Outstation is firing a rifle up at us. He has bandaged hands. The man on horseback is heading off cross-country to the south-east."

Major Hammer replied, "Roger Echo. Keep well up. Follow the man on horseback. Victor Delta Bravo, take over watching the man at Saltpan. What do you want us to do Inspector?"

"Pick up three of my men at Box Flat and lift them to Saltpan. I'll tell them."

"Victor Delta Delta. Pick up three police at Number One, Box Flat and take them to Number Eight, Saltpan. Be careful. There is an armed man there, over."

By this time the command helicopter was over Emu Creek and the Saltpan Outstation came into view on their starboard side. Beyond it the helicopter watching Frankie the Drover could be seen circling like a giant dragonfly. Barbara saw 'Bravo' arrive and begin circling. The dark green and black of the helicopter's camouflage paint now showed up clearly in the dawn light.

The Command helicopter held its course.

Major Hammer commented, "There's that truck. He's got the wind up, I reckon."

They raced low along a dirt road and over a cloud of dust. The truck passed beneath them and Barbara saw the driver's face peering up at them. The Inspector told his road block to get ready to stop him.

"That's the fellow who left the Tucker Box a few minutes ago. See, there's the other one that just came in off the highway. He's stopped at the turnoff to the Saltpan. He must be wondering what the hell's going on."

"He might have been warned by radio," Major Hammer suggested.

"Too bad! He's in the net. Let's check on Emu Pump," the Inspector replied.

They circled over Emu Pump and got the thumbs up. Sharkey and Steve were already sitting under guard out in the open. By the time the command helicopter circled back 'Delta' had moved three police to Saltpan.

"The man with the gun has surrendered," the Inspector said. "Now, let's go back to the Tucker Box and check on things there."

Barbara heard that with intense satisfaction. *They've got Johnno. Good!* she thought.

She had calmed down now and was really enjoying herself and she wasn't even disoriented by all the twists and turns and circling. Her track from the previous night and day was obvious to her. She could even see the blackened areas she had burnt out. Seeing the blackened shell of the drover's blue van also gave her a spurt of satisfaction.

From up there she was able to pick out the line of the creek where she had fled from the pigs and dogs. Those memories caused her to shudder with revulsion and she trembled with reaction.

The helicopter zoomed up over the low ridge at the end of the Tucker Box valley and swooped around the base of the hills behind the hut and shed. The helicopter circled and came down to land on the open area near the shed and hut. Dust blew outwards and the machine settled.

Barbara looked through the front. There was a line of police over near the yards. Standing with them were the Colonel and Capt Royston. Seated in a widely spaced line in two distinct groups were the crooks and the truck drivers. The trucks and cattle yards were behind them.

The Inspector tapped Barbara's knee to attract her attention. "Hop out and wait near the chopper. I'll just check things are sorted out and safe and then I'll call you over to identify people." He climbed out and walked quickly forward out of sight.

Barbara fumbled with the seatbelt. The crewman reached across and unclipped it. She rose and went to climb out but he gripped her arm. Puzzled, she paused and looked at him. He grinned and reached up to take off her headset.

"Sorry. I forgot," she said, then felt foolish as he obviously couldn't hear above the engine noise.

Carefully she stepped down, feeling a bit shaky and unsteady. Once outside she paused, unsure where to go. Major Hammer looked out his window and motioned for her to go forward.

Still a little uncertain about where to go she walked quickly forward until clear of the rotors. Looking back she saw Major Hammer hold up his hand. By then her legs and lower body felt very stiff and she thought her leg muscles were going to cramp again. Scared of that happening she stopped to stretch and ease them.

As she did she glanced at the shed and vehicles ahead of her. Parked just to her left near the shed was a brown Toyota Landcruiser with a steel cage on the back. In the cage was a huge wild boar, and in the back were four vicious dogs on chains.

Lenny's truck, she decided.

She turned and looked down at the line of men who were seated about fifty metres away, her eyes scanning for Lenny. The Inspector was now with his men who were guarding them. But Barbara could not see Lenny.

Where is he? she wondered. Anxiously she again ran her eyes swiftly along the line. Castledine was there. *And there is Wally with his right arm in a sling. So I did break it! Good!* she thought.

But Lenny was not there.

Where is Lenny?

Chapter 33

AS YE SOW…

Barbara looked again to be sure. She saw the Inspector reach the leader of the Tactical Response Group and start talking to him. Barbara stood there, unsure whether to call out or go down.

The helicopter motor suddenly revved and she heard a shout. Alarmed she looked at the helicopter and saw Major Hammer's arm was out the window, pointing behind her. Suddenly anxious she looked over her shoulder.

Lenny!

He was running forward from the shed and was holding a rifle.

Barbara froze for a second. Then she screamed and turned to run. But he was too close. At that critical moment her left thigh muscle was seized by a fierce cramp. Even as she started to hobble away, he caught up and struck her with the rifle. The barrel whacked into her right temple and she reeled on the edge of unconsciousness. As she stumbled and fell to her knees, he lunged at her.

His hand grabbed her hair and hauled her to her feet. Through a red haze of agony she had an impression of men looking, the TRG sergeant pointing, of policemen raising rifles. She saw the Inspector spin round and run towards her, then stop, his face a mask of dismay.

Lenny changed his grip. His massive arm wrapped around her throat. Barbara felt something hard against her skull behind her ear and knew it was the rifle muzzle. She pictured the angle at which the man must be holding the rifle to place the muzzle there and her knowledge of firearms made her freeze.

A single twitch could send a bullet smashing through my brain, she told herself.

Then she realised that Lenny was yelling and that she was trying to scream. It was deafening when added to the helicopter engine noise.

Still gripped by an agonizing cramp, Barbara saw the Inspector stop 20 metres away. Lenny was yelling threats, which only now penetrated her consciousness, paralysing her with terror.

"Keep back, you mongrel coppers or I'll shoot," he screamed. His arm tightened, crunching her teeth painfully together. "Shut up, ya bitch!" he added.

Driven by the instinct of self-preservation Barbara bit on her lip and controlled herself. To her immediate relief the cramp eased, but tears came to her eyes.

All the prisoners scrambled to their feet, but the hard-faced TRG sergeant shouted orders and half his men turned to cover the prisoners while the others took up fire positions aiming at Lenny, and at Barbara. She saw the rifle muzzles pointing her way and knew they had live bullets.

Terror swamped her, making her almost black-out. To her intense shame she nearly lost control of her bowel motions. Lenny saved her that indignity. He was holding her in front of him and he wrenched her head so hard she thought her neck would break. Anger surged through her but she dared not struggle.

Lenny yelled again. "Back off coppers or I'll kill her."

"Don't be a fool. You can't get away," the Inspector yelled back.

"I'm goin', so don't try ter stop me or she gets hurt," Lenny replied.

The Inspector almost danced with mortification. "We've got every road blocked. You haven't got a hope," he yelled.

"Then unblock 'em! And don't try to follow me. And," he gestured with his head towards the helicopter. "If I see or hear one of those bloody things the girl gets hurt, and I mean hurt. So get rid of them!"

Barbara could feel herself blacking out because Lenny's grip was so tight. His arm was sweaty and he stank of stale sweat and unwashed clothes. She saw the Inspector chew his lip in indecision. Then the Colonel moved to stand stony-faced beside him. He made palm-downwards sweeping motions with his hands towards the helicopter.

Almost at once the machine's engine cut out. There was a whining swish-swish which continued for a while.

Lenny shouted again, half-deafening her. "Now put your weapons down and back off!"

"No," the Inspector replied.

"I'm warnin' ya!"

"And I'm warning you. Harm her and you will be a dead man."

"Don't try ter stop me. I mean it," Lenny said, his desperation clear in the silence. He began walking sideways holding Barbara beside him. No-one else moved except the marksmen. Their rifles swivelled, maintaining their aim.

Lenny dragged Barbara across to the door of the Toyota. "Don't try anything silly little girl, my finger's on the trigger," he hissed. He released the grip on her throat and used his left hand to open the driver's door. Then he grabbed her again with an ape-like paw around her neck.

For nearly a minute he stood there, breathing heavily. *He must be wondering how to keep me covered while he gets in; or how to keep the gun on me while he drives,* she thought.

He squeezed hard. "Can you drive?"

"Argh! No."

"You ain't lyin' ter me?"

"No. Ouch! You saw me crash Wally's ute," Barbara answered.

"Yeah, I did. But that's an idea," Lenny snarled. He yelled again, "I want Wally. Let him go you coppers."

Wally made to get up but a policeman's rifle forced him back down. The Inspector looked behind him and said, "Let him go. We don't want Cadet Brassington hurt." He faced Lenny again and spoke in a calm voice. "Look Lenny, this is stupid. You can't possibly get away. Every policeman in Australia will be after you. And if you hurt her, you only make it worse for yourself."

"Don't try and con me with your smooth talk, Mister Pig. I'm goin'. Come on Wally."

The buzz of a helicopter in the distance came to them. Lenny screamed, "Get rid of them helicopters. Piss 'em orf!"

The Inspector nodded and called across to Major Hammer who called on his radio. A very nervous looking Wally stood up, dusted himself and walked across to join Lenny.

"Bloody hell mate! We ain't got a chance," he said.

"Shut up Wally! We're doin' it. Get in and drive," Lenny hissed viciously.

Wally indicated his arm. He licked his lips and glanced nervously at the policeman aiming their automatic rifles at him. "I can't drive with this arm."

"Then I'll drive. You take the gun. Come round the back where them coppers can't see so good," Lenny said.

Lenny dragged Barbara to the rear of the Toyota. The chained-up dogs in the back set up a savage barking and snarling. They hurled themselves at their cage. In the cage beside them the huge black boar glared at the humans with baleful eyes and began grunting and crashing against the steel mesh. Barbara was so close she could smell the creature. A horrible musky urine smell caught at the back of her throat. The boar grunted and thrust at the steel mesh. It had wicked curved tusks which it clashed on the steel cage.

Lenny gestured to the back of the vehicle. "Grab that rope and tie her hands. I don't trust her. She's a cunning bitch," he ordered. He jerked Barbara's head painfully. "No tricks bitch, I'm warnin' you!"

Barbara said nothing. She just wanted the ordeal to end. Still stunned by the awful turn of events she looked up at the clear blue sky and noted the first rays of sunshine bathing the hilltops in gold.

I don't want to die! It is too nice a morning. This can't be real, she thought.

Wally bound her wrists tightly in front of her. As he did, she saw his eyes studying her shirt front. To her dismay she saw that one of the buttons had come undone, revealing half her right breast. A wave of intense embarrassment added to her turmoil of emotions.

To add to her shame Lenny noticed it as well and gave an evil grin. "Later," he said. "Now get her in the truck, Wally. Keep in a bunch so them coppers ain't game ter risk a shot."

Wally edged in behind her and Lenny passed him the gun. Barbara felt the muzzle leave her skin, then return to press against her. She prayed Wally had a steady hand but could tell the man was trembling with fright. In a tight huddle they shuffled up the left side of the Landcruiser. Lenny opened the passenger's door and climbed in, dragging Barbara painfully after him. Barbara saw Wally was holding the rifle in his left hand. He was shaking so much she was afraid he would fire it accidentally. It was some sort of bolt-action, sporting rifle and she guessed it would make a nasty mess.

Wally then clambered in painfully. As he did the rifle waved around and poked into Barbara's ribs.

Lenny snarled, "Watch out, yer mug! Don't point that bloody thing at me!" Then he snarled again. "Never mind the bloody door!"

Wally had been puzzling over how to close his door with a broken right arm and a rifle in his left. Barbara sat wedged between the two men and found tears streaming down her face. Lenny started the vehicle and slammed his door.

Barbara looked through the front. None of the watching people had moved. Lenny leaned out. "Now remember coppers, don't follow us or she gets hurt," he yelled.

With a roar the vehicle lurched into motion. Barbara cringed. If there was to be shooting it would have to be now. There was none. Lenny swung the vehicle left onto the track and accelerated. Barbara felt utter despair start of overwhelm her. It just couldn't be true!

Then a fresh fear came to her; more immediate than the vague terror of what these animals might do to her. Lenny was driving so fast that they were bouncing over the rutted track in a way that made her afraid the gun might go off accidentally.

Lenny looked in the rear vision mirror. "Ha! We've done it Wally," he gloated.

They roared down into the first small creek. At the bottom they struck a washout so hard they all bounced out of their seats.

Bang!

Barbara screamed. She landed on the seat and bounced again. The rifle barrel struck her in the face and she smelled cordite. Lenny yelled an obscenity and braked the vehicle to a standstill on top of the bank.

"Did you shoot her?" he yelled.

Barbara sat numb, wondering the same thing. Wally replied with a stammer. "S... s... shit! It... it... just... just bloody went off."

"Is she hit?" Lenny shouted.

"No. No she ain't." Wally replied. Using the gun muzzle he pointed to the roof just above Lenny's head. Barbara looked up and saw the bullet hole. She felt so sick she wanted to faint, but it just wouldn't happen. She gasped with relief and more tears came. Then she broke down into uncontrollable shaking.

Lenny looked at the bullet hole and changed colour. "You stupid drongo! Keep yer bloody finger orf the trigger! She's our passport, we don't want her dead premature. Christ! Yer nearly shot me. No, don't reload the bloody thing. If she gives any trouble I'll break her neck."

Wally stopped trying to re-cock the weapon left-handed. Lenny swore again, glanced in the rear-vision mirror, engaged the gears and started driving again.

The vehicle bounced and rattled up over the stony ridge at the eastern end of the valley. Barbara could hear the wild pig snorting in rage as it was knocked about. The dogs kept barking at it.

At the bottom of the slope the vehicle turned right and headed south. They dipped down through a creek bed with a trickle of water in damp sand then up across a flat covered with cattle. Barbara saw a red and white road-train parked there and a windmill beyond. There were people standing there, including three policemen and three in army uniform. The policemen had rifles but did not point them. Barbara recognised Captain Conkey. He stood beside the road with a radio on his back and his face a picture of distress.

As they roared past Barbara met his eyes but knew there was nothing he could do.

Wally said, "More coppers. I hope they're the last."

"They won't be. That ain't a roadblock," Lenny replied.

"Where we goin?" Wally asked as the vehicle dipped through another dry creek.

"To Rocky Mill first."

"What for?" Wally queried.

"Use your bloody loaf. Ter get me money and stuff. Ya can't run without money," Lenny sneered.

"What if there's coppers there?" Wally asked with a distinct quaver in his voice.

"We tell 'em ter back orf," Lenny replied.

They were heading east Barbara realised, almost directly into the sun as it rose above the tree tops. Lenny drove very fast, hammering the vehicle over the bumps and corrugations with scant regard for either safety or comfort. Barbara was repelled by the way his huge hairy hands kept clenching and unclenching on the wheel. He kept wiping them on his filthy grey trousers.

Equally repellent was the way he kept glancing at her front. As the vehicle bounced over the bumps it sent her front bouncing as well. She was acutely and painfully aware of this and burned with embarrassment and fear.

Oh! I wish I'd worn a bra, she thought. To add to her shame another button came undone.

Almost as bad was the pain from her shirt rubbing on her sunburn.

Blisters had begun to form across her back and shoulders and the cloth rubbing on the inflamed and dry skin was so painful and irritating she wondered how much longer she could endure it.

After only a couple of minutes they came to a four-way road junction. They turned right, then left towards another hut set in a dusty yard and flanked by the usual litter of dunny, shed, windmill and a pigpen. Behind the hut a line of trees marked a largish creek.

Lenny swung the vehicle and braked to a halt in front of the hut. "Can't see no coppers... ah, shit!" he coughed as their dust billowed around them. "Ya better cock that gun though Wally. Don't point it at me, ya twit!"

Lenny opened his door and stepped out. He reached in and grabbed Barbara by her wrists and hauled her out. As she did she banged her head on the top of the door frame and then went sprawling in the dust. He hauled her to her feet with her shirt and pushed her towards the back of the vehicle.

Barbara stumbled and fell again. Her mind was frantically searching for an escape. Not for anything did she want to enter that hut. She rose and tried to run.

"Bitch!" Lenny yelled. He lunged and grabbed her shirt. Barbara felt it rip and was dimly aware that a couple more buttons had come off or undone. She struggled but he grabbed her around the throat. His right arm came around her front. She tried to kick at him but he held her firmly from behind. Wally came to the back of the vehicle.

"What ya doin' Lenny?" he asked.

"Bitch tried to get away. I'm gunna teach her a lesson," he grated. Barbara cried out but the arm around her throat tightened so that she could only see the sun. To her horror she felt his huge paw grasp her right breast.

Not again! her mind howled.

"Let her go, you animal!" someone yelled.

Lenny swore and turned. Barbara looked.

It was Gordon!

He was racing across the yard from the creek line.

"Bloody army!" yelled Wally.

"Shoot him!" Lenny screamed.

"No!" Barbara croaked through his choking gasp. "Gordon, no!"

317

She saw Wally swing the rifle up in an attempt to fire left-handed from the hip. At once she jumped against him and jostled him.

Bang!

Suddenly Barbara was flung on her back in the dust.

"Missed him, you stupid bastard! Give me that gun," Lenny shouted.

Barbara rolled over in time to see Lenny snatch the rifle from Wally who was struggling to cock it one-handed. Gordon was twenty metres away but still charging. Lenny worked the bolt and brought the rifle into his shoulder.

Desperate to save Gordon Barbara scrambled to her feet. She hurled herself forward, crashing into Lenny.

Bang!

Missed! Lenny staggered, then struck at her with a savage back-hander. It sent her flying. Again she had a bruising fall in the dust. As she hit the ground, she saw Lenny re-cock the rifle.

Just in time Gordon grappled with him.

Barbara screamed and struggled to regain her feet. It was too unequal. *Lenny is too strong!* she thought. Gordon gripped the rifle for dear life but Lenny kicked viciously at him.

Bang!

The rifle discharged into the air.

More shouts. Barbara was on her knees, her senses reeling. Then she saw Capt Hamilton, Lofty Ward and Sgt Oakwood pounding across the yard.

"More of em!" Wally shrieked.

"Let the dogs at 'em," Lenny snarled.

He suddenly let go with his left hand and delivered a smashing blow to Gordon's face. Blood spurted. He struck again and Gordon went down, still clutching the rifle barrel. Barbara was up by then and again rushed at Lenny. Now furiously angry, she kicked him hard on his left knee and punched with her bound fists. He was distracted and turned to hit at her.

Barbara was half-stunned by a blow to her face. She fell heavily. Lenny kicked her savagely on the left hip. He was demented with rage and was screaming obscenities.

Wally sprang to the back of the Toyota. He clawed at the latches on the cages, then, after a fearful glance over his shoulder, fled around the right hand side.

As Barbara tried to shield herself from another kick, she was dimly aware that at least one of the cages had swung open. Wally clambered into the driver's seat and started the engine. But as he did, the wild boar sprang out.

The enraged animal attacked at once. Barbara saw it and tried to shout a warning.

Too late!

A quarter of a tonne of bone, muscle and gristle slammed into Lenny from behind. Barbara saw his feet go up and his arms fly out. He screamed. The pig had got its tusks between his thighs and he tumbled in the dust.

Barbara rolled aside and tried to scramble to her feet. The Toyota's engine roared and it began moving after a savage grinding of gears. The barking and snarling of the dogs added to the gross snorting sound of the pig and the yelling of the people.

Gordon snatched up the rifle and ran to stand between Barbara and the pig. She stood up and looked, then looked away and vomited.

Lenny screamed and screamed. The boar had ripped his stomach open and now began biting and gouging at his neck. He flailed at it. Blood spurted and splattered. Entrails were entangled in the animal's tusks and these were being ripped and stretched like strings of blood-soaked sausages. Capt Hamilton, Lofty, and Sgt Oakwood stood transfixed by the horror of the spectacle. The screams became desperate gurgles. More blood spurted, spattering into the dust.

Gordon cocked the rifle. Barbara stood behind him and could feel him shaking. He raised it, aimed and fired.

The bullet took the beast in the skull. Bloody chunks flew. The boar squealed in rage and torment and spun round. It staggered, then recovered. Its black fur was matted dark crimson. Its eyes glared murderous hate. They fixed on Gordon and Barbara.

"Run Barbara!" Gordon yelled. He re-cocked the rifle. The animal charged. Barbara tensed to spring aside. Gordon aimed, without a tremor.

Bang!

The monster's knees buckled. Its snout ploughed the dust and it crashed on its side. Its legs twitched and its sides heaved. Blood flowed in a scarlet stream from its nostrils. Dirt caked the gore on its tusks.

Gordon straightened up and worked the rifle bolt.

"Whew! That was the last round," he said. He tossed the weapon in the dust and turned to enfold Barbara in his arms. "Don't look Barbara. You are safe now."

She clung to him, wracked by tears of relief and trembling with shock. She was dimly aware that the Landcruiser had stopped at the road. A Land Rover was blocking its path and police were aiming rifles at it.

Captain Conkey came running across towards them, relief on his face. Lofty rose from examining the mangled remains of Lenny. "He's dead sir," he said shakily.

Barbara buried her face in Gordon's chest and sobbed.

Chapter 34

TOO FARR

Forty-eight hours later, Barbara sat on a bench seat on the edge of the grass parade ground near the big shed. Beside her sat her father who had driven down from Cairns on that horrible Monday morning. On the parade ground the four companies of the Graduation Parade were being right dressed by the CSMs. Standing in a cluster with Barbara were the about-to-graduate CUOs, nervously adjusting their uniforms. The Staff sat in a row on forms and chairs to her right. There were also a few interested parents and families who had made the long drive to see their sons or daughters graduate. And a TV crew. Barbara had never seen a TV crew at a cadet parade before and gave them a sour look.

The sun was just peeking over the trees beside Hill 376, its rays illuminating the roof of the big shed. Barbara looked at the dark outline of the Tucker Box Range and shivered. Her father felt it and put his arm around her.

It was only 0715 but they had all been up since 0445. The parade was to have been at sunset the previous day but events had forced it to be postponed. The early start was needed not just to avoid the heat but to get people on coaches for the long trip home, ten or eleven hours for the Rockhampton cadets.

Fiona came over and stood in front of her. "Will you be okay Barb?" she asked.

Barbara smiled. "Yes. I'll be fine. Well done!"

"Thanks," Fiona answered. She turned and moved off to her position on the side of the parade ground.

The CUOs were all happy and excited. Gordon stood there pretending he wasn't nervous but Barbara could tell he was by the way he fingered the sword in its scabbard. Then she felt a little stab of jealousy as he reached forward to help Sharon adjust her Sam Browne.

"You want to hope the Colonel doesn't see you doing that," Barbara said, niggled by his attention to another girl. "He is hot and strong about boys not helping girls to get dressed."

They looked down at her and Sharon grinned. "Gordon is just being a gentleman," she said.

Gordon blushed but smiled. "Wish me luck then," he commented.

Barbara rose stiffly to her feet and smiled back at him, seeming to be swallowed up in his eyes. Noting that Gordon's lapel was caught under the shoulder strap of his Sam Browne belt, she reached forward and twitched it free.

She had just opened her mouth to murmur good luck when Sharon cut across her by saying, "And girls dressing boys!"

Realizing what she had just done, Barbara blushed and then smiled. "And poo to you too!" she replied with a grin.

Karen came over and interrupted. "Come on children! Enough silly games. Time we were in position," she said.

The others nodded and Barbara gave Gordon one last smile and whispered, "Good luck!"

The new CUOs all turned and moved off to their positions along the front of the parade ground and Barbara eased herself back down into her chair. Watching Gordon march to his position along to her left she thought how handsome he was, and how lucky she was.

The Parade RSM's voice cut across such thoughts. "Parade. Eyes... Front! Parade, Stand at... Ease!"

Barbara looked at him. It was Barker from Heatley. He looked the very picture of what a Sergeant Major should look like. *And he looks very handsome too,* she thought. She watched him about turn and stand at ease. *That Heatley mob!* They'd taken out top of the Warrant Officer Course and most of the top quarter of the Sergeants Course.

Barbara closed her eyes. Her face still felt very numb and she knew that it was a mass of bruises and that both eyes were so 'black' that from a distance it looked like she was wearing a mask. Her skin was still blistered and scratchy from the sunburn but the worst of the pain had gone. Now it just felt dry and irritable. She could just tolerate a uniform shirt on it.

Gently flexing her shoulders to ease the irritation she looked around. Oh, what a hectic three days it had been!

After her rescue they had wanted to send her straight to hospital in one of the helicopters but she had refused.

"No. I've got exams to do. I came here to pass a CUOs Course. I'm alright," she had insisted.

She had travelled back to camp in the Land Rover with the Colonel, Capt Conkey and Gordon's Patrol. Gordon had held her all of the way. Nobody, least of all the Colonel, had seemed to think that unusual and she had found it very comforting.

Back at camp there had been more arguments. Barbara had been able to persuade the Colonel she could do the exams. He had decided that was a good idea to take her mind off the horrors she had just witnessed as he feared she was in some kind of shock.

So the exams had been rescheduled. The army had provided some extra staff to help with the assessment of the Sergeants and Corporals. The CUOs and WOs Courses were given the rest of the Monday and Monday night off, to rest and study. A doctor had examined Barbara and after a hot shower, solid breakfast and several long drinks she had been put to bed.

She had slept for twelve hours, had another meal and then slept soundly through the night. On Tuesday morning she had woken feeling stiff and sore but mentally alert, although by the end of the day she had been exhausted.

Four exams and a Graduation Parade practice had so drained her that she had gone straight to bed after dinner and missed the end of camp concert.

At least they had found all her belongings. Monica had confessed to removing them, at Weismann's insistence. They had hidden them in one of the empty store sheds.

Poor Monica! Barbara thought.

It was sad. She looked along the line of CUOs, now spaced along the front of the parade ground and ready to march on. Only 20 out of the original 24 were present. Weismann was in police custody. Monica had been sent home in disgrace. So had Wilmot and Stephens.

Wilmot had been marched off for several acts of misbehaviour: breaking camp to sneak into town, drinking alcohol and worse. Monica had implicated them in her confession. Weismann had then corroborated her story. It certainly cleared up one of the mysteries which had puzzled Barbara.

Apparently, Weismann had caught Wilmot and Stephens doing something forbidden together (that wasn't quite how Barbara had had it described to her, and she wrinkled her nose in disgust at the memory) and he had then blackmailed them both. That was how Gordon had been set up. Monica had stolen Barbara's books at Weismann's instigation, but Stephens had planted them in Gordon's gear and then made the false allegations.

No wonder he looked nervous that day! she thought.

And she now knew the sordid details of the business down at the creek the other night. Monica and Weismann had snuck out before lights out during study time (the supervision had been made too strict after then) to have a little debauch down the creek. Once there and undressed, Monica had found that Weismann had promised the army driver sex with her in return for him driving to town and for providing alcohol.

Barbara sighed. She turned her attention back to the parade and watched Roger saluting the Parade RSM. *Good old Roger! He has a heart of gold and is brave as could be!* She watched affectionately as he about turned to face them. He had come 8th and was acting as Adjutant.

"Officers!" he called. "Take Post!"

Twelve of the CUOs came to attention, saluted and marched forward. Barbara ran her eyes along the line of marching figures. There was Fiona on the end. She had come 9th and was 2IC A Company.

She looks just perfect, she thought.

So did Jennifer, who had come 12th, so was only one of the platoon commanders. Millett, from Rockhampton, had beaten her by one mark and was 2IC D Company.

At least all of Cairns are in the top half, Barbara thought. But overall they hadn't beaten that Heatley mob. Barbara gave a wry smile. *Oh well! It is only pride and I do like them. After all they are all girls and the girls have won four of the top five positions.*

When he had heard that the Colonel had shaken his head and muttered, "I don't know what's gone wrong with the young men of today. It wasn't like that in my day. Talk about the 'marshmallow generation'!"

Barbara smiled. She was glad. But some of the boys had done well. Near her was Lofty, who had come 7th. Barbara watched him draw his sword and march forward to take over the parade from the Adjutant.

"What a splendid young man," Barbara heard Capt Conkey murmur to Capt Royston. She glanced at the two officers, both in their ceremonial uniforms with Sam Browne belts and medals. She did like Capt Conkey.

He's got a heart of gold! she thought affectionately.

Camille had come 2nd. She stood at the eastern end of the parade ground holding the flag, flanked by four sergeants with red sashes. One of them was Wendy, conspicuous even at that distance by her physical attributes. She had come 2nd on the Sergeant's Course.

Good old Wendy!

Seeing Wendy's proud front made Barbara blush with shame at her embarrassment at Rocky Mill when she had eased away from Gordon and had realised that her shirt had come undone. The memory of the expression of wonder and concern on Gordon's face when he looked down made her smile. Somehow she had not minded. Very tenderly he had drawn her shirt closed and then kissed her forehead.

Then Barbara thought of that desperate nude run through the bush to escape. *I'm as bad as Chloe,* she thought.

That caused her to scan the ranks of B Company until she found Chloe. Even at 50 metres and in an army uniform Chloe stood out. She looked beautiful and every inch the part, while still looking voluptuous.

At least she didn't misbehave, and she has passed, Barbara thought.

Lofty saluted the Adjutant. His sword went down and up in glittering arcs as the sunlight began to illuminate the parade.

What a lovely morning! Barbara thought. *Everything is so green. And the cadets look so good!*

She admired the scene as brass buckles and gold badges began to twinkle in the sun. The scarlet sashes of the RSM and CSMs made a vivid contrast and the white belts and sparkling instruments of the small band at the rear added a nice touch.

Gordon met her eye. She smiled encouragingly and he smiled back. It seemed to make the day even brighter. He adjusted his Sam Browne for the umpteenth time and drew his sword.

Oh, he looks so handsome. So much the soldier! Barbara thought. She wanted to cry out for love.

Gordon came to attention on the Parade 2IC's call and marched onto the parade. Off to Barbara's left Karen did the same. Good old Karen! She had tried so hard and so much wanted to top the Course. But she had managed 4th and, as OC B Company, had one of the coveted swords. Gordon had come 3rd and was OC A Company. The other two company commanders were Sharon and Cosgrove, who had achieved 5th and 6th respectively.

Major Wickham will be pleased, all his girls in the top jobs, she thought.

Barbara started. She had been so absorbed watching Gordon halt and about turn that she hadn't noticed Capt Conkey speaking to her. He touched her arm.

"Ready Barb? Sure you are okay?"

"Yes sir," Barbara replied.

She swallowed nervously and levered herself to her feet. Her father helped her and squeezed her arm encouragingly. She gave him a smile and pretended her stiff muscles didn't hurt.

"Good luck Bub," he said.

She smiled her thanks, then noted that Lofty was facing her and standing at ease. *That's my cue,* she thought. She came firmly to attention. Her right had went across her stomach to the sword guard. With a sharp motion she flicked the sword up and grasped the hilt. In a single smooth action she drew it out and held it at the carry. The blade glittered.

It just didn't seem possible. She had done it. She had topped the Course.

The only exam she had not done was the Navigation Test on Sunday. The Staff had unanimously given her full marks for her feat of making her way through 30 kilometres of bush without a map or a compass. On all the other tests—the Written General Knowledge, Organising of a Training Program, Planning of a Field Exercise, Conduct of Field Training and Giving of Verbal Orders—she had gained the highest marks.

She met Sharon's eye and they smiled at each other. Quelling a nervous flutter in her stomach, Barbara marched forward to take command of the parade.

*****

Two hours later, after photos, changing into casual clothes, last minute packing, and a substantial morning tea, the cadets were clustered around the line of coaches. They were busy saying farewells and loading their gear. The Townsville cadets were all still in uniform as they would not leave until after lunch. They had the job of dismantling the camp, cleaning up and returning the stores but they had been allowed a break to say goodbye.

Barbara went from one to the other saying 'Merry Christmas' and 'Good Luck' and 'Don't forget to write'. The boys she shook by the hand but the girls all hugged each other and the tears flowed.

What nice people they are, she thought. She had done three promotion courses with them now and felt she knew them really well. *I hope we will be friends for life,* she thought.

She was in a huddle with Sharon, Camille and Karen when she noticed Gordon standing there. He was trying to appear happy but his eyes looked miserable.

The others just seemed to fall away and they came together. She wrapped her arms around his neck and kissed him. Tears flowed. She couldn't help herself; she didn't care who saw.

They kissed and kissed and clung to each other. Barbara realised she was being spoken to. It was her father. "Ok kids. Sorry, but it's time to go."

Captain Conkey nodded. "Yeah. Let the poor bugger get some air," he commented with a chuckle.

Barbara stepped back but held Gordon's hands. "You'll write?"

"Of course."

"Perhaps we could see each other during the holidays, after Christmas?" she suggested.

"I'd like that. I'll try to come up."

Barbara looked at her father. "Please dad, can he?"

Her father smiled. "We'll see what we can organise."

Barbara stepped forward and hugged Gordon again. She kissed him again. Gently he wiped her tears.

Roger broke in. "Hey, don't we get a hug?"

Barbara looked at him and smiled. "Hug Lofty."

"Not likely!" Lofty snorted. The group laughed.

Barbara stepped back and let go of Gordon's hands. Suddenly she felt all choked up and cramped in the chest. She was the centre of an admiring circle, all patting her back and wishing her well. Her father took her arm and steered her through them to his car. Fiona hopped in the back with Wendy. They had opted for that rather than the bus ride.

Gordon came and stood talking while they did up their seat belts and the car was started. He looked thoroughly wretched but tried gamely to smile.

Wendy sighed. "Oh, isn't love wonderful!" she cried, tears flowing freely down her own cheeks.

The car started. Barbara's vision blurred from tears and she waved. They pulled out onto the camp road.

"Oh, I hope he can come to Cairns after Christmas," she cried.

Her father shook his head. "It's a long way from Cairns to Broadsound Sweetie, over 800 kilometres," he pointed out.

"Could we go down there Dad?"

"It depends on my work. It's a long way."

Fiona leaned forward. "I hope it's not too Farr, get it? Too F-A-R-R."

Barbara tried to smile but couldn't answer for the lump in her throat.

Too Farr! It probably is, she thought unhappily. *I can only hope that love is strong enough to conquer the distance.*

Enjoy more C.R. Cummings stories

The Air Cadets

The Navy Cadets

The Army Cadets

 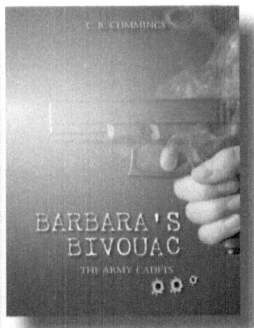